THE TRILLIAS GAMBIT

THE TRILLIAS GAMBIT

Book Three of the Warminster Series

J. V. Hilliard

Paperback ISBN 978-1-77400-060-1
Ebook ISBN 978-1-77400-061-8

Printed on Acid Free Paper

DragonMoonPress.com

ACKNOWLEDGMENTS

Writing a novel is not a solo effort, but instead is the definition of a team sport. Without a crew of supporters, contributors and other creatives, authors would be lost. It is to these unsung heroes I offer my eternal gratitude.

First, let me thank my family and friends for their continued support and encouragement. Andrea, you have sacrificed so much to let me chase down this dream. For that, I say again and again, I love you.

Secondly, I need to thank the rest of my Warminster team for helping make the series a success. To Dane Cobain, my literary compass; Gwen Gades, my patient publisher; Shai Shaffer, Abigail Linhardt, Katelyn Buschbacher, Sarah Brownlee and Brianna Toth, my beta readers and development sherpas; Larch Gallagher, my champion illustrator; Phil Athans and Pam Harris, my fantasy wordsmiths; Victor Bevine the voice of Warminster; Jan and Susan Dickler, my media giants; Ann Howley, Maria Simbra and Sarah McKnight, my JAMS session members; Auggie Tagabunlang, my social media guru; Hannah Nathanson, my poetess extraordinaire; Luke Bruss and Creator, for my coats of arms; Emily's World of Design for my family tree, Cathedral "flow chart" and all of my cartography; Chris and Gabriel Ithen, the geniuses behind my merchandise store; Dave Prokopec and Aaron Smith, the eyes and voice of my book trailers; Todd Waites and Andy Jackson, my Twin Tales brethren; Henry Roi, my PR machine; my "Professor Howley" classmates; and of course my Dungeons & Dragons group, Brent Burich, Joey Davis, Chris Niziol, Markus Rauhecker, James Stefanyak, Jim Stillwagner and Kent Szalla.

Lastly, of course to you, my readers. I hope you've enjoyed your third trip into the Realm of Warminster, and I hope you continue your journey throughout the series.

RUKKEVA SEA
HAMMERSTEAD
THE DRAGON'S BREATH MOUNTAINS
WRATHMOR TUNDRA
HROLT
RAWCLIFFE FORGE
GELVAR'S GORGE
NORSE COVE
VALLANCE
CONNOR BRAY
RAVENSHIRE
THORNCREST HILLS
DARK WOOD
RAVEN WOOD
SARACEN
FINCH'S GROVE
HALIFAX
QUEEN'S CHAPEL
FOGHAVEN VALE
HARDIN'S DUSK
FIRTH OF FURY
THRONCHELM
KILLEAN DESOLATES
PHOERESIAN MOORS
THE HEARTH
HUNTERS MANOR
SEABROOKE
GLOUCESTER
SHERBOURNE ORCHARDS
SHADOW MOUNDS
THE VILCHOR HIGHGRASS
THE FOX SHALES
THUNDER COVE
LAKE ALDREDD
COSTERE MEADUWS
CRESWICK HILLS
ALDREDD
LEHANE
AERENDASH
ALIESTER OVENS
SYLVAN FOREST
THE EMERALD DALES
CASTLESHIRE
MARRISTER COAST
LAKE HIRRUS
CROWS
FLOWERDOWN
SYPHEN
ANDARYNNE FIELDS
SYLVAN VALLEY
MYRRABEL
JIN JI REEF
ABACUS
N
W
S
THE SEA KINGDOM
THALASSIAN SEA
DEADWATERS FORK

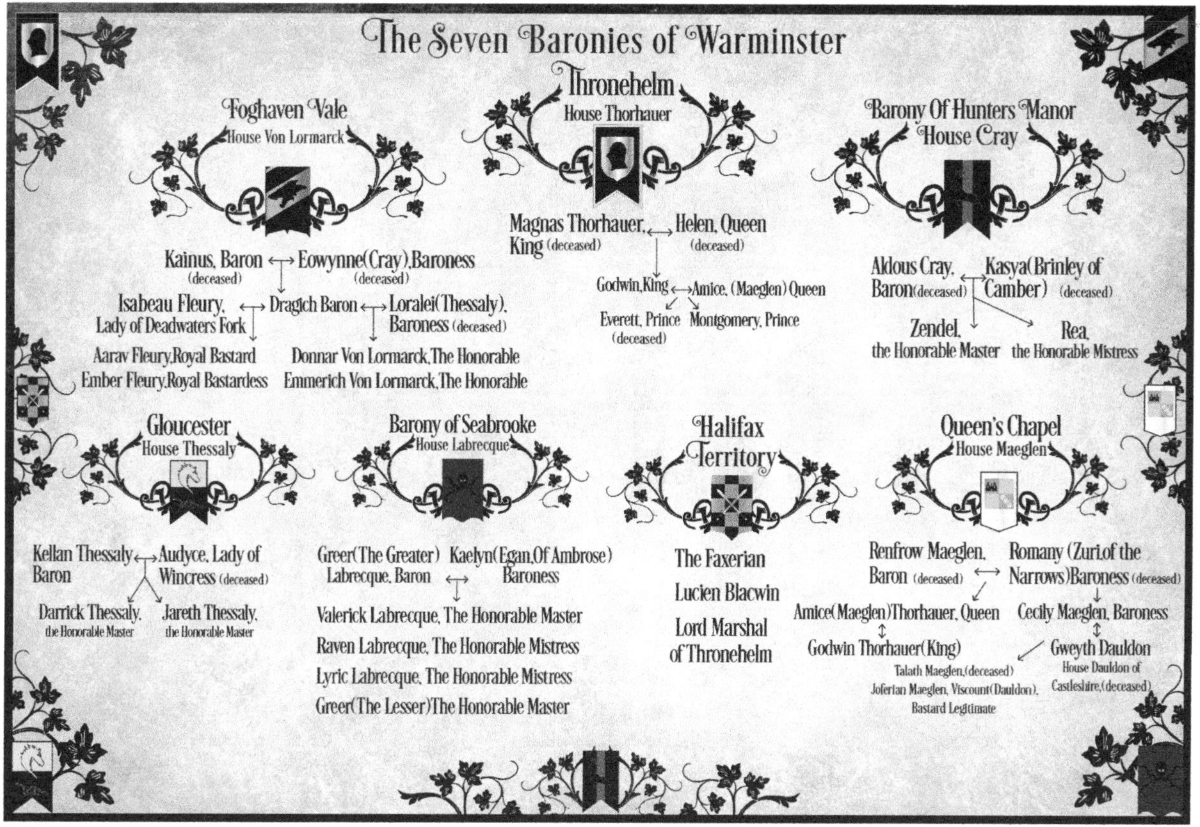

The Seven Baronies of Warminster

Foghaven Vale
House Von Lormarck

Kainus, Baron (deceased) ⟷ Eowynne(Cray),Baroness (deceased)

Isabeau Fleury, Lady of Deadwaters Fork ⟷ Dragich Baron ⟷ Loralei(Thessaly), Baroness (deceased)

Aarav Fleury,Royal Bastard
Ember Fleury,Royal Bastardess

Donnar Von Lormarck,The Honorable
Emmerich Von Lormarck,The Honorable

Thronehelm
House Thorhauer

Magnas Thorhauer, King (deceased) ⟷ Helen, Queen (deceased)

Godwin,King ⟷ Amice, (Maeglen) Queen

Everett, Prince (deceased)
Montgomery, Prince

Barony Of Hunters Manor
House Cray

Aldous Cray, Baron(deceased) ⟷ Kasya(Brinley of Camber) (deceased)

Zendel, the Honorable Master
Rea, the Honorable Mistress

Gloucester
House Thessaly

Kellan Thessaly Baron ⟷ Audyce, Lady of Wincress (deceased)

Darrick Thessaly, the Honorable Master
Jareth Thessaly, the Honorable Master

Barony of Seabrooke
House Labrecque

Greer(The Greater) Labrecque, Baron ⟷ Kaelyn(Egan,Of Ambrose) Baroness

Valerick Labrecque, The Honorable Master
Raven Labrecque, The Honorable Mistress
Lyric Labrecque, The Honorable Mistress
Greer(The Lesser)The Honorable Master

Halifax Territory

The Faxerian
Lucien Blacwin
Lord Marshal of Thronehelm

Queen's Chapel
House Maeglen

Renfrow Maeglen, Baron (deceased) ⟷ Romany (Zuri,of the Narrows)Baroness (deceased)

Amice(Maeglen)Thorhauer, Queen ⟷ Godwin Thorhauer(King)

Cecily Maeglen, Baroness ⟷ Gweyth Dauldon House Dauldon of Castleshire,(deceased)

Talath Maeglen,(deceased)
Joferian Maeglen, Viscount(Dauldon), Bastard Legitimate

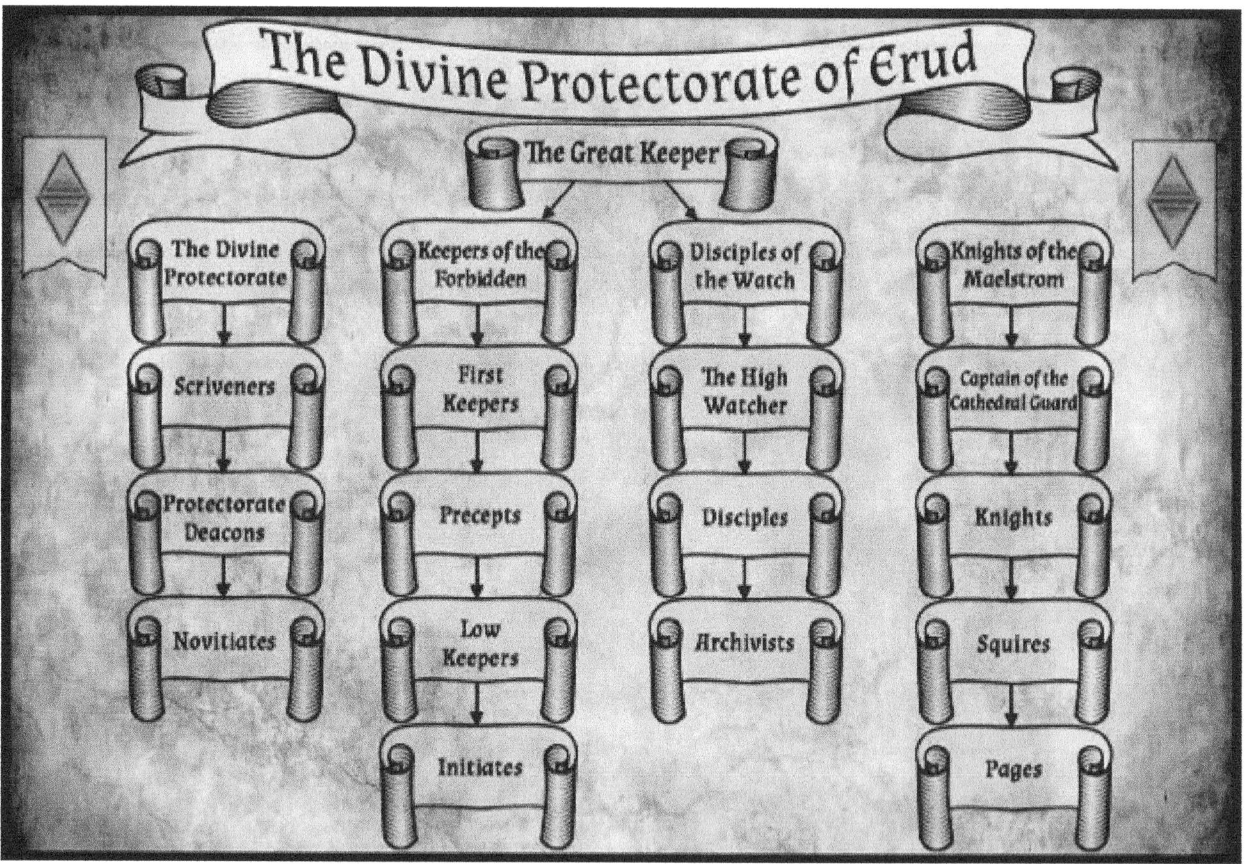
The Divine Protectorate of Erud
The Great Keeper
The Divine Protectorate
Scriveners
Protectorate Deacons
Novitiates
Keepers of the Forbidden
First Keepers
Precepts
Low Keepers
Initiates
Disciples of the Watch
The High Watcher
Disciples
Archivists
Knights of the Maelstrom
Captain of the Cathedral Guard
Knights
Squires
Pages

PROLOGUE

"Vengeance earned swiftly tastes bitter. It must age like a fine wine to taste justly."
—King Dragich von Iormarck

"INCANUS... STOP. THEY'LL HEAR."

Covered by the cawing of a passing crow, the whispered words of desperation didn't disturb the serenity of the forest. The magpie circled twice before soaring off into the darkened sky.

"They won't hear me climbing over the distance," came the quiet reply, one that oozed with confidence.

"But the bird," the second voice managed. *"What if that was Iris? What if—?"*

"Fala, you worry far too much." Incanus grunted from his perch in the tree. "That's not my mother's crow. And if it was, I'd feather it with an arrow before I'd let it return to her and tell our tale."

The young Bone elf knew his reply held little substance. His mother instilled fear into the hearts of everyone in their village of Bereslangum, including him. Killing her pet would only enrage her.

Fala shook her head, a scowl on her face. *"You are terrible."*

He met her gaze with a forced but blank expression, attempting to ignore his heart thudding beneath his chest. He couldn't stop a smile from spreading across his face, though he was glad it was not yet dusk so Fala couldn't see him very well.

Never give too much away, he reminded himself.

A petite young Bone elf only a year younger than he, Fala possessed silken, jet-black hair, rare for their kind, and a smooth, pale complexion that softened him when he dreamt of kissing her neck. But it was her eyes that captivated him. They were almond-shaped, like that of a Raven elf, black as pitch, with flecks of silver when he looked deep into them. From the age of six, he'd been enchanted by Fala, developing a deep-rooted yearning for her over the years. One day she would be his. He would make sure of it.

The small cluster of trees they'd hidden in overlooked the concealed village of Bereslangum, a surface outpost of the Bone elves, tucked away deep in the Dragon's Breath Mountains. In part, Bereslangum sprouted from a shallow cave system bored by the picks and awls of his forebearers. The caves surfaced near an overgrown grotto of white roses, twisted in briars and brambles too thick for passersby to dare to pass through. If any of the aldermen discovered they were there, there would be blood to pay. But Incanus wasn't worried. He was too stealthy, too clever.

"Your Rite of Investiture," muttered Fala, edging closer to him on the thick branch. "They must be here for your blooding."

"It's not dark enough for the sires to be here," Incanus reminded her. "But I can see a group of aldermen gathered in the grotto."

"Is your mother amongst them?"

His focus narrowed. "Nay."

"Do you think it's time?" She hesitated. "Will it be tonight?"

Incanus's eyes flicked down to her, but he didn't respond.

"Are you nervous?" Her brow knitted, and he could see concern for him on her face.

"I am ready."

In truth, he was more anxious to pass the Rite of Investiture than nervous. He was one of the most skilled hunters in camp and perhaps Bereslangum's best tracker, even better than his own mother. His blooding was overdue.

Fala shifted closer, perching next to him. Her hip grazed his, and in her gentle way, she reached for his hand. When she took it, he felt her quivering.

"I will be fine," he assured her, trying to steal a look into her eyes.

Her mild character stirred something within him. She recoiled from melee practices where Bone elves would engage in hand-to-hand combat and she possessed a fondness for living creatures that, to him, only had one purpose: to be hunted and harvested. Such weakness was frowned upon in the Dragon's Breaths. His people were not there to make friends or fall in love. They were bred by their creators, the Shadow elves, many centuries ago, to do their bidding during the lighted hours. They were designed to hunt and slay, and little more.

Deep in his heart, he knew she was not a hunter like him. But there were consequences to pay for those who did not follow the way of the sword. Bone elves who weren't considered "gifted" enough to exist for the reasons they were bred had two options: marry a true Bone elf warrior for the purpose of breeding, like his father did, or meet a tragic end.

Fala would never pass the investiture, and Incanus knew it. But she wouldn't have to if he did. He would demand her hand as part of his accolade of ascension, taking her as his mate, thus saving her from this test of tests. Some may think she had no choice, but he'd know better. They had a love, even if it was unspoken. And damn those to the Trials of Threnody if they didn't believe them.

"This is dangerous," she reminded him. Her body tensed. "Please be careful if they come for you this evening."

Incanus turned back to the group of aldermen standing in the grove and offered her a kind smile. "If they are here for my investiture," he said, "then I shall pass their test."

"Incanus... wake up."

At the sound of his mother's familiar voice, Incanus snapped his eyes open to find her slouching silhouette leaning over him.

"It is time for your blooding," his father's voice came from somewhere behind her. "You have the burning of one candle to prepare."

Their footsteps receded until the door closed behind them.

Incanus didn't bother to reach for the small candelabrum next to him but instead slid into his leather armor in the near darkness of their den and buckled on his longsword. He reached for his longbow in the rugged corner of the cave and made his way through the narrow cavern halls where his parents were seated at the table, feasting on pigs' ears.

"Here." His father held a bowl out to him. "You will need your strength for the ceremony."

Incanus took the bowl and began to munch on a crunchy ear. It was a near sacramental meal prepared for all catechumens, a name given to those seeking investiture before the rite of passage.

The three sat in silence, the noshing of their teeth the only sound in the cavern. For the first time, Incanus felt the pressure of the moment encroaching on him. Perhaps it was the evident tension in the den or his own nerves standing on end.

"You are ready?" his father mumbled, his mouth full of hog flesh.

Incanus nodded.

"Do us proud." His mother rose from her seat, followed by her servant-husband, and both turned to leave the room. "Come."

Bone elf parents rarely, if ever, showed affection for their children. Conversation was kept brief and limited, focusing on training or other duties, always with a distant target, the Rite of Investiture, for their offspring.

Incanus followed his mother through the rough-hewn corridors to the darkened skies of the surface world. The vastness of the Hall of the Ancients still shined down from the heavens above, the moon hanging low in the sky. He knew it would not be long before sunrise would come. Not only would he have to hunt, but he'd have to do it against the time of the rising dawn. He snorted in contempt at the needless trick and gripped the pommel of his sword as he strode.

His parents led him through the grotto, where they passed by the entrance of Fala's den. His eyes darted to the cavern opening, where he knew he wouldn't find her.

He looked anyway.

By this time tomorrow, he would be a hunter of the Bone elves of Bereslangum, and he could at last begin the life he had charted for them.

As they neared the training ground, his father stopped. Incanus turned a curious eye to him, but his father only offered an encouraging nod.

"Keep moving." His mother's tone was serious, and even tipped with a little fear.

The two proceeded into the open field before stopping in the center of the low grass. With a twitch, he glanced over to his mother to see her scanning the horizon. He turned and soon his elven eyes detected movement from a copse of trees and a cluster of jagged rocks. Shadows slithered toward them from every corner of the field, creeping ever closer.

At first, he looked up to see what creatures may be flying overhead, but as the mass of darkness moved nearer, he understood he wasn't looking at a mere owl or giant hawk above.

His fingers twitched, realizing the moment was upon him.

The Shadow elves had arrived.

Incanus strained against the urge to run from the encroaching darkness, but his mother stretched out her arm to stop him. The moving shadows encircled them before transforming in front of the pair. The darkness boiled and frothed in a primordial pallor, taking shape within seconds. Two Shadow elves now stood before them, their sunken faces emotionless.

It was the first time Incanus had seen a Shadow elf up close. Until now, he'd only heard the stories of their sires, told by the aldermen as folktales to scare the children of Bereslangum. He now knew the tales were more than just legends told to frighten or cajole. Their sires did live—or exist—in whatever form they'd taken in front of him.

"Incalia," one intoned, addressing his mother.

The cold, raspy voice chilled Incanus's soul, bubbling past his ears like an evil whisper. The Shadow elf wobbled when it spoke, the slight movement leaving the barest of traces. He couldn't help but cringe, but his mother shot him a sideways glance, stilling him.

She nodded and knelt, tugging Incanus by the arm to join her in genuflecting. "Sire."

"Your charge?" said the other, its voice no less disturbing.

"Yes." She cast her eyes to Incanus with the slightest of turns. "He is to embark upon his Rite of Investiture this night."

The Shadow elves looked down their slender noses at him.

"The woods are tricky for the eyes of a Bone elf this close to dawn," said one.

"Yes… Sire," Incanus dared to answer. "I prefer to hunt at this time."

"Prefer?"

"My prey feels the closer to dawn, the safer they are."

"We shall see." One of the Shadow elves gargled over the words, leaning toward him. As the figure drew nearer, Incanus felt a chill wind settle around him.

It breathed, Incanus thought. *It must be alive, after all.*

Without another word, the Shadow elves slipped back into the darkness, slinking away until Incanus couldn't see them anymore. He took a deep breath and stood tall, tightening his gloves.

"This way." His mother guided him from Bereslangum and the pair approached the edge of the forest, and then they moved deeper into the pre-dawn woods.

Incanus kept following, waiting for his mother to give him instructions, but he soon lost track of not only where they were, but how long they'd been walking. Perhaps it was nerves, as Fala suggested. He shook off the thought and looked up. They were surrounded by nothing but rustling trees and the dark night sky above them.

His mother came to a stop and turned to face him. "Are you, Incanus Dru'Waith, ready to take the solemn Rite of Investiture, to prove your worth to Bereslangum?"

"I am," replied Incanus.

"Are you, Incanus Dru'Waith, ready to swear your fealty to the Shadow elves, our lord masters and sires?"

"I am."

There was a brief silence between them.

"Then you are ready to begin your Rite of Investiture." His mother angled her face away, attempting to hide her emotions. "Bring the ears of the prey that dwells within this forest back to me by dawn. There is only one."

Incanus's face quirked, somewhat surprised with the challenge. Kill only one target and he'd pass the test? He had not imagined it would be so easy.

He dropped to one knee and bowed. "It shall be done."

When he raised his eyes, his mother had vanished. He cracked a half-smile, knowing he couldn't have asked for a better teacher. She was as silent and stealthy as he.

Incanus scanned his surroundings, his attention drifting toward the grass and mud beneath him. Within moments, he'd caught a trace of his prey: a set of odd indentions in the ground. These were not the claws of an animal or cryptid, but the booted footprints of a Raven elf.

"There is someone else here with us, Mother," he whispered to himself as if she was still there. It was an old habit formed from long hours of training with her hovering over his shoulder. In an odd way, the hollow act comforted him.

You have spotted it well, he thought she'd say. For tonight, for the first time, his prey was not an animal.

He started.

Moving in near silence, Incanus climbed a small rise, following the trail, and readied his bow. With great care, he drew an arrow from his quiver and placed the nock on his bowstring.

He dropped to one knee and inspected the trail, hoping he hadn't lost it. The elf's boot prints turned back and then back again. He smiled to himself. His mother must've known it was following them, and perhaps tracking the two of them for some time. Was this a scout from Ravenshire? If so, they'd gone too far north. A foolish and deadly mistake. Or was there a spy in their midst, hoping to find the well-hidden Bereslangum?

Then a rogue thought crossed his mind. It was unexpected he'd be chosen to dispose of the elf, rather than the warriors being sent to dispatch or even capture it, but he brushed the thought aside and continued to concentrate on the trail as he closed in.

His senses sharp, he kept his nose to the wind, hoping to catch any advantage. But something was amiss. If this were a scout or spy, why would it not retreat and report? His acute hearing detected a rustle behind him, and it was then he learned of his mistake.

The elf was hunting, too.

In a flash of instinctive reflex, Incanus arched his back just as an arrow skimmed his armor, sailing aside into the overgrowth. He spun and caught sight of his enemy's shadowy frame darting between trees, its hands scrambling to ready another shot.

Without thought, he rolled sideways, drew his string, and turned to fire.

The nimble elf had disappeared, but he knew the direction it had run. Taking another spin, he rose to one knee and took cover behind a mossy stone.

He waited. He listened.

The humming of a second arrow pierced the night sky, soaring by him. Then the shaft of a third, another near miss, exploded with a crack against the boulder in front of him.

He ducked and smashed himself as close to the boulder as he could. He heard the elf running and he sneered. This wasn't just some scout. This elf had been trained well. To displace after every shot was a wise tactic, never letting your enemy hone in on your position.

Incanus used the elf's motion against him. Instead of staying pinned, he sprinted in the opposite direction, back down the small slope, and then broke to the left to avoid a shot that never came.

With patience beyond his years, Incanus took cover, leaning in on a gossamer tree that split at the trunk, giving him cover and multiple lines of sight. He counted to himself, working to control his breathing, and listened.

Seconds felt like minutes, minutes like hours. He reflected on his training, hearing his mother's voice in his head: *The first to move in a stalemate is dead.*

He didn't care that the sun was approaching. He knew any clue to his presence would be his last. He remained still.

The slightest of noises rose on the wind. He strained his senses and heard the familiar sound of a bowstring stretching. With a pirouette, he spun from behind the gossamer tree and lurched to his right, nocking an arrow in the same flurry of motion.

The screeching of a loosed arrow whistled by, the sniper forfeiting his position. Even still in a roll, Incanus discerned the shape of his elven target leaning out of his superior position atop the hill.

Incanus raised his bow and fired on the run—a near impossible shot, even for a practiced warrior.

The arrow leapt from this bowstring and zoomed at his target. Even before it reached the elf, Incanus nocked another arrow.

The sound of his arrowhead embedding itself in the tree in front of the elf popped in his ears and he heard his target gasp.

The stunned sniper fell back from the tree, allowing Incanus the freedom he needed to make the killing blow. His lips curled as he let loose, arrow hurtling for his elven prey.

The dull thud of the arrow hitting home rose above the quiet forest, and for a second the figure stopped to look down at the arrow embedded in his chest. With a feeble stagger, the elf stumbled down the hill and collapsed.

Incanus glowed in pride. His first true kill lay only fifty paces away, and now it was time to collect his trophies. He approached, bow still drawn, watching the elf clutch at the mortal wound. Blood spattered across the jagged rocks as he lay gasping on the ground.

He knew deep in his heart he'd pass this test and now he just had to make it back to Bereslangum before dawn to claim his prize—to save Fala.

When he arrived at the grisly scene, he knelt over the elf, drew his dagger, and moved to carve off his ears.

"That will teach you not to skulk around our land," Incanus boasted, triumph surging through him. "Where are you from, anyway?"

He'd expected a Raven elf from Ravenwood, a sworn enemy of his kind. But the smirk vanished from Incanus's lips when he noticed the delicate features of the near white elf and the distinct markings on his armor.

This was no Raven elf. This was a Vermilion.

Incanus stood, his blood curdling. He, like all other Bone elves, knew from legends that the Vermilion elves only appeared from behind their walls of Eldwal in times of great need. A Vermilion elf near Bereslangum was no mere scout from a rival tribe. It was more than that. It spelled something sinister, something malevolent, something…

The sound of an explosion in the distance stirred him from his own thoughts.

Panic gripped at his chest, his heart racing. He turned in the direction of Bereslangum already knowing it was under assault.

In an instant, he sprinted through the forest, catching sight of the burning light of flames in the distance. As he raced along, he could hear screams and cries coming from somewhere in front of him. At that moment, his only thought was of Fala.

Darting between the trees with reckless abandon, he reached the training fields where hours ago he'd left his mother.

Mother.

Howls emanated from deep within the caverns, and even at this distance, his elven eyes revealed white stallions of the Vermilion cavalry riding in a phalanx to cut off those trying to escape the slaughter.

He ran as hard as he could, as fast as he could. His legs burned and his lungs heaved in desperation, tears welling in his eyes. Without fear, he made his way toward the grotto, staying low and skirting around the edge of the hidden grove. There were too many for him to kill, and he knew he'd surely fall to their blades if he wasn't careful. His breath nearly escaped him when he crested the rise in front of him.

It was a massacre. Bone elven bodies, strewn like bloody and broken dolls littered the ground of his once-proud home. Some had fallen to arrows, others to the sword. But the smell from the smoldering flames that flushed out the underground dens struck him the most. The hale of white-hot magic still plumed in an ebb and flow from the entrance where the fires burned.

Incanus grabbed at his chest, hoping against all hope that Fala had escaped. She was no warrior, but she had magic and knew the woods better than any other of their kind.

Then a dozen Bone elves and the two Shadow elves he'd met earlier were rounded up and led from the fiery caves, weaponless and unarmored, surrounded by a patrol of Vermillion elves. Each of the Vermilion donned the same distinctive armor as the one he had killed.

Incanus squinted and shielded his face as the Vermilion lifted their torches and threw them at the Shadow elves. With a powerful voice, one of the Vermilion called out a magical incantation and orange flames burst forth from the torches, encircling the Shadow elves in a wave of light. Screams of agony echoed across the night sky as the Shadow elves dissipated, wilting in the illumination of the magical spell. Their ethereal cries only grew louder as they disintegrated into wisps of black smoke.

Incanus couldn't stand to witness more. Suppressing the terror he felt, he ducked into the shadows and approached Fala's den.

That was when he saw them. His parents.

His mother and father, slain outside their den. His mother's mouth hung agape, her black blood still dripping from it, her eyes lifeless, impaled to the hilt on a Vermilion sword. His father's neck hung by a shred of skin, a beheading that had not fully done the job.

Frozen in his own tracks, Incanus's mind drew blank, as if his body had separated from his spirit. It was only when he heard a familiar voice that he wrestled himself out of his stupor.

It was Fala.

"Please! Please, no!"

Incanus's sharp senses caught the direction of her voice, and fury coursed through his veins.

A lone Vermilion had dragged her from her den, her family already executed at her feet. Her simple frock had been ripped and shredded in the struggle, and she cried out for help, tears streaming down her muddied cheeks. A Vermilion soldier stood before her, his sword out, his face hardened.

Incanus raised his bow, his fingers fumbling to nock an arrow. But the Vermilion's blade flashed before he could fire, showing no mercy to his beloved.

Fala crumpled atop the bodies of her dead family, her black blood tainting the once-white roses that shielded their grotto.

Incanus's jaw dropped, his hand stalling, knowing she was lost. His screams echoed in the night, but no one heard him, for the roar of his dying village was too strong. The flames of the slaughter raged behind her body, casting him into shadows. Unable to bear the sight, his eyes averted themselves from her body and fixated on the blackened petals of the white roses near her.

He was empty. Dead inside. Nothing mattered anymore.

"Come, Lord Dacre," one of the Vermilion commanders called to the bloody elf that stood above his beloved. "Our work here is done."

CHAPTER ONE

"The dead truly never leave us. They shall hunt you as long as you allow."
—Threnody, the Ancient of Death

"NOT MUCH FARTHER, MY LIEGE. The port of Abacus lies this way." Skullam's raspy voice shook Incanus from his thoughts.

Even with the Ophidian's potion, Incanus Dru'Waith's blurred vision persisted, and he knew he was dependent on his servant creature for the moment. His left eye, swollen and bloodied, remained closed, useless to him. The falcon's talons had missed blinding him by the slightest of measures, but the wound it left tore flesh from his face, exposing his jaw and teeth.

In time, he'd heard the Ophidian say when he and Skullam slipped into the dark alleys behind the crooked walls of the Twin Snakes. *In time your wounds will close, and your vision will return.*

Time was something he didn't have.

He hugged a wall and peered ahead with one eye, staying in the shadows as Skullam checked the streets ahead.

"The way is clear, m'lord." Skullam motioned for them to hustle between the streets while they could.

Incanus grunted and leaned forward, lumbering from alley to alley and halted when the imp did so. He could only see a few feet in front of him, so he stared down at Skullam's hunched figure, using it as his guidepost. His Bone elven night-sight should have been an advantage, but Ritter's war falcon stole that from him with the scrape of its talons. His keen ears still heard the harbor bells though as they neared, and his nose detected the slightest salt of the warm Abacunian sea breeze.

The two slipped by the final few streets, appearing at the

far edge of the harbor. The unique port was lit with tall poles, a soft yellow-green magic spilling in a frothy churn like waves in the sea from the high sconces, illuminating the docks.

"Where to?" Skullam asked.

When he turned, Incanus saw the open wounds on the imp. His bulbous nose, twisted and broken, still dripped a putrid, brackish blood. The tear in his wing from the arrow had ceased smoking—another scar wrought from Sir Ritter's bow. But it was useless to the beast, grounding him until the powers of the creature's dark trace healed it. In that moment, he took pity on his companion. For all his eccentricities, Skullam had been a loyal companion. Dauntless, the imp performed his tasks without complaint or consequence, save for the fear of not completing them.

"Can you still conceal yourself?" he asked.

"Aye, Master," the imp replied, understanding what Incanus wanted. Skullam closed his eyes and with the faintest of magical hale, disappeared into his innate spell of concealment.

Incanus leaned against the wall of the fishery, finding a moment of respite, while staying hidden in the dark shadows. He heard the quiet footfalls of the imp trailing away, creaking on the seaworn boards of the docks. He exhaled and closed his open eye, recalling the battle from hours earlier, the pain a constant reminder of his missed opportunity.

When they'd left the Twin Snakes, few thoughts occupied his mind other than revenge. A revenge filled with the worst pain and suffering he could possibly inflict on any other living being. A pain equal to the one brought to him those many years ago in Bereslangum.

Yet the lingering visions of how he'd been thwarted hours ago floated back into his mind's eye. The golden mace of Abacus—Peacemaker as it was known—brought with it a sorcery he'd hoped to avoid. But the weapon flooded the quad with its golden aura, taking him by surprise, and rendering him, for just a moment, without hate… without cause.

The humiliation.

The ordeal opened old wounds; wounds found on his darkened heart. Wounds, he thought, that couldn't hurt him anymore. *Fala…*

He wasn't blind to it. The connection—one between his trollborn adversary and the Vermilion princess. He had watched as Ritter stood, ready to forfeit his life for her. He knew that feeling.

Once.

Once, he too felt the same for someone—and he understood what compelled Ritter to stand in the way of any threat to keep her safe. Even though he'd not felt love for a long time, he knew why, yet he couldn't remember *how* it felt. And that lack of emotion made him burn with anger and rage, a reminder of the same love he'd been denied long ago.

He hated the trollborn Longmarcher for it. Hated them both—Ritter and Addilyn. It had become more than just revenge. Since the day he'd killed Dacre—Addilyn's father—his focus on the Vermilion princess had been more than just a desire. It had become an obsession, one that grew in strength with each passing day. He would end the Vermilion's line of succession with his dark blade and cherish dropping his black rose on her bosom, his revenge complete. Fala's honor and the honor of his family would be restored in the most fiendish of ways. Blood for blood. The illusory vision flashed by his closed eyes, and he fought the urge to smile.

The pain would be unbearable in his current condition.

"Master, I've found a vessel." The imp reappeared at his feet. "Empty, I believe."

"Take me there," Incanus mumbled, his voice garbled in blood and hanging flesh. He pulled the cowl of his cloak tighter and tried to maintain an unrushed gait. But he knew the Castellan were looking for him, and if the wizards of the Horn of Ramincere were employing their scrying spells, they'd be found.

The imp took Incanus by the cloak and used its magic to conceal itself once more, leading the man through the docks at a measured, unassuming pace. The Bone elf struggled to see and staggered from his wounds, appearing more like a drunken sea dog than a merchant or sailor. But the hour was late, and the Fates for once appeared to be on their side.

"Here." Skullam's tugging stopped and Incanus peeked from behind his hood. It was then that he saw it. A magnificent ship of ashen wood, not too large to catch attention but small enough to harbor a couple of stowaways. It was distinct from the others, featuring a purple-colored head of a roaring dragon at the front, its marbled face carved into scales and its eyes aglow with the reflection of mystical gems, casting a spectrum of fractured light into the calm waters of the bay.

"Is this the one? Are you certain no one's aboard?"

"None that I've seen, Master." Skullam looked up at the ship and sniffed the air. "But I must warn you. There is something about this vessel. It does not feel right. Powerful magic comes from it. It's empty, but perhaps we should look elsewhere?"

Incanus ignored the creature. He knew they couldn't spend all night searching for the perfect vessel. The Castellan could find them at any moment. "Climb on my back."

Skullam held on to the assassin's shoulder with his uninjured arm and hoisted himself up. Incanus moaned with the added weight as the imp's awkward clinging pulled at his wounds, but they had no choice. The creature couldn't fly and there was no plank lowered. He'd have to jump onto the rigging and pull them both aboard.

With a muffled groan, the Bone elf leapt and climbed, the imp's breath heating his neck as it seeped through his cowl. The wounds on his face reopened with the tugging, but it was a small price to pay for escape. Within seconds, he hefted them aboard, and with caution lowered the imp to his feet.

Incanus needed a moment to rest, but a moment he didn't have. With practiced silence, his blade slid from his leather scabbard as he motioned for Skullam to search the vessel. His eye scanned the deck, looking for any sign of a crew. To his surprise, they found no souls topside.

The assassin straightened, his shoulders easing a bit. But he knew they weren't done. He raised his blade and pointed to a small cabin amidships. With a flick of his outstretched sword, he waved for Skullam to approach. With careful steps, the two approached the cabin and his eye affixed on the door's handle. He readied his blade and flung the door inward, extending his sword and sliding into the cabin. Ready for battle, his heart pounded in his chest, expecting to have startled a sleeping crew. Instead, he found the room empty.

The interior of the quarters stunned the assassin. For a ship this size, it was a grand, near opulent quarters. The space seemed larger once inside the chamber than from out, with pristine wooden flooring and a long dining table stretching from one end of the cabin to the other. Several bronze lanterns adorned the tabletop and a cabinet full of whiskey and port waited at the back of the table, diamond glasses complementing the drinks.

A peculiar speculum hung to the left, framed in the same ashen wood of the ship. Its mirrored surface reflected, catching the swift reaction of Incanus as he turned away. His blurred vision captured only the vague figure of himself in it.

In truth, he didn't want to look. The sight of his face, as he had discovered at the Twin Snakes, repulsed him. But the mirror, so out of place for where it hung, lured him anyway.

"Master," whispered Skullam, "the mirror possesses of dweomer of sorcery. Be cautious."

"Hush." He moved closer to the mirror, his face still hidden in the depth of his cloak's cowl. He drew to a halt in front of it, resisting the urge to smash it with the pommel of his sword. He didn't move. He didn't dare. Even he, untrained in the ways of wizardry, could feel the magic of the speculum emanating from the polished glass in front of him. A strange and unfamiliar awareness seized him. There was something… behind the mirror… calling out to him. Not in a language, not with a voice, but with a feeling. A sense. A touch.

He reached his hand out slowly toward the mirror, but then a voice from outside the cabin startled him. "Hey lad, watcha doin' in me quarters?"

Incanus reacted with anger, his blade twisting as he spun to face his adversary. Deep down, he knew this ship couldn't have been left unmanned. How could he have let someone sneak up on him?

An old man with a bent back, an unkept beard, and a crooked smile stood grinning at him. The grin flipped into shock when he saw Incanus's fleshy mouth and jawbone wetting his cowl in black blood.

"By the Ancients." The old man cringed at the sight. "What happened to yer face?"

"Get off the vessel, old man." The Bone elf pointed his sword and motioned to the docks. "Unless you want my blade to remove whatever teeth you have left."

Rather than seem perturbed by this threat, the old man started cackling. "Fix yer mush of a face before makin' yer threats!" he hooted, and then looked to Skullam. "Oy, what's this? Yer pet?"

"How did you get in here?" Incanus barked, the cold anger still in his voice.

"Get in? This is me ship! I should be askin' ye that question instead."

"*Your* ship?"

"Aye." The hunched figure scrutinized the pair with bloodshot eyes. "Now, how aboot ye tell me what *yer* doin' on the *Ashen Dragon*? Did the ole' girl call to ye?"

"Ashen Dragon?"

"That's her name, boy," the broken man continued, one hand stroking the ashen walls as his eyes drifted, lost in thought. "A beauty she is, ain't she?"

"I have no patience for your delusions, old man," Incanus managed, stepping toward him. "Or should I call you *Captain?* This vessel is ours now."

"Oh, lad," hooted the old man. "Yer makin' a big mistake. Me girl takes care of me. And yes, you may call me Captain, or Thiago Amyr if ye prefer."

Before Incanus or Skullam could react, the old man clapped his hands and the speculum on the wall glowed a purplish hue, like the jewel encrusted eyes of the dragon figurehead carved on its prow. The Bone elf spun, this time catching his full image in the face of the mirror. Magic tendrils rushed from the speculum's surface, weaving in between Incanus and the imp, spinning and darting, and with a flash tightened around the assassin's torso.

Incanus tugged at the glowing tentacles, but his sword arm had been pinned down at his side by the amethyst-colored force. The magic tightened around him and lifted him from the deck. As he dangled, his sword slipped from his grasp and clanked on the floor. He fought to escape, and his good eye caught Skullam ensnared beneath him, twisted upside down and as helpless as he.

The captain laughed and walked by him, helping himself to a glass of whiskey at the far end of the room. After a few swigs, he leaned against the wall and smiled at the Bone elf. "Aye, she's gotcha good," spluttered the old man. "An' the little flyin' rat of yers."

Incanus grunted and tugged against the grip of the spell. He was drained from the battle earlier, injured and desperate, and the final wisps of energy left him. Escaping the tendrils wouldn't work. With a final sigh, he went limp, his face stoic. He and Skullam were caught. Surely, the hangman would await them. But worse than death was the knowledge that his quest for vengeance would go unfinished. His thirst for Vermilion blood unquenched.

"Oy!" squealed the man. As he approached, his whiskey breath washed over Incanus. The captain took another swig and put the glass down on the table. He leaned in and peered into Incanus's open eye. "Are ye sure?" he called to the mirror. He cocked his head back and stared into the speculum. "Both of 'em?"

Incanus, suspended in the air, tilted his head sideways, trying to look at the magical mirror but could only see the amethyst tentacles spilling out from the wall.

The man turned back to the assassin and approached, leaning in again. "Seems like me girl has taken a shine to ya. An' yer pet."

"What is to be done with us?" Incanus asked.

"Not up to me, no more," the captain sneered. "It's up to her. It's up to the *Dragon*. So, where is it ye wants to go then? Seems like stayin' here ain't an option no longer, eh, me boy?"

Incanus stared, suspicion and doubt cast upon his face. "What does it matter? You have us trapped here."

"The *Dragon* says she'd take ye where ye wants to go." The captain's jittering eyes bobbed between Incanus and Skullam. "Can't you hear her, elf? Ye should be on yer knees thanking 'er. So, boys, where'll be? The port at Lehane? The bay of Queen's Prey?"

Incanus thought for a moment. He saw no use in telling this old lunatic where he needed to go but at the same time, if there was an offer being made that didn't involve being exposed to the Castellan, he wasn't about to refuse.

He'd lost Addilyn but knew she'd eventually go back to where this all started. By that point, his wounds would be healed, he would be at full strength again, and he could resume his mission.

"Thronehelm," the assassin muttered.

The man grunted. "Aye, it's been too long since I sailed the Firth of Fury. The *Dragon*'ll take ye there."

He patted the wall as he exited the room, leaving Incanus to wonder how he'd get out of this mess.

CHAPTER TWO

"Those who find themselves lost will discover the value of finding their way home."
—Trillias, the Ancient of Sports and Tests

"YOU HAVE MY EYES!" Graytorris's haunting words echoed in Daemus's mind for days, even drowning out the incessant beating of his gryph's wings as they made haste in the skies toward the city of Abacus. The memory of the horrid man's eyeless face played over in his mind, staring down at him atop the Cathedral of the Watchful Eye, his putrid spittle wetting his brow with the bitter words.

"You have my eyes."

Their terrible shared secret—the source of the cursed man's crucible of vengeance now revealed—weighed on Daemus's soul with the gravity of an immovable lodestone. Was the mysterious visitor that granted him sight so long ago been Erud itself? Had their Ancient visited him as a blind infant, bestowing upon him both Graytorris's physical vision and the fallen Keeper's one true Sight before his banishment? Is this why Graytorris stalked him in his dreams—nay his nightmares—since childhood?

His heart sunk at the thought. *Why would their Ancient curse one and steal the innocence of the other, setting this unavoidable struggle into motion? For what purpose? Toward what end? And will my death lift Graytorris's curse? Why would that be so?*

The chains of his fate rattled in his mind and the fingers of reality gripped at his throat. A lump rose in his chest and he shook in unbridled rage and confusion. A helpless, blind child, unaware of Graytorris's sacrilege, was to be cursed with the torturous "gift" of their Ancient?

"No!" he screamed into the deafening winds, forgetting for a moment he was alone in his self-torment, tears streaming from the corners of his eyes.

Why would my Ancient steal my life away before I'd taken his first step? Said my first words?

Rolf, his hippogryph, cocked its eagle head toward him, its avian eyes twitching to understand the misperceived command.

Daemus leaned forward and stroked the feathers on the creature's crown. "It's all right," he said over and over, as if he were reassuring not only his gryph, but himself. "Keep going."

For days, the beating of Rolf's wings had been the only sound to reach Daemus's ears. Too tired to speak a word, he managed the barest glance at Katja. She sat ashen faced behind Caspar, atop their gryph, Syl. Once again, the Fates had cursed Daemus, forcing another innocent like her into a life-and-death struggle, simply for the crime of trying to help him. With his anger for his god renewed, he refused to give honest thanks to Erud that she hadn't been killed. Instead, he offered a silent prayer to Nothos, the Ancient of Good Fortunes, for her safety.

A voice sounded behind him, the exact words lost to the wind. Startled, he turned before realizing Caspar had called out to him.

"We've gone too far," Caspar repeated. "Got to turn back around. We missed Abacus."

"Arjun," Faux half-shrieked into the wind shear, trying to make herself heard, and Daemus nodded in agreement.

Following his friend's lead, he turned Rolf around and tapped three times on the gryph's wing, which he thought he remembered as the signal for the gryph to begin a slow descent.

Rolf and Syl obeyed their riders and began circling back, heading for the scholar city below. Within minutes, the beasts alighted on the wall near the Faye Tree and had to be cajoled by their riders to land on the ground. Daemus nearly fell off Rolf, trying not to feel envious of Faux as she dismounted with ease behind him.

"Which way is he?" Daemus asked, but Faux shook her head, looking distraught.

"I'm just—I don't—" She cringed. "I'm so tired. I can't remember."

"Gather around please, for just one moment," Katja ordered in a surprising but steady tone. Her face was still waxen, and she didn't look any less exhausted than the others. Faux shambled over to her, and Katja raised trembling hands and closed her eyes.

"Ssolantress, I beseech thee," Katja's appeal to her Ancient began, "bless these weary warriors and bring them into your healing arms."

Blue light descended over all four of them and their hippogryph steeds, shining brightest over Faux and Katja. Daemus sneezed at the magical shock, feeling energy surge into his limbs and clearing his mind of its fatigue. He reopened his white eyes. Katja looked even worse, but when she glanced over to meet his gaze, he could see a steel in her spirit that he hadn't noticed before.

"Thank you, Blue Lady." Katja bent then slipped to one knee, her voice harsh from the obvious toll the healing spell exacted on her. "Feeling better?"

Faux, still haggard, nodded with what energy she could muster. "Thank you."

Caspar, looking the fittest of the bunch, pointed in a familiar direction. "I think it's… I think it's this way."

The group didn't need to tie up the gryphs, as the semi-sentient creatures knew to stand by, and Daemus thought that anyone crazy enough to try to steal one deserved the swipe of a swift talon or the bite of a piercing beak.

They staggered forward, even with the respite the spell had imparted, and followed the winding streets of Abacus, Caspar gravitating toward Daemus.

"That little priestess sure is something," he remarked, drawing a look from Daemus.

"You're that impressed by a prayer? You've served Erud for more than half your life. You know what it's like to call on the Ancients for blessings. It's almost never how you think it's going to be."

Caspar looked surprised. "You've changed." His voice was somber.

"How do you mean?"

"Well, you used to be..."

"Weak?" Daemus supplied, trying to temper the edge in his tone.

"No. You just... you were like the rest of us." Caspar opened his mouth then closed it. "You used to have faith."

Daemus's lips tightened. "Sorry. I'm sure it's hard for you to see me like this."

"No, you're just being honest," Caspar replied with a shake of his head. "It's strange. But I suppose it's better than you just being terrified all the time. For you, I mean. You were always having those horrible visions, always wondering if the realm was out to get you."

"Well, now I know the realm *is* out to get me," Daemus mumbled, which earned him a grin.

"You're funnier now, too."

"Here," called Faux as they rounded a corner into the Mistchapel Quarter.

Ahead, Daemus recognized the scene of their recent battle, the spot of the Boiling Beaker.

Just a week ago they'd run for their lives here, evading the Knights of the Maelstrom. It felt as if he returned to the scene of a crime, one that he was somehow responsible for, yet in no way caused.

The red-haired rogue raised her fist and pounded on the door of the Beaker, perhaps a little harder than necessary. Uriah, the alchemist's assistant, opened it with a harried expression on his round face.

"Oh, it's you. You knocked so loud I was afraid you were the Castellan. Or—it doesn't matter. Come in, come in."

With haste, the orange-haired lardal shepherded them inside, and led them upstairs to a spare bedroom, one that used to house Anselm Helenius, the great cryptid hunter. Daemus took a deep breath, hoping to find his friend and champion, Arjun Ezekyle, doing well.

When the door opened, his eyes met Arjun's, who had managed to sit up on his own in his makeshift cot. Kneeling next to the captain sat Anoki, the Athabasica of Abacus, who by her weary demeanor appeared to have not left his bedside since Daemus fled for the cathedral. When he saw the captain bedridden, he knew something was wrong.

"Arjun!" Faux rushed to his side and took the hand that wasn't holding Anoki's. To Daemus's near shock, the man cracked a smile.

"You're safe." His hoarse voice scratched as he spoke, and his eyes wandered to Daemus and then to Katja. "You're all safe. I'm so glad. What happened?"

"We lost *The Tome of Enlightenment*." Daemus averted his gaze in shame.

Faux shot Daemus a glance, her brow furrowing. She

squeezed Arjun's hand. "We rescued Katja and injured Graytorris, but his antlered beast aided in his defense, and we had to flee before we could finish the job."

Arjun gave a short nod of acknowledgement, his smile falling.

"Never mind that, how are you?" Faux all but demanded. "Are you injured? Why are you still in bed?"

"Leg is gone," Arjun pulled the blankets aside, revealing a fresh amputation. His leg had been removed just below the knee, and it appeared the area around the wound, although dry, remained an unnatural black. His usual demeanor appeared unbroken, and the captain raised his head and turned back to Anoki at his side. "But the priest of Ssolantress was able to stave off the bleeding. And the alchemical serum that Jeric and Uriah concocted saved me from the poison."

Daemus heard the word "poison", but the shock of Arjun's apparent nonchalance staggered him. He struggled not to turn from the grievous injury and stopped himself from crying out or showing any expression of despair. He felt a bead of cold sweat on his forehead. For several months, Arjun had been invincible by his side. The old captain had trained him with his mace and crossbow, fought off the trollborn mercenaries that hunted them across the Vilchor Highgrass, and attacked cryptids where others would have run. Now, even though he seemed undaunted, Daemus wondered if his bravado was true.

Faux's shoulders slumped, and her lips quivered. "I'm so sorry."

"Faux, we have means to restore him," Anoki reassured her, though her pinched expression revealed she only half-believed it. "The wizards of the Horn of Ramincere have constructed a limb for him, one that moves using their magics. He can walk."

Daemus's eyes widened, and he noticed the device Anoki

referred to resting next to Arjun's cot. The artificial leg seemed to be fabricated from a form of metal, but a type he was unfamiliar with. He'd seen peg legs among sailors and crutches used by old soldiers, but this magic was beyond wondrous.

"I will stumble along like an old beggar," Arjun mumbled. A bit louder, he added, "The leg does work, but I need to learn how to use it. Don't know what use I'll be to you now, my lady."

Faux's eyes narrowed at his slip of the tongue, and she gave him a light and playful shove, though her face remained humorless. "No calling me 'Lady' until the Regency restores my title. And no talking that way. You're coming along no matter how slow we must walk. Right, Daemus?" She whirled around to look at him, her eyes filled with desperation.

Having no idea how else to respond, but just as reluctant to leave Arjun behind, Daemus offered a stiff nod. "If you want to come, that is," Daemus amended.

Arjun's eyes flashed. "I'm no charity case."

Anoki pointed at the device. "This will allow him to do more than walk. Once he's adjusted to it. The wizards of the Horn tell us it will move as one with him.

"We will go. I'm coming too."

Daemus, shocked, opened his mouth to protest, but Anoki cut him off. "Please, Daemus, for my sake, do not argue. I have already informed the city of my decision to step down from my position. I won't be separated from Arjun again." Her tone brooked no argument, but her expression was just as intense as Faux's pleading had been.

Feeling uncomfortable at the naked display of devotion, Daemus nodded again.

The proprietor of the Boiling Beaker appeared in the doorway. "Where are we off to?" Jeric Tuttle asked.

Daemus turned and hugged his friend, glad to see that

he'd survived the battle. "Thank you so much for helping with Arjun's recovery."

"It was my honor." Tuttle stepped to Faux and hugged her next. He nodded to Caspar and looked to the healer. "So, you must be the woman Daemus sprinted off to rescue? Katja, I assume?"

Daemus's eyes flicked to Katja's, and his face flushed red. His feet shuffled beneath him. Tuttle's words, although playful and innocent, stung. "More like rescued me. She saved my life by opening the Tome and stunning Graytorris with the light of Erud, long enough for me to escape the powers of his spell."

"We saved each other," Katja demurred, her expression soft. "If it were not for Daemus's bravery, Faux's sword and Caspar's daring flight, none of us would be here."

Daemus thought there was one name missing from her account. Radu. His old precept had been killed as they escaped on the back of their gryphs. Another friend dead, giving his life to save him. His face soured in the memory. "Jeric, you don't need to come with us."

"Nonsense." The alchemist shook his head. "Arjun will need me, so if he goes, I go, too. His wounds are healing but the Venom of the Abyss is the most dangerous of poisons. Its effects may return at any time. I'll bring my alchemical kit. Now, what's this I hear about losing a tome?"

Daemus's efforts to stop his friends from putting themselves at risk yet again ended in miserable failure. His lips drew into a serious line, and his eyebrows fell. "It is called *The Tome of Enlightenment*. It's our religion's most precious artifact. Before I could recover it, the fallen Keeper cast it into a magical mirror, and it spun away." Daemus's arms reached out as if the book was just outside his grasp. "I saw an image in its reflection… before the Tome all but disappeared."

"What did you see?" Tuttle asked.

Daemus swallowed hard. He knew what he was about to say would scare anyone. "The Laurentian Labyrinth."

"I'VE WRITTEN YOU A poem," Anoki whispered, not knowing Daemus was just outside the door. The Keeper halted and gave Anoki some time.

"*Where My Tide Leaves You,*" she began, unraveling a small scroll and reading the title of a poem she'd scrawled her thoughts onto. She read in a soft voice and bent to be close to Arjun's ear.

"My forgiveness flowers into a flood of petals, my love.

"Years ago, my heart bloomed,

"as I tossed water over my simmering soul.

"Our love grew like a thick meadow,

"where stems are stronger every spring."

"Oh, had I known the Ancient, Illustra would shorten our time.

"I would have challenged her, begged her.

"Given up to her."

"As my tears fall, they cut my cheeks,

"Sore and aching touches

"Shattered shards of my voice fall,

"Lost and muted,

"my cries as weak as ribbons."

"If Nothos divides us with the turn of his cards or throw of his dice,

"my knees will lose the strength that's meant to hold me.

"I will sink to my ankles in the quicksand of a battle gone wrong.

"Threnody, she of the Dark Wings and Sudden Doom,

"will plunge my soul into the shadowy realm of regret."

"May Ssolantress make every dewdrop of my tears
"potions of flowing cure, returning to you your strength.
"You are the eye of my storm,
"The winds that hold me tight,
"like your grip on pommel of your sword."
"Arjun, we need faith, but faith alone cannot be trusted.
"Our new beginning cannot be an ending that we can't fathom.
"Our love shan't be a snipped tightrope,
"that might have taken us to a new dawn together."
"You are my resilience,
"and if I could make the scrolls we passed
"hold tiny bits of power,
"to pull you through this battle,
"I would go back and do so."
"As I watch you disappear slowly in front of me,
"I wish I could tell you what a new beginning could feel like.
"It would have healing, like water over a waterfall.
"It would be new land, fresh to the steps of our feet.
"It would have smooth sand betwixt our toes, after finding a shore of seashells.
"It would be a place where we find each other again, Arjun.
"I will make sure you have our new beginning.
"You will start over, where my tide leaves you."
"I love you."

Daemus stood in the open doorway to Arjun's room, listening to the Athabasica recite her poem. When she'd finished, Daemus waited a few moments and knocked on the frame.

"Yes, Daemus?" Anoki looked to him.

"Katja and I are ready. We'll be waiting in the Gatehouse."

At her nod, Daemus left the two to their privacy.

MINUTES LATER, DAEMUS SIPPED his Abacunian verjuice and stared over the brim of his wooden cup at Katja, who sat across from him. The pair had stolen some time apart from the others, returning to the Gatehouse while Faux and Jeric made provisions for their travels and the former Athabasica saw to her final duties before their departure.

It had been a day since their arrival in Abacus, and he'd been waiting to find some time alone with the priestess. Much needed to be said, but he didn't know where to start. Then she spoke first.

"Thank you." A gentle smile appeared on her face, and he couldn't help but smile back. "I never had a chance to say those words when we fled the cathedral."

Daemus's mind struggled to find the correct response. His heart called for him to say more, but his voice stumbled. "I—I, uh…"

She continued, interrupting his awkward reply, "I am sorry we lost the Tome."

"I came for you, not the Tome," he blurted, nearly stunning himself. His countenance betrayed his true feelings, and the priestess blinked, then fell silent. A pregnant pause seized them, and the young Keeper bit his lip and drew a deep breath, unsure if he'd gone too far.

"You did?" her unsure voice whispered.

He knelt by her side, and she spun in her chair to face him. "When Caspar told me you were taken, I—I could think of nothing else but finding you." Sacrilege dripped from his tongue, but he didn't care. It was the truth. His truth.

"Daemus, I…" It was her turn to lose her words. She glanced sideways to the floor and fought the smile that began to curl at the corners of her mouth.

He battled every urge to reach for her, just to touch her face once. "As I said at the cathedral, it was the first time in my life I felt Erud had placed me in the right place at the right time."

Her gentle eyes teared, but she blinked them back. "But the Tome?"

Daemus struggled to answer. He wanted to profess his growing feelings for the priestess, but she'd reminded him of the dangerous path they were about to walk.

"Katja, I don't want anything to happen to you. I think you and Caspar should stay here." The moment the words left his mouth, he regretted them.

"Absolutely not," snapped Katja. Her face frowned at the thought, and she leaned away from him.

"But too many have died for—"

"You need a healer." Katja's blue eyes widened. "Besides, how could you ask me to stay behind when Erud's sacred artifact has been lost?"

"You serve Ssolantress," Daemus pointed out, and she scowled.

"You should know better, Daemus. I serve all the Ancients, and the good of this world. As do you. And you're mad if you think Caspar's going to listen to you."

"Not to mention selfish." Caspar appeared in the door, startling them. "I'm a Keeper, too, you half-wit. It's *our* Tome that's out in the labyrinth. Where would I be, where would any of us be if you failed? What would I tell the others? That I just let you go off on your own to die, letting our order die with you?"

Daemus mumbled in a smaller voice, "Of course you should come. Sorry."

Caspar's expression eased; Katja looked away.

"As I was saying," Anoki's approaching voice echoed in the Gatehouse's halls, "we really ought to get moving soon."

Daemus sighed at his ruined moment with Katja before he could stop himself. His pubescent attempts at navigating a budding romance had fallen flat, and Katja stood, turning from him as Anoki and Arjun entered the room.

To Daemus's surprise, the captain's magical leg didn't click or clack on the floors as he made his way inside. But Arjun struggled to hide the clumsiness in his gait and the frustration on his face. His eyes were dark, and his face sunken.

Katja, in her mild way, stepped through the group of friends and looked at the prosthetic. "I see you can use it, Captain. Is it not too painful?"

"I'll manage." Arjun's voice was resolute, although his face lacked any of his usual confidence.

"I sent word to the Horn of Ramincere," Anoki explained to the gathered group. "The wizards have stayed at the ready. They should be able to use their combined magics to transport us most of the way there. They assure me that the gryphs from the cathedral, captured or abandoned after the battle with the Knights of the Maelstrom, will make fine steeds for our return and will not fear their magics. They've been conjuring a riftskimmer spell for nearly a day now without rest or food, so our time is dwindling."

For our return, Daemus heard her say, but after every battle or dangerous encounter, someone often didn't return. Learning the hard lessons from Flowerdown Syphen, he swallowed his pessimism instead of voicing it. They hadn't even left yet, and he already wondered what Addilyn would say. And he knew they'd sorely miss Jessamy's sword and Ritter's bow, if not the keen senses of his war falcon, Storm. With a hobbled Arjun and a patchwork group, he wasn't sure if they were ready or even able to retrieve the Tome.

"Daemus." Caspar elbowed his friend. "C'mon, we're leaving."

"I'm sorry," Daemus managed to whisper to Katja, but he felt the distance in her eyes as she said nothing in return.

"HOW DID THEY BUILD that?" Faux muttered, her eyes glued to the mystical structure known as the Horn of Ramincere. The conical building twisted as it rose, thinning at its top, forming a point. The tip vaulted into the skies of Abacus, glinting in the afternoon sun.

At its base, Daemus noticed a row of hippogryphs, one for each of them, awaiting at what appeared to be a gate. All had been saddled with full packs and supplies. Syl and Rolf curled their heads back and forth in greeting as Caspar and Daemus approached. He reached out and petted Rolf on his neck.

"I am sorry, boy," he whispered in its ear. "This flight may be our last."

The gryph contorted, seeming to understand Daemus's tone, but appeared otherwise unfazed. He'd forgotten for a moment how courageous these creatures were.

He mounted Rolf and glanced to Katja, hoping she'd offer some sign of forgiveness. He found none, though the healer was preoccupied with mounting her own gryph. He knew how poor of a flyer she was when she first climbed atop the steeds from the cathedral, and she'd yet gotten better at flying at all, even getting sick a few times on their way back to Abacus.

With a flash, a gate on the base of the Horn began to undulate in the hale of a powerful magic. Soon the ensorcelled door cracked wide, and a grey-faced old man in worn, blue robes appeared.

"Thank you for your help, Tempest." Anoki bent at the

waist in a show of respect for the Horn's highest ranked wizard.

"The Horn recognizes the gravity of your quest, Athabasica." The Tempest extended his arms in an equal display of respect. "We are here to serve the Keepers and wish to see the cathedral restored. Recovering the Tome is a moral imperative."

Behind him, Daemus heard the incantations and conjuring voices of a gathering of the Tempest's fellows, setting off into a long and elaborate chant. A small gaggle of wide-eyed acolytes hustled from the gate, leading the group inside once all had mounted their gryphs.

Daemus exhaled, torn as to what to do. He missed his Uncle Kester, and Disciple Delling, and even, in a perverse way, his father and mother. He felt as though he were falling into an abyss, a future that he could not clearly see, all but abandoned by Erud and left to turn the fate of the entire world on his own. Looking at his friends made some kind of emotion stir in his chest, but his heart still felt too numb to know what it was.

Dread, maybe, because he felt sure they would not all make it out alive.

Moving without thought when Anoki gave the signal, he urged his gryph. The wizards' voices grew into a thunderous crescendo, then stopped all at once. A moment of silence passed, followed by a quiet hissing noise that resolved with a small crack, and then there was a hole in the air where there hadn't been one before.

"Quickly, now," Anoki said. "They won't be able to hold it for long. Everyone into the rift."

CHAPTER THREE

"One may walk, run, or even fly. But know your road will always lead you home."
—Xevvex the Wanderer, of the Rukkeva Glaciers

ADDILYN LOOKED FONDLY ACROSS the sky at Ritter and then Jessamy as they soared through the air, the cold winds of the Dragon's Breath Mountains whipping at their cloaks. They were traveling light, but that hadn't stopped them from wrapping themselves up against the weather.

The Kingdom of Warminster lay spread out below them like so many marks on a cartographer's map, and the stars of the Great Hall of the Ancients above them seemed to sparkle with a knowing glow, lighting their way as they soared through the air on the back of their hippogryphs. They'd been flying on and off for two weeks, snatching a couple of hours of rest every time the gryphs tired or needed water, and the journey from Abacus had by no means been easy. But it had also been something magical, like one of the tales from the lips of her father, Dacre.

The memory of Dacre brought a tear to her eye, or perhaps it was the bitter wind blowing motes of dirt from the fields below her. She raised a hand and wiped it away, then glanced back at Ritter, who maintained a resolute gaze on the horizon.

"Not long to go now," Ritter shouted, struggling to make his voice heard over the beating wings and the howling wind. "See how the fields have changed."

"It's too dark, Ritter," Addilyn replied, the hint of a smile playing across her lips. "I can't see anything."

"What about those elven eyes of yours?" Ritter teased.

Addilyn enjoyed her playful exchanges with Ritter. Her

sharp eyes noticed the changing colors of the trees. These weren't the wilds or the occasional farm. The fields below were marked and arranged into rows, the work of the nearby farmers of Hunter's Manor. She knew there were getting closer to the city, but she wasn't about to admit it.

Instead, she made a noncommittal noise and winked at the Longmarcher. "I prefer to gaze up at the night sky than to risk glancing down and losing my head for heights."

The final two hours of the journey proved to be the toughest. Time crawled along the closer they came it seemed, and she found herself counting down the minutes. They were due another break, but Ritter wanted them to push through to Thronehelm. Addilyn found herself nodding in agreement, despite how tired she felt and how her gryph needed to be fed. The finish line was in sight, the moment they'd been working toward for more days than she cared to think about.

They touched down in the cobbled courtyard of Castle Thronehelm and were greeted almost immediately by a phalanx of guards, their halberds held upright but in such a stance showed they could be lowered at a moment's notice. Captain Anson Valion recognized the travelers from their previous visit and gave the order for them to stand down.

"Thank you, Captain," Addilyn called, taking the lead by stepping down from her gryph and handing the reins to one of the guards, who looked bemused and uncertain, especially when the beast flapped its wings. "We've traveled long and far with news for the king and queen."

"I see," Valion replied, and Addilyn thought he probably did. The weeks of travel had taken their toll on her. Her face was wind-burned, and her elven ears were echoing from the shear. She still wore the same clothes and armor she'd been wearing in Abacus, battered and blood-stained. She had the look of a woman who'd gone through a great ordeal, and Ritter and Jessamy fared little better. "Please, follow me. My men will take your gryphs to the stables and I'll show you to the great hall without delay."

THE SKIN-STEALER THAT HAD taken the form of Meeks Crowley bided its time, carefully choosing the right place to strike. With the ever-present Makai now gone from the queen's side and the king immersed in late night preparations for war, Meeks had been left to serve the will of the queen.

It had waited for Godwin to commit to a late session with Blacwin and the prince before choosing to strike.

The queen was returning from a short visit to the parlor with her sister before retiring for the evening. Meeks, as always, turned her bed down, and one of the queen's handmaidens helped her out of her dress before departing the room.

It stood respectfully at the door as Crowley was trained to do, just outside of the room, as the queen was no longer presentable. It waited for the servant to disappear down the long hall and thought about how pathetic humans were with their clothes and shiny baubles. The skin-stealer needed no clothes; it only needed to feed.

"Is the king coming to bed soon?" Amice asked through the door.

"No, my queen," the skin-stealer replied. "He's discussing matters of state with the generals."

"Very well," the queen's voice called. "That is all then, Crowley. Good evening."

"There's one other small matter," it said, opening the door and slipping back into the room.

The queen turned to cover herself in the heavy blankets from the bed and gasped.

"I'm not Meeks Crowley," the cryptid admitted, its voice changing in its metamorphic state, "And I need your skin."

THERE WAS A GENTLE rapping at the door.

The cryptid spun, caught between the pleasure of feeding and the fear of being caught in the act. It peered back toward the chamber's entrance.

"I'm sorry, my lady," the handmaiden announced as she re-entered. "I forgot to leave your—"

The door opened and the woman gasped at the morbid sight, dropping her woolen blankets, and raised her hands to her face.

The skin-stealer hissed, half absorbed into the queen, who in her death throes twitched in pain, convulsing as the creature diffused throughout her. Reflexively, the cryptid lashed out at the surprised maid, a transmuted and deformed hand grabbing at her throat.

The woman's face contorted in fear as she stared into the honeycombed eyes of the beast, its true form revealed. She tried to scream, but the cryptid squeezed harder. It was all she could do to wheeze.

"Fool." Its voice bubbled, looking deep into his second victim's eyes. "I must kill you now."

With its hand wrapped around the woman's throat, it pulled her in from the archway and slammed her onto the floor, next to the dying queen. It couldn't let her escape and risk exposure, nor could it leave Amice's body while it was half finished. Its only solution was brutal and bloody.

The woman choked under its strength, her hands flailing, trying to escape.

The skin-stealer cracked the handmaiden's skull onto the castle's stone floor, again and again, until his victim stopped struggling. Blood drained from the back of the handmaiden's head, the light leaving her eyes.

With a heavy sigh it let go of the dead woman and returned to its feeding. Amice's skin bubbled and popped as the creature consumed her from with.

The three became two as Crowley's skin was shed, and the pair lay in a puddle of bloody sludge, a mixture of primordial goo from the cryptid and a sanguine red from the maiden.

For a brief second, the cryptid-queen stared at the poor handmaiden and wondered what to do. Then it made haste, closing the door and locking it from the inside. It worked feverishly to clean the messy scene of its transformation and kill. The queen had struggled, and some of her blood and bodily fluids had soiled the blankets and dripped onto the floor. Parts of her body remained, as the handmaiden's interruption stopped the skin-stealer from feasting on her from the inside out. Flustered, it knew it had made a mistake. Perhaps it should have waited until she was asleep, but time had been of the essence.

It rushed to gather the messy coverings and used them to wrap the remains of the dead handmaiden and her queen. The skin-stealer rushed to the privy chambers, lifted the wooden seat, and stuffed them into the hole, making a sloppy disposal of the bodies. It didn't have time to take care, so hiding the evidence in the long column that washed the excrement away below would have to do.

There'd be questions about the handmaiden's whereabouts and Crowley's, but the skin-stealer had no choice. The rudimentary beginnings of a plan began to form in its mind as Amice's knowledge seeped into its consciousness. When the chance availed itself, it would have the privy emptied and bury their combined remains outside the castle grounds. Until then, the new queen had to return to bed and await the king.

THE THREE TRAVELERS ENTERED the hall with the pomp of a full fanfare, the noise grating at Addilyn's ears and setting her teeth on edge. She felt her stomach rumble as she looked at the grand table, though it had long since been cleared of the evening's meal. She was so tired she found herself leaning on Ritter for support. And yet despite the royal welcome, the hall was quiet—unusually so, even for the late hour.

"The nobles must be preparing for the winter ahead," Ritter murmured when Addilyn asked him. But there was worry in his eyes that hinted at an unspoken thought.

The worry was matched in the lined faces of King Godwin and Queen Amice Thorhauer, who seemed to have aged ten years in the brief time since Addilyn last saw them. The king had lost some weight from his considerable frame, and Amice's face was drawn with worry. They were both attired in black.

"Ah," King Godwin bellowed after the fanfare subsided and Addilyn had curtsied in his direction. "The travelers have returned. Armed with more bad news, I trust."

"More, sire?" Addilyn struggled to not turn to Ritter, choosing to stare at the king. Diplomatic protocol pulled at her, but she sensed the king and queen would suffer no formalities this evening.

"Indeed." The king motioned for them to sit. "I'll have food brought to the table. In the meantime, we have much to discuss."

He clapped his hands and summoned a servant to carry a message to the kitchens.

"Before we begin, let me express condolences on behalf of the entire Vermilion nation at the loss of your son and also your nephew." Addilyn bowed her head as she spoke, her eyes drifting to the queen, whose face was painted in grief. "We fought by their side on the decks of *Doom's Wake* the night they both perished. They died... fighting for—"

"For what?" Godwin interrupted. "For the kingdom? The unity of the seven baronies is no more."

There was a pause, and Addilyn exchanged knowing looks with Ritter and Jessamy.

"Sire, we've heard news of the civil war." Ritter's face stared across the long table at the king and queen. "We learned of it in Abacus before we left."

"Poor news travels fast, I see," the king affirmed with a nod. "Von Lormarck seceded alongside the Thessaly family and took with them the Barony of Gloucester." He pointed to the arrows of war from Foghaven Vale and Gloucester hanging precariously over the thrones. "It is he who lies behind this treachery. Erud has abandoned us, deserting the realm, and leaving us to fend for ourselves in the darkness. War has come to Warminster, a war that divides the realm and will soon birth rivers of blood."

Addilyn said nothing, her mind racing at the reality of war. Her loyalty was torn between her friends and her people, and she wondered where her aunt, the Coronelle of Eldwal, would stand if the elves were called to the battlefield. Her people were secretive and preferred to avoid the conflicts of men, and yet...

"Come, Princess Addilyn." King Godwin clapped his hands together, jerking her from her introspection. "Let us speak from one royal to another. You've flown all the way from Abacus. The last we knew you were headed for Castleshire. Why have you returned? What news do you bring? Did you find Anselm Helenius?"

"Good news, and bad I believe, sire." Addilyn stopped when the doors to the hall opened, and four servants entered carrying meat and bread beneath silver cloches. The smell had her salivating, and yet the food would have to wait. "Helenius is dead, killed by the same assassin—"

"That killed our son and nephew?" Godwin interrupted.

"Yes." Addilyn tried to remember her father's lessons of diplomacy, even as the specter of his death still haunted these halls.

"What of good news?" Queen Amice's voice broke, and her eyes fluttered as she scratched behind her ear.

"Aye, Your Grace," Addilyn affirmed, attempting to steady her voice. "Our mission to Abacus met with success. The Caveat had sent us with a young Keeper, one who still possesses the Sight, to find answers to not only the visit of the tetrine to your kingdom, but to learn why Erud's light of knowledge has faded from their collective's eyes."

"And?" Godwin waved away an encroaching butler and leaned in.

"And the Athabasica helped us. She gave us a key that opened the magical doors to Vorodin's Lair, and we spoke with Vorodin himself. It appears the Sight has been fading because of the return of a fallen Keeper, a man known as Graytorris. He has taken control of the Cathedral of the Watchful Eye and closed *The Tome of Enlightenment*, severing Erud's connection with the Keepers of the Forbidden entirely."

"Was this Keeper Daemus Alaric, by chance?" A new voice rose from the corridors behind them, and Addilyn peered over her shoulder to see an old, squattish man waddling into the room. He wore the robes of the cathedral.

"First Keeper Amoss," the queen acknowledged their new guest, "please meet Princess Addilyn Elspeth of the Vermilion nation."

Addilyn noted the queen ignored both the presence of

Sir Ritter and her champion, Jessamy, but didn't interrupt. She stood and bowed, offering her traditional Vermilion greeting to the older Keeper. "Why yes, Daemus Alaric was our traveling companion."

"Was?" Amoss's eyebrows rose, his face prepared for bad news. "And where is Daemus now?"

"He left our company to travel to the cathedral," Ritter put in. "He and another Keeper named Caspar. One of our companions, Faux Dauldon, accompanied them."

The king shifted in his chair and looked to the queen, whose head sunk. "The cathedral has fallen into the hands of Jhodever, the former Keeper of Foghaven Vale and a puppet of Von Lormarck," he explained.

"Graytorris was cursed by our Ancient, Erud, two decades ago," Amoss added, "and his return reveals much, including an alliance with Von Lormarck. If Daemus returned to the cathedral on his own, he's likely captured, or dead."

Addilyn had no words, and so she simply shook her head in silence.

Ritter saw her discomfort at the thought. "We don't know what happened to him, sire. I wish we did."

"Much like my remaining son," the king murmured.

He sat back in his chair and stroked his chin, appearing deep in thought. Exhausted as they were, the travelers waited for him to elaborate.

"Monty has traveled north, to Rijkstag," said the king.

"My lord?" Ritter replied, his confusion evident in the tone of his voice. "You've delivered your only heir into the hands of your enemies?"

"Perhaps." Godwin's gaze met Ritter's. "The situation is... complicated. It's true that the Norsemen have been the enemy of my family and my people for many generations, but these are unusual times, and we must take every ally we can get."

"Still, sire, is that wise?"

"If I wanted your advice, Valkeneer, I would have asked for it," Godwin growled. "You mimic the worries of Keeper Makai."

To his left, Queen Amice looked imperiously on as though gazing out not upon the great hall but at the body of her murdered son.

"I apologize, my lord."

"Yes, well..." Godwin muttered. "Sending Montgomery north was a risk, but a calculated one. If the Norsemen come to our aid, it could turn the tide of this war in our favor. I've also dispatched Master Zendel Cray to Saracen to negotiate with Sasha Scarlett. Perhaps his silver tongue can bring the guildmistress back to our side. With her help and supplies from the merchant city-state, we can wait out the winter and wage war until Von Lormarck breaks."

King Godwin paused and signaled for an aide to pour him a glass of ale. He took the glass once it was proffered, downed it in one, then handed it back to be refilled.

"I have other news," Godwin continued. "And as part of that, I have a surprise for you, Princess Addilyn."

He stood up abruptly and nodded at his heralds, who raised their instruments and blew another short fanfare that echoed around the empty hall like the ghost of a laugh in a cathedral. As the sound died away, the great doors opened, and a wing of Vermilion filed in.

"My contingent has returned!" Addilyn exclaimed, clapping her hands together with delight. "The Vermilion haven't forgotten you in your hour of need, King Godwin."

But Godwin shook his head, and Addilyn's excitement faded as quickly as it had come, to be replaced with confusion and uncertainty.

"My lord?"

The leader of the Vermilion stepped forward and Addilyn turned to look at him in the light of the great hall's candelabras. The man removed his helmet, and Addilyn's face flushed in embarrassment.

"Lord Evchen Vischer." King Godwin gestured for the Vermilion to enter. "Your betrothed, Lady Addilyn Elspeth."

She felt Ritter stiffen beside her, and she didn't need to look to know what expression was on his face. It must have looked similar to her own.

"I'm not betrothed to Evchen Vischer, my lord," Addilyn managed in a sweet voice, though the words tasted like bile in her mouth. She wondered if the rest of the court could hear her heart as it fluttered in her chest like a chick that had fallen from the nest. "We've only begun to court, as the tradition of our people dictates. I mean no offense to either yourself or to my fellow Vermilion, of course."

"No offense has been taken, my lady," Lord Vischer replied, advancing on her and taking her hand in his. He kissed it and quickly returned it.

Addilyn risked a glance at Ritter, who looked as though he'd just swallowed a bad piece of meat that had stuck in his throat. She offered him a reassuring smile, but she sensed her sadness had shone through for all in the room to see.

"Why are you here?" Addilyn asked, turning back to look at her suitor. "When last we met, you were serving the coronelle, teaching politics and warfare at the Red Priory."

"I remember it well, my princess," Vischer replied. "I traveled here with First Keeper Amoss, accompanying him from the cathedral to ensure his safe arrival to Thronehelm. We live in dangerous times, and the coronelle thought it best that a man of such importance be given a guard to protect him should the enemies of Warminster make an attempt on his life."

"You've performed a great service to the realm," King Godwin added.

"And yet our work isn't done," Vischer countered. "I come bearing another message. Our coronelle has pledged to help in your war against the Von Lormarcks."

"I thank you." Godwin turned to Queen Amice, who cracked a forced smile. "We'll need every sword we can get."

CHAPTER FOUR

"Many that choose the path of shadows mistake the darkness for the light they truly seek."
—Warminster the Mage

THE NECROMANTIC LIGHT THAT glowed from the back of the eyes of Graytorris, now Master Mortus, swept across the room. It had been too long since he'd been able to see, and every sight, every image was pleasurable to him. The broken windows and cracked walls of the Cathedral of the Watchful Eye stood testament to his vengeance, his plan nearly fulfilled. He smiled, as best as a lich could, at his incantatrix, Zinzi, next to him.

"Bring me my chronicle," he ordered Zinzi.

"Yes, Great Keeper." Stepping from her light reverie of prayer next to him, Zinzi rushed to retrieve Mortus's magical diary and quill, taken from the tail of a vulture of the Killean Desolates. As she approached, the grey quill levitated from her hand and stopped, and she opened the pages of the chronicle, holding it fast. The quill spun and stabbed at her arm before returning to dip its nib in her blood.

Zinzi winced, hesitating to come any closer to Mortus, but he didn't react to her reticence. With his powers, he concentrated on the quill, letting her blood drip onto the pages, activating the magic.

With a thought, his spectral eyes drifted to images of King Dragich Von Lormarck, who possessed one of the three chronicles linked by the madman's necromancy.

"*The time has come.*" His mere thoughts controlled the quill, which began to scrawl a message into the chronicle. "*Begin the war against Thronehelm.*"

The message glowed faintly on the parchment and then settled itself, confirming that it had been transferred to Von Lormarck before vanishing.

Several moments passed before Von Lormarck's response came. *"I shall leave Dragon Ridge today and march on Thronehelm with twice the forces of Thorhauer."*

Mortus waited for the returned message to fade and began to pen his second missive, the quill dipping again into the small wound on Zinzi's arm. This time, the images of Zamiel, the Black Vicar of the Moor Bog appeared in his mind's eye.

"Zamiel, begin your descent upon Castle Valkeneer. I will join you soon." He still had a few things to accomplish before leaving the cathedral.

Several moments passed by and Zamiel's response came. *"And our deal? Our divine Mother awaits."*

"She shall be returned to you," Mortus promised, his temper short. How dare this mortal question him. He couldn't wait to see Zamiel's face once his "divine Mother" was restored. He, the Great Keeper, would control her—not some obscure and barbaric cultist from the Dragon's Breath Mountains. *The foolishness of mortality*, he thought, hoping to sway the interests of the gods.

He closed the book and looked to Zinzi, who returned it to the nearby shelf. With a slight *wuff*, the Antlered Man appeared behind her from the shadows.

"You will go to the lair of the Moor Bog ahead of me," Mortus said, "and deliver my orders."

The Antlered Man made no sound but moved toward the great mirror, Dromofangare, whose magical hale began to glow when Mortus turned to it.

Zinzi bowed to him, gathered herself, and moved to the front of the mirror.

"Exel vander bis," Mortus incanted in the conjurer's tongue and with one hand motion, the mirror's surface flared in a cold blue color. He felt the rush of Dromofangare's essence emote onto the ground next to them.

"Take Traumefang with you," he ordered the Antlered Man, and the near ten-foot-tall beast lifted Dromofangare's sister mirror from the floor with ease. "Careful, Rrhon." Mortus warned, using the Antlered Man's real name to underscore the need for caution. "If either you or the Black Vicar loses Traumefang, you will not be able to return to me."

With a slow nod, the creature that was once Rrhon Talamare, captain of the cathedral's Knights, bowed in understanding.

With one final glance at Dromofangare's surface, he watched his servants disappear into the bubbling froth of magic around them, where he saw them for an instant reappear in the lair of the Moor Bog.

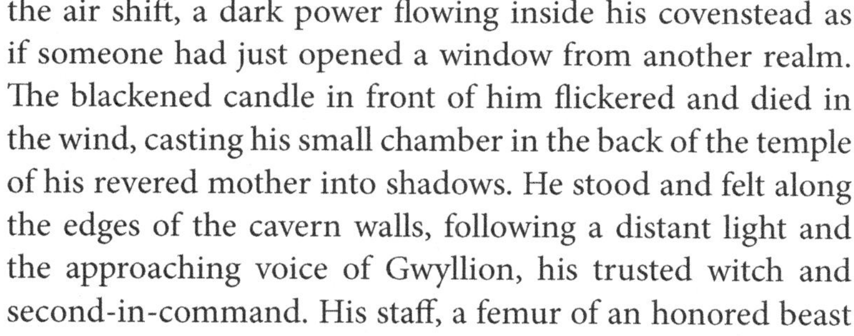

IN THE SPACE OF a breath, the Black Vicar Zamiel felt the air shift, a dark power flowing inside his covenstead as if someone had just opened a window from another realm. The blackened candle in front of him flickered and died in the wind, casting his small chamber in the back of the temple of his revered mother into shadows. He stood and felt along the edges of the cavern walls, following a distant light and the approaching voice of Gwyllion, his trusted witch and second-in-command. His staff, a femur of an honored beast lost long ago, scraped on the temple's floor, and as he neared the light of the inner chamber, three shadows stretched along the side wall.

"They have arrived," Gwyllion said as he entered the sunken chamber. "The Great Keeper is not with them," she included in a hushed tone.

Zamiel noticed a pique of curiosity on Gwyllion's countenance. Perhaps it was a vague hopefulness that the transformed lich would have been among them. After all, it was the cult's recovery of a tetrine's horn that led to Mortus's transformation and of course the younger witch would have wanted to see their handiwork. But she had not become the Black Vicar's favorite by asking stupid questions.

Zamiel nodded as if he already had this information and floated through the crooked archway and into the inner cavern. In front of him was one of the most spectacular creatures he'd ever witnessed. The Antlered Man appeared gargantuan in the den of the Moor Bog, dwarfing Zinzi, Mortus's incantatrix, at his side.

"Master," Zinzi offered the kind title to her former leader.

Zamiel ignored the pleasantry. She had been trained here, and he had helped place her with Mortus when the two had struck their deal. Seems he would benefit from this arrangement after all.

"We have been awaiting your arrival, honored one," he said. "It is a true honor to meet you, Rrhon Talamare." His face contorted in a mixture of depraved love for Mortus's necromantic creation and the wicked abomination of Rrhon's existence. He bowed low to the cryptid, meeting Zinzi's eyes when he arose.

"Does it speak?" he asked of Zinzi.

"Nay," she replied. "But he hears. And understands, of course."

"Rrhon," Zinzi motioned, "the mirror."

The Antlered Man leaned Traumefang against the cavern's wall but made no other acknowledgement of the Black Vicar's presence.

Zamiel's hopeful gaze wilted, and he looked to Zinzi.

"We shall bring your companion before the covenstead to honor him, and then you and I shall speak in private." He extended an arm to her.

Zinzi didn't take the arm but instead walked alongside him. He noted the change in her demeanor but didn't question it. The Antlered Man followed a short distance behind her.

As they exited the corridor into the main hall, the Harkening Bell tolled thrice. Their trio came to the center of the chamber, the covenstead gathering in clusters around the periphery, all in awed silence save one sobbing figure held fast and gagged by three cloaked men.

"My children!" the Black Vicar called across the vast chamber. "We have been graced by the arrival of an honored beast, servant of the Great Keeper himself."

The crowd oohed in near harmony, a low pitched and rote response to his declaration.

The Black Vicar addressed the Antlered Man. "O champion of our lost mother, be pleased with our offering."

At these words, the cloaked men pulled forward the sobbing figure, who had started to struggle, twitching against the cloaked men, and mumbling under the tightened gag. Two of them held his arms outstretched as he fought, while the third took a knife from his robe and made a shallow slice down the man's chest before they shoved their human sacrifice toward the Antlered Man.

Zamiel touched Zinzi's arm and gestured for her to follow him, and they turned away from the cryptid and his meal before the feasting began, followed by the crowd's cheers.

The Black Vicar wasted no time traveling back to the privacy of his quarters. Once there, he relit his tallow candle and watched Zinzi produce a scroll from the folds of her robes.

With eyes of steel, she handed it to him.

Zamiel broke the waxen seal on the message and unraveled the skin-like scroll. The missive was penned by Mortus's spidery hand, no doubt. He read its contents, holding the document to the candlelight in the cave.

The Black Vicar summoned his assistant with a deep call, and she appeared by his side in an instant.

"Have the covenstead stay in the great chamber after the Antlered Man has finished eating." The Black Vicar's eyes filled with dark delight. "The time of the return of the great mother is nigh."

"MY LADY," KAIL ILIDARI said, "the king orders your immediate departure." A flurry of servants flooded into her chambers from behind the enormous chamberlain to help Lady Isabeau pack her belongings.

"And what of Ember?" Lady Isabeau inquired, as she watched the servants begin to hastily filter through her things. "Has he sent word for her retrieval?"

"I know not, my lady."

"Kail, I will leave as ordered," Isabeau assured him, "but I must speak with my field marshal, Cherica Lambert, before I do."

"I will fetch her for you." Ilidari stepped from the room and Isabeau used the time in his absence to compose a scroll for Lambert. The attendants were working feverishly as ordered, so she didn't worry about her things. In fact, she cared little for them. She only cared for Ember and her safe return to Deadwaters Fork.

Minutes later, Ilidari returned with Field Marshal Cherica Lambert in tow. Lambert's light armor, made for a cavalrywoman, featured the blue and silver of the Fork and a silver trident brooch that held her cape behind her. Her face, drawn tight in the curiosity of the summons, betrayed her lines of age and the scars of battle. The Fork's leader of their legendary Tritons took a swift knee and bowed her head to Isabeau. "My lady."

"Thank you, Field Marshal," Isabeau said, "for coming on such short notice."

Lambert saluted Isabeau, crossing her heart with a bent elbow and fist. "I am at your service."

"Are the Tritons well?" Isabeau asked, handing her the newly inked scroll.

"All present and accounted for."

"Excellent," Isabeau replied. "You will stay here, under the command of King Von Lormarck and assist him in any way. He will need our Tritons if he is to defeat the Thorhauers."

"As you command," Lambert replied.

"I, however, am leaving to return to Deadwaters Fork." Isabeau saw the surprise in Lambert's eyes. "I have left orders for you." She pointed to the scroll she had just handed her. Isabeau knew Ilidari was watching, so hiding her note in plain sight might fool the trollborn.

She then reached over and hugged her field marshal, kissing her gently on the check. "I wish you good fortune in the coming battles. I will send reinforcements to you when I return to the Fork."

"Very good, my lady," Lambert agreed, then left the room, passing by the looming trollborn chamberlain.

"I am ready, Kail," Isabeau said with a kind smile, trying her best to distract him. "Would you be so kind as to escort a lady to her carriage?"

"I would not miss our goodbye," Ilidari responded, bowing to her.

Isabeau smiled once more and Ilidari helped her into her long coat. The two made their way with a mob of servants to the gates of Dragon Ridge where her carriage awaited. She looked up at the balcony outside the war room to find Dragich looking down at her. For the briefest of moments, she waited to see if he would wave. Perhaps one last farewell for an old flame.

But he did not.

She huffed and waited for Ilidari to open the door. As she climbed in, she turned back to kiss and thank her only friend in Dragon Ridge. She owed the man an apology, even if he didn't understand why. But as their eyes met, he directed her to a small box sitting on the other seat across from her.

"Farewell, my lady," he said, in a tone made for a final goodbye.

She could feel the tension between them and saw the old warrior's eyes fighting back tears. He closed the door without her kiss. She then heard the driver snap the horses to attention and they began the winding descent from Dragon Ridge with her royal retinue leading the way.

She sat alone, looking at Ilidari through the rear window, and then turned her attention to the mysterious box across from her. Fear told her not to touch it, but she had faith that Ilidari would never poison or trap her. She waited for the carriage to make a full round of the hill, far enough from any spying eyes and then gently lifted it to her lap.

The box was light and unlocked. She steadied herself and drew a deep breath. Summoning her courage and offering a fleeting prayer to the Ancients, she opened it. A small, awkwardly folded parchment laid inside. She recognized Ilidari's unpracticed handwriting hidden on the inside of the folds and smiled at his kind effort.

A love note, perhaps?

She unfolded the parchment and began to read. Her worst fears were confirmed. She would never leave Foghaven Vale alive.

CHERICA LAMBERT WAITED FOR Ilidari and the rest of the attendants to get far away from the confines of Lady Fleury's chambers before she opened the scroll. The ink hadn't even dried properly, and she knew it had been penned in haste.

The letter read in the lady's code. She hadn't trusted the king in many years, as their failed love affair had only led to tragedy and embarrassment. Yes, their two children had grown up well but apart, and in different directions as Aarav favored his father and Ember her mother.

But the missive was revealing. Cherica Lambert had her orders. Now all she could do was pray to the Fates for her lady.

She cast the scroll into the burning hearth, leaving no trace of the communication. As she watched the parchment turn red with flame a voice entered the room from the hallway.

"What are you doing in the lady's room?" said the voice.

She spun to see King Dragich Von Lormarck in the doorway. She bowed to him, but positioned herself in front of the flame, hoping to shield his eyes from the burning scroll.

"I was summoned here, my lord," Lambert replied. "I have new orders from my lady."

"And?" the king asked.

"I am to avail the Tritons to you. And guide them into battle under your orders."

"And?" the king pressed.

"That was all, sir," Lambert replied.

"Are you sure there was nothing more, Field Marshal?" the king asked.

"I am certain, Your Majesty," she added, lowering her eyes in a slight bow.

"Very well. Ride out with the Tritons to join the Thessaly's in the field. They may need you in Gloucester. If not, you will ride north to meet the bulk of the army. Your cavalry will be instrumental in our victory, I am sure."

"Of course, my lord," she replied. "I will next see you on the field of battle."

CHAPTER FIVE

"And now i've come to it, the labyrinth of my life.
My ancient lies before me, and i shall not fail."
—Daemus Alaric, Keeper of the Forbidden

THE GRYPH'S WAILING PIERCED the sky, and Daemus leaned into his steed, unable to lift his hands from the reins to protect his ears from the shrieking. He squinted in the strobing of the light and moaned, hearing the other riders and gryphs crying out alike. But as the seconds passed and they emerged from the riftskimmer spell, the golden tapestry of the magic fell away, crackling in its last moments of potency.

He blinked, and appearing in front of him were clear blue skies and clouds above. A rush of cold, thin air gushed at his face. His grip tightened and he winced, gritting his teeth. All those days of flight to the cathedral and back to Abacus still didn't lessen the woozy sensation of being off the ground. Even the straps that held him fast to the fashioned saddle offered little respite from the inevitable churning in his stomach.

Moments ago, they lifted off in Abacus as the wizards of the Horn of Ramincere cast their spell, and the sudden change in pressure and temperature made him sick. His ears popped and he turned, vomiting into the rushing winds, afraid to lift his white-knuckled hands from the saddle horn to wipe his mouth.

Something moved in the corner of his eye, and he turned: Anoki rose on her gryph next to him with a harried look, tears wetting her face. It seemed she fared no better than he in their transition. She pointed, indicating that they should descend.

He dared a glance down and saw their aerie of gryphs circling over a small landmass. In haste he nodded, and then turned to relay the message to Faux and Caspar on his other side and Katja behind him before tapping his gryph three times.

The gryphs began their wide, circling descent toward the sandy beach. As they got closer to the ground, Daemus's heart slowed, and he felt the sun on the back of his neck. When they touched down, he took a few deep breaths and wiped his brow before dismounting.

"Sorry, Rolf," he muttered, trying to apologize to his beast for his poor riding skills.

Rolf nuzzled him with his beak, and Daemus hugged him around the neck. The pair were making strides in their budding friendship, but he knew the hippogryph wasn't used to bearing such an unseasoned rider.

From the sands, Faux approached and handed him a waterskin she'd recovered from her saddlebags. Daemus took a long swallow, realizing he didn't know if there was more water nearby. He coughed, glancing sidelong at Katja.

"Where are we?" Blue Conney's usual gruff voice sounded distant, nearly lost in the crashing of the breakers of the Thalassian Sea. They'd managed to hit the beach, far enough inland to avoid the water, but close enough to drown out Blue's usual bluster.

"The Devil's Crest," Anoki called out from behind him and pointed a beringed finger at a reddish mountain that curved out of the horizon like a dragon's tusk.

Blue scratched his head. "I thought we were headin' for the Crown Islands."

"We're in the Crown Islands," Anoki assured him, motioning with her arms. "Due east of Deadwaters Fork and south of the Vale Mountains."

Marquiss smiled at Blue. "By the Ancients, you look even

shorter not mounted on Jericho."

The springheel balled up a fist and waved it at his friend. "No way the dog coulda made it 'ere on the back of one of those. I hope he doesn't give Uriah too hard a time. If that fool tries addin' him to your Marvelria, Tuttle, you may be returning to a few less creatures to protect."

"Enough of that," Arjun ordered, his tone serious, and Daemus realized he had been struggling to dismount his gryph with his magical leg. Anoki and Faux both moved to help him, but he held up an impatient hand and continued trying by himself while his uncomfortable gryph shuffled beneath him.

"The Devil's Crest is supposed to be the home of Trillias." Caspar's solemn voice held the slightest tinge of worry as he petted the neck of his gryph, Syl. "Trillias, brother of Erud, the only Ancient to never leave for the Great Hall and live with us in our world."

Daemus wanted to roll his eyes at the orthodox explanation taught to all Keepers. From everything he'd heard, Trillias held little interest in humans beyond treating them as a game. Though then again, Erud's deep involvement in human affairs had brought him nothing but suffering. He considered whether Trillias's approach might be better. For a fleeting moment, he half-wished the Ancients did not exist at all, and then banished the thought from his mind with a surge of shame.

Yet Graytorris's words crept back into his mind. His cursed eyes connecting the two men in some mystical way. The divine Sight. Was this just another game? One of Erud, and not Trillias?

Katja's voice parted Daemus from his thoughts. "*With us* might be a bit strong. From what I've learned from my Matron Mother, he rarely leaves the Crest, let alone his island." She turned to Daemus for silent affirmation.

The young Keeper nodded and said, "But he will hear challenges."

"How are we are supposed to *summon* Trillias?" Anoki asked, turning to Daemus and Caspar for help. "Does he know we're here to accept a challenge from him? Or do we need to walk the Crest to find him?"

"A sacrifice perhaps?" Marquiss wondered aloud.

"Are we sure we need to summon an Ancient?" Faux asked in a hushed voice, white-faced. Her lips tightened, trying to control her nerves. "Can't we just fly over the labyrinth on our gryphs and find *The Tome of Enlightenment* from the air?"

"No one can enter the labyrinth without his permission," Caspar explained. "Even flying above, tunneling underneath, or using magics as we just did is forbidden. Only he can grant us entrance to the labyrinth. After accepting his terms of challenge, of course."

Daemus had forgotten that most of his friends had little experience with the Ancients as he and Caspar had for most of their lives. Of course, Faux would be nervous. If Daemus had any common sense, he reflected, he would be nervous, too. It was as though all his fear had drained away when Delling died, like rainwater sinking into the ground, and all that remained was anger.

"How's this done?" Faux scratched at her head, the other hand resting on her hip.

"There's meant to be a riddle, I think," Caspar put in, an air of doubt hanging from his words.

Daemus didn't remember anything about that, but then again, their week of exegesis on Trillias had begun shortly after his horrifying recurring nightmares of Graytorris.

"We're not long on time," Faux pointed out.

Anoki nodded, her eyes still on Arjun. At last, with a loud

grunt, the soldier rolled off his gryph and fell onto the sand. Faux hauled him up.

"He had to know we were coming." Daemus turned to the distant Crest, feeling a little irritable when the thought occurred to him. He might not be on good terms with his Ancient now, but he was still Erud's chosen.

With sudden clarity, the idea of the gods forcing all his friends to fight through these struggles just to waste time in finding or summoning Trillias when the fate of the realm was at stake seemed unimaginable, even petty. His blasphemous thoughts from earlier started bubbling up in his mind again. He exhaled and schooled his mind into blankness, not sure anymore if he was doing it out of ingrained habit or because he simply couldn't handle where he might go if he followed the thought to its conclusion.

"The Ancients are not known for being easily contacted." Anoki covered her brow with her hand to stare into the sun, looking up at the distant Crest.

"I know what might work." Faux pointed. A piece of driftwood stuck out of the sand, appearing as though it had just washed up the night before.

Daemus squinted and realized it was covered in a script that seemed too tiny to have been written by any physical means. He hesitated, and at last went over and picked it up, having to yank a little to wrench it out of the sand.

"Here writ is the riddle of mighty Trillias, he who presides over Game, Sport, and Test and bears reverent witness to both victories and losses. For ye who find this ancient note, let the challenge of the Ancients begin. Three men enter a room with three doors. One of the doors leads outside, and two lead farther in. One man has a key. Two of the men are soldiers and the third is a prisoner, but only one of the men knows which is which. Upon—"

Daemus cut himself off, scowling at the driftwood. "I'm not reading all this. That wasn't even a tenth of what's on here. Trying to solve this would take days."

Anoki grimaced and made a grasping motion with her hand. "Let me see?"

Daemus handed her the driftwood, disgusted.

"*This* is your test?" he called at the mountain, making Caspar, Faux, and Katja all glance at him, wide-eyed. "This is your game, Trillias? Do you delight in making mortals think in useless circles, make your sport of wasting our time as this realm approaches ruin?"

"Sacrilege!" an earsplitting voice echoed in his hear, knocking the young Keeper to the ground. He grabbed at his forehead, raising his hands in a feeble effort to stop the intrusion into his mind. Tears streamed from his eyes, the deific voice booming in his skull once more. *"How dare you, Keeper? You, of all that seek my help, hurl insults at the one who could offer you a chance for victory?"*

The force of the voice made it impossible to understand, each word resonating as if caught in a ringing belfry. For the briefest of instants, Daemus thought to take a chisel to his skull in an effort to allow the words of the Ancient to escape.

After an excruciating moment, one that seemed to last an eternity, it finally stopped.

Daemus took a long, shuddering breath and fought to regain his composure.

Katja was at his side in another moment, helping him up, even—to his embarrassment—trying to wipe his eyes for him.

"I'm fine," he mumbled, and with a gentle touch moved her hands away. He staggered, punch-drunk from the effect.

"Was it really that bad?" came a loud, clear male voice

from atop the beachhead in front of them.

The group turned to the figure, and Arjun even dared to unsheathe his sword.

The man strode toward them, speaking with the practiced projection of a bard. As he drew closer, the figure's eyes glowed a gold so radiant it was as if they were peering into the sun. In the sweltering heat, it was easy to imagine that his presence had even raised the temperature a few degrees.

Daemus didn't know how to respond. The shock of the man's voice gone, he strained to squint and cover his eyes. He moaned, and the man—Trillias—shook his head.

"Not your experiences," he replied, waving a dismissive hand. "I meant the riddle, Daemus, *the riddle.* Was it really that bad? I spent forever composing that one."

The brightness in Trillias's eyes diminished as he approached, making gazing at his visage more tolerable. Daemus lowered his hand but stared at the swirls of sunlight dancing in the Ancient's glowing orbs. He looked to the gryphs, which he expected to scatter in the presence of a god, but instead, they bowed their avian heads in reverence. The act reminded him of Addilyn's horses and the story she told as the tetrine greeted her at her camp. But somewhere it registered that gryphs came to Solemnity at its founding. And as the history tells, perhaps by some instinct, they recognized the presence of the brother of their god.

" 'Forever'?" Katja mumbled from the sand next to Daemus; upon Trillias's arrival she had gone into a bow so deep she was almost prone.

"Yes, Priestess," Trillias complained, frowning at them. "I was here when this realm was created—before the beginning of your time. I was here before even the air you breathe. A perfect riddle for the perfect time. And yet, you just gave up before completing your read, Keeper? Is this how you behave toward me, the brother of your ever-faithful deity, knowing you have come here for my help?"

To Daemus, Trillias's bizarre tone sounded more like his mother scolding him than the voice of an Ancient.

"Might I speak, Lord Trillias?" Daemus asked, managing to find strength he wouldn't have possessed a few months ago. He bent to one knee and felt the Ancient's radiant eyes lower to him. Even from several feet away, the heat from his stare began to burn Daemus's skin. It was as if he'd stayed too long out in the fields of Solemnity. "As Erud's chosen, of course."

The Ancient paused. "I know why you are here, young Keeper. You seek my brother's tome, lost in my Laurentian Labyrinth. You believe the answers to all your questions lie within. The answers of who you really are, and knowledge to defeat the one who tossed the book into the depths of the maze."

"I am," he remained in a bow, joining Katja, even though his was less sincere. In truth, genuflecting to Trillias was more out of fear than respect, wanting never to hear his terrible voice again. "But my good lord, if you are testing my faith and knowledge of your history, understand that I know you lie. According to the knowledge imparted by the great Erud, you didn't exist until after Melexis, the Ancient of all elves, came to Warminster. And she's one of the youngest of all of you. There weren't any sports and games for you to preside over until mortal societies were born."

Trillias scrunched up his face, pursed his lips, and scrutinized Daemus for a moment. "I don't like you," he stated, almost petulant. "You're far too much like your patron, Erud."

Daemus, unthinking, dared to look up and started forward. But he felt a touch at his ankle and another touch on his shoulder. It was Katja, and Caspar, who had inched over to his side. He took a moment to breathe. "You aren't on good terms with Erud?"

Trillias glanced off to the side. "Neither here nor there, young Keeper."

After a moment, the Ancient continued, "I do admire you, and the courage it takes to seek my help. I was planning to help you. I suppose I see no reason to go back on those plans, particularly when there is—" he wiggled his fingers at them—"at stake."

"The realm," Anoki braved. She pulled at a piece of hair stuck to her neck.

The Ancient hummed. "This realm," he corrected. "Part of why I don't like my sibling. You know, they think they know all there is to know."

"Don't they?" Caspar's tremulous voice managed, his hand still resting on Daemus's shoulder.

"About this realm," Trillias retorted, his annoyed tone hard to miss. "Only this one, here and now, from its beginning until its death, and nothing past that. How is that everything? If I knew something about another realm, and I made a riddle of it, Erud wouldn't know the answer, would they?"

Katja tried to steer the philosophical conversation back to the matter at hand. "We are only here to ask for your help." Her voice sounded strained. "Lord Trillias, we beg your forbearance. We don't have much time. We need entry to the Laurentian Labyrinth in order to find the lost Tome of Erud."

Trillias's eyes fell on her for the first time. "Oh, little healer." His tone made Daemus's hackles rise. "You serve Ssolantress, I suppose. Have you been fighting with the young Keeper, yet? I'd imagine it's much easier to be devout when all you receive from your god is the gift of the healing touch, wouldn't you say, Daemus? No nightmares for her."

"I've had nightmares," Katja admitted, so soft it was nearly inaudible, and Daemus looked at her. She was still on her knees, her fingers wound together in reverence, but dauntless and diplomatic in the face of a god.

He felt a surge of pride.

"Please," Anoki added, "and we understand that this request comes with a price."

"It does, poetess." Trillias rolled his brilliant eyes and began to speak as if reciting a script. "You have traveled far and at great risk to seek my help. Oh yes, I will grant you entry to the Laurentian Labyrinth—on the condition that you accept my challenge. You must find the center of the labyrinth, where you will find my sibling's tome. And if you reach the center, you shall be doubly rewarded. There you will find the Heart of Laurentia, a gem of inestimable beauty and power. The Heart will help you to defeat your adversaries. When you first enter the labyrinth, you will hear the Heart's distant thrumming. If you listen close enough, it may even serve to refine your course. The louder you hear its call, the closer you are to finding it."

He squinted, appearing to consider something, then continued, "Know that the labyrinth grows each day you are within its walls. If you don't find your book in seven days, you'll be trapped inside—forever. And Keepers—" he pointed at Daemus and glanced at Caspar, who flinched and covered his eyes—"I don't allow the Erudian Sight to work inside the maze. My sibling will be cut off from you whilst you are within."

"And the gryphs?" Caspar asked.

"My sibling's pets may stay here on *my beach*." Trillias drew a deep breath and took a moment. "I'll keep them alive for you… *if* I think of it."

"Truly, Lord, you are too gracious," replied Anoki.

"Do you accept my terms or not?"

"Yes," Daemus said, his voice hoarse from both fear and excitement. His mind was fixed on the opportunity to be separated from Erud for the first time in his life.

Trillias did not wait for the rest of the party to confirm his acceptance. With a single gesture, he raised his hands and clapped once. There was a flash of light so bright that Daemus shouted in pain, and then the beach was gone.

CHAPTER SIX

"Magic, the undiscovered science."
—Athabasica, the Sorceress

THE ROCKING OF THE SHIP awoke Incanus. He opened his eyes to find himself in a tiny, bare room, lying on a hard bed with a drab of fabric as a mattress.

By his feet was Skullam, leaning against the wall. The creature never slept.

For a moment his mind was blank, but then Incanus recalled the events of the night before. The crazy old man, the pain in his face that continued to throb, the strange vessel they had found... Now their destination. They were going back to Thronehelm.

Back to Addilyn.

He struggled to his feet. His wounds were still fresh. His hand reached for his weapon, which lay at his side.

"Master," Skullam rasped. "You slept well?"

Incanus nodded in response. Without another word, he strode to the door and opened it, Skullam following at his heels.

The chamber door opened into the captain's quarters, but Incanus didn't recall the chamber being there the night before. Or the door, for that matter. He passed through the grand room with its long table, whiskey cabinet—and that alluring mirror.

This time, he didn't look into it.

The pair made their way onto the deck where they found the old man steering the vessel. The weather was fair and mild, a good day for sailing. The sun hid behind the clouds, but Incanus squinted anyway, his Bone elven eyes never adjusting well to the light. But the horizon was clear and the sky a bright blue, and he knew this meant their sailing ought to be smooth.

"Awake, are ye?" the captain said, that familiar grin spreading across his withered old face.

"How far have we traveled?" Incanus approached him, not sure whether to believe they'd set sail for Thronehelm or if the old coot was taking him somewhere… *else*.

"Four hundred and seventy-two leagues," replied the old man.

"Impossible." Incanus strained to turn to the captain, shielding his eyes from the sun. "How long have we been sailing?".

"Five hours, three minutes, and twenty-seven seconds."

"What?" Incanus gasped, and when he crinkled his face in disbelief, he was reminded of his wounds.

"Aye." The captain appeared to enjoy the look on the Bone elf's countenance.

"How so?" Incanus shook his head in disbelief. "At the speed we're going—it's impossible."

"This 'ere be a magic ship," the man assured him. "She… my love… makes us go fast when it looks like we're goin' slow. Ye should thank 'er, lad."

Incanus didn't know what to make of the statement. Was the strange man lying? His eyes seemed genuine, even if he was so twisted that he miscalculated the distance.

"Skullam?" he muttered.

The imp stared at the old man, his beady eyes searching for the truth. "I find no deceit in his words, my liege."

So, the ship *was* magical. Incanus hadn't forgotten the magnetic feeling that had captured his attention when he faced into the strange speculum and wondered if that was the source of the magic, where the mysterious "love" of the captain dwelled.

"Ye will travel a month on a normal ship and a week on this 'ere *Dragon* of mine."

The captain's proud words echoed in Incanus's ears. "How's that possible?"

"Lemme tell ye inside over a drink 'n nibble." The captain hobbled away from the wheel and toward his chambers.

He was a lot friendlier this morning, but Incanus wasn't letting his guard down. He could be laughing and joking with them one minute and have a knife at their throat the next. He'd learned that last night and as he and Skullam followed the captain, he kept his hand on the pommel of his sword.

The three of them entered the cabin and the captain made a line to the drink cabinet.

"A concoction of sorts fer yer imp?"

"He does not drink." Incanus's voice was stern.

"Water?"

"Nothing." Incanus sat and leaned on the table. "Ever."

The captain froze, gazing at Skullam for a moment before bursting into laughter.

"Well, where's the fun in 'at?" He took two glasses from the cabinet and a bottle of whiskey. Then he went into Incanus's room at the rear of the cabin and emerged with a tray of cheese, bread, and ham. The Bone elf sneered, knowing full well there was nothing in that room moments ago.

" 'Ere, Eat up. Or does yer imp not eat either?"

"Skullam doesn't eat anything from... *here*." Incanus shrugged.

"More for us then."

Incanus looked at the plate of food in front of him. Even though his stomach growled, the pain in his face still hurt too much to try to eat. He pushed its contents away and let the proffered whiskey sit. The mere thought of the burn in his torn mouth turned him sour. But the old man didn't seem to care, and before Incanus realized it, the man had cleaned both their plates and refilled his glass.

The ship continued smooth sailing with no one at the helm. As the captain swigged his drink and sloshed it around in his mouth, Incanus's shrewd eyes stared at him. He was calmer today, and not so keen to get his hands around their collective throats. And for what it was worth, he was being oddly hospitable. Incanus wondered what had brought about this change in manner.

"She likes ye!" said the old man after taking a swig of his whiskey.

"Excuse me?"

"She likes ye! The *Dragon*… is fond o' ye. Told me to treat you well… and I is."

Incanus stared at him, his expression blank.

"She tells me what yer thinkin'. How's yer wound?"

Incanus stiffened at the thought of the ship's magic, and apparent sentience. "Better."

"Want me to take a look? Got some old ointment in the cupboard. Might be able to speed up the healin' process."

"Perhaps later," Incanus said, his patience running short. "Why don't you tell us more about yourself?"

The captain chuckled. "Wouldn't ye like to know?"

After a pause to belch, he seemed to reconsider. "An' why not? We got time fer it."

He polished off his glass and reached to refill it, but Incanus stopped him, and poured a generous amount from the decanter for the man.

"Been a cap'n fer many a year. Started off as a young'un. Me ole man was a cap'n, a famous one at that. Fought in all manner of battles, did me ole man… famous fer it, too. Always said to me, 'Son, you follow in me footsteps, ye hear?' An' I says, 'Yes, Dad, I will.'

"So, I did. Fought me own battles, faced me own monsters, found me own women—not that they stayed around fer long!" He hooted with laughter.

"So how did you end up on *this* ship, Thiago?" asked Incanus.

The captain stared at him with a glint in his eye.

"Ah, there it is." He pursed his lips and downed half his glass, his eyes squinting. "This is the tale ye want to hear. All right… well, I'd not introduced meself before now but no time like the present. I was a cap'n of a Warminsterian vessel known as *Skyward Wind*. A naval mariner for King Godwin's father before Godwin 'imself became king."

"So, you worked for the royal fleet," said Incanus.

"Aye. And I was good at what I did. Won many a battle fer king n' country. Saw off threats to Thronehelm several times. It was after one of me greatest victories that I became cap'n of this 'ere ship… the *Ashen Dragon*. A beauty she was then. A beauty she is now." A whimsical look came over his browbeaten face.

"So how did she come into your possession?"

"It was one night," Amyr paused, taking another swig of his drink, his tone becoming darker, "and we were huntin' a pirate vessel. She'd been prowling the Firth of Fury an' we were expectin' an attack. We went a'huntin' fer her instead and fell upon the *Dragon* near the coasts 'round Seabrooke. Near the Horn, you see."

Incanus leaned in and Skullam crawled onto the table, his eyes staring into the captain's, who didn't seem to notice.

"Me and the men… we boarded the *Dragon*." He hiccupped and wiped his mouth before continuing, "It was a fierce night—wind n' rain was not on the side of the sailor. We found them… the enemy. Turned out to be one man."

"Like you," Incanus pressed. "One man."

Amyr took a hearty swig and stared out a porthole. "It were an Abacunian wizard o' sorts. He was the one that made the *Ashen Dragon*. 'Twas a fierce battle. The wizard's name was Jayvier Sevyn. He found a way to give the ship a life of its own—the ship was his, you see? 'E commanded it. But that's the thing… with magic. Abuse it too much and it drives ye insane in the end."

"You won, though, correct?" Skullam chimed in, startling the captain.

"It speaks," Amyr managed, his tone still dour. "Yer right, littl'in. We fought the wizard, me and the men. We won. I was meant to sink the ship. But before I killed this wizard…" Amyr pantomimed a stabbing gesture, and his eyes glazed over as he seemed to replay the image in his head. "Stuck a sword right into his gut. But 'afore I did, the bastard smiled at me… an' thanked me 'afore he died."

"Thanked you?" Incanus pondered aloud, leaning in.

"Aye," Amyr smirked. "He thanked me. An' then he freed *the Dragon* from his command."

He took another sip of whiskey, and a long, forlorn look came into his eyes.

"And then?" Incanus prompted him.

"Well, a ship can't just be released," said the captain as if he was stating the obvious. "It needs a master, you see. When the wizard set it free, *the Dragon* she… she, uh… she reached out and latched onto the nearest cap'n… which was me."

Incanus leaned away with the weight of the man's words and didn't reply. He could tell, even through the booze and insanity, that the man spoke with conviction, with truth.

"I was tricked, lad," Amyr admitted at length, fury now in his eyes. "That's the thing… the wizard knew. He knew what would 'appen if I killed 'im. An' he let me do it anyway."

For a second, Incanus thought he saw tears in the man's eyes.

Amyr straightened and took a deep breath while the Bone elf poured him more whiskey.

"The ship cannot exist without a cap'n," Amyr repeated, then choked down another burp. "And no cap'n can destroy *the Dragon.* At first, I thought I could control it. I said to her that I'd be the cap'n but… no. Good thing is, no crew needed, ya know. It's a magical ship. But no… the *Dragon*'s power is too strong. The *Dragon* controls… me."

"What happened to your crew?" Incanus asked.

Amyr slammed his drink onto the table, splashing whiskey everywhere, and howled, "No, my love! I is not unhappy with ye! I love ye! Forgive me!"

Tears began gushing from his eyes and Incanus, who had jumped up at the sudden movement, his hand gripping his weapon, relaxed. The old man was having another of his batty moments. Incanus looked at Skullam, who stared up at him, hissing.

"My love allows me, as gracious as she is, to leave her long enough to gather supplies," said the captain. Then, his voice as hushed as much as possible, he leaned over to Incanus, his bad breath wafting in the elf's face, and whispered, "She calls to me like a woman or babe… in the mind."

He sat back, and Incanus let the man's revelation sink in, their two gazes locked until Amyr managed one last sip.

The old man found a moment of sobriety enough to say, "Abacus is our home, lad, our port o' call. We been sailin' the high seas together ever since…"

Incanus shook his head, his eyes sliding to meet Skullam's as the captain rubbed his face.

"Well, I'mma go check on 'er. Remember, lad, we're at yer

service now. The *Dragon* has told me to tend to yer every need—even fixin' that face of yers. Me ointment could still do somethin' about yer mug, if yer'll allow it."

He patted Incanus on the arm and Incanus watched him hobble to the door and disappear in the fading morning sun.

"Skullam." Incanus turned to his only companion. "We need to kill him."

"Master?"

Incanus remained quiet and calm. "We'll kill him and then take control of the ship."

Skullam's leathery face puckered in confusion. "My liege, are you certain?"

"And why not?"

Skullam's eyes widened, and his demeanor changed. The creature looked wary, scared almost. "The hale of magic this ship possesses is unpredictable, sire. Perhaps it is because the captain is himself troubled in the mind. But I fear if we take his life, the ship may turn on us. Or worse. You heard his story."

Incanus stared at him. He knew Skullam, and if he was reacting in this way, with such fear, there was likely to be truth in what he said.

He sighed, annoyed. "Perhaps you are correct. In that case, we should wait until we near Thronehelm. But this ship is far too conspicuous to sail into her harbor. You heard the man's ramblings. Someone in that port, no matter how long ago the battles were, will identify her."

"Still, my liege—"

"We cannot afford to allow the old man to live. He's seen too much of us."

Skullam shook his head. "But, Master, who would command the *Dragon?*"

"Who exactly *is* this *Dragon*?" Incanus scoffed. "We will

see what happens as time passes. I think this sailor's tale is just that—a yarn spun from the old man's head to justify his lonely existence. The boat may have the hale of magic, but he's in control. No ship is *alive*. Come, let's go and join him on deck and learn what we can from him until it is time."

Skullam nodded and the two made their way on deck, just as the wind outside began to howl and droplets of rain spattered down from the sky.

CHAPTER SEVEN

"Regret not a life being yourself. Regret only a life chasing what others would have you be."
—Erud, the Ancient of Knowledge

KING GODWIN WAS TALKING to her, but Addilyn Elspeth was barely listening. His words stung her, and the pain had been made worse because she knew that he hadn't meant to hurt her. He wasn't to know how she felt, how her heart burned when she thought of Ritter. The king couldn't know how it was drenched in ice water when she thought about Evchen Vischer. She held no hate for the man, nor even disdain—in fact, she felt nothing, except perhaps for some slight gratitude when she thought about how his Wing had come to the realm's aid. It was hardly the kind of love that stood the test of time, but her people were a practical race and she'd always been raised with the expectation that she'd marry to secure an alliance. Vischer had been pursuing her for many seasons with the blessing of her aunt, the coronelle.

So why did his appearance make her feel as though she'd swallowed a lead ball that was stuck somewhere inside her stomach?

She glanced across at Ritter and saw the pain in his eyes, and that gave her an answer. Chance or not, this meeting had hurt the Longmarcher and placed their fragile relationship in jeopardy before it had even begun. She wished she could see inside his head and know what he was thinking and how he felt. And she wished that the two of them were alone so they could talk it over.

"...untenable situation," King Godwin was saying, as Addilyn dragged herself out of her reverie and tried to focus on the gruff sound of his voice and the meaning of the words issuing forth from him. "Let us ask Amoss for his wisdom."

"As the king mentioned, Princess." Amoss's face sank as began his tale. "The fall of the Cathedral of the Watchful Eye and the closure of the great tome place us at a grave disadvantage."

Addilyn's heart sank at the notion. "First Keeper, we were in part informed of this while we fought in Abacus but didn't realize the extent of the revolt." She snuck a peek at Sir Ritter, whose face had taken on a pallor she assumed was from a combination of Vischer's arrival and the news from the cathedral, as well as the long nights on the backs of their gryphs.

"I am sorry," Amoss replied.

"Tell me, Amoss," Addilyn's voice piqued once the First Keeper had finished his tale and started tucking into the bread and wine that had been brought out for them. "What news is there of Daemus?"

"I wish I had something to tell you." Amoss offered a baleful shake of his head and swallowed the last of his wine. "The boy hasn't been sighted, but the Keepers are still blind and Erud's voice remains silent. I fear the worst."

"Speak plainly, First Keeper," Godwin said.

Amoss hung his head and said, "We believe he's either captured or dead."

"But what's to be done, my lord?" Ritter asked.

"Indeed. What is to be done?" Godwin picked up his empty goblet, his gloomy stare distant for a moment, then he signaled for an aide to refill it. "Well, young Ritter, your place is at your hometown of Valkeneer. You and the Longmarchers must defend the Bridge, as Valkeneer will be critical for the coming war. We must hold the Bridge at all costs, allowing us to bottleneck Von Lormarck's advancing forces and providing cover for our twergish allies from Clan Swifthammer and Clan Battleforge along the Garnet Pass."

"As you wish, my lord." Ritter bowed, and Addilyn noticed the slightest tinge of relief cross his face.

How ironic, she thought, that being ordered to stand—and perhaps die—would give him relief. Ritter was a complex and dutiful man.

"Jessamy and I will accompany him." Addilyn stood before either Ritter or the king had another chance to speak. Her cheeks flushed as she felt Jessamy shooting daggers at her from the seat beside her, but she was resolute and in no mood to back down. "Ritter and I have traveled together for many moons. Our place is at his side, and Jessamy's sword will be a valuable addition to the Longmarchers."

"I'm not sure—" Godwin began, but he was interrupted by Evchen Vischer, who rose from his seat at the great table with an imperious glare.

"My Princess." The Vermilion commander's face didn't hide his concern. "I can't permit you to head off on this fool's errand. It's my intention to take you back to the safety of Eldwal, where our people can protect you against your enemies. The coronelle herself—"

"The coronelle will need to wait for my return," Addilyn insisted. "Or else you'd need the whole of your Wing to force me back to Eldwal."

"My Princess, I—"

"I believe I've made myself clear," Addilyn continued. "I'll travel with Ritter to the Bridge, with or without the approval of the coronelle."

Vischer seemed taken aback, and Addilyn noted that King Godwin fought to hide the amused expression on his face. It had wiped away the tension from his troubled brow, at least for a moment. Or perhaps it was just because his tankard had been refilled.

Vischer looked at his soldiers, who remained standing in formation at the entrance to the hall as though they were guarding it from an enemy at the gates. Then he looked back at Addilyn, sighed, and sat back down.

"Very well," he conceded. "I can see that your mind is made up, my lady. If you're to refuse the coronelle's summons and wish to travel to the Bridge, my troops and I will accompany you to Valkeneer. If we can't take you to safety and you insist on placing yourself in danger, we can at least defend you against our enemies."

"Then it's settled." Godwin smacked his lips together and took a deep swig of his drink. "You'll ride for the Bridge come morning."

LATER THAT EVENING, AFTER they'd retired to their chambers, Jessamy Aberdeen maintained a guard at the door while Addilyn washed the dust from her face in a basin of warm water. They were both exhausted, and the parley in the great hall of the castle had done little to improve their moods or morale. Their beds were calling to them, but Addilyn had something on her mind.

"I can't believe it," Addilyn murmured as she toweled herself off with the fine linens the Thorhauers had provided. "I—I can't believe it."

"My lady?"

"Evchen Vischer and his Vermilion… here," Addilyn replied. "And King Godwin telling everyone that he was my sweetheart. Did you see the look on poor Ritter's face?"

"I did, my lady." Jessamy paused for a beat, just long enough for Addilyn to notice it. "He looked… well, heartbroken."

"Then it wasn't just me imagining it?"

"I don't believe so," Jessamy admitted. She paused again, glancing at the door as though she expected someone to break it down. The expression on her face revealed that she was wrestling with a different decision, and Addilyn thought Jessamy would have preferred it if the door did explode into the room. At least then she would have faced a challenge she could solve with the stroke of a sword.

"Jessamy…" Addilyn's eyes narrowed. "You're not telling me something. What is it?"

"It's not my place, my lady."

"Jessamy, you may be my champion and my protector, but you're also my closest friend. You can always speak your mind to me."

"As you wish, my lady," Jessamy replied. Her face had softened a touch, but she kept her eyes on the door. "And forgive me if I speak out of place. Ritter isn't Vermilion, and protocol dictates that a princess should marry within her race. It's tradition… an unwritten rule, but only because it's considered so obvious that it doesn't need writing."

"I know all of this." Addilyn turned, disappointment rising in her breast and threatening to spill out through her throat. "I was taught the ways of our people as a child, and you've hardly hesitated to remind me."

"That was before we spent many moons traveling with Sir Ritter," Jessamy continued. "And it was also before we saw Commander Vischer."

"And?"

"I am certain Commander Vischer will make a fine husband, my lady." Jessamy paused. "But not for you. As much as it pains me to admit it, Ritter is a better match for you, though it's against *all* of our customs."

Addilyn broke out in a smile, stunned with her champion's honesty. Jessamy had never been one to mince words, but her plain spoken response set Addilyn aback.

"I've been thinking the same, Jessamy," Addilyn confessed. "In truth, it's a dilemma I've been wrestling with for more nights than I care to remember."

"I know, my lady. You talk in your sleep."

"I don't!" Addilyn protested, playfully tossing a pillow at Jessamy, who dodged it without taking her eyes off the door.

"No, you don't, my lady. If you did, Ritter would already know how you feel."

"Did you just make a joke, Jessamy?" Addilyn asked. Without waiting for an answer, she continued, "It seems our journeys have changed us."

"For the better, I hope."

Addilyn hardly heard her. Her initial relief at Jessamy's words had faded to dust in her mouth as she realized they made her feelings for Ritter even harder to deal with. If even her Raven elf champion saw Ritter as a better match than any other suitor, where did that leave her? Doomed to a loveless future with Evchen Vischer? Or shunned by her people for breaking with tradition and choosing Ritter?

She finished her ablutions in silence, a storm cloud brewing in the darkness of her mind, and then changed into her nightclothes. With that done, she climbed into her bed, and for a moment found peace in the comfortable mattress and the soft pillows she'd missed for months.

"Jessamy, you're dismissed for the night." The princess motioned with her hand and closed her eyes.

"But, my lady—"

"Go and get some rest," Addilyn insisted. "You've earned it."

As Jessamy left the chamber, Addilyn waited for the door to close then slipped her token from around her neck. It was the simple one Ritter had woven for her from turkeyfoot, fashioned from the sturdy flower that grew along Harbinger's Run on their travels to Abacus.

A small smile appeared on her face as she remembered the flush of her cheeks when he explained how it reminded him of her hair in the moonlight. She held it up to the rising moon that peered through her window and kissed it, replacing it around her neck before the comforts of her bed raced her off to sleep.

LATER THAT EVENING, ADDILYN'S quiet introspection was interrupted by a knock at the door.

The moon was high in the sky and the hour was so late that by all rights, she should have been asleep. She wondered who her visitor was and why they'd flouted social conventions by disturbing her at such a time, especially when all in the castle knew how hard her journey had been. She told herself it could only be one person, and that Ritter had come to comfort her after the scene in the great hall.

That thought was enough to get her out of bed and into the fresh set of robes the Thorhauers had provided her. She knew she looked tired and that the endless days of travel had left deep lines in her face, but it didn't matter. Ritter had seen worse.

She opened the door, not sure what to say to Ritter to cure this dilemma.

"Good evening, my lady."

"Oh." Addilyn's brow raised, her heart sinking like a stone in the waters of Loch Keefe. "It's you."

"You don't sound pleased to see me." Evchen Vischer

gestured to the inside of her room. "May I come in?"

"Of course. My apologies. It's late and I'm tired from a long journey. It seems that my manners deserted me."

"Then I'll keep my visit brief." Vischer eased past her, and Addilyn closed the door behind him as he made his way to one of the simple wooden stools that furnished the quarters. "I bring you tidings from Eldwal."

"Oh? What news?"

"When your father's coffin returned from Thronehelm with his honor guard, your aunt was deeply concerned," Vischer explained. "She sent me and my men to save you, but we learned about the upheaval at the cathedral and arrived too late to be of much use, though we were able to save Amoss."

"You told us as much in the great hall."

"That's true." Vischer seemed taken aback by the princess's response. "I must confess that there's another reason for my visit. I… I feel for you, Princess Addilyn. Perhaps King Godwin spoke out of turn, but he meant well. I believe he knows the extent of my feelings for you and wished to play matchmaker."

"I don't want to talk about this right now, Evchen." Addilyn frowned. "I have great need of sleep. Perhaps we can continue this discussion tomorrow."

Privately, she hoped he'd forget all about it. She doubted Vischer's motives and suspected he was motivated by the thought of a seat beside her after Coronelle Fia passed and the mantle of leadership was handed over to her. She knew Vischer well, and she knew his family. The man was a fearless warrior and a worthy husband, but not for her. She was no prize to be won—and if she was, then Ritter had already won her.

But there were political niceties to be involved and a game to be played.

"As you wish, my lady." Vischer stood and bowed before

heading for the door. "I have no desire to deprive you of your sleep after such a lengthy voyage. In the morning, my Wing will escort you to Valkeneer. I will commandeer Ritter and Jessamy and roll them into our Wing for the time being. I will send word to Eldwal tonight via my war wizard's magics and implore the coronelle to dispatch another Wing to help guard the bridge."

Addilyn paused. "Thank you, Evchen. I appreciate everything that you're doing for the realm."

"I'm not doing it for the realm, my lady. I'm doing it for you."

With that, he offered up a formal bow and took his leave of the room. Addilyn locked the door behind him, de-robed and returned to her bed, but sleep was a world away from her. Even the comfort of the silks and pillows couldn't calm the carousel of her mind.

And so instead of sleeping, Lady Addilyn Elspeth returned to her introspection, and to her own growing feelings for Ritter.

ISABEAU WAITED, HIDING THE dagger in the folds of her long coat. The knife, no more than a ceremonial dirk, had hung like a noble ornament from her hip since her childhood, never drawn in haste or anger. That was not her style. She feared—nay, knew—now would be the first time she'd ever raise it in her own defense.

Her nerves stood on end, and she rubbed the feeling back into her hands. Her body twitched in anticipation, knowing the moment was near. Ilidari's warning was a blessing; one she'd have no way to repay, save for using his gift to save herself. She would not let it go to waste.

Once outside the city of Krahe, the carriage slowed then after several excruciating miles, halted. The time had come.

"Driver," she called, knowing silence would look suspicious.

"Is there a problem?"

She felt the carriage shift around her as the weight of her driver leapt down from steerage.

"Aye, mum," the man's voice called back. "One o' the wheels loosened on the way from the castle."

The carriage door opened and her driver, a man in the middle of his life, looked upon her. She tried not to look to his hands for weapons but instead offered him a pleasant smile.

"I assume you need me to step out so you can fix it?" Isabeau struggled to keep calm and her voice from shaking, hiding the readied dagger in her long sleeve.

"Aye," the man nodded, offering a hand to assist her.

"Thank you." With her free hand she took the man by the palm and stepped on the lowered stair, and then plunged her dirk into the man's neck. She felt the cool, smooth metal meet little resistance before coming to rest when it reached its hilt.

For the briefest of moments, the driver's eyes widened in shock before his knees wobbled and he fell. The garrote, hidden neatly in his other hand, fell to the ground.

Isabeau stepped away from the fallen assassin, her body trembling and her eyes not leaving him until the last death throes shook from him. The jewel encrusted dagger she'd carried since adolescence was stained red in death.

Choking back tears, she looked around to see where they'd gone. The driver was smart enough to pull into a secluded grove to hide from passersby and complete the horrible deed. His loss was her gain.

In haste, she stripped her bloody jacket off and wiped her face and hands clean. She then hurried to release one of the horses from the train. Even without a saddle and bit, these were trained horses, and she was a skilled rider, born to ride in the horse fields of Deadwaters Fork.

She mounted her steed and looked back to the road. Her countenance turned south, the pathway back to safety and the protection of the Fork. But instead, she turned north, and headed back to Dragon Ridge.

CHAPTER EIGHT

"To be victorious in war, one must win first, then seek the battlefield."
—Koss, the Ancient of War

SOLVEIG JINS AND FIRST Keeper Makai rode in the royal carriage among a forest of Black Cuffs on their high steeds, donning the livery of House Thorhauer. They meandered their way through the outskirts of Ravenwood, their journey taking them back to the Garnet Pass.

The Black Cuffs listened to Jins but deferred to Makai. She knew where the pass was, but he outranked them all. Even though he was a newcomer to Thronehelm, a First Keeper held sway on all matters, stopping shy of direct orders from the royal family. Jins didn't mind, though. She preferred to be more of a guide than in charge.

In the morning of their third day, they reached the foothills of the Dragon's Breath Mountains and had entered Queen's Chapel. She knew they were only a half day from the subterranean entrance to the pass, and they were making good time.

Her mind swirled with ways to introduce Makai when they arrived in the Forge. In fact, she wasn't sure what to do with him at all. She didn't know the *krol* but hoped that Makai's presence and his return to his native home would earn them an audience. And although she owed no fealty to the Thorhauers, she felt their cause was just and welcomed the opportunity to position herself as close to the king and queen as possible. After all, there were golden palmettes to be earned here for Tancred, and then, of course, herself.

"Aliferis," Jins said to Makai. "May I call you that?"

"Of course," he replied, "as long as I may call you Solveig?"

She smiled back at him, her full cheeks widening at the thought of being casual with a First Keeper.

"I must confide I am not a well-known figure in Rawcliffe Forge, and I am a half-twergish trollborn at that. I don't know how the twergs, let alone the *krol*, will react to our arrival."

"Some will have a memory of me." Makai's voice was reassuring. "And I will tell them I came on a dual mission. First, to offer an alliance from Thronehelm, as the king requested, and second, to show Yen, my old friend, the runes that you discovered."

"And what do I do?" she asked. "I am a simple merchant girl, not a diplomat. This role has been thrust upon me."

Makai laughed and ran his hand over his beard. "You return with a prize worth more than its weight in gold. You are the queen's new personal jeweler, are you not?"

They both shared a laugh, but their amusement was interrupted by the sound of metal penetrating metal and the streaking of arrows from all sides.

Jins looked from the carriage window and saw two Black Cuffs fall from their horses while the other guards began to duck for cover. More arrows streaked by, clipping a horse and sending it and its rider charging wildly away. The rider wrestled to stay in his saddle until an arrow sliced through an opening in his armor, knocking him to the ground.

"Solveig, with me!" Makai yelled, then he jumped from the carriage.

The chaotic flurry of battle churned around them, coming at her from all quarters. Jins jumped from the carriage and rolled safely to the ground. She sat up as Phanna, her pack mule galloped away with Makai's pony, but she'd lost track of the First Keeper when she leapt.

She ducked through the legs of a riderless horse and saw Makai lurking behind the thick trunk of a nearby tree.

Two arrows zipped by her and stuck in the tree near her head. She fell to her knees, hoping to make use of her size and hide as best she could. Her heart pumped, and her mind raced. She fought to take stock of what really was happening, but she couldn't catch up to the battle that surrounded her. The dissonant uproar of the Black Cuffs barking orders jumbled with the growing clamor from their charging attackers.

"What do we do?" Jins cried, looking to Makai.

The First Keeper adroitly spun his quarterstaff in his calloused palms and pointed to a nearby thicket. The two sprinted for it.

The pitiful calls from the wounded and the neighing of the horses behind them created a bowl of chaos in the shallow dale they had found themselves in. The rushing footfalls of their attackers closed in from all sides, their war cries ringing in her ears.

The Black Cuffs, many now unhorsed, fell into a defensive circle, raising their shields as they had been trained. But the attackers were too many.

"Stay down," Makai whispered to her before he turned to run to help their guards.

"Aliferis, no!" She reached to stop him, but the determined twerg had left her behind.

She peered over the hill as he raised his hand, calling out in a language foreign to her. For the second time in her life, she saw magic appear. A yellow ball of energy emanated from his hand, and before she knew what it was, the First Keeper tossed it at the ambushers. The fiery orb landed in a pack of on-rushing soldiers and exploded in all directions. The shock of the magic hit her like the startling sound of a nearby church bell, and even the tree shook in front of her, casting its foliage about.

Yellow flames seared through their ranks and two of the marauders fell dead on impact, the fire still burning on their cloaks. Two others screamed out in pain, rolling and writhing, trying to extinguish the flames. But his magical effect did not dissipate, and moments later, their squirming stopped.

Two of the remaining ambushers turned to face the Keeper, their black cloaks and orange sashes spinning away from the surrounded Black Cuffs, but Makai's quarterstaff was ready for them. The first man lunged at the twerg, but the Keeper rolled through the man's legs, knocking him to the ground with a flourish of his staff. The blow connected with a resounding *ding* on the back of the man's helmet. The attacker fell to the ground, dead or unconscious.

The second assailant swung his sword down at Makai, but the twerg blocked the swing with his staff. The blade cut through the pole and clipped Makai's shoulder on the way, sending him into a roll. The attacker pressed on and stomped toward him, but Makai's voice called out for another spell. This time, his fingers launched a wispy volley of streaking lights that reminded Jins of arcs of lightning without the thunder. Each burrowed through his target's armor, disappearing into his chest. He screamed as the battery of bolts tore into his torso, dropping to his knees and then collapsing to the ground, dead.

Jins couldn't look away but wanted to hide her eyes. Her knees knocked, and she couldn't blink. The sound of the battle raged all around her. Regardless of what Makai wanted, she had to join this fight. She reached for the pickaxe she had at her side and pushed herself to her feet. She made a beeline for the battle and swiped at the back of one of their attackers. The axe's sharpened head punctured his armor and lodged in his back.

The man cried out and reflexively reached back, but Jins kicked him to the ground and removed it herself, finishing him off with a second swing of its hammerhead.

She stared for the briefest of moments at the anonymous enemy she had just killed, watching the blood pour from inside his helmet.

Blessed Ancients, what have I done?

"Jins!" Makai yelled to her, just in time to wake her from her stupor. She turned about and ducked away from the arcing swing of a polearm, tipped with a vicious blade and hook.

Without a thought, she threw her pickaxe at her enemy, and it struck true. The weapon spun perfectly in the air twice, as if she were at an axe throwing contest at the Forge and impaled itself in the man's face. His visor was knocked clean off his helmet and for a second, he wrenched back and dropped his polearm. He let loose a groan, stifled only by the pick buried deep within his face. Then he dropped backwards, arms and legs splayed apart, and stopped moving.

She rushed to the man to recover her axe, but when she tugged on it, the curvature of the pick only dug deeper into his skull. She let go of the handle and turned away, not wanting to see his distorted face. She instead stole the man's dagger from his belt and turned to look for Makai.

The battle seemed to be turning in their favor when a second row of men rose from the hillocks and descended on their position. Black and orange flowed down the hill like a swarm of bees, and for a second, Jins locked gazes with the man leading the charge. Her enemy wore a familiar coat of arms, the Jackal head of Foghaven Vale. His armor, more regal than his regulars, stood apart from the rest, and he wielded two longswords.

But the small circle of remaining Black Cuffs stood strong.

They awaited the next line of attackers who arrived with the resounding clang of metal on metal. Outnumbered as they were, the Black Cuffs weren't outclassed.

The screeching of more arrows came from behind thickets and from the trees around her. She ducked, assuming they were meant for her, but when she looked around, the arrows had found their marks. Cries rose from the ranks of the orange and black. One after another, the ambushers began to fall, some dead, some still alive and clutching at wicked wounds from the anonymous arrows.

A cheer rose from the Black Cuffs as they welcomed the help.

Jins looked for Makai and found him on top of a man, beating him to death with his own helmet. Blood dripped from the Keeper's face, and his eyes finally met with hers for the briefest of seconds. His shoulder bore a gash, but the wound seemed not to slow him.

Onrushing help emerged from the woods. These troops wore different colors of browns and greens and had forgone their bows to enter the fray with their swords. One of the men leading them into battle stood nearly seven feet tall and swung a sword above his head that was almost the length of two twergs. The first arc of his sword landed, nearly cutting a man in half. He waited for the body to fall and then ran to the next.

Jins stood to rejoin the fight, brandishing her dagger now, when two other men in brown hustled by her, one wielding a flail and the second a mace. Both had raven-colored hair and pointy ears, and for a moment, she thought the elves of Ravenwood had come to their rescue.

The leader of the Jackals tore his sword from the carcass of a downed Black Cuff and headed for the tall man, calling to him. The two met and engaged in a quick exchange of steel. The large man used his size to keep the quicker, smaller man at bay by kicking at him. His greatsword swung horizontally in front of him in short strokes, preventing his nimbler opponent from sliding underneath the defense. Their steel clashed again and again while the fight roared on around them.

"Surrender," one of the Raven elves yelled at the Jackal. "You are defeated."

"Death first," the leader spat, finding a brief stalemate against the giant human. Two of the Raven elves surrounded the leader, while the others joined the Black Cuffs to subdue the remaining attackers.

The leader growled in defiance, holding one sword to the tall man, the other to the elf that spun his flail behind him.

"Drop it, Jackal," the tall man bemoaned, but it only enraged the leader, who lashed out, his dual swords banging in defense against the greatsword.

As he turned, he hadn't seen the third man close ranks on him. Another Raven elf landed a full swing of his mace high on his back. The Jackal's armor bent, and he gasped for air as he fell, dropping his swords. The man curled up for a moment in pain and reached for his swords, but the large man kicked them away and pointed his blade in the face of the injured leader.

"The man asked you to surrender nicely," the bulging warrior said. "I would take his advice if you want to survive this."

The remaining Jackals, their fearless leader downed, cast their weapons to the ground in defeat. The Black Cuffs and their new allies swiftly moved in and bound their arms with hemp rope and placed their prisoners in a small circle together. In all, eight of the Black Cuffs lay dead among thirty dead Jackals.

"Solveig," Makai said, rushing to Jins as she fell to her knees. Her eyes welled with tears, and she cast the dagger she had stolen moments ago into the woods. Her hands shook, and the Keeper caught her before she swooned.

"I… I killed two men," she muttered as she took comfort in the strength of Makai's arms. She pulled at his riding cloak and saw his wound still bled.

"Are you all right?" With anxious eyes, she looked him over. "Oh, please tell me that you will survive."

The twerg smiled, and his white tail wagged from under his cloak. He removed her hand from his wound. "I will be fine. His sword merely glanced off of me."

"Let me look at it." One of the Raven elves approached them and dropped to one knee. His face was youthful, like any elf's, with a sharp nose and almond-shaped eyes. His hair was as black as the mines of the Forge.

"Please help him." Jins's voice wavered. "And thank you, good elf, for coming to our aide."

The man, preoccupied, didn't answer her at first. His hands searched through a pouch on his side and produced a small vial, which he opened.

"This may sting," he warned Makai before pouring a molasses-like liquid onto his wound. Even from several feet away, it smelled of hibiscus and honey to Jins. The old Keeper gritted his teeth.

"It stings," he grunted, "but the wound is now numb."

"It will heal." The elf half-smiled. "But try not to move it so much. Apply this once a day for several days until the wound closes." He handed Makai the bottle and then turned to Jins.

"You are welcome, my lady." He picked her up from the ground. "Are you hurt?"

"No, this blood is the Keeper's. And from the dead men."

"Keeper?" the elf said, his tone inquisitive. "I am Marr Larkin, a Longmarcher from nearby Castle Valkeneer."

“Thank the Fates for your arrival.” Makai grabbed the man’s hand in gratitude.

“We had been following you from a distance since you crossed into Queen’s Chapel and this part of Ravenwood,” Marr replied. “Our scouts found the Jackals waiting in ambush, and we arrived just in time. I am sorry that many of your escorts have been slain. We will make sure to take them back to the bridge, and I will sing a Lament to Threnody for their safe passage to the Hall of the Ancients.”

“You are most kind,” Jins managed, her nerves calming a bit. “Dare I ask, what is a Longmarcher?”

“We are rangers tasked to keep this part of Ravenwood safe.” Marr’s gaze lifted. “We serve the lord and lady of Valkeneer, under King Godwin and Queen Amice.”

“It is good to see you then,” Makai offered. “Very timely, if I may say so. We are from Thronehelm ourselves. I know of one of your nobles. A man named Ritter.”

A few other Longmarchers drew closer at the mention of the name.

“What of Ritter?” the tall man asked. “I am Wilcox de la Croix, his first lieutenant. We expected to hear from him by now.”

“Sir Ritter and the Vermilion princess made their way to Castleshire,” Makai explained. “But I fear I may bring sorrowful news. Talath Maeglen and Everett Thorhauer were both killed on the journey.”

A collective groan rose from the Longmarchers with the news of Talath, who was first in the Maeglen line.

“And of Ritter?” de la Croix asked.

“Sir Ritter went on to guard the princess, and one of my kind, a young Keeper named Daemus Alaric. They were to travel from Castleshire to Abacus, far to the south.”

"At least he still lives," Marr said, smiling in relief for the group.

"There's more. War is upon us. Foghaven Vale and Gloucester have left to form their own kingdom and have delivered arrows of war to Thronehelm. I expect you will be called up to defend the kingdom soon."

"My name is Til Aarron," a second Raven elf said as he emerged from the ranks. Jins recognized him from his fight against the Jackal leader. "We thank you for this information but must get this word back to Valkeneer—with haste."

"Would you like us to escort you to the safety of the Bridge?" Marr asked Makai and Jins.

"A kind offer, but Solveig and I are tasked with reaching Rawcliffe Forge with messages for the twergish *krol*. We were being taken there by the Black Cuffs until this assault, but I am afraid our messages will not allow us to return with you. We must press on."

"I see," Marr said, then looked to de la Croix.

"Rufus, Til," de la Croix ordered, "take five of our Longmarchers and finish escorting them and the remaining Black Cuffs through Ravenwood. Where exactly do you need to go?"

"The Garnet Pass." Jins pointed in the direction of the grounded carriage. "I can guide them once we near the mountains."

"Excellent." De la Croix nodded. "We will take the prisoners back to Valkeneer for questioning. Especially that royal over there. I've met him once from a distance at Castle Thronehelm. He's Aarav Fleury, Von Lormarck's half son. He was there the night the Vermilion ambassador was killed. I am certain the king will want to speak with him."

Hearing his name, Aarav Fleury spat blood in the direction

of de la Croix.

"What are you doing so far away from Foghaven Vale, I wonder?" De la Croix's voice was mocking. "So far… north?"

Aarav cast an evil eye toward the towering Longmarcher and remained silent.

De la Croix smirked. "I can't wait to introduce you to the dungeons of Castle Valkeneer."

CHAPTER NINE

"Ships asail invite mutiny, with n'er a deserter to be found."
—Captain Thiago Amyr, of *the Ashen Dragon*

INCANUS WAS READY TO make his move. Thronehelm's shore awaited them not two full days away. Over the past week, Incanus drew close to ending Thiago's life and taking command of the *Ashen Dragon* several times. Each time, Skullam protested, sometimes mentioning the *Dragon*'s magic, and other times noting how Thiago may be of use to them.

As the sun set, casting a dark orange glow on the oak of the ship, Incanus clutched his sword's pommel tighter by the second. He eyed Thiago, ready at the helm and lovingly stroking the wheel.

"There, girl," Thiago mumbled. "Feelin' a bit twitchy today, eh? What's 'a matter, huh?"

Incanus grimaced at the captain, spying Skullam watching his master from nearby. Incanus's anger rose in him like the coming of the inevitable tide. He answered to no one, especially not an *imp*.

"They'll recognized the *Dragon* in Thronehelm," Incanus worried aloud to his companion. "You heard the ol' man. Even if it's been twenty years. She's too unique a vessel for all eyes to have forgotten."

"Yes, Master." Skullam clung by his feet to the rigging next to the assassin. "But how do we get there otherwise?"

It was a less than ideal situation for someone so accustomed to life in the shadows.

"Easy, now!" Thiago cried, causing his passengers to spring to attention.

Incanus white-knuckled his sword's hilt.

"What is it?" Skullam asked the captain.

"I love, ye, darlin'. Ye must know that," yelled Thiago into the sky as the *Dragon* hit rough waters and bobbed. He left the helm and headed for the center of the deck, all the while pleading with an unseen entity. He dropped to his knees, his hands clutched in supplication.

"He's lost his mind," Incanus whispered to his imp.

Skullam flew to perch on the wheel, steadying their course. "He sees something."

"He sees nothing but hallucinations."

"My love, please!" Thiago yelled. "There is only ye. Yer loveliness is all I need. Ye are my jewel!"

A knowing of sorts overtook Incanus.

The time had come. Incanus *would* do something. Something he should've done the moment he was freed days ago.

Seeing the look of determination in Incanus's eyes, Skullam rushed to persuade him otherwise. "Master, no. You shouldn't. The magic is too powerful."

Incanus grunted, his patience evaporated. "Enough. I don't want to hear any more about the *magic*. From now till Thronehelm, you will hold your tongue, or I shall hold it for you."

Skullam shrank back and pulled his wings in close.

With the calculated footing of a masterful assassin, Incanus crept behind Thiago. The old man sobbed, occasionally pleading and muttering to himself.

The light *ding* of Incanus's sword as he unsheathed it fell below the captain's despairing hiccups.

Thiago was a miserable excuse for a man. The Bone elf felt as if he were performing an act of mercy as he brought his weapon to Thiago's throat and cut deep.

The old man's eyes flashed up at Incanus for a brief second and he blinked. His hands rose to stave off the blood that began to pour down his neck. He tried to say something and with bloody arms reached out for the assassin. But with failing hands, he dropped with a slight gurgle and a *thud* to the wood below, his blood puddling around him.

Skullam fluttered his wings but remained silent.

Incanus waited for the man's eyes to go dark then gestured to the corpse. "Come. Help me with the body."

Skullam obeyed, lifting Thiago's shoulders as best he could while Incanus handled the legs. They hoisted the former captain onto the railing, and gravity took over from there. The body fell into the ocean with a final splash.

"Captain. My captain."

The whisper came to him on the wind.

Incanus spun on Skullam. "What did you say?"

The imp shook his head. "I said nothing, Master."

Incanus knew before his companion answered him that it hadn't been Skullam who had spoken. The voice had reached out from inside his mind. But it didn't just come to him as a whisper. Accompanying the strange voice was an even stranger sensation, as if his limbs and even his brain had gone numb.

"Incanus," the voice said, tingling and caressing parts of the Bone elf that no outside force should be able to reach. It was not entirely unpleasant. Odd? Very.

Incanus gripped the railing with both hands to steady himself. He knew Skullam must be chattering away, but he couldn't discern what the creature was prattling on about. Skullam's lips moved but the words… the words were silent.

"Captain,"

The voice inside his head was hollow and distant, reminding him of the overwhelming feeling of serenity brought on to him by Millen Bane's Peacemaker mace back in the streets of Abacus. Without thought, he closed his eyes. Incanus's mind floated away, and he began to envision each part of the ship. The captain's quarters came to him first, then the brig, the stern, the boards of the ship with the *Ashen Dragon* painted on it, even the mast and crow's nest high above. He saw it all as if the *Dragon* was taking him on a tour of his new home.

For an instant, Incanus presumed this sensation must be close to how Ritter communicated with his falcon, that cursed creature. Or his mother had, with her crow.

The pain in Incanus's face returned and he breathed deeply, trying to lean into his new connection.

The ship buzzed with excitement at her new captain's acceptance. Her masts billowed, and her wheel spun, correcting their course to Thronehelm.

"My liege!"

Skullam's voice broke Incanus from his concentration. He glanced down to see the worried imp staring at him.

"No, my liege, fight it. It's the *Dragon*. It's too dangerous!"

Incanus huffed and blocked out what he could, focusing on the *Dragon*'s more dulcet tones.

SOLVEIG JINS WATCHED AS Til Aarron and Rufus Crag chose five of their fastest scouts and spent the rest of the afternoon helping the wounded onto their horses and wrapping the dead in their cloaks, placing their bodies on their steeds for their return to Valkeneer. As for the dead Jackals, the Longmarchers dug graves for them and buried them at the site of the battle. Marr said a short prayer and sung to Threnody as he'd promised.

After the other Longmarchers departed for Valkeneer with the prisoners, Til and Rufus approached the twergs.

"I am afraid we will need to ask you to abandon your carriage," Rufus Crag explained. "The road through Ravenwood may find us stumbling onto more Jackals. We have recovered your ponies and must ride offroad.

Jins turned to see her pack mule returned. "Phanna!" she cried and hugged her steed. Then, with careful eyes, she checked to ensure the queen's golden palmettes were still there.

"We don't mind," Makai replied. "I can use some fresh air after a battle. It's been centuries since my last melee."

"I actually prefer the ride to the carriage." Jins tried to sound upbeat, but she couldn't help her eyes from scanning the trees for more assailants. "I can guide us to the pass."

"Very well." Til Aarron mounted his horse. "We will take you as far as you will allow. I know the twergs keep their paths hidden and prefer to keep outsiders away."

"Thank you for understanding," Jins replied. "Although I think the Longmarchers have earned the trust of Clan Swifthammer. Will you return to Valkeneer after we depart?"

"We will first go north to Ravenshire, the capital city of the Raven elves." Til pointed north toward the thickening Ravenwood. "They need to know of this treachery. They are friends of Queen's Chapel and often fight aside the warriors of Valkeneer."

CHAPTER TEN

"Fear and courage are siblings. To be triumphant, you cannot have one without the other."
—Admiral Valerick Labrecque

THE SUNDOWNER RETURNED TO the port of Thronehelm, this time with Prince Montgomery Thorhauer on deck with hope in his eyes. They left the port of Hammerstead with two thousand Norsemen sailing their longboats behind them.

"Are you ready to return home, Prince?" Admiral Valerick LaBrecque's voice stirred Montgomery from his thoughts. The two men were not alone on deck but stood apart from the others.

"We shall see." Montgomery turned and offered honest eyes to his friend. His negotiations did not go as planned, but it was the best he could do. He hoped the king and queen would accept the terms of his blood oath and unexpected betrothal.

"You've done well." LaBrecque leaned on the rail of the ship and with a thoughtless spit into the Firth of Fury, he turned to face Monty. "What worries you?"

"Joferian," Monty admitted. He bade farewell to his cousin in Hammerstead, who was on his way with a second army to the Norse settlement of Hrolt and then to invade the Saracenean trading town of Vallance. But even on this short trip, his thoughts were of his murdered brother and cousin, Everett and Talath. And for the first time, he and Joferian were truly alone.

He knew his parents would have reservations, if not outright objections, to the Viking's plan, but time was of the essence and any ally was a good one. Even now, the nearing winter winds bit at him as they arrived in the chill harbors of Thronehelm.

LaBrecque patted him on the back as he started for the dock. "Come, Prince."

Before following the admiral Montgomery paused to hug the captain. "Thank you, Halford."

Halford bent at the waist in a respectful bow. "We are here to serve."

Montgomery pursed his lips and offered a respectful half-nod. As he disembarked with Admiral LaBrecque, they were greeted at the port by triumphant bells from the castle.

"The bells ring for you, Everett," he whispered to himself.

Anson Valion, the king's captain of the guard, met them in the harbor as always, and led them back to Castle Thronehelm with a contingent of Black Cuffs. The prince offered little in the way of explanation to Valion, asking him only to extend the courtesy of protection to their guests, Konungr Atorm Stormmoeller, and his family. And of course, his new bride. He wasn't being evasive, but his mind was elsewhere, tumbling through various scenarios he may find when he met with his parents.

As they rode through the town, they and their northern allies were greeted by throngs of cheering citizens, many of them offering prayers and thanks as they rode by, with some cries of "savior," or "champion," reaching Montgomery's ears. He let himself look into the eyes of the citizenry as they made cries of jubilation. Unsure what he expected, the looks of relief on their faces as he and his Norse friends rode by took him by surprise. Montgomery could almost feel it, like a balm on his battered spirit.

"Valion, what has happened?" Monty asked.

"War arrows from your uncle," Valion replied with his

usual stoicism. "They were delivered just four days past. Your return signals hope for all of Warminster."

A surge of rage and understanding shot through Montgomery. He bit his tongue in anger and pain. The news burned like a healing wound had just reopened to the stinging wind. His uncle. *King Von Lormarck.* It was clear now he arranged the events that led to Everett and Talath's deaths.

"Your father has summoned the Faxerian, Lucien Blacwin, from Halifax to lead the armies," Anson went on. "He arrived today. He and the king are meeting to devise a battle plan as we speak. I am to take you to them now."

Monty said, "The *konungr* must attend as well. The Norsemen are with us. Their armies are already on the move to Saracen," he added, letting his pride at this one accomplishment ease the painful revelation—if only a little.

"And Joferian?"

"He leads them," Monty explained. "He and the *konungr*'s youngest son, Argantyr."

"May Koss bless their swords," Valion replied. "And Baroness Maeglen's last son."

MONTGOMERY AND HIS RETINUE were ushered through the gates of Castle Thronehelm and into the great war room in the heart of the keep. The cavernous room stretched wide, built to seat many. Great frescoes of the seven baronies, serving as a map to the entire kingdom, etched the sides. Ancient flags, tapestries, and relics won in wars past decorated the walls, the freshest of which were Talath Maeglen's sword and Everett Thorhauer's armor. Monty glanced only briefly at them, knowing he would return to them later when he was alone.

Instead, he focused on his father and the Faxerian who

stood at the end of the long council table in front of a blazing hearth. Both the queen and Baroness Maeglen sat next to them.

"Mother, Father," Montgomery announced his own arrival. "I have returned."

The group looked at their prince with smiles and greetings. Queen Amice rushed to hug her son. She embraced him tightly and whispered, "You look well. You are unharmed?"

"And my son?" Cecily Maeglen asked, her eyes scanning for Joferian.

"He is safe," Monty replied, pulling away from his mother's arms. "He travels with a Norse army to attack Vallance. Then he will go on to Saracen."

"Under whose orders?" King Godwin asked with a cautious frown. He joined his wife in greeting their son.

"Under the direction of the Ancients." Einar Skullgrimsson, the Norse runecaster, appeared from the rear of the troupe speaking in broken Warminsterian. He lifted his hands in reverence before grabbing Monty's hand. Twisting the prince's palm, he showed the scar to the Thorhauer contingent. "We are allied, by blood oath."

"And who are our guests?" the queen asked, turning her attention to the barbarians in her war room.

"These are our allies." Monty offered a pointed bow. "This is Konungr Atorm Stormmoeller, son of Wolfrick, and king of Rijkstag."

"Son of Wolfrick?" Godwin approached the huge *konungr* and looked him over. "You are the spitting image of your father. He was a ferocious warrior."

"He died well," Atorm responded. "At your hands."

Godwin raised his head and his lips parted. Monty swallowed hard, eyes watching the two men. With a respectful nod from Godwin, the *konungr* extended his hand. The tension in Monty's neck passed as the two men shook hands.

"We are honored to have you as our allies," Godwin announced to the room. "I am proud of you, son." Breaking from Atorm, Godwin placed one hand on Monty's shoulder, the other on the ample shoulder of the *Konungr*. A look of cautious pride creased his brows.

"Father, this is Atorm's son, Faxon the Red, and their runecaster, Einar Skullgrimsson. He is a wizard of sorts, like our war wizards of Thunder Cove. And this is my… my translator, Ulf Skuli, who has been invaluable to me in our dealings."

Ulf's head remained staring at the floor, but he acknowledged his name with a deeper bow.

"I see." The king shook hands with each of the men, including Skuli, whose reaction was stiff. His eyes then went to Freya. "And who may this be?"

Monty took a deep breath. "Allow me to introduce you to Freya, shield maiden of Rijkstag and daughter of Atorm." He wasn't sure if he had gotten the titles or protocols correct, but the Norsemen didn't seem to mind. "And my betrothed."

"Betrothed?" Amice gasped, her eyes going wide. She recovered as quick as the words passed her lips and extended a hug to Freya while shooting a sideways glance at her husband and sister.

"Yes," Monty assured her. "I accepted the offer of her hand as part of our arrangement."

"What else was part of our arrangement?" Godwin inquired. His eyes scanned the party before them.

Before Monty could respond, Faxon the Red unslung Wolfrick's axe from his back with a great, arcing motion. He held it out in both hands, presenting it to King Godwin.

"My king," Faxon muttered in the broken Warminsterian

tongue, "while we appreciate this token of friendship, our culture doesn't allow us to accept such gifts until they are earned."

The son of Atorm turned to his retinue, which included Ulf Skuli, Monty's thrall. The men lifted the chest of gold offered to the Norsemen and placed it on the council table.

"This too must be earned," Atorm added with finality.

Godwin took the axe and placed it back on the wall where it used to hang. "It will be here along with your gold for you to claim at the end of this war."

Atorm agreed with a solemn nod of his head, seeming to seal the deal.

Then the king hugged Freya. He locked a curious gaze onto his son over her shoulder. "Welcome to the family."

At the conclusion of the introductions, Godwin asked their new allies to stay and participate in the planning of the war. Atorm, Faxon, and Freya stayed, and Einar joined from farther down the table. Monty sat nearest his father, with the dutiful Ulf Skuli standing behind him, head bowed low.

The Faxerian gave a situation report, pointing to the painted maps on the wall.

"Our spies in Krahe discovered that Von Lormarck's forces have been on the move, but not *with* the Jackal. He remains behind in Dragon Ridge. An army of ten thousand at least left his castle even before the declaration of war."

"Ten thousand?" the queen whispered. "May the Ancients be merciful."

Blacwin nodded in resignation. "Seems our enemy has sought trollborn forces as mercenary conscripts to swell his numbers."

"If they left when our spies said they did, they would be here any minute then?" Montgomery asked. "Where are they?"

Blacwin pointed to the map. "They headed north toward the Dragon's Breaths. At the time, our spies assumed they were headed to Rawcliffe Forge, with Baron Von Lormarck remaining in Krahe. But fortunately, they have not turned toward Thronehelm, yet. This is a mistake. It has given time for our forces to muster, and now for our northern allies to join us." The Faxerian offered a soft salute to the contingent from Rijkstag.

"If true, they have left a path to Dragon Ridge for us," the king offered. "And perhaps we can secure a quick surrender."

"Not so." Blacwin shook his head. "It is a trap. The Jackal wants us to attack Dragon Ridge. Troops from Gloucester are sweeping north, providing a reserve of several thousand, and our armies would be crushed between the two if we were to advance."

"Do we attack south and face Thessaly before they combine with the Jackal's forces?" Montgomery asked.

"Nay," Blacwin answered. "I agree, Prince Montgomery, it does appear a juicy target. That's also what they want us to do. This gap between their forces is no mistake. The Jackal is too clever for that. Our forces, even without the Norsemen, would overwhelm Baron Thessaly."

"Why expose his ally troops to slaughter and incur losses?" Monty asked.

"If we head south, the Thessalys will retreat to Dragon Ridge and lure us farther east while his greater numbers swing in behind us and capture Castle Thronehelm, leaving us in the field between the two for a long winter."

"So, what's your plan, General?" the queen asked in a measured tone.

At length, the general said, "We meet the Jackal's forces in the Dragon's Breaths."

"And face them head on?" the king asked.

Blacwin nodded, his face serious. "With the combined forces of Rijkstag, they will still outnumber us two to one. But if Keeper Makai can convince the twergs of the Forge to attack, we would have turned the tables on Von Lormarck. It would be he instead that is trapped; Thorhauer on one side and the twergish forces on the other. He would have to attack in both directions, dividing his forces and bringing the fight to level. I would bet a Halifax trained sword against a mercenary sword any day."

"And if the twergs refuse us?" Monty's eyes narrowed.

"Then we fight as the Ancients intended," Atorm interrupted with a smile. "A glorious death will lead you to the Hall of the Ancients, prince."

"What if we stayed within the walls of Castle Thronehelm?" Baroness Maeglen asked. "It seems that we would then have the advantage."

"The great castle will hold," the Faxerian agreed. "But that too is what the Jackal wants. If we stay here, he will lay siege, and our people will starve through a harsh winter. Our supply lines are thin and unpredictable, only by sea at this point. We'd trap not only ourselves but our people as well."

"If Joferian is successful, he can march south with supplies and relieve us," Monty offered.

"If," Blacwin murmured in an ominous tone. "He will be slowed by the Jackal's forces, if not destroyed. Success in Vallance will incite the rage, and mercenary forces of Saracen to join the war against us."

Baroness Maeglen took a deep, shuddering breath and raised her head above the horror of the thought.

"Koss will not allow that to happen," Einar interjected, his spindly finger pointing to the map on the wall. "We will die here, in blood and glory."

His finger rested near an area of treacherous peaks known as the Falkenwraths.

"How do you know, Runecaster?" the king asked, doubt dripping from his tongue.

"We are not meant to die in hunger, my great king," Einar said. "The Ancient of War demands blood in return for your kingdom's restoration. It has been marked as so. Thus, we shall die in open combat."

"We have brought food and supplies for our own army," Atorm interjected. "And we are prepared to ration it with your troops."

"Thank you again, Konungr," Godwin replied. "Your contribution to this effort is well received."

LaBrecque spoke up for the first time. "Sire, let me sail for Castleshire to negotiate relief from the regency."

When no one stopped him, he went on, "Lady Chessborough owes Thronehelm for many years of our support, and if Joferian and Argantyr do fail to relieve us, we need to assure the trade route."

Godwin inclined his head in soft agreement. "I would send my son, but he must stand with me and our realm. And I need my admiral on the seas with our navy. I will send word to our ambassador, Duncan Alberic."

"My lord," LaBrecque tried again, "Alberic visiting the Regent will tip off Lady Thessica Camber and our enemies in court. They will expect an order to come from you to him. They won't see me coming. I will take the *Sundowner* and sneak in under the guise of an average seaman on a familiar vessel. I will be in and out before they knew I was there."

"But the navy..." Godwin protested.

"It will be ordered to sail," LaBrecque promised. "With

me sailing with them. Or so they will think. Let our enemies know I am there, while I sneak in the back door to Castleshire and rejoin them when my work is done, sailing home on *Doom's Wake*."

"Von Lormarck is landlocked and doesn't have a navy," Monty added. "He must have thought through this contingency. There is a piece to his strategy that we are missing. We must set sail the navy and look for his move on the seas."

"I cannot argue with that," LaBrecque replied. To Godwin he said, "But I beg of you, let me lead this."

"You are not known to the Lady Chessborough. How do you know you will succeed?"

"I will ask Jaxtyn Faircloth, Ranaulf Alaric, and Tribune Greyson Calder to come to our aid. Each of those men owes us for what we are doing for the realm. They understand the importance of the Keeper's survival, as well as the Vermilion princess. They will rally to our cause.

"And besides," LaBrecque said with a coy smile, "women like me."

Monty smiled at the attempt to lighten the mood.

"Very well," the king agreed with a begrudging sigh, finding no humor in LaBrecque's attempt. "Do not fail Warminster, Admiral. And make haste in your return."

His admiral bowed. "Consider it done."

AS THE WAR COUNCIL came to an end, Queen Amice and King Godwin asked Atorm Stormmoeller, his family, and Monty to stay behind to discuss the arranged marriage between the prince and Freya.

"So, tell me of the alliance, and its conditions," Godwin asked, holding his wife's hand under the table.

"I have sworn a blood oath with the *konungr*," Monty

began. "In return for the Norsemen's help, we are to forfeit half of the spoils of war south of the mountains, and they keep all the spoils from Vallance and Saracen."

"And?" Amice pushed.

"And I am to marry Freya." Monty shared a glance and a smile with his bride-to-be.

"A blood oath?" Godwin asked.

"It is an oath taken between our kingdoms," Atorm put in. "One that cannot be broken. A marriage of our families will assure both blood lines continue, and peace among our peoples. No longer shall we be enemies and look south to Warminster for conquest and land. In fact, in the eyes of our people, they are already one."

"What do you mean?" Amice asked, a slight frown on her face.

"They coupled after we swore our oath, under the eyes of Ulthgar the Forger. A seal from the Forger cannot be broken."

"Coupled!" Amice sputtered. Her eyes shot to her son.

Monty affixed his eyes on Freya to hide his shame. Freya, however, held her head aloft, unfazed by the exchange.

"That is unacceptable for our people," Godwin murmured in a steady tone, trying to remain calm. "The people of Warminster will want a ceremony under the eyes of *our* Ancients."

"And they shall get one," Atorm agreed, showing his matching scar. "For our part, it is already done. But you may keep your traditions as you like. And no one will be the wiser."

GODWIN AND AMICE RETIRED to their quarters for the evening, leaving Montgomery and Blacwin to finish the details in the war room. The servants turned down their bed and helped them out of their regalia. They crawled into bed, and Godwin looked to Amice, who kept her eyes fixed to the ceiling, avoiding his gaze.

"Blood oath…?" Godwin complained with a growl.

"What other choice did he have?" Amice whispered.

"We sent him with gold enough to buy a kingdom." A sense of defeat hung in his voice.

"Sometimes, blood is more important than riches," she quipped. "It seems we are now destined to have barbarian blood taint our line."

Godwin turned to his wife, seemingly taken aback by her vitriol. He reached over and pulled Amice closer to him. Her eyes never left the darkness above, even when he gently kissed her forehead.

"Let us see what transpires," Godwin whispered. "And where has Crowley been? I have not seen him all day."

"What if the girl is pregnant?" Amice hissed, avoiding the question. "I always hoped for an agreeable match that brought an alliance for Montgomery." Her voice drew thick. "And for Everett for that matter."

"This is bringing us an alliance that may save Warminster," Godwin tried. "Without it, I fear the Jackal may win the day."

"But a barbarian girl." Amice turned her face away. "Barely in her teens?"

Godwin sighed again. "You were eighteen when we were betrothed."

"Sixteen," Amice countered.

"Then not much different for Freya," the king replied. "And Montgomery has been ready to be married for nearly ten years. Halifax training has been in his way. Now, he is ready."

Amice waited a moment before replying, "When will the men be ready to march?"

"Soon," Godwin replied.

"Any word from First Keeper Makai?" she pressed, the tension leaving her throat now that they spoke of different matters. "I worry the twergs may ignore us, as they have so many times in the past. They are as reclusive as the Raven elves when they choose to be, except when they want to trade."

"You are on edge, my queen." He ran his hand through her long hair. "Let's get some rest."

"I cannot sleep."

"I am exhausted," Godwin said. "I will find answers to your questions in the morning. Let us try and catch a wink, my love."

The skin-stealer that was Amice rolled over, choosing not to press too hard and hid the poisoned dagger, laced with the Venom of the Abyss. Von Lormarck wanted news of the twergs alliance before the king was to be dispatched.

Godwin would live one more day.

CHAPTER ELEVEN

"Behold, the storm gathers. And on its winds calamity comes."
—Amoss D'brielle, Former First Keeper of the Cathedral of the Watchful Eye

AS THRONEHELM BECKONED TO them on the horizon, Incanus further explored his connection with the *Ashen Dragon*. He knew the unmistakable ship and its presence at the harbor would be recognizable and conspicuous. This would not do.

"We won't be able to sail this into port," he told Skullam. "A ship with no crew will draw unwanted attention." He nodded to the lifeboat on one side of the ship. He knew the *Ashen Dragon* could control it, as it was a part of its magic. "We'll use this to come ashore."

"As you say, my liege," answered Skullam, but his voice still dripped in suspicion about the *Dragon,* and Incanus felt the imp was anxious just to get off the vessel.

The ship rocked, knocking the Bone elf and imp off-balance. Its wood creaked, and cabin doors that had been ajar slammed shut.

"What's happening?" Skullam asked, his beady eyed shifting from side to side.

"Calm down," Incanus spat, forgetting himself. His patience with the imp's paranoia was nearing an end.

He switched to the telepathic link with the *Dragon*, closing his eyes. *"I'm not leaving you. I need information that I cannot get from the Firth of Fury. I will return when my business on shore is finished."*

When he opened his eyes, the *Dragon* eased its rocking

and grew still. Before it could change its mind, Incanus entered the lifeboat, and Skullam followed close behind. The *Ashen Dragon* lowered the boat to the sea, its oars magically rowing the assassin and his imp toward the shore.

Incanus said nothing on the long trip. He kept his mind on gathering food and other supplies, trying not to upset the sentient vessel. His years of practiced mental preparations for his killings helped him focus, and he repeated his false chores in the same manner and mantra he'd do before an assassination. Each step was thorough and detailed, and this deception was no different. He struggled to admit that Skullam had been correct all along, but he'd never let him know it. The *Dragon* was more than a boat with a free will. He'd felt the magic's hale and knew perhaps one day, if he couldn't solve its riddle, he may end up on the high seas, doomed to the same fate as Thiago Amyr or Jayvier Sevyn. He needed to learn more and being ashore would help him test the *Dragon*'s range and control.

What would have been hours of rowing passed by in minutes, and the *Ashen Dragon* disappeared on the horizon as he commanded. The lifeboat's magic catapulted them toward shore and the harbor at unbelievable speeds until they neared the first of a group of ships leaving the docks for the Firth.

Incanus contacted the vessel. *"Slow us, Dragon. We must appear as fishermen at this distance."*

"My Captain."

The Bone elf sensed the dragon's despair at their departure, and in his mind's eye, visions of her ashen boards rolled through his consciousness. Yet within seconds, the *Dragon* responded and slowed the boat to a near halt. Incanus grabbed the oars and started for shore, even as the ship moved him along without the need to row.

"Are you all right, Master?" Skullam's voice came from thin air, as the imp had already called upon his dark trace to conceal himself. There was a telling tone in his words, the first time Incanus had sensed dissention in his voice.

He chose to ignore it and continued to feign rowing until the approaching ship sailed by. The harbor couldn't come fast enough.

A CLOAKED INCANUS AND invisible Skullam made their way through the streets of Thronehelm until they reached the market just outside the castle gates. A wool merchant hobbled his way over to the Bone elf, a few of his wares in his hands. Incanus pulled his hood tighter around his face as the merchant peered up at him.

"Morning, sir. Newly made trousers? Cloak?" the man pitched.

"No, thank you." Incanus envied Skullam and his power of stealth. The imp could always avoid unwanted attention.

The merchant was not to be deterred. "You sure? I have ladies' capes as well if you're looking for someone—"

"I'm not." Incanus's blunt tone stopped the man. "Leave me be."

The wool merchant huffed, but hobbled back to his stand, muttering unintelligible words as he went.

"Insufferable."

The now too-familiar tingle of the *Ashen Dragon*'s impatience returned to the back of his mind. A flash of the ship's bow penetrated his consciousness, flooding his vision. Incanus shook it away and placated the *Dragon* as best he could.

"He's merely trying to earn a living," Skullam pointed out.

Incanus ignored him and changed the subject. "Where were we to meet this skin-stealer?"

"Around the side of the castle. To the left, in the gardens where we can find privacy," Skullam's disembodied voice answered.

Incanus moved closer to the castle, following Skullam's direction away from the gates and the pair disappeared into the depths of Thronehelm's outdoor gardens, now brown with the onset of the Season of Long Nights. He ducked off the well-manicured walking trail and disappeared into a copse of trees, where Queen Amice waited.

Incanus braced himself. He knew the skin-stealer had changed many times before, but its new form was stark. Of course, this wasn't the queen, but the skin-stealer's last appearance had once been of Meeks Crowley, the castle steward. Meeks either had yet to master the queen's posture or currently enjoyed the break from royal etiquette as it hunched in the shadows.

Skullam withdrew from his invisible form and climbed a nearby tree, blending in and standing guard for their conversation.

"It's bad business to keep your acquaintance waiting, you know," the skin-stealer bemoaned. "What took you so long?"

Incanus grunted. "I would appreciate if we could skip the pleasantries and get to the heart of our meeting, *Your Majesty*, if that's even what I should call you."

"You may call me Honored Beast, like our dark allies do. What's happened to your face?" Her eyes flickered with the slight taunt.

"It heals." The Bone elf's temper grew short. "You have news?"

"The Vermilion princess is here."

A thrill shot through Incanus. His prey was here, and vengeance was again within his grasp. A more expressive man may have shouted in triumph, but Incanus stayed solemn, no expression crossing his face.

But it wasn't all good news.

"She arrived not long ago with a Longmarcher and a Raven elf," the skin-stealer continued.

This wasn't much of a surprise to Incanus. He knew Addilyn was glued to Ritter, Storm, and Jessamy.

"Is that it then?" Incanus asked.

"In such a rush, eh? It's not as if the Vermilion will walk right out that door to you. As it happens, there *is* more news if you're inclined to hear it."

"Get on with it," Incanus spat.

"The prince, Montgomery Thorhauer, and Viscount Joferian Maeglen have returned from the Viking capital of Hammerstead. It appears the prince was successful in forming a new alliance with the Norsemen's *konungr*, Atorm Stormmoeller."

"An alliance?"

"Yes. It seems Prince Montgomery is to marry Atorm's daughter, Freya."

"I see," Incanus thought aloud. Godwin's support had increased. For a moment he considered finishing the job Von Lormarck had paid him to do, killing Montgomery and Joferian. But Addilyn was right *here*. The new alliance and Von Lormarck's wishes were issues for another day. The Vermilion princess was all that mattered.

But the honored beast wasn't finished. "Master Aarav Fleury, Von Lormarck's bastard, is heading north to the Moor Bog in the Dragon's Breaths Mountains. Together, they will ambush the twergs at the Bridge in Valkeneer."

The *Ashen Dragon*'s mast flickered into Incanus's vision.

This time, Skullam must have noticed his master's agitation, even from afar. The imp fluttered his wings, but before he could broach the subject, Incanus reassured him, "I'm fine."

"Are you?" The false queen's brow dipped in confusion.

The Bone elf guided the skin-stealer back to the only topic of true interest to him. "The Longmarcher will need to leave for the Bridge to defend it from the Moor Bog and Von Lormarck's approach, yes?"

"Yes. He will leave shortly. And the princess intends to accompany him there."

Incanus mumbled, lost in thought as a plan took shape in his mind. "I will need you to forge a note to the Vermilion," he explained to the skin-stealer. "One that would have come to her from your royal messengers. Perhaps from the Athabasica herself."

"Go on," Amice's devious smile returned.

"Tell her that her 'magical ally from Abacus' has arrived to help her and her Longmarcher. Have her come to the harbor and that an ashen lifeboat will bring her to my ship. A ship that awaits her in the Gossamer River. I will be waiting there."

"And Von Lormarck's orders?" the false queen sneered, not hiding its concern. "Will you finish the job when you have your Vermilion skull?"

"The royals will never leave Castle Valkeneer," he said with conviction.

Appearing satisfied, Amice rose, straightened her bustles, and disappeared back to the garden's paths without a farewell.

Skullam dropped from the naked branches and slunk to Incanus's side. "What's next, my liege?"

"Supplies for the *Dragon*." Incanus wasted no time returning to the false narrative playing over in his mind.

All the way back to the lifeboat docked at the Firth of Fury, Incanus fought the thought of his sword slicing into Addilyn's

Vermilion flesh. He struggled against the sublime vision of her face, the color of her blood as it poured out of her.

At last, revenge was at his fingertips. She wouldn't get away again.

CHAPTER TWELVE

"One that walks in the footsteps of their ancients shall see the wisdom in their journey."
—Nasyr, the Great Keeper of the Cathedral of the Watchful Eye

"ARE WE READY?" DAEMUS turned to the party, his face steady. Inside, though, his spirit wavered. With a subtle glance at his trembling hands, he balled his fists and covered his nerves with the length of his sleeves.

The Laurentian Labyrinth's lone gate opened before them. The maze's high, grey walls towered into the sky, making it impossible to get a glimpse of what twists and turns awaited inside. The labyrinth's smooth surface offering no handholds, and Daemus recalled the Ancient's warning that climbing or any attempt to fly over the walls were forbidden. Trillias made no mention of what punishment would come for violating the rules of the challenge, but he didn't want to find out.

"Let's go, lad." Blue Conney motioned to the massive gate with his drawn daggers, but Daemus wasn't sure. It was the first time he'd heard Blue's voice hold the slightest hint of fear.

Daemus swallowed hard and glanced at Katja, who took a brave step toward him. She took his hand in hers, and the warmth of her reassuring grip calmed him. He drew a deep breath. The rest of the group remained silent and followed as Daemus stepped forward.

The wondrous structure—a gargoyle gate—formed a monstrous gaping jaw of a dragon's head. The carved creature loomed ahead, its dead eyes staring at the distant horizon. The dragon's jaw splayed open, and there was room enough to walk through a gap in its teeth. Horns from the dragon's head spired into the morning sky, their spindled design curving away, mimicking the rays of the sun.

From the gate, a mysterious spray of silver magic emanated. The power of the spell wafted onto the beach creating swells of luminescent waves, gently ebbing and flowing with the nearby tide. The hypnotic patterns vacillated in and out of the dragon's mouth, and Daemus swore he felt the gentlest of breezes from within. His hair rustled as he approached.

"This is it." He looked into Katja's eyes for courage. "No turning back once we pass the threshold."

The blue priestess smiled and squeezed his hand, and the pair stepped into the mouth of the dragon. As they passed into the twirls of silver, Daemus's head pounded with the flap of each mystical wave as they washed over him. He blinked and shook his head, and when he turned to Katja, his vision distorted. She looked bent and refracted in the pearly light, like the surface of a cracked mirror.

A tug on his hand made his head turn, and he found her pulling him through the last of the fluttering spell. He staggered forward, stepping from the powerful enchantment, and his eyes cleared.

"Better?" Katja asked.

He bent at the waist and fought for a second to recover. "Yes."

He took a deep breath and looked back, watching each of his friends' fractal figures emerge from the enchanted barrier. One by one they stepped into the labyrinth, until Marquiss, the final member of the group, breached the spell. As he did, the entrance began to transform. The argent waves diminished and with them, the wall sealed itself, as if the entrance was never there.

"By the Ancients, what was that?" Marquiss heaved and puked against the wall. Faux put her arm around her half-brother and he spat, wiping his face with her cloak.

"Too much for ye, eh?" Blue teased, but Faux shot him a look that shut the springheel up.

"Let's move," Arjun ordered.

Daemus stared down a long corridor of flagstones covered in weeds and moss. Sunlight wavered onto the path ahead, stretching so far, he couldn't see an end—only openings along both sides, presenting turns and other paths. An infinite array of endless options lay ahead, and if Trillias was to be believed, the choices would only grow in number. Daemus had no idea which path was the right one. The very thought thrilled and scared him.

"I can't feel it," mumbled Caspar, with a tone of disappointment. "I thought I'd be able to sense it. The Tome."

"Steel yourself." Daemus took him by the shoulder. "We're already closer to it than we were an hour ago. The book will be back in Keeper hands before you know it."

Or it won't, Daemus thought. Erud might know how things would turn out, but for once in his life, Daemus didn't.

"Stay focused," Arjun observed, squinting at him. "Let's get a move on. No way of knowing where we're going, so we'd better just start."

"Jeric, would you mind mapping our way?" Katja suggested.

"I'll do one better." Tuttle produced a blank ledger from his pack to trace their paths but handed Katja a bottle from his alchemical kit.

"What's this?" she asked.

"It's a simple unguent made from a terrie root that's been dried. If you rub some of the terrie root on the walls, it will leave a mark, showing us the way we came. It's harmless, I assure you, and it glows at night like a firefly."

Katja dabbed her finger into the substance and drew an

arrow and the word "start" on the wall.

"Which way?" Faux asked.

"For now, straight ahead," Daemus offered, feeling it was riskier to take one of the numerous turnings and lose sight of where they'd started—and their only point of reference.

As they walked, Daemus noticed messages on the walls. *This way for water*, read a message scratched into a wall by a turning. *Do not go here—Cryptids* read another in what appeared to be dried blood.

For some peculiar reason, the scrawled words all looked recent, as if they'd just been left within a week, even though there were so many that Daemus thought people had to have been leaving them for years.

When they reached yet another turn, Katja pointed to an etching that read *Please tell my wife I am sorry*, with the name Momac carved in the surface and the name of a city, Notre Nouveaux, scratched in alongside it. The thought made Daemus's skin crawl.

"No use dwelling over it," Arjun called from the rear. "Let's keep moving."

"May Ssolantress bring you peace," Katja whispered in hushed tones as she marked the spot with a yellow heart.

They continued ahead, avoiding any turns until the long corridor seemed to close around them except for the lone path forward. No turns or alcoves presented themselves. Just one eternal hallway lay in front of them.

Daemus halted for a second and looked to the group. There was no sound but their footsteps and Arjun's harsh breathing as he struggled to move with his prosthetic leg.

"How long have we been walking?" asked Caspar, peering back the way they'd come. "I can't see where we entered anymore."

"Trillias doesn't want us leaving." Anoki's tone was grim. "We aren't supposed to go back."

"Or it's a trick to get us to waste time," put in Faux, and to Daemus's slight surprise, Anoki nodded.

"Yes. I wouldn't put it past him."

"You are all being blasphemous," remarked Katja in a conversational tone as she marked the wall. "My high priestess would have a fit if she…" Her voice wavered, but she went on, "If she heard a word of this. Trillias is helping us by—"

"All of us have seen firsthand how the Ancients treat mortals." Daemus knew his voice was a little sharp.

Katja raised her hands in concession. "Oh, no, I believe you." An awkward silence fell as she peered at him. Self-conscious and now feeling shy in a way he didn't think he had since he left the cathedral, Daemus contrived a smile for her. Satisfied, she flashed a grin back and touched his arm before drawing away. He tried to convince himself his skin wasn't tingling.

"Something up ahead," grunted Arjun with a jerk of his head. "Light. You see?"

The passageway did look brighter up ahead.

"More light is… good?" Katja's voice was uncertain.

"That's odd," remarked Tuttle from the back of the party, breaking his silence as he mapped. "I'd think the main corridor would go on for longer than this."

"Do you know how long we've been walking?" asked Caspar, eyeing him. The young Keeper looked to the sky and others followed his gaze.

"The sun," Daemus remarked. "It hasn't moved. But it feels like…"

"Like it's been too long for it not to have moved," Tuttle replied, adjusting his spectacles.

"If this is true, how will we tell time? How will we know when we are nearing the seventh day?" Marquiss asked.

"Perhaps we're not meant to," Anoki lamented. He looked to Arjun, who stared down the endless corridor.

"Keep moving," the captain ordered, pointing to the growing illumination. "Perhaps this light ahead will provide a new landmark. Something we can reference for our exploration."

They picked up the pace and drew their weapons. Faux nocked an arrow and took the lead, with Anoki and her katana a step behind. Blue followed next, leaving Daemus, Katja, Caspar, and Tuttle in the middle while Arjun and Marquiss guarded the rear.

As they drew closer, the source of light intensified, and they found the corridor opened into an expansive courtyard basked in the mid-morning sun. Daemus shielded his eyes and scanned the area. Remnants of an abandoned town, little more than a hamlet swallowed by the labyrinth, spilled in all directions. Unlike the messages on the walls, the buildings were obviously old and unmaintained, with many collapsed roofs and broken walls overgrown with plants. The surrounding stone walls seemed to amplify and distort any sound.

"What is this place?" Anoki murmured.

"Looks like a village unlucky to be in the way of an ever-growing maze," Marquiss surmised. "It appears to have grown all around it. How can that be?"

Blue looked ahead. "Cursed, to have fallen in here."

Anoki pointed to Faux with the tip of her katana and waved for her to circle to the left. She motioned with her blade for Blue and Marquiss to do the same, but to the right. Arjun stepped next to her, and they both looked back to Daemus and the rest of the group before starting for the town.

"Spread out," Arjun whispered.

Daemus struck off with Katja, as Arjun had ordered, and crept into the outskirts of the abandoned village. He pointed to a small, single-room house, one of the first in the town and one whose roof was partially destroyed. Katja nodded and they slid up to the dwelling. Daemus hugged the side wall and lifted his gaze to peek inside.

The shack, a peasant's house no doubt, appeared to have stood uninhabited for quite some time. His eyes scanned for signs of recent activity but found none. The room seemed to have been left in a hurry, its original residents not given the chance to take their belongings with them wherever they went. Cookware sat undisturbed and covered in dust near a tiny fireplace. Around a broken table where a piece of the roof had fallen in what looked like a child's wooden doll, writing implements, and someone's nearly finished knitting lay scattered about. The names Fryga and Narl were scratched into the wall in human script, surrounded by a flowered circle.

A faint, intermittent hooting noise made Daemus look up. As he raised his head, he thought he saw something move out of the slit of a window in one of the walls, but when he looked closer, he could identify no other sign of life.

"Empty," he whispered to Katja, and they moved away, heading for the next structure, a building that looked to be a traveler's inn.

The hooting sounded again, and after a moment he identified its source as Faux, standing outside the village chapel. When she spotted him, she beckoned in silence with a flick of her hand. Looking around, Daemus could see his other companions emerging from their own areas of investigation, and all of them hurried to converge on the chapel.

"I've found something," whispered Faux in a tone of

excitement when they had all ducked inside.

"This place feels like a grave," Tuttle said a little louder.

"Keep quiet." Arjun's grim face betrayed his emotions. "Something doesn't seem right here. It's not safe."

"No part of the labyrinth is safe," Anoki asserted, also taking care to keep her voice low. "What did you find, Faux?"

"Maps." Beaming, Faux pointed to the chapel's altar where they found an ancient-looking, leather-bound book.

Tuttle and Daemus stepped forward to inspect its drawn contents, while Caspar leaned over Daemus's shoulder.

Tuttle turned several pages. "Somehow, this atlas has been maintained… with care."

"It's a good thing we kept going straight, or else I would never have found this," Caspar smiled.

"Well done, Faux," Arjun congratulated.

"How do we know they're accurate?" said Tuttle, squinting at the group while cleaning his spectacles. "Could be a trick from the Ancient, you know?"

"It's not from Trillias." Faux flipped to the first page and pointed to the name written on it: Renfrow Wilkes. "A person made these. This Wilkes fellow."

"I see," Tuttle replied, and with a grunt, subsided.

Daemus flipped back to the maps. The spidery drawings were marked by notes, like *the nest of cryptids here* and *alternate route*. Looking at them, Daemus was struck by how meticulous and detailed they were, and yet how they showed no sign of a path to the center of the labyrinth. The man looked to have spent his entire life mapping the maze, only to be left to pass his life's work on to someone else, with no reward for himself.

"How old do you think this is?" Caspar asked.

"Couldn't say," Tuttle replied, shaking his head.

"Let me see." Anoki reached for the book, and Daemus

handed it to her with a glance.

"Fifty years at least," Anoki proclaimed, though she didn't elaborate as to how she'd reached that conclusion. "Must have been lost around the time the village was destroyed."

"Where is this place on the map?" Katja inquired, blue hair falling into her face as she leaned forward to look. Daemus fought the urge to brush it back for her.

Faux started to point. "I think it's—"

A loud crash sounded on top of the roof, making them all jump.

Anoki tucked the book away in her cloak and spun, katana in both hands.

"What was that?" Daemus dared to asked, and a split second later, a familiar chittering noise echoed through the courtyard. Daemus's skin crawled: it wasn't quite exactly like the noises the Antlered Man made, but similar enough that he knew what it was.

Cryptids nest here.

CHAPTER THIRTEEN

"Those that seek death shall not find it, for only i may meet you in my own good time, granting permission for your sublime crossing."
—Threnody, the Ancient of Death

MASTER MORTUS STOOD AT the edge of the broken parapet, surveying what remained of the Divine Protectorate of Erud. The masses gathered beneath him, converted Keepers clustering together in the center of the throng, surrounded by larger clusters of Knights of the Maelstrom and the Disciples of the Watch on the outside.

The lich approached the edge of the ruins of the once-proud observatory of the Cathedral of the Watchful Eye, now lain in rubble from the starfall. His new eyes surveyed the abandoned town of Solemnity in the distance. Hours after his overthrow of the cathedral, the denizens of Solemnity abandoned its streets, taking little with them in their haste.

He didn't bother to have his Knights round them up or pursue them. They were simple farmers and tradesmen, here to serve the protectorate for generations—nothing more. But the cathedral would soon be abandoned, and their withdrawal from the town was inconsequential.

Leaning forward he tapped his obsidian staff on the broken rocks at his feet, sending a distant rumbling of quiet thunder rolling across the plains. His skeletal jaw cracked open, his spectral voice issuing forth on waves of mystical wind, amplifying his words throughout the compound.

"Brothers and sisters of Erud's protectorate," his voice rang out, "the time to defend our order is upon us! For far too long did our blind Keepers lead this realm to the brink of oblivion.

It is we that shall return Warminster to lawful rule, rule under the one true king. King Dragich Von Lormarck."

He paused as the low grumbling of approval from his followers rose from below.

"Our Ancient, Erud, demands this," he continued. "I've seen the true king's ascension, a vision granted to me in the reflections of Dromofangare. Erud speaks to us. Erud commands us. The Sight of Erud leads us to victory. It is we who shall purge the realm of its heretics. The great cathedral shall rise again!"

Cheers again arose from the crowd gathered below.

"The day of battle is upon us. Unchain the traitors of our faith," Mortus commanded, "and let them depart our great cathedral in shame. Let them bear witness to the will of Erud and its loyal and true servants, so they may warn the realm Erud's vengeance is coming. They are free to leave and scatter far and wide."

Jiro, the new captain of the Knights of the Maelstrom, strode to the front of the crowd on the back of his gryph. His plate mail armor, dark as Graytorris's obsidian staff, reflected the torchlight from the crowd as he bowed to his master before shouting an order to some of his men nearer the castle walls. They came forward, dragging forth a dozen former Keepers, what remained of the traditionalists, bound in chains.

The Knights did as they were told, and Jiro gave the sign for his troops to release them. But the Keepers did not run as might be expected. They looked as though they had been kept in total darkness for a long time, and even the torchlit night sky was too much for them as they stumbled and held onto one another.

"Run," Mortus commanded, his voice empowered by his spell. "Carry the new word of Erud to the whole of Warminster."

"Never!" One of the traditionalists cringed forward, her shackled hands by her side. "Erud hasn't chosen you," she yelled toward the tower in the direction of Mortus. "We, the rightful Keepers of the Forbidden felt the return of the one true light to the cathedral nights ago when Daemus Alaric challenged you. Murderer! Heretic! False Prophet!"

The throng, silenced by her courage, lifted their gazes to what remained of the cathedral's eye. The woman stood firm, helping some of the others to their feet.

While this spectacle of defiance was taking place, Johonnum the Black, chosen as new high watcher by Mortus himself, approached the Great Keeper from the shadows of the inner sanctum. Mortus's necromantic eyes flickered green as he registered the approach of his second-in-command.

Johonnum had long been a friend to the creature that was once Graytorris, perhaps his closest associate, as the two ascended through the ranks of their orders as young men. Mortus allowed him to join him on the parapet.

"Shall I signal for Jiro?" Johonnum asked. "Perhaps demonstrate the new weapons the inventors of Abacus have provided?"

The lich heard Johonnum but didn't respond. He wanted them to flee. He wanted them to believe that mercy was theirs. He wanted his vengeance to taste as sweet as it could. And killing them too soon would rob his corrupted soul of this greater pleasure.

"What do those from Abacus call these new magics?" he asked of Johonnum, his voice crackling.

"They call them granattus, my master," the high watcher explained. "When our forces activate them, they can be thrown and will explode on contact."

"And then?" the lich asked, at last turning to his second.

"These." Johonnum loosened the strings on a pouch producing sharpened metal caltrops. "The magic powder inside ignites and launches these projectiles in all directions."

"Do the Knights need to train in magic to do this?"

"Nay, my master." Johonnum shook his head. "The magic has been bestowed already. The hale lies within the powder."

If a lich could smile, Mortus did. His eyes flared in the knowledge of what was to come, and he turned back to his followers below. With the raising of his staff, a closer, louder thunderclap sent Captain Jiro into motion, taking to the sky circling over the crowd.

The small group of dissenters looked to the gryph, as did the crowd, and after a few circles in ascent, Jiro steered his mount in a steep dive. The protectorate watched from a distance, as did Mortus and Johonnum. The group of traditionalists appeared to sense what was coming next. Some scrambled away, tripping on their chains, while a core group of half a dozen linked arms and began to sing aloud prayers to Erud, others to Threnody, the Ancient of Death.

The nervous crowd below began to sway, and some muddled voices rose in futile protest, but Jiro was already committed to his attack. The captain swooped by and hurled a granattus at the chained Keepers before banking and rising into the sky once more. When the granattus contacted the ground, a bright explosion of red light flashed and boomed, silhouetting the traditionalists in the distance.

The protectorate ducked nearly as one with awestruck faces and confused cries for themselves if not their former brothers and sisters. Screams from the faraway group of dissenters echoed within the walls of the compound, half of them scattering from the site of the explosion, running in terror and extinguishing their cassocks by rolling on the ground. The others, less fortunate, lay scattered on the ground in pieces.

Captain Jiro circled back and tossed two more grannati at a trio of the dissenters who had run off in the same direction in a pack, making a last effort to reach the cathedral's gates. The shells fell and exploded and when the smoke cleared, Mortus could no longer see the traditionalists from his perch atop the cathedral. Only black scorch marks on the ground remained.

"*Raucher wolk feuer schweben,*" Mortus muttered in the conjurer's tongue. His staff flashed in a smoky red, emoting a billowing crimson magic that manifested in the form of a semi-solid cloud of fire and ash.

The lich stepped from the edge and balanced himself on the wisps of the fiery cloud. The plumes of flame wafted at first above the protectorate, carrying their leader toward what remained of the dissenters. The surprised crowd cried into the night sky, but the Knights and Disciples corralled the converted Keepers and those that remained from the protectorate in a semi-circle under him.

On magic wind he drifted, gliding to the pile of churning flesh across the courtyard, and scanning for any surviving traditionalists. Seeing some bodies still squirming below, he maneuvered the magical cloud closer, soon hovering a few yards from his impaled enemies. The grannati had done their job, their Abacunian design and purpose wicked in their trial exhibition.

The last of the dissenters cried out, lying scattered and impaled, pinned with dozens of caltrops among two shallow craters created by the explosions. Mortus's flaming creation floated behind him, and the lich stepped from the scarlet mist and walked to the blackened ditches. The rising cries of pain fed him. He tried to breathe it in but failed, a remnant reflex of his human form.

As he crested the first crater, he saw body parts torn and strewn, and even some remains buried under darkened soot. Some of the dying moaned for help, but Mortus knew none would come for them. He looked down, his skeletal visage catching the attention of a particular survivor—the woman who had called out to him from afar. She lay face up, her broken and impaled body motionless, but her eyes tracked his approach.

"Heretic," she gargled over a mouth of blood. "Erud shall ensure you find no peace, Graytorris. You may hide behind the façade of what you've altered yourself to be, but Erud knows what you are. Soon, too, shall all the realm."

"Graytorris is dead," the lich stated, "but Mortus lives for him, in undeath."

The Keeper choked, her head stilling but her eyes still alive, if but for a few moments more.

"Say your last prayers to Erud," Mortus mumbled in his spectral voice, "and let this hole be your funeral pyre."

He stood next to her, looking deep into her fearful eyes as his fiery cloud crawled into the crater with them.

Her eyes flared before the flames engulfed them both.

AN HOUR HAD PASSED, and Mortus returned to the inner sanctum of the cathedral. He entered a room that used to house a classroom, one that was designed to honor the Keepers from Cascadian Forest. A brushed fresco of a snowy mountain chain covered in fir trees adorned the walls. The furniture within was carved from white oak, a tree found only in the Cascadian Forest.

In the center of the converted room stood an old lectern, and by it waited Johonnum and Keeper Tarrant Cynric of the

Sea Kingdom. Both genuflected as he entered, his ghostlike figure ambling toward them.

"Keeper Tarrant Cynric." Mortus wasted no time. "Has the Sea Kingdom agreed to dispatch their armada to the shores of Thronehelm? Their blockade of food will serve our new king."

Cynric appeared nervous and wrung his hands together as he stood. "Great Keeper, I am afraid the royal—"

"I care not for excuses, First Keeper," Mortus warned. "Their armada should have set sail several weeks ago. They must destroy the navy of Thronehelm and blockade the harbors of the Firth of Fury."

"But Great Keeper," Cynric tried, "I am but their counsel and sage. I cannot make the Valdostan family do anything. I can only advise."

Mortus shambled closer to the Keeper, each of his staff's clicks on the hardwood floor echoing in the small chamber. His eyes flared and his jaw closed. He stared into the countenance of Cynric who did his best to step back, but he only bumped into Johonnum, who'd used the distraction to sneak up behind him.

"I… I will return to the Sea Kingdom this evening and make them understand," Cynric conceded, swallowing hard.

"I will send you through the magic of Dromofangare," Mortus ordered. "There will be no return trip, Keeper. I expect to see you with the Valdostans in the waters of the Firth of Fury within ten days."

"But Great Keeper, the waters and winds this time of year—"

Mortus stopped the man with a burning glare. "Enough with your delays and excuses. I will watch you with my mirror. You will not fail Erud, First Keeper. Dromofangare will always find you, always see you."

Mortus sensed Cynric neared a breaking point, recoiling

from the stench of his breath and closing his eyes.

"Do you understand?" Mortus asked, already knowing the answer. "Don't make me send Johonnum to find you."

Cynric nodded, his meek voice threadbare. "Y-yes, Great Keeper. Thine will be done."

Mortus stepped back from the quivering man, letting him escape into the hallway as Captain Jiro entered the room.

"Jiro." Mortus turned to face his captain who appeared unfazed at the cowering Cynric.

Jiro rested his helmet on his hip, his other hand on the pommel of his sword. "Yes, Great Keeper?"

"Erud has shown me more enemies have allied themselves against us." Mortus extended his hands and turned one palm to the sky. A wisp of golden wizardry appeared between his hands, and from the spitting cloud of sorcery appeared an image of the Norsemen forces marching in the snow. "The Norsemen have joined with the Thorhauers, Jiro, and Erud demands they be punished for their treachery against their divine truth. These heathens and their blasphemy must be disciplined for their hubris."

"As you wish, Great Keeper."

"You shall take the majority of our Knights and join forces with King Von Lormarck at the gates of Foghaven Vale. Leave at once on the wings of your hippogryphs and aid King Von Lormarck, our ally, in his coming battle against the forces of Thronehelm."

"Yes, Master." Before he left, Jiro said, "We shall succeed in battle, with the love and knowledge of Erud lighting our way."

"And me, Great Keeper?" Johonnum asked. "What shall the Disciples of the Watch do?"

"High Watcher, you are to activate your Disciples as spies in all cities of the baronies that are not in our control. They are to learn what they can and take action to benefit the war effort."

Johonnum's face remained impassive, except for his eyes, which flicked in curiosity. "Action, Master? What would you have the Disciples do to aid and serve you?"

"Whatever is necessary to cause chaos among our adversaries."

Johonnum nodded and turned to go.

"High Watcher." Graytorris stopped him. "You will be traveling with me, on another mission."

Johonnum turned back to Graytorris, visibly interested. "Of course. How shall I prepare." Johonnum was good at asking questions in his indirect way.

"We are going to Rawcliffe Forge, in the depths of the twergish subterrane." Mortus's necromantic glare flared green. "It's time to release an ally who has been trapped for far too long."

CHAPTER FOURTEEN

"Sometimes, victory can be found in a retreat."
—From the Annals of Halifax Military Academy

"THERE!" DAEMUS POINTED AND Faux drew her bow back and waited for whatever it was to emerge from a hole in the ceiling.

Timbers creaked and dust shifted from the rafters of the chapel as the creature on the roof moved. The beast, a massive, bloated humanoid, dropped into the cathedral and landed on two cloven feet, its scaled wings fluttering it to a soft landing. The cryptid's body was covered in a natural armor, resembling the plates of a dragon's hide. Its oversized arms, bulbous and scaled, ended with sharpened claws and its head resembled a helmed knight, featuring a singular, sunken eye that glared out at them. Dried blood was crusted on its sinister maw, and a gurgling voice rose from deep within, giving Daemus the sense that it relished the arrival of new prey.

"By the Ancients, what *is* that?" he shouted, reaching for his mace.

Arjun grunted in reply, drew his katana, and positioned himself between Daemus and the unimaginable beast.

An arrow screamed past Daemus and snapped itself against the scales of the beast's protective hide. The Keeper flinched, startled at the shot.

"No use," Faux mumbled, her eyes affixed on the predator.

The abomination chattered louder and lunged with its oversized arms at the trio, slashing first with its deadly claws at Faux. The red-haired rogue rolled away and in the same motion dropped her bow and unsheathed her sword. Arjun, less nimble, stepped into the monster and swung, meeting its second hooked arm in the air, deflecting its attack wide and away.

"There's more!" cried Katja, and when he looked, Daemus saw that another creature was trying to come in through the window.

Tuttle fumbled through his bag and produced a yellow vial and tossed it at the peering, one-eyed lurker. The bottle shattered and splashed, spraying in a hiss and a puff of smoke. In an instant, the chapel filled with the odor of the bottle's acidic contents.

The second cryptid's chittering turned into a gargling sound, a whooping of some kind, as the acid took its effect. Stunned, it waved its burning arms erratically in the window, its brutish claws caught in the framework of shattered glass. In an animalistic panic, it tugged itself free, smashing what little wooden frame remained, and retreated away.

The first monster lunged again, and with a yell Anoki leapt and spun her sword, plunging her katana deep between the draconic plates on the humanoid's shoulder, making it squeal.

Blue Conney yelped and joined in the assault from the side, trying to turn the creature's attention to him. His twin daggers slashed at the creature's right flank with little effect, the blades deflecting off its thick hide. One of the beast's hooved feet kicked sideways at him, catching Blue in the chest and launching the springheel across the room. Blue slammed into the chapel wall and slid to the floor. He groaned and shook his head, trying to regain his senses.

"Blue!" Katja rushed to the springheel's aid and reached to pull him to his feet.

Blue's lip was split, and he spit a tooth on the floor. His face reddened and his legs bulged as only a springheel could do. He winked at Katja, said, "Thank ya, lovely," and then launched himself into the air and back into battle.

Daemus turned to see a third cryptid running outside past the entryway, looking for a way in. "Find another way out of here!" he called as Marquiss and Caspar moved to block the front door with an empty pew. "There's too many."

"I'll find an exit." Marquiss, his face set, turned and sprinted to the rear of the chapel.

The third creature slammed its considerable frame into the failing front doors of the chapel, sending splinters flying, but the door held against the first assault.

"What do I do?" Caspar leaned into the door in a feeble attempt to stop the raging beast from entering.

"Stab it!" Daemus yelled to Caspar, whose face paled, his sword hand shaking.

The inexperienced Keeper gritted his teeth and screamed in fear, but he somehow found the courage to attack. With a high-pitched war cry, he stuck his blade through the cracks in the wood. Daemus watched the blade strike true as the sound of the creature's whooping intensified. It backed from the threshold, and for a moment, seemed to withdraw.

Then a searing pain lanced through Daemus's shoulder, and his body turned from the force of the first cryptid's blow. Its piercing fingers had caught him when he'd turned his attention away—a mistake made in the chaos of battle. Blood drained from the wound and his right arm fell limp, his mace falling to the ground.

Before he could react, the creature tugged at him, its vicious grasp tearing at his flesh, digging deeper into him. He howled, a helpless feeling racing through him as he felt his feet leave the ground.

With one claw buried in him like a fishhook, the beast lifted him toward its awaiting mouth.

Stunned and flailing, a numbing sensation coursed through his body. He tried to pull away, but his other arm was now numb and a vain attempt to cry out fell into a garbled mishmash. His eyes fluttered, his view now turned upside down while dangling in the air, and he began to swoon.

He caught the faintest of cries from Faux somewhere near him.

"Kill it!" she cried, and his wandering and helpless eyes caught a glimpse of terror on Katja's face before the swirl of blackness took him.

"DAEMUS?" KATJA'S SOOTHING VOICE reached his ears. "Daemus, don't move."

The young Keeper's eyes opened and wobbled, trying to focus on the healer's voice.

"We're going to have to remove it before I can heal you." Katja leaned closer, her eyes looking into his. "But this may hurt."

"Get it over with," Blue protested, and Daemus noticed the springheel leaning against his left shoulder, pinning him down. He felt the flat of a table on his back and Arjun and Anoki's hands holding down his legs.

"Wha… what—?"

With a swift tear, Katja pulled what remained of the cryptid's sharp claw from the hole in his shoulder.

Pain shot through him, and he screamed, fighting against his friends and the shock of the claw's removal.

"Attaboy," Blue said above the anguish, patting the injured Keeper's chest. "Almost done."

Daemus couldn't see the wound but the expression on the faces of his companions told him the story. He knew it was bad.

Katja moved to stave off the blood with a roll of bandages

she'd produced from her healer's kit and applied pressure, which only made the pain worse.

"Stop, please!" He squirmed against his restrainers, and for a moment he thought he'd lose consciousness again.

"Look at me." Katja lowered her face.

Her blue eyes caught his and he looked back. Time seemed to slow, and her calm demeanor stunted the pain.

Are her eyes sparkling?

He stared into the deep blue ocean of her mystical gaze and saw her Ancient's mark of healing glow under the skin of her delicate face.

"I have to stop the bleeding first, before my magics will work."

Daemus found a strange serenity in Katja's voice, the voice of a goddess perhaps, and he wasn't sure if it was a spell she'd cast or if it was his desire to listen to her pulled to the surface. He trusted her. He knew she'd be there for him. He…

He loved her.

Her attention drifted back to her work, but his countenance never left hers. He felt the grip of his friends loosen as his body relaxed. He tried to concentrate on his breathing by mirroring the healer's and his mind reflected on the first time they'd met in Forecastle, where she'd treated his wounds after the Battle of Homm Hill against Misael and Clan Blood Axe.

Moments passed, but how long he wasn't sure. The pressure she'd applied to his shoulder hurt less and less, and her eyes began to flutter.

"That's better." She looked back at him with a smile.

"What happened?" he managed, trying to fight the urge to move.

"The creature nearly ate ya." Blue informed the Keeper, making a mocking noise of pincers and mandibles. "But we got 'em good."

"Ever the diplomat," Faux admonished the springheel for his bluntness.

"Where are we? Everyone else make it?"

"We're in the basement of the chapel," Anoki explained. "We chased away the cryptid that attacked you—"

"Arjun cut off his arm and it flew away." Caspar's excited voice carried over the group. Daemus didn't dare tilt his head to look, but out of the corner of his eye he could see Caspar winding up through a pantomimed swing of Arjun's katana.

"Marquiss found a system of tunnels," Anoki motioned for the other Dauldon to approach.

Marquiss brushed his mint green hair out of his face and placed his hand on Daemus's good shoulder. "Your idea to find an escape route saved us all. We found a system of tunnels hidden under the altar. Without it, we'd be dead. Looks like Erud still stands by you, Keeper."

Daemus said nothing. For the first time in his life, he'd been without the omnipresent sensation of his Ancient, just as Trillias had promised. The decision to run came from him and him alone, not ordained by some divination or augury from his dispassionate companion since his birth.

"I'm glad," he relented.

"So are we," Arjun admitted, "else I fear we'd all be food for cryptids."

A soft blue glow emanated from Daemus's side and with a gentle turn, he noticed that Katja had started her supplication to Ssolantress.

"*Aida la santius.*" Katja's prayers had begun, and the aura of blue grew stronger in her hands. "*Hilfe vho Ssolantress, mi blauen bleu.*"

Daemus closed his eyes and turned away. Not sure what

to expect, he could only hope her spell worked.

With a delicate touch, the healer laid her flickering hands on his shoulder, alit in the healing powers of her Ancient. Through closed eyes Daemus swore he could still see the azure hue of Ssolantress's magic as it blossomed around him. There was a magical, almost caressing sensation taking hold, and he'd never felt safer in his life. The fears and anxieties of entering the labyrinth flushed away and his body relaxed. He felt as if he cuddled in the familiar arms of a mother, and he hoped this feeling would never end.

As fast as it had come, Ssolantress's touch seemed to fade, and the darkness of the tunnels returned.

"How do you feel?" Katja asked, removing her hands from his wound.

He wanted to tell her to stop. To keep her loving hands on him, but when Blue leaned in, his toothless smile glaring down at him, the fleeting moment had all been ruined.

"How ya feelin' now, kid?" the springheel asked.

"Try to sit up," Katja instructed, and helped him rise from his back.

His shoulder was stiff, but with a glance at a horrific and bloodstained scar, the pain was all but gone.

"I—I don't understand," he managed, trying to pull his tattered cloak over his disfigured flesh. He didn't want to see it anymore.

"Ssolantress blesses you."

"Thank you, and thank the Ancient of healing for this blessing, but that's not what I mean. Why is my connection, and Caspar's for that matter, with our Ancient severed while yours remains? I expected Trillias to stop all powers of the Hall of the Ancients from reaching here."

Katja's face turned a bit at the revelation, and she shook

her head. "Perhaps even Trillias grants small mercies."

"Is he all right to move?" Arjun asked Katja, his intentions poorly hidden in his tone.

Daemus looked at the captain, who appeared to have regained some of his confidence after the battle.

"I'm fine," Daemus answered for the healer. "Time is of the essence."

"Are you certain?" Katja looked worried.

"No." His honest answer stunned her, but his smile softened her gaze. "But I am going to try. I will let you know if I need to rest."

Arjun and Katja exchanged a quick glance, and the captain pursed his lips and handed Daemus's mace back to him. "You dropped this. I think you'll be needing it."

"Thanks for saving me," Daemus said with a half-smile as the captain helped him to his feet and then he felt a tap on his back.

He turned to see Anoki gesturing for him to follow. After a few steps, Daemus could see the mouth of a narrow, man-made tunnel that smelled of carrion.

"We don't know how far it goes." Blue pointed into the darkness. "But we found a small lantern 'ere and were able to get it workin'."

As Marquiss held the light into the tunnel, the darkness retreated but only by a few feet.

"You first." Marquiss handed him the lantern's handle.

For a second, Daemus froze, but Marquiss relented. "Blue, you're up."

The springheel bumped his way to the front and took the light, looking back at his companions with a smile. "Follow me."

Blue disappeared into the tunnel, followed by Marquiss and Caspar. Daemus looked to Arjun and Anoki.

"You ready?" Anoki glanced at Arjun's false leg.

"It'll hurt, but I'll manage." The captain went next. At first, he struggled to fit and move his enhanced limb, but seemed to find a workable stride.

Anoki followed with apparent concern on her brow.

Faux motioned to Daemus. "You next. Katja after and I will bring up the rear, just in case."

"In case of what?"

"In case those purple things figure out a way to get down here."

Daemus shrugged and half-laughed at the suggestion. Those beasts would never fit into the tunnel. It was barely big enough for them. But he knew it was Faux's way of offering him protection, hidden in the middle of the group, and Katja was no warrior. Her guarding the rear was impractical.

He looked one time at Katja, who forced a smile on her face.

"Oh, just get goin' lovebirds," Faux mumbled in her brogue.

Daemus dived, falling headfirst into the mouth of the tunnel. He belly-crawled his way through, following the panting of the group in front of him. The lantern's light was long lost ahead but the confines of the cave and running into Anoki from time to time guided him forward. A slight turn led to a distant glimmer of light and the smell of fresh air. Soon he could see an opening that led outside.

One at a time, the group crawled out into the evening air and Daemus stood and stretched his shoulder. He put his hand on his mace, wiped the sweat from his forehead so that it didn't drip into his eyes, and helped Katja and Faux out of the hole.

"Where are we?" Tuttle asked, looking to the sky for a hint.

Daemus looked around, seeing several apparent directions to head.

"This way," Anoki waved. "I think I see a… a light."

The party followed her and ducked into the opening in the courtyard wall. Anoki made silent hand gestures as she scouted ahead, which Arjun interpreted for the group, which followed back into the main part of the labyrinth. Daemus counted three left turns, and Anoki stopped in a small dead-end chamber. The rest of the party followed her in, with Faux keeping watch outside in case the creatures managed to catch up.

"Left one alive," said a voice.

Daemus whirled. What he'd thought was a heap of rags in the corner moved, revealing itself to be a man, shaggy-haired and covered in dirt.

"Cryptids? Be ye new to the labyrinth?"

"Who are you?" demanded Arjun, half-drawing his blade, though the man had no weapon and looked, by Daemus's reckoning, too feeble to pose a threat.

"I be Wilkes," said the man with a somber tone. "Came ye from the village? Most of us know better than to venture there. 'Tis long since lost, and the cryptids nest within."

"Wilkes," repeated Anoki, then said slowly, "Renfrow Wilkes?"

The man's brows shot up. "How'd you guess?"

"I think we found your maps," Anoki went on, pointing to the atlas they'd found in the chapel.

The man hummed. "Haven't seen that in a while." He paused and looked to the group as though considering what to do or even say next. "Come along, I'll show you to my place."

Without another word he shuffled out into the passageway.

Glancing at each other, the party followed.

CHAPTER FIFTEEN

"A wise nation doesn't march to war without knowing the limitations of its weakest allies."
—Dirdrenum, War Wizard of Thunder Cove

IN THE SKY AS the *Sundowner* sailed into the busy port of Castleshire. The port, as expected, brimmed with merchant vessels, and Halford expertly guided them into the docks and set his crew to unloading the false cargo. They had brought with them a small load of Hoar fox pelts, courtesy of the Norsemen. Without something to trade, the spies of the thieves' guilds that operated in the town would have noticed a merchantman sail into harbor empty, sending up red flags and sending rumor mills to churn within minutes.

The wreckage of the *Phantom* still sat in the harbor, its mainmast poking just above the surface of the water. LaBrecque didn't care, though. His first thought was of *Doom's Wake,* and his eyes scanned the docks for her as they approached. On the far side of the port, away from the hustle and bustle of the warehouses, he could see the *Wake*. His eyeglass scanned the hull to find much of the damage repaired. He could see his crew assisting a group of fiery haired tinker lardals pounding away at last minute fixes. He slid the conspicuous eyeglass away and smiled. She should be fit for sailing soon, he determined, if not already.

"Admiral?" the familiar voice of Declan Raynor called, and he turned to see both he and Birch Hallowell approaching. The two were dressed as they'd discussed, donning the garb of merchants rather than seamen. LaBrecque, trying to remain as inconspicuous as he could, did the same, and kept the cowl of his cloak above his head to hide from prying eyes.

"I'd come with ye if it wouldn't look too fishy," Captain Halford mumbled as he approached. "I wish ye well."

"Thank you." LaBrecque shook the captain's hand. "For everything." He handed Halford a bag of coins for his troubles.

"This is far too much," the captain argued, but LaBrecque stopped him.

"It is far too little for all Warminster has asked of you. The king commandeered your vessel without a thought as to who you were. You were gracious in the eyes of desperation."

"Should I count it then?" Halford said with a wry smile.

"It's not mine," LaBrecque quipped. "It's the king's, so you know it will spend well."

The two shared a last laugh and a hug.

"I'll be here in the harbor for a few days reprovisioning," Halford offered. "What's yer plan?"

"I will return to Seabrooke with my crew and the *Wake*," LaBrecque replied.

"I know you lost mariners. Good sailors of yers. Bring Raynor and Hallowell back safely to me. The two bastards are me best men, and I know they cannot make up for all the lives lost, but their hands and experience will help ye on a safe return. I know it isn't much, but those two have manned the *Sundowner* by themselves at times. And may the eyes of Nothos watch over you today."

LaBrecque disembarked, cloaked and in disguise, traveling in anonymity with Raynor and Hallowell at his hip. The men loaded the pelts onto the back of a cart and rode for town. LaBrecque resisted the urge to go to the *Wake,* trying to escape the ever-watchful eyes of the guilds.

But before they could leave the docks, they were stopped by the harbormaster, Aldusa Vho, and several of her attendants bearing their various weights and measures.

"And where do you think you're going?" Vho hissed, stopping the cart by standing in front of it.

LaBrecque waved for Vho to approach. "We have pelts for Lady Chessborough."

The woman sauntered over to the cart, and LaBrecque flashed her his smile from under his hood.

"Not before I—" Vho stopped, recognizing the admiral.

LaBrecque tilted his head and hoped the powers of his handsome gaze would win over his female foe.

"I've got this." She motioned for her crew to board the *Sundowner*, leaving her alone with the admiral. "Think you were going to sneak into town without paying for your repairs?"

"Nonsense," LaBrecque replied, glancing at the chest in the back of the covered wagon. "Just needed to abate the 'interested parties' here at the docks. My plan was to visit you on the way back."

"Show me." She pointed to the chest behind him. He opened the chest, revealing enough gold palmettes to commission a new ship.

"I see you are a man of your word."

"And you a woman of yours," LaBrecque replied. "From afar, she looks brand new. And the speed of repair was unexpected."

"Tinker lardals sometimes can go days without rest once their minds are set to a task." She tilted her head in the direction of her craftsmen. "They are worth every sheaf of copper."

"I plan to inspect the ship upon my return," LaBrecque assured her. "And my men? Have they behaved themselves?"

"Yes," Vho replied. "Sailing Master Tamsyn kept them in check. But I need to show you your new rudder. It is, as I said, new technology from Abacus called a pintle-and-gudgeon. It is mounted on the stern but allows you to forego the use of your quarter rudders. It will make the *Wake* highly maneuverable. She's the first naval ship fitted with it so far. It should give you a clear speed and maneuverability advantage in the open sea."

"I am looking forward to setting her a'sail," LaBrecque said.

Vho fumbled around in the pelts for a moment or two, keeping up with the charade, then gestured for their wagon to continue through.

"WORDS OF WAR?" JAXTYN'S face sagged with disappointment. He hugged LaBrecque and the two exchanged pleasantries before proceeding to the Faircloth manse to find a more private setting. When they entered, Jaxtyn sent for ale for his guests.

"Aye." LaBrecque nodded, pursing his lips. "We are long past words. Von Lormarck is on the move. He has shown himself for the usurper he is. He's gathered trollborn mercenaries and declared war on Thronehelm. He and Baron Thessaly have allied and march as we speak."

"What of Thronehelm? Of Montgomery?"

"We sailed north, to the Norsemen of Hammerstead, for help. A blood oath was sworn, and Monty is to marry the young daughter of Atorm Stormmoeller."

"Who is that?"

"Rijkstag's ruler," LaBrecque explained. "Their armies have split, some heading for Thronehelm to help. The other marched east, intent on breaking the embargo that will starve Thronehelm this winter."

"What do you mean?"

"There is much to tell, Jaxtyn." LaBrecque leaned in and whispered in his friend's ear. "But as much as it pleases me to see a friend, I didn't come to speak with you. I came to see Lady Chessborough.

"The Regent?" Jaxtyn's face drew up, concern evident on his brow.

"Aye, my friend." LaBrecque smiled. "And that's why I came to you for help."

"Before we leave," Jaxtyn added, "any word from our Keeper friend and their efforts?"

LaBrecque shook his head. "I have heard none. Although I was north for some time, and then back to Thronehelm before departing here. I am no source, I fear."

"I understand," Jaxtyn's eyes wandered for a few seconds.

"The redhead?" LaBrecque inquired.

"Aye." Jaxtyn smirked and let out a small sigh.

LaBrecque offered a knowing look. "Don't worry, Master Faircloth. She seems to me a survivor. I have no doubt she will return to your arms."

THE FOUR MEN SET out from the Faircloth estate and arrived unannounced at the gates of Chessborough Castle in the heart of Castleshire. The estate was the city's first, the Chessborough family being one of the founding members of the Shirian society. The wondrous city grew up around the storied keep, and until the Caveat was built its hallowed halls served as home for the regency.

The castle's spires, topped with golden, diamond shaped roofs, rose from every angle of the white stained structure. The painting and appointments were immaculate, freshly maintained by the storied family. It was a task never completed. The keep had never seen a siege or bore the scars of battle. How different that was from the walls of Thronehelm or the stones of Firstgate at the Bridge. LaBrecque puzzled over how one family maintained such peace over the centuries, and how the inhabitants of such a dwelling would ever understand the fog of war that had descended upon Warminster.

As he, Raynor, and Hallowell watched Master Faircloth negotiate an audience with Lady Chessborough from their cart, Raynor tapped him on the shoulder. "How does but one family live there? It's the size of fifty galleons."

Hallowell peered out from the covered wagon. "More like two hundred."

"Where are the guards?" Raynor asked, lifting his gaze to the empty towers.

"There are none, save for at the front gate, it appears," LaBrecque confirmed. "The Chessboroughs must think themselves safe in the city they helped to found."

A few moments later, Jaxtyn returned, pulling them away from their sightseeing. "The lady will see us."

Jaxtyn's half-smile gave LaBrecque pause, but what choice did he have? The men shared a sigh of relief and guided their cart into the front gates. The guards, donning their gilded white uniforms and polearms, led them to the inner bailey, which featured a bricked, circular drive that surrounded a large statue of a golden dragon in its center. One of the guards removed his ornamental helmet and approached a second set of sentinels at the towering set of double doors at the entrance of the castle.

LaBrecque looked around at the manicured hedges and opulent fountains that decorated the courtyard. He noticed Raynor and Hallowell taking turns pointing at the wonders in every corner.

"We are not here for a tour," LaBrecque grumbled, and the two sailors ceased their gawking.

The guard soon returned, and he and five others escorted them into the heart of Castle Chessborough. The wonderment of the outside only served as an appetizer on the inside. The long, decorated hallway that opened before them fascinated, with gold leaved vaulted ceilings accompanied by shiny chandeliers that hung at the center of every archway. The pillars were of polished marble, and the walls were adorned with tapestries and lavish frescoes painted perfectly, depicting different views of Castleshire in each of its seasons.

The guards led them to the end of the hall and through a set of matching double doors LaBrecque expected would open into a cavernous throne room. But instead, the doors led into a small corridor that emptied into a conservatory. The four men found themselves in a greenhouse, replete with the rarest of plants and flowers, culminating in a glass dome above, through which warm light descended onto a sunken veranda in its center. Birds sung from somewhere in the high plants and small trees above them.

On the veranda sat Lady Chessborough, a human woman of old age. Her hair was expectedly grey, but well groomed, and she wore a gown of gold and white, with a gold dragon brooch, the coat of arms for her family.

"Forgive me if I don't rise to greet you." Lady Chessborough sipped a spot of her tea. "My old bones need some rest after my gardening."

LaBrecque wondered what kind of gardening she could have done, as her gown was impeccably clean, presentable for court.

Jaxtyn offered a sharp bow to Castleshire's regent. "Of course."

"And I do recognize you, Admiral," she said, "from your appearance at the Caveat that day with the Vermilion and the prince from Warminster. But who are your friends?"

"This is Declan Raynor and Birch Hallowell, my lady," LaBrecque turned to his sailors, each taking sweeping bows.

"They are part of my crew."

"For a crew of seamen, you look more like townsfolk to me," she noted.

"That's the idea, my lady. Anonymity… for now. Thank you for receiving us."

"Would you like some tea?" she offered. "Perhaps some food for your men?"

"No, thank you. We are here in search of more food than a lunch."

"I see." Her knowing eyes turned up to meet the admiral's. "I expected this visit but didn't anticipate it would come at the request of one of the Regency's own in Master Faircloth. My guards tell me Master Faircloth has brought you here to discuss the civil war in Warminster."

"You are aware then?" LaBrecque asked.

"Of course. This city has eyes and ears across the realm. Ambassador Camber and Ambassador Alberic of your own realm have been here to see me, yet I have heard nothing new in several weeks."

"That is why I sailed here and am dressed as I am," LaBrecque replied. "I am here on orders of King Godwin Thorhauer to seek your help."

"You know, my dear Admiral, Castleshire does not engage in such matters of sovereign governance. As does Master Faircloth." Her eyes wandered to Jaxtyn, her tone nearly scolding her associate. "We are a free city here and as such we expect Warminster to solve her own affairs."

"Even at the cost of lives and treasure?"

"They are the usual costs of such matters," she replied.

"Baron Von Lormarck has effectively stopped Saracen goods from entering the realm and Gloucester's food now belongs to him."

"And what does this have to do with Castleshire and this Regency?"

"It is my sovereign's desire to open a second trade route to Thronehelm," he answered. This one by sea. One that Von Lormarck cannot account for. My hope is that we can find such an arrangement here in Castleshire. With you."

"Admiral, as I've explained, it has always been an edict of the Regency to remain neutral in times of war. Especially between regions and families that share part of our Regent Court, as both King Godwin and Baron Von Lormarck do."

LaBrecque moved and sat next to her, taking the regent by the hand. He flashed his eyes and smile but before he could say anything, the lady removed her hand and turned her face.

"Valerick," she said with a diplomatic tone. "Your charms may work on the ladies, but I am too old for such games. Your attempts to woo me will not help."

"May I respectfully remind the Regent that this matter is greater than the baronies of Warminster itself," Jaxtyn interjected. "With the fall of the cathedral and the appearance of the Vermilion there seems to be a greater threat afoot."

"I saw what the Keeper did with my own eyes, Master Faircloth," the regent replied. "I need no reminding."

"Then you will remember Von Lormarck's cousin, Thessica Camber, rose against Thronehelm in the Caveat that day," Jaxtyn went on. "Admiral LaBrecque believes the war in Warminster is only part of this unfolding plot. The fall of the cathedral and stories of the return of a fallen Keeper may wrap into the war, as may the sightings of the tetrine and, of course, the Keeper's visions."

"Do you have proof of this Von Lormarck plot that ties all things together?"

"Proof? No," LaBrecque admitted, "but instinct and

wisdom guide us. Can you not feel the same?"

Lady Chessborough sipped her tea, and LaBrecque hoped what he had said was registering with her.

"The Chessborough family cannot help you," she said, with a resolute tone.

LaBrecque shared a look of disappointment with his men and Jaxtyn.

"But," she continued after a longer sip of her tea, "I feel you should speak with Greyson Calder, the Tribune of the Caveat. As tribune, he is a man of the people it isn't subject to the same laws and expectations the regent is. He may be able to help you more subtly than I can. I am sure, however, his help will be expensive."

"Thank you, lady." LaBrecque rose, his voice tinged in disappointment. "We shall visit the tribune as you request."

The four men bowed and turned to leave.

"Oh, Admiral, one last thing." The lady waved for him to approach. He bent and lowered his ear.

"I might be willing to help," she whispered. "But it cannot be linked to me."

His eyes met hers and he saw a bit of a sparkle in them.

"My contribution must remain secret. Food cannot surface in Thronehelm from boats owned by the Chessboroughs. I hope you and your sovereign understand."

"I believe I do," the admiral replied with a smile, and the four men headed for the Lighthouse Inn to meet with Tribune Greyson Calder.

SOLVEIG JINS AND MAKAI finally reached the Forge. The subterrane basked in the subtle glow of orange, a light cast from the ovens and forges not far from the city proper.

They were arriving during the twergish night, so much of the subterrane was asleep.

They plodded their way through the barren city, finding their way by lanternlight and stopping just outside Jins's guild.

"I haven't smelled home in a century," Makai said, taking a deep breath of the stale, cavernous air. "I was reared not far from here before being sent to the cathedral."

"We must go by it tomorrow," Jins said. "I am sure it will be the same."

She knocked on the front door of Tancred's shop, hoping to wake her boss from his slumber. A few minutes passed, and Jins heard the familiar footsteps of the limping twerg inside. A slot in the door opened, his spectacled face stared back at her.

"Jins!" he said, his voice concerned and angered. "What in the name of Anvil Ironjack are you doing back? Do you know what time it is, girl?"

"I have sold it all," she said.

Tancred's eyes stared through the hole in disbelief.

He closed the portal, and she heard the door unlock. It swung open to a dark and cold shop. The only light emanated from a single candle on his desk behind him.

"Who is this you have brought with you?" Tancred asked, eyeing the Keeper standing next to her in the door.

"I am Aliferis Makai," he said, "I am the First Keeper of Castleshire."

"Have you come to buy more of our wares?" Tancred asked.

"No," Makai replied. "I came home to speak with the *krol*, but Solveig insisted we see you first."

"The payment?" Tancred asked of Jins, turning his attention back to the task at hand. He removed his glasses and rubbed his eyes, waiting for Jins to empty her pouch.

Instead, Jins flopped the saddle bags from Phanna's back

onto his desk with a heavy thud.

"It's all there," she said. "It will take you some time to count."

The greedy twerg cracked his knuckles and began to undo the ties on the bags.

"Please have a seat," he offered to both. "I may be a while. How did you move all the jewelry so quickly?"

"You are looking at the official jeweler to Queen Amice Thorhauer," Jins boasted, hardly containing her enthusiasm. "She bought the lot from me and plans to wear them at court. We will have many more clients in Thronehelm very soon."

Tancred raised his head with a smile wider than Jins had ever seen.

"That's my girl." He rubbed his greedy hands together and painstakingly began to count the various coins from Thronehelm.

Jins paced, mulling over how to approach the next subject. "Any news of the cave writings we discovered a few weeks back?"

"I warned you, Jins." Tancred's eyes peered up at her over his spectacles. "That is none of our business. You are a merchant, not a miner."

"She asks on my behalf," Makai replied. "I am here to also learn more about this. We Keepers often have visions of such things."

"Well..." Tancred began reluctantly, "the miners have been digging around the ancient ruins and have found some sort of underground chamber. Just today, news came from the mine that their efforts tripped a cave-in. Some kind of trap set by those that left the markings. Three miners are missing so they called off the dig until they could figure out what had happened."

"I have an old friend who may be able to help," Makai

offered. "A friend even older and wiser than me. A twerg named Yenroar Silentall. Do you know of his whereabouts?"

"I am sorry, Aliferis." Tancred shook his head. "But Yen disappeared into the mountains a number of years ago. No one has seen him in a decade, maybe two."

"Perhaps I can find him." Makai tilted his head and raised a furry eyebrow, his tail swooshing about beneath his traveling cloak.

"You will need to see the *krol*," Tancred replied. "She is the chieftain of both clans Swifthammer and Battleforge. She may know more about where he went."

"Makai has business in front of the *krol*," Jins said. "He travels with a message from Thronehelm. One of an alliance."

"Then you should ask to meet her in the morning." Tancred stopped inspecting the queen's silver, appearing to grow tired from their interruptions. "I can arrange an audience for my favorite guildswoman after dawn comes, but no earlier. Why don't you both stay here in the shop tonight? I am sure you can use the rest, and my counting will go on for several hours."

The two tired travelers needed no further invitation.

TISHARA AND AERENDARIS VALKENEER, accompanied by the young Fira Carling, sat atop the perch overlooking the two-story pendulum clock that kept time in Castle Valkeneer. Tishara needed to rest from her overnight training where she had stood guard at Firstgate. It was part of the journey of becoming a Longmarcher, even though some days her destination was a rough one.

She laid back flat, her knees bent, on an uncomfortable stone bench. Her wool cloak kept her warm from the mountain stone that had been growing colder with the nearing winter. The castle was so high in the Dragon's Breath Mountains that its inhabitants needed to guard themselves from frostbite caused by the stone's touch on the coldest winter days. The stones themselves never really warmed until the onset of the Season of the Rose.

She was still in her Longmarcher gear when her adoptive little sister Fira intercepted her at Castlegate, playing an early morning game of hide and seek with Aliester, her stray cat. The girl had a tough time adjusting without her father and to life at the Bridge. Aerendaris eventually found them, and the three sat up talking, waiting to be called to breakfast.

Tishara was tired, but it was hard for her to fall asleep right after standing guard. Captain Driscoll always assigned her night watch, which she hated. He'd carry on in from the troops, claiming that not even a Valkeneer would be shown favor over others. But in her private thoughts, she'd hoped it was because of her half-elven sight, which gave the guards at Firstgate an advantage in the dark.

"To become a Longmarcher," he would say, "you must train to march long." Long days and long nights followed for her, but she knew if Ritter could do it, so could she. If she ever wanted to serve Valkeneer as he did, the days of cozy fires and early nights were over.

She was soon startled by the castle's horns, signaling the return of the Longmarchers.

"Come, Tishara," Aerendaris said, "let's welcome them home."

The three girls jogged to the parapet above the bridge and watched the Longmarchers enter Firstgate. as was tradition. They crossed the long bridge to the keep but it was obvious to Tishara that their retinue had swelled. As they got closer, she noticed they were leading a line of prisoners, many of which wore the dirtied armor of Foghaven Vale.

Wilcox de la Croix and Marr Larkin waved to them from

the front of the troupe, and then passed through Castlegate into the courtyard below. It appeared from afar they were no worse for wear, but they were accompanied by two soldiers wearing the livery of Thronehelm.

"What's this?" Aerendaris tapped her sister on the shoulder and looked to her for an explanation. It was one Tishara couldn't give.

Their jog turned into a concerned walk as they descended the steps of the parapet into the courtyard where their father and mother had already arrived. Both sisters noticed Lord Hertzog wore his Longmarcher armor and had a bow strapped to his back while her mother donned leather armor, deep green in color. It was an outfit Tishara had never seen her wear. Her mother adopted the customs of a human lady when she married her father and left the elven culture of Ravenwood. In all her years, she had only seen her mother wearing dresses and acting the part. But here, Lady Amandaris wore the armor of Ravenshire and carried her bow on her back and short sword about her waist.

When the girls arrived in the courtyard, de la Croix was already offering his report.

"Eight dead, but two survived," he explained to the lord and lady. "The First Keeper and the half-twerg continued to the Forge. I asked Rufus Crag and Til Aarron to escort them there and then go on from there to warn the Raven elves of war."

"While you were away, we learned of the presentation of the arrows of war," Hertzog's disappointing glare told the story. "Word had arrived from Thronehelm, and of the prince and viscount's demise. We must ready ourselves for the call to war from Thronehelm. I am certain it will come."

"Any word of Ritter?" Amandaris asked, with the barest strain of hope.

"Yes," de la Croix replied. "He went on to Abacus with the Vermilion princess and one of the twergish Keeper's associates. A man named Daemus Alaric of Castleshire."

"Abacus?" Tishara's face crinkled with the revelation.

"It's far to the south." Amandaris shook her head. "I've seen maps and drawings of it. It's the distance to Castleshire twice over."

Tishara sighed. Their brother was far from the Bridge in a time of war. The Longmarchers, she felt, would need him here.

"Why would Ritter be helping her?" Tishara continued.

"Shh," Aerendaris said, "I am listening."

The two turned back to their father and mother and watched as the other Longmarchers solemnly went about the duty of unloading the corpses of the soldiers from Thronehelm from their horses.

"And the prisoners?" Hertzog asked.

"Jackals," de la Croix replied. "But we do have a special guest. Aarav Fleury, the bastard son of Dragich Von Lormarck."

"*King* Von Lormarck," Aarav called from across the courtyard.

The lord and lady walked to the young royal, as Tishara and Aerendaris followed behind. Aarav was just a bit taller than Tishara and his armor had been dented and bloodied from battle. He wasn't much older than she, but seemed calm as a prisoner of war, where she thought she could never be.

"Cut him loose from the rest," Hertzog ordered. "I am pleased to meet you, Master Fleury."

"Prince," Aarav complained.

Hertzog and Amandaris shared smiles.

"Just as your father, I see," Hertzog replied. "Worried about titles when he should be worried about the welfare of his people."

"Do you plan to ransom me?" Aarav asked, with a hint

of condescension in his voice. "From the looks of it, Castle Valkeneer can use the silver laurels. You have children guarding your entrance."

Tishara took offense to the comment but said nothing. She just registered the insult and paid close attention to how her father and mother handled the unruly bastard.

"No," Hertzog said. "You will spend the rest of this war in my dungeons, regardless of the laurels and palmettes your treasonous father may throw at us. I am not sure the king and queen would want one of his sons returned during a time of conflict. I will send them word. Perhaps they want you in Thronehelm?"

Aarav spit at the feet of Hertzog and was rewarded by a swift kick from Marr, knocking him to his knees.

"I am sure you will grow to learn what an embarrassment your capture was." Amandaris scolded Aarav as if he was her own petulant child. "So early in this affair too. Dungeons have a way of doing that. Lots of time on your hands, you see."

"Place him in his own cell," Hertzog ordered. "Far away from his men."

"Straightaway, my lord," De la Croix half-bowed. "Come on now, Master Fleury. Let us show you your new accommodations and help you out of that ruined armor."

De la Croix lifted the bound man to his feet as the other Longmarchers laughed aloud as they departed.

"What of that strange one?" Hertzog asked, pointing to the man in dark robes. "He is no Jackal."

"Correct, my lord. He appeared to be assisting the Jackals but was unarmed. He did try to cast a few spells, but we surprised and subdued him."

"A wizard, then?" Hertzog said loud enough for the man to hear him. They walked closer to get a better look at him.

"Or a priest perhaps?"

The man just smiled back with a mouthful of blood-stained teeth.

"I recognize you." A worried look formed on the lord's brow. He tugged at a simple necklace the man wore, consisting of a thin line of dried sinew from some unfortunate creature and a razor-sharp tooth from another. "You are of the Moor Bog. I thought your cult existed no more."

Again, the man said nothing.

Hertzog stepped away from the man and asked the others to join him.

"This troubles me. If the Moor Bog have resurfaced and are in league with the Jackals, it may explain why the bastard was so far north."

"My lord?" Marr asked.

"These cultists worship all manner of cryptids," he continued, "which is why they live in the Dragon's Breaths. They have been banished, even before my father's time, but on occasion one or two cultists are found."

"Send word to Thronehelm of this," Amandaris ordered Marr.

"At once, my lady." Marr scrambled off to find a rider.

"Captain Driscoll," the lord called to his captain of the guard.

"Yes sir," Driscoll replied, having returned from Castlegate.

"Prepare us for war."

CHAPTER SIXTEEN

"I am no longer a slave to the shadow elves, but a slave to the shadows."
—Incanus Dru'waith

RITTER CHECKED THE STRAPS and buckles on his saddle for the third time. He had been to the stables before daybreak, having barely slept at all the night before. His mind swarmed with thoughts of Valkeneer, being reunited with his family, and above all else, Addilyn.

He hadn't sought her out the night before, instead alternating between pacing in his room and trying to sleep in the soft, oversized bed. Now, he was sure he had made the wrong choice by not going to her. He had no idea what he would have said to her if he had seen her. But he supposed that he almost never knew what he was going to say to her, until it happened. It was so natural, being with her. Ritter wondered if it would still be that way now that she was reunited with Evchen Vischer. An embarrassment at these thoughts and feelings burned inside him. He remembered Addilyn's hurried explanation of her non-betrothal to Vischer. What did it all mean?

Before long, the Vermillion arrived at the stables, making their own preparations. They were swift and efficient and didn't seem to notice him in the slightest. They wore an amalgam of powder white, matte black or crimson red scale mail armor, designating their ranks, and went about saddling their horses and checking their arms in a very similar manner as he and the Longmarchers did. Could they truly be that different? They threw one leg over their steeds at a time, just like he.

One of the Wing noticed him and tilted his head. "Sir Ritter,

Colonel Vischer wishes to speak with you before we ride."

"Of course." Ritter nodded at the man and directed his horse out of the stables. He wondered what his rival could want.

As he emerged, he caught sight of Addilyn approaching from the castle with Jessamy, but before he could go to her, a voice called from over his right shoulder, "Sir Ritter!"

He turned and saw Vischer striding toward him.

Vischer extended his hand and Ritter took it, dismounting out of respect for Vischer's position.

"I wanted to thank you again for keeping my lady from danger on her journey to Abacus. With the assassin plaguing her travels, I am glad to know you were with her. She was lucky to have you."

Vischer's subdued Vermilion smile caught Ritter off-guard. For a moment he was stunned by the comment, alluding to him as a useful tool and not a person, but it wasn't much different than the treatment he received from most nobles. He had to remind himself that the Vermillion weren't used to being around lower elves, let alone trollborn.

"It was an honor," Ritter replied. Addilyn was walking toward them, within earshot now. "I look forward to continuing to serve."

"Good morning," Addilyn said to the two men, acknowledging each in turn. "Are we ready to depart?"

"Yes, my lady," Vischer indicated before Ritter could respond to the greeting. "I was about to give Sir Ritter his assignment on our journey."

"Assignment?" Ritter repeated.

"Yes, you and Princess Addilyn's champion here have been folded into my contingent."

Vischer's lazy gesture to Jessamy reminded Ritter of his days at Halifax Military Academy, and how his betters would treat him: more a servant than an equal. And he wasn't even sure if Vischer remembered Jessamy's name. "You will ride at the front of the contingent taking point. I understand you are skilled in this, are you not?"

"Aye." Ritter's eyes moved to Addilyn's, and when they met, her gaze flicked away.

"Good," Vischer continued, "we will need you to scout ahead. I understand you have a falcon companion for such things?"

"Yes, I—"

"Excellent. That will be all." Vischer turned away, taking Addilyn's arm.

Addilyn locked eyes with Ritter for a moment but looked lost for words before she allowed herself to be guided away to her royal caravan.

Ritter's spirit numbed, and he took his place at the front of the company, waiting for Jessamy to join. The feeling of being subservient, being an "other," had been thrust upon him so fully it shocked him. He hadn't realized how good it had felt to feel like his status as trollborn didn't matter in the time he had traveled with Addilyn, until its heavy weight had been placed on his shoulders once again.

The betrayal and embarrassment he felt kept him quiet but focused on his task. When Jessamy reached him, he said nothing and rode off to gain distance from the retinue. Distance from Evchen Vischer, and Addilyn Elspeth.

THE CONTINGENT TRAVELED FAST with Ritter guiding them through the familiar confines of Ravenwood toward the Bridge. When Jessamy neared, he'd find a reason to ride ahead. His mind wandered at times but with the luck of Nothos, day one of their travels brought nothing notable.

He let his thoughts wander, thinking rather of his return to the Bridge, the reunion with his family and his troops. It felt strange to be coming home again under such different circumstances than when he had left; the war between Thronehelm and the deserters, and the changes he'd undergone in his own life.

As night fell, Ritter returned from his duties and helped the Vermillion Wing break for camp. When they dismounted, Jessamy found Ritter as he was rubbing down his horse after the long day's journey.

"It seems you and I are camping together tonight, if it pleases you." Jessamy's voice brought her usual stoicism with it.

"I have no problem with that, but what do you mean?" Ritter asked.

"The Vermillion, while they seem fine with you running point, they don't seem keen on having a—

"On having two Raven elves make camp with them."

"You can call me a trollborn," Ritter said, irritated. "It's what I am."

"Yes, but—"

"Come, let's find a spot for us. Away from them." Ritter took his pack and saddle from the ground and led his horse off a little way, not turning to see if Jessamy followed.

Soon, they were sitting around a fire with their camp set up, but Ritter didn't eat. He had no stomach for it. He thought of hunting a winter hare or a forest boar, as time shared in simple connection with Storm always calmed him, and but he decided against it.

Jessamy tended the fire, while Ritter sharpened his sword and two daggers. He wasn't making any progress, he knew, as the blades were already razor sharp, but he felt if he didn't do something with his hands, he was going to explode.

"How does it feel, being close to home again?" Jessamy asked.

To start any conversation was rare for the swordswoman, Ritter thought. "I'm anxious to see my family." His voice was sullen. "And to get away from this lot."

"Yes," Jessamy agreed, "it's a much different experience than running from cryptids."

"The differences seem to trickle into our previous company as well."

Jessamy narrowed her eyes. "What do you mean?"

Ritter sighed and debated whether to discuss his feelings. Jessamy was no conversationalist and a fierce loyalist of the princess. But if he didn't say something, Ritter felt he may go mad. "You are too honest to play coy, Jessamy. You know well what I mean. Addilyn won't even look at me. I suppose she was just pretending to overlook my low born status while it was convenient for her to do so."

Jessamy stiffened. "Do not disgrace my lady that way. That is not what she thinks of you."

Ritter froze, looking up from his work. "*You* know what she thinks of me?"

Jessamy poked the logs on the fire with a stick, softening a bit. "She speaks to me often of you. It's not my place to say," she muttered.

They were silent for a few minutes before Jessamy spoke again.

"When we first met, that is when you and Addilyn first met. She told me about you, and I cautioned her to stay away from you."

Ritter placed the dagger on his lap, giving Jessamy his full attention.

"I understood, as we all do, her place in our society, and our places in it as well. And I understood your heart, as it's like the one that beats in my chest."

Ritter's eyes focused on the swordswoman, who seemed to struggle with every sentence.

"What do you mean?"

"As a Raven elf. We're stubborn and devoted to those we love. When we fall in love… we fall in love for life. I wanted to protect both of you from what I saw as an inevitable heartbreak, should you come closer together. But now I see that I was wrong… for trying to keep you apart. You are a perfect match for Princess Addilyn, and I cannot imagine anyone better for her."

Ritter's eyes widened with her revelation. At first, he didn't know how to respond, remaining silent, but the wellspring of emotion growing in him pushed him to say something, say anything.

"I love her."

There it was. He hadn't even truly admitted his feelings to himself, but here he was, saying them aloud, to Jessamy of all people.

Jessamy turned to him and for the first time since he'd met her, he saw emotion. Her face quirked, her eyes opening wide, and she half-smiled.

He ran his hands through his dark hair and sighed. "All I've been able to think about today, even with going home and the war approaching, is the crossroads we've come to." He stared into the fire. "I've enjoyed my time in her company more than any other time in my life, but now… especially now that she has someone close by who is more suitable for her, perhaps I should step back. I'll focus on my duty to my family and to restoring Warminster… and keep my feelings to myself."

Jessamy peered at him for a while but said nothing. Ritter didn't expect her to.

"I'll take the first watch. You should get some rest," Ritter said. Then he walked a little way from the fire to be alone with his thoughts.

THE ASHEN DRAGON BOBBED at the narrow passage that was the Gossamer River. A two-day journey down it would lead Incanus and Skullam to the Bridge. The only problem: the Ashen Dragon was too big to traverse the river.

Skullam paced behind Incanus as the assassin lowered the anchor.

"What do we do now, Master?" Skullam asked. "Should we leave the ship here and continue on foot?"

The *Ashen Dragon* didn't like that idea. It cried out wordlessly, forbidding him to choose that option. Incanus cringed at the high-pitched sound. "No," he said to Skullam. "We can't leave it here. It will take too long to travel through the Ravenwood."

The familiar hum of the ship's telepathic link nudged at Incanus as he finished with the anchor. He tilted his head, throwing up a hand to a babbling Skullam who fell silent.

Command me and I shall be, Captain.

Incanus heard the *Dragon*'s words in his mind and as if she gently turned his head, his eyes settled on the ship's wheel, now glowing in a whitish ethereal aura of magic. He saw an illusory form of himself, standing in front of the wheel, controlling the stopped ship.

Take control of the wheel, Captain, and your desires will come true.

Incanus pushed past Skullam who gave him a quizzical look before following him to the helm. "Master?"

He walked to his illusory self and stood within the mystical hale of the aura, just where the *Ashen Dragon* had guided him.

"My liege, be careful." Skullam warned.

Incanus shushed him as the *Ashen Dragon* spoke once more. *Ask, my Captain. Your every desire is my command...*

Incanus stood for a moment, befuddled. He placed his hands on the wheel and began to feel his connection with the *Dragon* flourish. At first, her touch was pleasant to the senses, and soon his palms no longer felt the wood of the wheel, but the gentle touch of a woman's fingers interlocking with his own.

He looked down in disbelief.

His torso, now shrouded in an ashen aura, pulled him away from the deck and into a dimension of his own. In front of him appeared the emerging shape of a woman—the wheel gone from his grasp. Soon her features began to form.

Think of her, my Captain.

He blinked and tried to pull away, but the ship's visage only grew in strength and clarity. Her ghostly hair turned raven black and her skin, smooth as alabaster, mirrored his grey pallor. Her smiling face took form last, and Incanus saw the countenance of his beloved Fala before him.

"This can't be," he murmured, his head shaking in disbelief. But he yearned for it to be true.

I am here. You can call me whatever you wish.

With the *Dragon*'s disembodied voice washing over him, he saw the name on the boards of the ship begin to change. As the words *The Ashen Dragon* were sponged away, he saw her name appear. *Fala.*

"What perversity is this?" His eyes flecked down and he tried to let go, but the *Dragon* held fast.

It doesn't have to be. I can turn into anything you desire.

"Even the dead?"

Nay. But you shall see me as you wish.

Before he could overthink it, Incanus did as he was instructed. He imagined the *Dragon* smaller, fitted enough to sail the Gossamer River.

The deck shuddered and groaned, and he felt the *Dragon* connect deeper, its mental bond stealing from him energy to make the change. A wave of exhaustion hit Incanus, knocking him to his knees.

Skullam reached but he stopped the imp's approach with a raised hand, as every inch of him felt the *Ashen Dragon*. Her form was his in that moment.

Focus on what you need, Captain.

He obeyed, pulling every ounce of remaining strength to focus his thoughts on narrowing the width of the vessel. His hands gripped the rough wood, fingers scraping with effort as the ship splintered into his skin.

Black spots dotted Incanus's vision as he swayed. His will was strong, and this would not break him. Every thought was of the *Ashen Dragon* even as his head pounded.

"You did it, Master!" Skullam yelled above the blood rushing in his ears.

Incanus collapsed at the confirmation, and his eyes fell closed to the humming of the *Ashen Dragon*.

Well done.

WHEN INCANUS AWOKE, THEY were well on their way to the Bridge. The trees in this part of the Ravenwood hung over the Gossamer River, the soft leaves gently stroking his cheek.

Castle Valkeneer stood small but mighty against the wilds of Ravenwood. Scars of age and distant battles riddled the grey walls of the great keep, retelling the stories of the repelled assaults of the past. The centuries-old structure went by its second name, "the Bridge," as it ushered many a weary traveler across the Gossamer River to the safety of Valkeneer. More a fort than a castle, the legend of the Bridge was known throughout Warminster—it had not fallen in all its years of protecting its borders.

A substantial reputation indeed, but Incanus knew from experience that something so sure, so unbreakable, could be taken away in the blink of an eye.

Now, Incanus wished to learn more about their surroundings and survey the comings and goings at the castle. He'd been familiar with the forest, helping the brigand, Veldrin Nightcloak assault villages and hamlets of the north for Von Lormarck before the Nightcloak's untimely death at the hands of Sir Ritter of Valkeneer.

"There has been no sign of their arrival, Master." Skullam returned to Incanus's side and stepped from his concealing spell into the shadows of the trees. "I believe we've arrived before Princess Addilyn and Ritter."

Incanus didn't answer his companion. He watched for the movements of the guards, their timed patrols, and he even tried to pick up on their habits. The expected arrival of the Vermilion Wing was nowhere in sight, and a mere handful of bored Longmarchers stood at the portcullis of Firstgate, on the forest side of the Bridge. He and Skullam had a two-day head start on the Wing, thanks to the magical sails of the *Dragon*, and he wanted to use that time to his advantage.

"It will be easier to kill the Vermilion from inside the gates," Incanus determined, looking up at his imp perched in the nearby fir tree. "Has your strength returned? Can you conceal me in the powers of your dark trace yet?"

"I can," the imp affirmed, "but I will need to rest upon your shoulders and concentrate on my spell of concealment. I will be useless to you otherwise."

"Do it," Incanus ordered.

Without further instruction, Skullam climbed atop Incanus's back and took his master by the shoulder. The Bone elf felt the rush of a heavy magical hale, like a blanket, engulf him. He blinked and the world around him appeared to darken, losing all color. But his eyes sharpened in the black and white of the movement around him while the imp's dark trace did little if anything to his other senses.

The two approached Firstgate, waiting for a time when a small group of travelers ambled toward the squat stone structure. Firstgate rose three stories high, a keep without walls, guarding the Ravenwood side of the Bridge.

As the weary mishmash of bards, travelers, and pilgrims reached the portcullis of the keep, Incanus ducked in behind the group, waiting and listening for the lead horse to be permitted to enter. Once they started to move again, he trudged slowly behind the procession, slipping by the guards unnoticed.

Inside, the Bridge itself appeared almost empty. The courtyard opened in front of them, half a dozen guards meandering about, waiting for orders and smoking their pipes. The castle gates stood open, and he saw no sentries guarding the entryway.

"There," he whispered to Skullam, and they took care in approaching.

Peering inside and finding the foyer and great room of the castle as empty as the courtyard, the pair found an unoccupied room to duck into. This was as good a spot as any for now. All that was left was to wait.

ONLY A FEW MINUTES had passed before a breeze flowed in from behind Incanus, the opposite direction he would've expected. On its back, a small cloud of black rode in, curving to rest right in front of him. It swayed in place at his eye level and stretched itself until it touched the stone floor.

A Shadow elf.

Incanus almost rolled his eyes. He'd only seen a sire one other time, on the day of his ascension. Its very presence reminded him of Fala and the last day he'd seen his love. The day of her death. The day of her murder. The Shadow elves were as much to blame for her senseless killing as the Vermilion to him.

He gritted his teeth and suppressed a growl. It was all he could do not to draw his sword. What did a Shadow elf want from him, and why did it have to be this day?

The elf did not speak, seemingly waiting on something. Finally, the spectral creature vacillated in place, before a bubbling voice emanated from somewhere within its pallor. "You do not bow to your master, Bone elf?"

Shadow elves' voices were as airy as their forms, their words whispers on the wind.

Incanus jutted out his chin. "Who are you, and why do you come?"

"My name is Master to you." The Shadow elf's tone bordered on anger.

"Not in many years." Incanus's eyes narrowed. He didn't know but should have expected that perhaps Shadow elves would see him through Skullam's spell. "Leave me."

"Hubrisssss..." the ghostly shadow expanded, stretching the length of the small corridor and then forward, pushing Incanus and Skullam against the rough stone of the castle. The elf's gale picked up, blowing Incanus's long hair behind his shoulders.

Incanus supposed he should be intimidated, but he couldn't

muster the emotion to his eyes, which seemed to only anger the Shadow elf further.

As Skullam trembled in his corner, the creature hissed. "A servile Bone elf should be on his knees, you ungrateful knave. For I could have killed you instead of helped you."

Incanus bit his tongue and backtracked, if only to save his position. Any more noise or shadows, and the Longmarchers would likely find him. He forced his eyes to the floor and dropped to one knee, recalling his mother's training from so long ago. Hatred burned inside him. "A thousand apologies… *Master.* But I am focused on the task at hand. A Vermillion will seek asylum here shortly."

"What do your sires care for your petty revenge?" the figure whispered, shrinking a little and allowing Skullam to sit straighter. "I have sought you, Incanus since your arrival. Our need is greater than yours. You will do well to remember that."

"What do you require of me?" The words hurt him as Incanus said them. He had no intentions of helping and just needed to escape this charade.

"Your target, assassin," the sire said, "is the lord of this stronghold, not the Vermilion you ssseek. You must kill Lord Hertzog Valkeneer. This is how you serve your masters… and the Moor Bog, Bone elf. Nothing less, yes?"

Incanus gritted his teeth. This creature expected him to let decades of revenge slip away for the skull of a simple frontier noble.

"Yes, Master." Incanus lied. "Will you please help to keep me hidden while I fulfill this task?" He hated every word that left his mouth.

The Shadow elf shrunk to his original size, and Incanus felt the tension leave his shoulders. He'd play nice for now, but the Vermillion princess never left his thoughts.

DAYS PASSED SLOWER THAN Incanus ever thought they could. Silence clung to the halls of Castle Valkeneer. They'd had to move rooms a few times, almost being caught twice. On day three, they found themselves in a closet and his Shadow elf sire helped to protect them, hiding them within its darkness.

Incanus had begun to think he'd been given bad information from the skin-stealer and was in the middle of considering looking elsewhere for Addilyn when trumpets blared.

Skullam jumped at the sudden noise, but Incanus smiled. That was the sound of an arrival. And who else could it be but Addilyn's?

In the hall, Longmarchers filed out to greet their guests. There were more than Incanus had expected. Once ensuring the hall was empty, he and Skullam slipped back into the concealment of Skullam's dark trace and made their way to an alcove a few paces back. They listened as news of the princess's arrival made its way through the halls of the castle.

Incanus smiled.

CHAPTER SEVENTEEN

"Some love is home. Other love, adventure. True love is both."
—Illustra, Ancient of Love

THE LAST TWO DAYS of uneventful travel passed, just as the previous day. But this morning was different. In a few short hours Ritter would be home. Minutes passed like hours and their retinue was slowed by some unexpected snow on the Tavastia Bridleway, but in the distance, he could hear the bells of Wendelin Abbey ringing as if their chimes rang just to call him home.

He closed his eyes and commanded Storm to the air. His war falcon circled at first then led the way, rising on the mountain winds. He connected with Storm, closing his eyes and allowing himself a glorious view of home. Through the falcon's eyes he saw miles farther, scanning for any signs of Valkeneer from the ground.

As their eyes paired, Ritter noticed smoke from the fires in the hearths of Valkeneer homes seeping into the morning sky. On its perch above the town sat Castle Valkeneer, teeming with activity. He fought back tears at his homecoming and his heart swelled upon coming into sight of the walls of the Bridge. Still riding at the front of the company, he let Storm bring them home.

As they took the castle road, children from the town greeted them along the bridleway in their winter clothes. "Ritter's back!" one child called to the others. "Ritter's home!" celebrated another. Ritter sensed Jessamy stiffen at the lack of protocol, but he didn't care. In Valkeneer, he wasn't a sir, or some trollborn half-breed. He was simply Ritter. He waved to them as they ran alongside the caravan until the road to Firstgate grew too steep.

"It's the first time I've seen you smile since we landed in Thronehelm," Jessamy stated, her tone flat.

He hadn't noticed until she mentioned it. He offered her the barest of assents and looked to the looming tower of Firstgate. The guards at the gate called to him as well, many lifting their visors or removing their caps as the procession passed through and crossed the bridge. Ritter could smell the fresh waters of the Gossamer River tumbling beneath them and welcomed the rising portcullis of the Bridge.

Ritter looked ahead and saw his sisters, Aerendaris and Tishara rushing to him first.

"Ritter!" they exclaimed in near unison, and he dismounted to hug and kiss them both. They were trying to speak to him but with the castle horns welcoming him home and the courtyard of the castle filling with Longmarchers and servants alike coming to greet him, his head spun.

From the threshold of the castle's keep he noticed his mother and father smiling, holding hands and waiting for him to make his way through the throng of well-wishers and curious onlookers. He saw his mother coming alongside him and met them in the middle of the courtyard with a young girl, cleaned and well-dressed, in tow.

"Mother." He embraced Amandaris as she placed a gentle kiss on his cheek.

"I've got a bowl of Einlauf soup waiting for you," his mother said, smiling from ear to ear. "We heard the abbey's bells harkening your arrival. We are so happy to have you home safe."

"And who's this?" Ritter bent to meet the noble girl at his mother's hip but as his eyes met her, her recognized her—Fira Carling, the poor orphan from Emberlyn, whom he'd rescued.

"Fira?" His face quirked and he bent to hug her.

The girl's eyes, glossed in tears, fluttered and she reached for him. "Sir Ritter, I—I…"

"I'm glad to see you safe, Fira." Ritter offered the girl a lifeline from the awkward reunion. He was sure it must've conjured mixed emotions in her. "I am so glad you made it."

"I wouldn't have if it wasn't for you. I owe you my life."

"Nonsense," he said, shaking his head. "That's what a Longmarcher does."

"Lady Tishara tells me I can be a Longmarcher one day." Fira's confidence surprised him. "I'm a page for her now, and that's the first step in my training."

"Let's talk more over dinner, Fira. I must announce my visitors to my family."

The girl stepped back, her flushed face nodding in understanding.

"Your mother and I are overjoyed to find you in good health and great spirits, son." From the crowd, Ritter's father and Lord of Valkeneer, Hertzog, emerged from the crowd to put his hand on his son's shoulder. "I see you've brought a company of friends."

"Yes, Father." Ritter pointed to the Vermilion Wing that had entered the courtyard behind him.

"You must come in, and tell us everything from your time away," his father said, "but we must first be good hosts."

Ritter and the entirety of his family approached the Vermilion Wing, making their way to the door of the white carriage, now stained brown in mud to meet the Vermilion contingent. The doors opened, and they all bowed to their royal guests. First to emerge was Evchen Vischer, followed by the princess. Ritter stood straighter, looking at the space between Vischer and Addilyn to avoid having to look directly at either.

His mother stepped forward and greeted them. "Welcome to Valkeneer." She curtsied, looking awkward in her Raven armor.

Vischer gave her a traditional bow and the princess returned the curtsy.

"It's an honor to have such esteemed guests in our home." Amandaris's smile widened. "I was very saddened to hear of your father's passing, Princess Addilyn."

"Thank you, Lady Valkeneer," Addilyn acknowledged. "These have been trying times for us all."

"Well, let's celebrate your safe arrival while we have a cause to." Lady Valkeneer's eyes slid to Ritter. "We will hold a feast in Princess Addilyn's honor, and as a show of appreciation that you come to aid us in defending our home."

Ritter looked to his mother, and then to Addilyn. Her cheeks flushed pink, but she nodded in her regal way.

"Your home is as lovely as Sir Ritter described it, Lady Valkeneer. Might I have a royal tour when it's convenient for you?"

"Of course, Princess." Lady Valkeneer smiled. "In fact, Ritter can show you around himself, to all the places he's told you about. After dinner, of course."

Ritter's stomach dropped. He looked at his mother. He could swear he saw a knowing twinkle in her eye.

"It would be my pleasure, Princess." Ritter's tempered response hid his mixed emotions well. The pair needed the time to speak in private, but he feared what may come of it.

Addilyn smiled, as did Vischer, and Ritter had to wonder if he was unaware of anything that might be going on around him in the subtext.

"My lord and lady, we look forward to tonight's festivities." Vischer motioned to his Wing, "But we must attend to our troops for the moment." Without further explanation, he and Addilyn turned and left.R

THE NEXT FEW HOURS passed in a flurry of preparations, the Vermilion setting up camp for themselves and the Valkeneer household readying the feast. Ritter, relieved that everyone else seemed distracted by other tasks, went up to his room to unpack some of his traveling things and get himself in order.

Being back in his bedroom was strange. His room wasn't small by any stretch, but it felt simultaneously small and empty to him now, after spending so many nights sleeping under the open sky, next to his companions. The wooden dresser, the comfortable bed, all these seemed to be things from another life, one of boyhood, and he didn't feel as if he quite fit into them anymore.

He allowed himself quiet reflection until it was time for the feast to begin, then he dressed himself for the occasion and made his way downstairs to the dining hall. Quite a few of Vischer's men were there, along with his troops of Valkeneer, but Vischer, Addilyn, and his father weren't in sight yet, so he took up a seat next to his mother.

Amandaris took him by the arm. "There's much emotion in your eyes, my son."

"Is there?" he replied.

"Is it love or loss that troubles you?"

He turned to face her, and she was gazing into his face.

"Or perhaps loss of love," she added.

"I—I don't know," he confessed. His mother could always read him well, and he felt as though he might cry. "It may be all three."

She took one of his hands in hers and offered a gentle and knowing squeeze. "When I met your father," she began, "I knew he was the man I was going to marry. But that still didn't make it easy. My father worried about the marriage, a Raven elf princess—his young daughter—and a human lord?" She shook her head and leaned back for effect. "There was a lot we had to learn about and from each other, and our families... They didn't always understand."

"I know." Ritter's eyes curled and he looked away. He understood what a union between two different races meant. He was a trollborn, after all.

Lady Valkeneer squeezed his hand again. "I'm telling you this because despite everything, I love your father. Everything we went through to be together was worth it, because I get to love and be loved by him."

Ritter locked eyes with his mother for a long time, and then nodded. He understood what she was trying to say.

The rest of the guests arrived, and dinner dragged on, with Vischer and Ritter's father taking the primary roles in the conversation. Soon, the plates had been cleared, and Ritter met Addilyn's eyes.

"If you'd still like that tour, Princess...?" Ritter asked.

"Of course," Addilyn thanked her hosts and stood.

Ritter ushered her to the main entrance of the hall, heading out into the clean night air.

They passed through the halls of the castle in near silence, interrupted on occasion by Ritter staggering through contrived explanations of rooms and ornaments, all the while his mind swirled with the right words to say.

Addilyn watched him silently for a few moments. "Take me to your favorite place to get away from everyone. I've had enough of pageantry and pleasantry for a little while."

He pointed her to a pair of stairs, and the two ascended into the lone spire of the castle, a tower that overlooked the splendor of Valkeneer. They climbed the winding staircase, their footsteps on the stones the only sound. At the top was a circular room with a large window, a crate and a pallet on the floor.

Ritter watched Addilyn survey the sparse room and then float to the window, sitting on the crate as if it were a throne. He smiled a little at that, despite the nerves he was feeling.

"The view from here is incredible," Addilyn remarked.

Ritter joined her at the window.

They could see the silhouette of the Ravenwood against the starry sky. "Just as you said during our first dance."

Ritter sensed the memory was both good and bad for Addilyn. While he was happy she remembered those moments, it was also the night of her father's murder.

"Out there," he pointed in the direction of Ravenwood, trying to distract her, "past the trees, lies my mother's lands."

As he glanced at her over his shoulder, he realized they were alone, and memories of their time clinging to one another in the crow's nest of *Doom's Wake* flooded back. The warmth of her breath on his neck, and the smell of her perfumed hair.

"What are you thinking about?" the princess asked.

"My mother used to tell me that if you counted the leaves in the Ravenwood during summer, and the stars in the night sky, you would find that the leaves were greater in number," Ritter remarked. "It is truly a beautiful place."

"It reminds me in some ways of home," Addilyn said. "The… feel of it. Or maybe—"

Ritter stepped closer, "Maybe…?"

"Maybe that's just the way I feel when I'm with you."

Ritter paused and their eyes met. He wasn't sure what to do, what to say. Could she really feel this way? The tension was too much to bear. She had to know how he felt. And now was the time to express it, regardless of outcome.

He went down on his knees in front of Addilyn, taking both her hands softly in his.

"I feel like home to you?" he asked.

"You make me feel like I'm a person. Not a Princess, not a ward. Since my father's death, you're the only person who has made me feel like I wasn't alone."

"I thought… When we were together on the journey before returning to Thronehelm, I thought you may have feelings for me." He gazed deeply into her crimson eyes. "And I knew that I had feelings for you. But then we got to Thronehelm and Vischer was there…

"Addilyn, why didn't you tell me?"

"Vischer wasn't on my mind, that I can swear to you. At any point in the journey. He had begun courting me before I left for Thronehelm, yes, but he had only come around in that fashion once."

"You didn't think of him?"

"I don't think of him." Addilyn's words left no doubt.

She must have realized the bluntness of her words and raised a hand to her face. "I know that I'm meant to, and I know that my aunt, the coronelle, favors the match."

Addilyn fell silent once more and Ritter squeezed her fingers in his.

"I understand. Well, I suppose I don't understand, I'm not a Vermilion Princess," Ritter admitted, and Addilyn smirked. "All I know is, the reason I've been distancing myself from you was allowing you to be with Vischer if you needed to. To make things easier… on you."

"That is not what I want." Addilyn's eyes flashed in the darkness. "I don't want you to stay away from me out of some ridiculous sense of duty."

Ritter paused, staring into Addilyn's bright eyes. "What

do you want, then?"

She looked into his gaze for a moment, then glanced toward his lips, and back to his eyes again. "I want you to be honest with me," she said softly, "And if you wish it, I want you to stay by my side. Today, tomorrow, and the days and nights to come."

"I wish it," Ritter whispered.

Addilyn smiled. "Then I want you to kiss me."

Ritter placed a hand on her soft cheek, bringing his face slowly toward hers. He brushed his lips on hers with a loving touch. She smelled like flowers. She laced her fingers around his neck, and he deepened the kiss. His fingers found her hair and she pressed herself against him, catching him off balance and sending them both, entangled, to the floor. They parted lips to laugh.

"I'm so sorry," Addilyn laughed.

Ritter kissed her cheek, then the tip of her nose, then her mouth again. He continued to kiss her as he scooped her into his arms and laid her on the makeshift bed. Her hands traced the muscles of his back and he shivered. He kissed her until he needed to draw breath, and then pulled back, looking into her beautiful face once again.

"Is this okay?" he asked.

She pulled him back to her, the frantic removal of his shirt over his head and her fingers at his belt the only answer.

THEY LAY TOGETHER, ADDILYN drawing idle circles on Ritter's chest with one finger, her eyes closed in contentment. Ritter kissed the top of Addilyn's head again, feeling whole with her tucked into his side. He looked at the way the shadows were reflecting on the ceiling of the tower. He had spent many nights up here alone, but something didn't feel right. The longer he looked at the shadows, the less correct they looked.

"I'm going to check on something," Ritter whispered, and Addilyn sat up straight.

"What's wrong?" she asked in alarm.

Still undressed, Ritter went to the window.

He cursed and Addilyn came to join him, covering herself with her dress but not wearing it. Off in the near distance, Ritter could see torches in the Ravenwood.

IT WAS LONG AFTER midnight and Firstgate was as silent as the late autumn skies above it. No insects chirped as it was beyond their time. No birds sung, as it was far too late to hear their melodies. Occasionally, the crackling of the fire pit atop Firstgate would echo into the woods and speak back, but the guards of Firstgate stood fast, nonetheless.

It was truly the dead of night.

Captain of the Guard Forbes Driscoll sat inside, warming himself by the hearth of the fire. The Bridge was too undermanned for a veteran and officer like Driscoll not to take a dead man's shift overnight, and tonight was his night to stand next to his most inexperienced trainees. He looked at it as a time to show the greenest of soldiers that duty called for even the captain of the guard. True, he would have preferred the warm comforts of his wife's bed, but after the Longmarchers had returned with their prisoner, he thought a shift or two with his newest recruits would keep him frosty.

Then he heard a soft rapping on his door.

"Yes," he said, loud enough for the recruit outside to hear him.

"A lone rider approaches, sir," the young woman's voice said. He recognized it as the voice of Tishara Valkeneer, who was working to complete her training as a Longmarcher. Nights like these would soon be common for his royal recruit.

"Take care of it, Private," he called back.

"It's not that, sir," she replied. "It's that he won't come any closer. He seems to be waiting for something."

Driscoll stood up. There was no way a Jackal could have made it this far seeking ransom demands for Aarav's freedom. In fact, he doubted they would even be missing him at this point.

"I'm coming," he said, and slung his sword over his back and donned his helmet.

He emerged from Firstgate with Tishara and she pointed across the open expanse that lay between them and Ravenwood. Cast in the grey pallor of moonlight, a large, cloaked figure strode atop an even larger horse, one that at a distance looked unnatural in its size. Driscoll could see the steam rising from both the man and horse's breath, dissipating quickly in the night breeze.

Driscoll and Tishara mounted up and he turned back to his young guards for a moment.

"We will ride out to meet this man," he said. "Be prepared."

"For what, sir?" one of the trainees asked.

"Anything," Driscoll replied, and turned his horse toward the figure.

He and Tishara rode side by side, eyeing the man as they approached. He didn't move.

As they got within fifty paces, their horses stopped and would proceed no farther. He urged his steed on, and it protested, snorting and whinnying, but eventually yielded to his spurring.

Driscoll looked to Tishara and her steed looked skittish too, yielding its leg and trotting diagonally to a halt.

They both stopped and Driscoll raised his hand to greet the rider.

The man's steed was gigantic, larger than some draft horses Driscoll had seen plow the fields of Valkeneer or turn the grist mill at Wendelin Abbey. He doubted he had seen anything of its size before.

The man himself sat over a foot taller than Driscoll and Tishara atop his giant stallion, his features shrouded in the cowl of his cloak.

"Do you wish to cross into Valkeneer, friend?" Driscoll asked. "It's a little late for us to allow entrance."

The man didn't respond.

He sensed something odd and searched the tree line not far from him. "Lower your hood so that we may see you better," Driscoll ordered, his tone changing from pleasant to official.

Again, the man didn't respond.

"Tishara," Driscoll turned to the young noble and whispered, "do your Raven eyes see anything in the forest, in the trees?"

"No, Captain," she replied. "All seems calm."

"If you don't lower your hood, we will have to arrest you," Driscoll threatened, his patience wearing thin.

"I am a messenger," the man finally spoke.

"So late?" Driscoll remarked. The excuse seemed implausible. "From where?"

"I bring word for the lord of Castle Valkeneer," he replied.

"From where?" Driscoll asked a second time.

"From Ashen Hollows," the man offered. "And from the Dragon's Breath Mountains."

Now it was Driscoll's turn to be silent. What he said made no sense.

He waited to see what the man's next move was and

scanned him for weapons. He saw none, save for a gnarled staff strapped to the side of his stallion.

When Driscoll was convinced they had reached a stalemate, he spoke again. "Lord Valkeneer cannot see you until the morning," the captain replied. "Perhaps you can pass along your message to me."

"We want the one known as Amaranth returned," he said.

Driscoll chuckled. "He was caught attacking our men and the soldiers of Thronehelm," he replied. "I believe he will stay in our dungeons for a long time."

"We also require the return of the Von Lormarck bastard," the stranger muttered, his voice turning clipped.

"Ride off," Driscoll ordered, "lest you join your friends in the dungeons of the Bridge."

"Lord Valkeneer has until the moon of the winter solstice to release him."

"Or else…?" Driscoll prodded.

The stranger struck out, the boney staff leaping from his hand and impaling Driscoll. The captain's eyes looked helplessly at the wound and back into the dark eyes of his slayer before sliding off his horse to the cold ground below, dead.

THE MAN'S HORSE REARED up, scaring their horses. Tishara did everything she could not to lose her place on her saddle, but it wasn't enough. She fell to the ground not far from Driscoll's body as the pounding of hooves retreated behind her. Even her own horse had abandoned her.

The strange stallion's eyes glowed red in the darkness of night as if they possessed an illumination of their own. A sickening took hold of Tishara, as the man tugged the staff from the captain's fresh corpse and pointed it at her.

"You shall take my message, girl. The prisoners you hold in

your cell. The one named Amaranth and the son of the Jackal must be set free. Tell your father he has to the coming of the winter solstice, or I shall return."

Then the man rode off, disappearing into the darkness of Ravenwood.

CHAPTER EIGHTEEN

"Neutrality is not an ally."
—Teachings From the Horn of Ramincere

DAEMUS JOGGED TO KEEP up with the man, who seemed rather too spry for the years Daemus had assumed he bore. He tried to keep track of the turns as he followed Wilkes through the corridors—second left, third left, first second right, straight, first left, fourth right, second left—but when he tried to think back, around the thirtieth turn, he realized he'd lost track.

He could hear the steady drumbeat of his companions' footfalls behind him as they all trailed silently along after the mapmaker. He kept half-expecting Faux to overtake him, far stronger runner that she was, but the whole group seemed content to follow in a line.

The only sound he heard for nearly three-quarters of an hour, other than feet and heavy breathing, was a soft "oh" from Katja when she stumbled over something. He turned his head in time to see her catch herself on a wall, and she shot him a reassuring glance before he looked for Wilkes again, only barely catching the man as he made the next turn.

When Daemus was starting to question how much longer he could go without stopping, Wilkes called at last, "Here." He stopped at a curtain of moss, which he pulled aside to reveal a narrow opening.

After a brief hesitation, Daemus followed him through it.

An inclined path led up to small cavern that opened up into a rocky overhang, barely large enough to fit all of them, but looked like it would have been comfortable for a single occupant. Wilkes's things—a tattered bedroll, an oddly unused-looking cooking pot, and what Daemus guessed was another journal—were neatly organized by the rocky wall.

"My place," Wilkes said with a simple gesture of his hand as the rest of them filtered out with caution onto the overhang.

Arjun, Daemus noted, was out of breath but seemed to be acclimating much better to his new leg, at least enough that he had not fallen too far behind to catch up. Everyone else looked exhausted but well. His eyes lingered for a moment on Katja again before he forced himself to look away. Once Daemus turned his attention to the view of the labyrinth below, he quickly became absorbed in the sight.

Wilkes shuffled closer to him and pointed. "See that glow? That be the Heart." He referred to a soft violet light Daemus squinted to see in the distance. "Center of the labyrinth."

"Where the Tome is," said Caspar, his voice sturdy. "What we care about."

"And there," Wilkes went on with a brief, incurious glance in Caspar's direction. "See that tree? Closer by. And the lady." He pointed to a massive weeping willow tree next to an even larger stone statue of a hunched figure covering its face. "That's Willow's Weep."

"You mentioned that in your atlas," said Faux with a sudden turn. "The one we discovered in the chapel. It's important? Willow's Weep?"

"Aye. Think so." Wilkes's mouth quirked. "Close by, but still haven't found the way to get there. Some of the old scratchings, the really old ones far in, mention doubling back to find the Weep. Someone must've uncovered some clue there. One that I couldn't find. That, or it's gone now."

"Trillias doesn't maintain it?" asked Katja with some surprise. "The puzzle?"

Wilkes gave her a funny look, scraggly eyebrows drawing down. "Why ought an Ancient do anything to help? Entertains 'em seeing us run around like rats, don't it? Up to us mortals to make our own way."

Katja pressed her lips together and frowned but didn't reply.

"You get cryptids coming this way?" pressed Arjun, who had caught his breath at last.

Wilkes shook his head. "Don't know why. Not as though they'd be fooled by the greenery over the entrance. Think maybe a wizard came through the maze this way, maybe put a spell over it—makes me sneeze nearly every time I pass through, like there's magic thereabouts."

"Magic makes you sneeze?" Faux inquired with a suspicious tilt of her head.

"He's not spinning a tale," Tuttle spoke up. "Magic sniffers are uncommon, but we exist. Thought I felt a prickle as I came through under that moss, but I figured it must be spores."

"What are spores?" asked Blue Conney, with a confused look.

"Particles that come through the air around—"

"Perhaps the lecture can wait," Anoki interrupted Tuttle with a gentle inflection, "until after we have uncovered our next step."

Tuttle paused, mouth still open, and subsided with a respectful nod. "Indeed. Remind me to explain it to you later, my springheel friend."

"If you wanna stay for the night I'd be happy to have ya," Wilkes offered. "I don't get much company and it may be a bit crowded, but…"

"Your generosity is very welcomed." Katja bowed, accepting his invitation for the group.

Daemus bit his lip, fighting the urge to keep going, but knowing they would be hard pressed to find a safer place from the cryptids in what seemed like the dwindling hours of the day. The light changed little in the labyrinth, which seemed to be cast under a perpetual twilight, but in the distance, they could see cryptids emerging to prowl around in the maze, more than they had seemed to before.

"Come, Master Wilkes." Anoki put her rucksack down. "Let's spend some time. I'd love to pour over your books and maps. Jeric, Caspar, care to join?"

As the little group began comparing the two atlases, trying to work out the best routes to try to reach the Weep, Daemus sat by himself near the edge, watching the glow of the Heart in the distance. A part of him wished he could remain here forever, although he knew the world would be doomed if he did. To wander the maze until the end of time, never knowing which way to go, felt safer and freer to him than to return to the outside world and be pushed toward an immutable destiny that he had to look in the eyes as it approached, seeing every move in the game but unable to truly influence any of it. At least here, for the first time in his life, it felt like he could be himself, whoever he was, without the weight of providence.

Someone came up and sat by his side. He half-hoped it might be Caspar, whom he still hadn't had much time to talk to since the two of them had reunited, or Faux, or—he registered with a tinge of embarrassment—Katja. When the figure spoke, however, he realized it was Wilkes.

"Gives me hope," the man's soft voice reached his ears. "The Heart does. It's still alive, and I'm still alive."

"How long have you been here?" Daemus inquired, and Wilkes tilted his head before scratching a long finger on the rock on which they sat. Daemus just looked at him for a moment, confused, and then glanced down, finally noticing a wiggly row of fine, shallow cuts into the rock that followed the edge but stopped about a third of the way in from the wall.

"Weeks?" Daemus guessed, but Wilkes's expression told

him otherwise. Unease started to color his feeling of tranquility at the man's somber gaze. At a glance he might have said there were around two hundred of the little scratches. "How old are you, Renfrow?"

"Thirty," replied Wilkes. "Was that old when I… when the labyrinth spread to Shiloh." Daemus recognized that he must be talking about the village. "Not many places to see your own face in this tangle, but I found that pot about a year back—" he jerked his head at his cooking pot, which rested in the corner—"polished it up. Couldn't say my face looks any different than it ever has. Don't feel any different neither… or just my mind does, anyway."

Daemus looked over at the pot, then back at Wilkes. "You… Haven't you eaten with it? Don't you use it to cook?"

Slowly, Wilkes shook his head. "May have noticed ye haven't had any hunger pangs since you came in, either. I just keep it to look at. The magic keeps us all frozen, I think, in every way. Like death."

"Death doesn't do that." Daemus rejected this, but Wilkes just looked at him, pity in his eyes.

"I just mean it's no better than. Not living in the world anymore, are we?"

Daemus saw the man's drawn conclusion: they might never leave the labyrinth again, just as a dead man could not return to dwell among the living. But Wilkes refrained from saying it.

Daemus couldn't think how to answer that. He wanted to tell Wilkes that living in the world wasn't always all it was cracked up to be, that he'd almost rather just stay here, but it seemed like the wrong thing to say to a man who had been wandering the labyrinth for years trying to find his way out.

"Trillias has given us one week to get the Tome. Seven days to find the Heart of Laurentia," Daemus explained. "How long did he give you?"

Wilkes chuckled. "He didn't."

"What does that mean?" the Keeper asked.

"Hey," said Katja from behind them, and they both turned, Wilkes's long beard brushing at Daemus's shoulder. "We think we have something."

It turned out that the spot in the corridor where Katja had tripped had looked like a marker of some kind, and that they thought the spot might be very near to a blank patch on the map that Wilkes had not been able to find a way to access. It did seem like a promising lead, one Anoki declared they would pursue tomorrow, after getting some sleep. Daemus didn't mention that after speaking to Wilkes, he wasn't even sure they could sleep inside the labyrinth.

They passed the night in silence, everyone lying very still, eyes closed. Daemus let himself drift, trying not to resent that one of the things he'd looked forward to most had been denied him: to dream again without even the chance of it being poisoned by prophecies.

CHAPTER NINETEEN

"The more you prepare for war, the less you bleed when it comes."
—The Faxerian, Lucien Blacwin

RITTER HAD ONLY TAKEN time to wash his face and arms before joining the others in the war council room, which on normal days was the Bridge's library. The large wooden table in the center of the room was surrounded by reading chairs, and Ritter's parents, Addilyn, with Jessamy standing behind her, Vischer, and Ritter's lieutenants Wilcox de la Croix and Marr Larkin of the Longmarchers were already assembled there.

"Who was it?" Hertzog demanded from Tishara, who still appeared in shock from the encounter with the unknown messenger.

"He wore no sigil," Tishara replied, her voice quivering. "He demanded first the man in the dungeons named Amaranth and then Aarav Fleury. By the winter solstice."

A tense silence pervaded for an indeterminable time before Amandaris spoke. "The stranger must be the Black Vicar. And this Amaranth a member of his cult. I know they've been thought to be long vanished but there's no other explanation."

"Ritter." Addilyn looked across the table to him. "Vorodin the Ageless warned of their return. As did Anselm Helenius."

Ritter rose, his face grim. "I see but two paths. We can give in to his demands or prepare to fight the Moor Bog."

"We could fortify Valkeneer and wait them out," Marr volunteered. "The cold is coming. They won't wish to stay camped out here for long and may simply return home to the Dragon's Breath Mountains."

"They won't." Hertzog shook his head. "They have magics, and I am certain he didn't choose the time of the solstice unless they had a reason. I am sure it has some significance to them or their plan. If we don't give them their prisoners, they will attack—swiftly and fiercely."

"We have heard of the Moor Bog, even in Eldwal." Vischer stood and began to pace the confines of the library. "If they have allied with cryptids, it may make our defense of Valkeneer difficult with the forces we have."

"It would seem we are all of the same mind," Hertzog agreed. "We do not stand to gain anything by surrendering the prisoners to the Black Vicar. The threat of attack lingers regardless of whether or not we acquiesce. Correct?"

Everyone around the table confirmed the statement.

"Excellent. Then we must prepare for battle."

Ritter sat forward as his father took a scroll from beside him and unrolled it on the table, revealing a map of Castle Valkeneer.

Hertzog pointed out places that would need to be fortified in a coming conflict, and the possible places that he thought could be used to their tactical advantage. The armorer and the tradespersons put in their own input throughout the conversation, and Vischer asked relevant questions about how they would use their respective forces most effectively.

Addilyn, who Ritter noticed had been listening, spoke up. "I believe I should go. We need more forces if the Bridge is to hold."

"No," Ritter and Vischer said in union before looking at each other.

"Let her speak," Amandaris said to the men. "Go on, Princess."

"I know that Ravenshire isn't far. If I were to leave my Vermilion escorts here, I could escape into the forest unnoticed and seek the support of the Coronel of Ravenshire. He'd be obligated to help a Vermilion princess."

Before Ritter could retort, Amandaris cleared her throat. All eyes turned to the lady of the house.

"As you know, Princess, my father is coronel, and I am well acquainted with the Ravenwood. The castle's tunnels can get me clear of any dangers until I am deeper into the woods. We don't have much time before the solstice, but a good woodswoman or two can move with speed and silence."

She locked gazes with her husband. "I believe I should take my daughters and our young page, Fira Carling, to my people, the Raven elves. Once there, Princess Addilyn, I will recruit my father to help in our cause. Like you said, he cannot refuse to help a Vermilion Wing."

Hertzog nodded his agreement with this plan, then looked to Addilyn.

"Of course, my lady," Addilyn affirmed. "I know of your lineage, and it makes best sense to me."

Hertzog addressed the room. "If there are no more questions or debates, we all have work to do. In three days, the Moor Bog attack."

RITTER SUMMONED THE LONGMARCHERS to the soldiers' dining hall near the practice arena, but found that they were already assembled, sitting or standing in small groups. He found the table where Marr, de la Croix, Til Aarron, and Rufus Crag were sitting, talking quietly together. An oppressive feeling hung over the entire company, but especially over his four friends. As Ritter marked the men's faces, he understood—they had gathered here to mourn Captain Driscoll.

Ritter walked with solemn steps, and when Marr saw him,

the man smiled. "I was hoping you'd come see us. You've been away too long."

Ritter gave Marr's shoulder a comforting squeeze and then took the empty seat next to Rufus, across from Marr and de la Croix. They exchanged pleasantries, but Ritter waited for their emotions to surface.

Of course, de la Croix voiced his opinion first. "Driscoll was a father to all of us. He trained many of us, sir. We can't just sit here and wait for an attack."

"That's exactly what we'll do," Ritter replied. "And that's what Captain Driscoll would be ordering if he were sitting here with us right now."

"We just can't do nothin'," Rufus Crag weighed in. "That feels like he died unavenged."

"The Longmarchers are not cowards," Ritter reminded him, "and we do not bow down to the threats of warlocks and their blood sucking ilk who attack in the night. We will stand and fight the Moor Bog, my friends, but we need to be smart in defending the Bridge and bringing honor to the spirit of Captain Driscoll. And when the Black Vicar shows himself, one of us will be ready to defeat him. For the Bridge, for Driscoll."

The men yelled and beat their fists on the tables.

"My mother, Lady Valkeneer, who has been like a mother to many of you, has left the Bridge in the hope of gaining us allies with her kin, the Raven elves. She will be successful and bring with her a second army of Ravenshire. What we need to do now is ready our weapons and steel our minds for the coming assault."

His men were silent for a moment, then Marr began rhythmically banging his mostly empty mug against the table. *Boom. Ba-boom. Boom. Ba-boom.* De la Croix and Rufus joined in, slapping their chests between Marr's beats. *Boom, whack! Ba-boom, whack! Boom, whack! Ba-boom, whack!* The men at the surrounding tables marched their feet in time under the tables and around the room along with them. *Left, right, left, right. Boom, whack! Ba-boom, whack!*

"Many men, one sword!" Ritter yelled over the chanting.

"Many chests, one heart!" the men yelled in return.

The drumming stopped with the end of the chant, and yells and cheers came from the men, who dispersed into groups and began preparing themselves, as assigned. Only Marr, de la Croix, Til Aarron, and Rufus stayed behind.

"Been practicing your pretty speeches since you've been gone?" Rufus said.

Ritter didn't grace him with a response.

RITTER LEFT HIS LONGMARCHERS and let his feet carry him at will, finding himself back at the base of the lone tower. He sighed and climbed the steps to the top.

It still smelled of her in there. He traced his finger along the groove of the grout between the stones and ran it along the circular wall until he reached the window, standing next to the crate where Addilyn had sat only the day previous when he had confessed his feelings for her.

Now, without her right next to him, he wondered whether or not he had made the right decision. The feel of her skin against his, her hair tangled in his fingers, was still fresh in his memory… but had the tryst been ill advised? Deep inside, he knew their union was ill-fated.

He was just about to head back down from the tower when he glanced out the window and saw Addilyn, walking side by side with Vischer from their encampment toward the castle. There was enough space between them for him to see the grass behind, even at this distance, but the sight of them together made his chest burn with jealousy. He wanted to walk next to her across the grass and share in conversation. He found himself wondering what they might be talking about, but they were too far away for him to hear.

He chastised himself and looked away from the window. He didn't own Addilyn or her time, and she could speak with whomever she wished to. Torn, he descended the stairs of the tower, determined to take the long way to the hall for dinner and avoid intercepting Vischer and Addilyn.

JESSAMY PATROLLED THE HALLS of Castle Valkeneer with no true destination in mind. She wanted to familiarize herself with her new surroundings but found herself in the hall outside Addilyn's chambers. As a reflex, Jessamy looked inside when she reached the open doorway and caught movement at the window. The rest of the room was empty save for a scroll on the bed, but the tip of a wing retreated through the open window.

Jessamy drew her sword and rushed to the opening, but she was too late. The assassin and his imp had just touched down on the ground below.

She sheathed her sword and watched them flee, unable to pursue.

Turning around, she crossed the room to the parchment. It bore Queen Amice's seal. Jessamy squinted in confusion and thought about bringing it to Addilyn's attention. Curiosity and caution got the better of her, and she opened the message, sure that whatever it said was lies.

"ENTER," LORD HERTZOG CALLED, and the doors to Castle Valkeneer's receiving room opened. Ritter looked upon his two younger sisters, with confusion in their eyes. He stood to the left and behind his father and mother who had worn their finest for the impromptu occasion.

"Approach," Hertzog waved from his makeshift throne, as the Bridge held no such fineries.

The two young women looked at each other and slowly made their way toward their parents. Aerendaris carried her cat, Aliester, and from behind the pair, appeared Fira Carling, whom had been inseparable from them since her arrival.

"Sir Ritter, what are we doing here?" Fira asked, innocence in her voice.

"Shh," Tishara answered for her brother.

"Come forward daughters," the lord said, "this is an important evening for you."

"What is going on, Father?" Tishara asked as the trio approached.

Ritter did his best to hide a smile, as he knew at least one of his sisters had been waiting for this moment since he could remember and hadn't yet recognized the purpose of her summons. If circumstances had been different, there'd be more pomp and circumstance around the evening's festivities, but as the situation called for, this was the best his parents could muster.

"My beautiful daughters." Hertzog stood, a proud smile appearing beneath his beard. "I wish we had more time to plan for tonight, but it seems the Fates have again reminded we Valkeneers that duty to country and kin comes before oneself. And tonight, we call you both to service."

"I don't understand," Tishara said, her eyes sliding to Ritter for help.

He gave her none, hoping to preserve the sanctity and gravity of the moment.

"We are need of more brave Knights." Lady Amandaris rose to stand in front of them. "Come, Tishara, kneel in front of me."

"What?" she asked, but before she could retract it, Amandaris had drawn her sword.

"There is no time for a white vesture and red robe," Hertzog said from behind his wife with some level of rushed incredulity, holding back a smile and a tear. "If you want to be a Knight as you've always said, you must be knighted. Now, kneel."

"But Mother, Father, my training has just begun."

"Some warriors die before they ever feel the touch of a lord's sword on their shoulders," Amandaris reminded her, her anger rising, pointing out the window to the bodies of the Black Cuffs lying in the courtyard. "That does not make them any less a Knight."

Tishara quieted and knelt, a tear forming in her eye. She looked to Ritter, who nodded in encouragement. For as long as he could remember, Tishara wanted to be a Longmarcher, and with Driscoll's death casting a pallor over the Bridge, perhaps his father was correct. Perhaps this simple ceremony would raise spirits.

"Tishara of Valkeneer," Amandaris began, "do you swear by the Ancients to defend to your uttermost the weak, the orphaned, the widowed and the oppressed?"

"I do, Mother," she managed, fighting back her own emotions. She looked up at her, and then back to Ritter, who knew her dreams were coming true in an instant.

The lady placed the flat of her sword on Tishara's left shoulder and lifted it to the right.

"Tishara of Valkeneer, do you swear on pain of death and by

threat of divine retribution to uphold the laws and protect the lands of Valkeneer until the day you enter the Hall of the Ancients?"

"I do," she said, her tears forming tracks down her face.

"Rise now, then, as Lady Tishara of Valkeneer."

As she stood, they took turns embracing until it was time for Ritter to hug his sister. As he reached for her, he whispered in her ear, "I was only a few years older than you when I felt the touch of the blade on my shoulders. You will serve us well. I am proud of you, Lady Tishara."

"This is what I have wanted forever," she replied as her mother and sisters hugged her in a weeping pile of Valkeneer women. Even Fira slipped in between them to share in their celebration.

"You next, Aerendaris," Hertzog ordered, taking the sword from his wife. "Even though you won't fight this war with a sword, you will fight bravely, like your mother did. An elven sorceress that will strike fear into the eyes of your enemies. Use your powers to their full advantage. The Longmarchers will need you in the field, speaking to the trees and the birds and the creatures of Ravenwood."

Aerendaris knelt and swore as Tishara had and rose Lady Aerendaris of Valkeneer. The two sisters hugged and then hugged their mother.

"What of me?" Fira asked of Lord Hertzog.

Hertzog laughed and looked to his wife for help, where none was forthcoming. It also brought a mean look from Fira. He turned to Ritter who could only shrug.

"What is it, Fira Carling, that you will have of me?" Hertzog asked, trying to diffuse her anger with a smile. He bent down to meet her face to face.

"I want to be a great knight and avenge the attack on my father and the good merchants that died," she said. "I can fight."

"War is too dangerous for a child," the lord replied. "You

must train first, like Tishara and Aerendaris. I will not have you fight. What would your father say?"

"I will not die." She stood, her hands shaking in defiance. "I am fast, and I know I am small and perhaps I can't lift a sword yet, but I have learned to survive on my own. And now look at me. I live in a great castle."

The group chuckled in nervous laughter at her fiery counter.

"Very well," Hertzog laughed. "I cannot make you a Knight. You're not of noble blood."

"I've heard the stories of your father," she replied. "And neither was he, sir. He fought bravely, as do you and Ritter. It is my turn."

Ritter looked to his father. He could hear the chuckling of the Longmarchers over his shoulder but refused to look, knowing he may end up laughing as well.

"Kneel then," Hertzog conceded, to everyone's surprise. The girl did as she was told, her anger dissipating in a fleeting moment. "I cannot knight you as you are too young. However, I decree that from this day forth, you, Fira Carling, shall be named Squire to Lady Tishara of Valkeneer."

He reached down and kissed her on the forehead.

Fira's elation drew cheers from the Longmarchers and the Black Cuffs. She then turned to Ritter and bad him to come closer with the curl of her finger. Ritter leaned over to her.

"What is a squire?" Fira asked.

"It is a step to becoming a Knight," he replied. "Perhaps one day you can fight beside the Longmarchers too."

Fira smiled and quieted, then picked up Aliester so she could tell him all about it.

"Oh, and Ritter," the lord said. "Have our newly knighted ladies outfitted along with their new… squire."

CHAPTER TWENTY

"The puzzle is only impossible until you solve it."
—Shirian Diplomatic Proverb

THE NIGHT PASSED IN silence, and Daemus spent the time lying on his back with his eyes open, feeling very conscious of the fact that everyone else was awake too. They had no sundial, water, clock or even the mechanical devices of Abacus to tell him time had passed, but he knew. He couldn't have said why they all felt the need to continue pretending, except that to acknowledge the fact that none of them needed something so basic as sleep would have been to face the very thing Wilkes had said—that right now, they were no better than dead.

At last Anoki sat up and with a soft voice asked, "Is anyone awake?"

"I think it's time we were away." Daemus sat up slower than he'd intended, finding himself falling into the game of pretending he'd been asleep without quite having a reason to.

With a gradual stir, the group rose, the feeling among them cautious, careful, as if none of them wanted to break the spell.

Daemus felt ill. Not at the abject absence of his Erudian nightmares, but at the ease he felt throughout much of what must have been the night. In a curious way, his routine of terror, ended by their presence in the labyrinth, made him uncomfortable, like he'd forgotten something. He sat there looking around at his companions, all creating a comforting illusion together, and the feeling began to dissipate. He could almost believe that it was real.

Renfrow Wilkes was sitting with his back to the wall, where he'd spent the entire night, watching them with an odd, wistful expression. Seeing him and his knowing look made it harder to pretend, although the man seemed to possess no desire to draw attention to their little facade.

"Time to be away," Wilkes echoed under his breath.

The trip back to the spot Katja had marked on the map was a short one, everyone walking at pace enough that Daemus kept half-expecting someone—maybe himself—to break into a run. Three left turns and one right, and there it was.

The spot didn't stand out at first glance, but then Katja pointed to a spiked sigil on the wall near the small nub of rock she'd tripped over.

"I'm not certain." The healer's voice held a tinge of doubt. "But it felt unnatural. It's if the rock had given way when I stumbled, like a switch on a door."

"Could be a trap," Tuttle warned, to an affirmative nod from Wilkes.

"But I didn't set it off before," Katja reminded him.

To Daemus, it seemed obvious that there was nothing to be done about that, and no one bothered replying. Katja stepped on the switch, cringing a little, before anyone else could offer to take her place.

With the grinding of stone and release of stale air, the rock nearby shifted and fell away, revealing a small tunnel. Katja snapped back and looked to Daemus, who offered a half-smile.

"I will go first," Arjun declared, his voice resolute.

Faux put her hand on his shoulder. "But—"

"Enough." With a gentle touch he removed her hand with an unconvincing smile. "I'm tired of being coddled."

Faux at last relented, and he proceeded through.

A few moments passed before Arjun called back. "Safe."

Caspar took a deep breath, rolled his eyes, and went next; then Katja, Anoki, Tuttle, and Daemus. Faux and Wilkes brought up the rear.

Unlike the tunnel under the chapel, Daemus sensed light ahead from his first step into the secret passage. The tunnel appeared to be worked, not from the craft of stone masons, but by the magic of an Ancient. The walls were smooth, and he felt his heart flutter in hope. This had to be the right way.

The group emerged inside the Willow's Weep, and he glanced around, taking in the measure of the magnificent sight. Before them sprawled a grand lawn of green, maintained meticulously, as if the gardeners of Castleshire themselves tended to it. In front of them stood the giant red statue, now bleached pink from years in the southern sun. The figure towered over a glassy pond, her hands hiding her face. Daemus registered that she looked much larger up close, but her size was nothing compared to the massive willow tree that hung over her. The place was altogether placid and stole Daemus's breath.

"Look here." Faux's order stirred Daemus from his thoughts and he noticed the rogue crouching near the base of the statue and pointing. "There's a plaque."

Daemus exchanged a glance with Katja and approached with the others while Wilkes scrambled to the front.

Wilkes read the script from the plaque aloud. " 'She wept tears enough to fill the whole well.' " He looked up. "It doesn't say anything else."

"That can't be it." Tuttle pushed his way to take a closer look. Wilkes pointed, his face unable to hide his disappointment.

"Wait." Caspar turned to Daemus. "I know that line. *We* know that line." He motioned with his arms in the space between them. "From our teachings at the cathedral. From Precept Radu's class. That's… that's from something."

Daemus ran his hands through his hair and strained at the memory. It had only been a few weeks, but the mention of their slain precept jarred him. The image of Radu dying at the hands of the Antlered Man raced through his mind.

"I wasn't in the best frame of mind in many of Radu's classes" Daemus replied. "My dreams… I was fatigued."

"I recognize it too." Anoki stood for a moment, thinking. "It's from a poem called 'The Song of Laurent' "

"Laurent," said Faux, in the exact moment Daemus had the same thought. "Laurentia?"

Anoki hummed, looking doubtful. "I suppose it's possible. I don't know the origin of the tale. But it could just be coincidence."

"It's on a statue in the Laurentian Labyrinth," Faux pointed out, earning a wry tilt of the head in assent from Anoki.

"What's the poem about?" Daemus asked, exchanging glances with Anoki and Caspar.

"It's folklore." Caspar knelt, staring up at the statue. "Precept Radu read it to us from the Scrolls of the Ancients."

"He's correct," Anoki confirmed, nodding as though she'd figured something out. "A woman lost her child and wept until she nearly flooded the whole world. Three kings were sent back from the Hall of the Ancients to convince her to stop."

"What does the story tell us happened?" Daemus asked.

"The kings stopped her, but in shame, she refused to uncover her face and remained silent until the day of her death." Anoki folded her hands. "It is a story about one who's lost a child. Something important to them. Something they love."

"More like a story about impossible quantities of tear production," quipped Tuttle, but he went silent at an annoyed look from Arjun.

"Something they love," repeated Faux under her breath.

"Why don't we take a little time to just sit and think about it?" Caspar suggested.

"We have all the time we need," Wilkes reminded them, his words laced in double meaning.

The group sat, contemplating the words on the plaque while Arjun, Marquiss, and Blue approached the pool to look for other clues.

Time passed, and Daemus leaned against the weeping willow, watching, and listening.

"Hang on." Faux paced then focused her attention on the statue again. "I have an idea. Everyone, cover your faces." She slapped her palms over her own face, shielding it from view.

The others peered at one another, sharing doubtful glares, but one by one they relented.

Daemus covered his last. He'd been staring at the statue with renewed interest since Anoki spoke and wanted to keep looking. There was something in her hunched posture that seemed familiar to him now, resonant. But he followed Faux's direction and put his hands over his face.

"Nothing," Anoki said after a few moments, her voice dour. "I thought perhaps—"

"A worthy effort," Caspar put in.

Daemus turned away to see Blue and Marquiss skipping stones across the pool. Apparently, their search turned up little but pebbles.

"Enough of that," Arjun barked at them.

The men frowned and dropped the remaining rocks.

Daemus's face quirked with an idea. He stood up and walked to the pool, ignoring the group's exchange of ideas under the hanging branches, and looked back over his shoulder at the statue of Laurent.

"Loss," he said to himself under his breath. "Something she loved."

He turned his attention to the peaceful surface of the pond and knelt like the giant statue had. His image appeared along the surface of the water, with her reflection looming over his shoulder. He found himself staring back at his own haggard appearance and he sighed.

If anyone knew of loss, it was he. The loss of innocence to the whims of an impassive Ancient. The loss of friends, sacrificing themselves to save him. The loss of the cathedral into the hands of a madman, and the loss of his Ancient's most powerful relic to the terrors of this magical maze.

The gravity of the moment washed over him. He felt Graytorris's fingers gripping at him, calling to him. *You have my eyes!*

Then the water beneath him began to change. His image floated away, replaced by memories that flooded out of his mind and onto the surface of the pond. At first, he saw his Uncle Kester, falling to the axe of Misael of Clan Blood Axe. Then the water replayed the death of his friends, Burgess and Chernovog, in the second battle of Homm Hill. As they disappeared in the ripples of the pond, a visage of Disciple Delling surfaced, and he watched him fall victim to the tines of the Antlered Man in the fields of Harbinger's Run.

Tears began to well in his eyes, but he fought the urge to cry in front of his party. They too had sacrificed to help him, lost friends in his defense. He pulled the cowl of his cloak over his head to shield them from seeing his emotion while perhaps shielding himself from embarrassment.

The pond showed him representations of his old cloistermates, taunting him as a child as he soiled his undergarments after uncontrollable dreams of Graytorris's return. Then his mother's scowl and her disappointment in him, followed by his father's face, frozen in doubt that he'd ever carry on the Alaric name.

He quietly sniffed and lowered his head, closer to the pool.

Oh, how he hated himself. Poor, helpless child, never to reach his potential. He closed his eyes hard, and began to rock back and forth, trying to drown out the squabbling and ramblings of his fellows behind him.

Visions of Radu, his murdered precept, flooded back and he felt a lump swell in his throat. He recalled Caspar's voice calling to him to get onto the back of a gryph as he chose to leave his friend to die at the hands of the Antlered Man.

Guilt ripped deeper and deeper. He bent nearer the water and looked at himself again. What a failure. He thought back to that fateful battle atop the cathedral when he lost *The Tome of Enlightenment* into the magical mirror and at the very moment, he thought he lost Katja—forever.

The cackling of the madman's voice echoed in his ears, the sound of his voice muffled as if his head was submerged under water, as he catapulted his love out of the broken inner sanctum of the once-great eye. Katja's countenance replaced his own reflection on the surface reminding him of the terror he saw plastered on her face as she spiraled away. The gut-wrenching feeling of helplessness that he knew so well at that moment must match the way Laurent felt when she lost her child. It had to be.

He glanced once more at the towering pink statue over his shoulder and wept as she did, tears running freely down his face, until another figure appeared next to him—a blue one.

He straightened but before he could stand, Katja's loving arms hugged him. "I am here, Daemus," her tender voice said. "Let it out."

He couldn't hold back anymore. Her slightest touch sent him into a convulsive cry, his shoulders heaving and his breath deepening. He started to gasp, and she held him tighter and tighter, a blanket of love and understanding comforting his soul.

His hands crossed his face, trying to stop his tears and bury his shame somehow, but he knew it was too late. His tears dripped from his fingers and spotted his image on the surface of the pond. He closed his eyes and leaned into Katja's warm embrace.

"I'm here," she said, comforting him. "I will always be here for you."

Daemus looked up into her eyes and saw his own reflection, his cursed white eyes staring back at him in her blue orbs. She had to be an angel sent from Ssolantress herself to help him.

"Look!" Faux exclaimed, and when Daemus turned his face he saw the statue of Laurent move. He blinked away his tears to uncloud his vision, but slowly, the statue lowered its hands, its gaze meeting Daemus's awestruck eyes.

With the creaking of stone, she rose from her knees and looked to the heavens and then back to the young Keeper.

"You, Daemus Alaric, understand my pain," the statue's voice intoned. Her words sounded like rocks grating against one another. "The labyrinth was created from my grief, my mind lost in the never-ending search for my child. I lost my heart to these walls and within their corridors I've left my soul."

Daemus stumbled to stand and didn't know what to say. A living statue, one that shared the burdens of perhaps a worse curse than he, looked upon him. He staggered, not knowing what to do.

Then it came to him. He was surrounded by those that loved him, fought for him—even died for him. And she fought the depth of her grief alone. He needed to do something.

"What can I do to help you, Laurent?" he managed, not sure if he wanted to know the true answer.

"Free me," she said before turning to the waters behind him. "Free me of my curse, and I will free you of yours."

With a few encumbering steps, she lumbered to the lake, the ground shaking as she stepped. With an outstretched arm, she touched the surface with her finger.

In that simple motion, the illusion that was the pond dissipated around them. First, the willow tree faded from their eyes, then the grass returned to the familiar flagstone floor of the labyrinth. Last to disappear was the statue of Laurent, fading into a pink mist before his eyes until there was nothing left.

The group fell silent in reverence.

Daemus turned to Katja, and the pair hugged. "Thank you," he managed.

She leaned in and kissed him on the cheek. He wanted more, so much more, but Arjun's voice interrupted their not-so-private interlude.

"Behind you." The soldier pointed at where the hallucinatory pond had once been. What looked like a massive well, with a set of stone stairs at the rim, led downward.

"Bone dry," observed the ever-stoic Tuttle, leaning over to peek into it.

"That means it's our way out," said Katja, struggling to hide the happiness in her voice. "Progress! Look, Renfrow!"

"I've looked," said Wilkes, an odd somberness in his tone. "Thought I'd be happier, but somehow, I feel as if I am about to leave home."

Daemus spotted a tear in the man's eye.

"Up here, you've made a *home*," Daemus found himself pointing out. "Makes sense you'd be sad to leave it." Wilkes looked at him, surprised, gratitude suffusing his expression.

"Everyone in," said Arjun, gesturing toward the spiraling stairs.

CHAPTER TWENTY-ONE

"Diplomacy is the art of stalling until your sword is ready."
—Master Zendel Cray of Hunter's Manor

"I'LL FETCH HER, MASTER." The merchant sat high upon a raised dais, hidden in part by a large wooden trading desk. To Cray, it looked more like a wall. "Please ask your men to wait outside. This is a free city-state."

Cray frowned but motioned to his lieutenant, and the woman nodded at him, removing herself and his guards from the guild.

Master Zendel Cray had made the long trip to Saracen and entered the town at midday. His presence in the merchant city was singular. He was to visit Sasha Scarlett in a last-ditch attempt to stave off a trade embargo with the merchant city. He arrived safely and he and his small retinue of guards from Hunter's Manor rode into town and straight to the Guild of the Copper Wing.

A few moments passed, and the man returned. "Follow me, Master. I'll escort you to her."

Cray removed his riding gloves and clapped the dust on his thigh. "Very well." He followed the merchant into an antechamber.

The man gestured to a seat around a small, uncomfortable looking table. "Wait here."

The room was cramped and stuffy, lacking any amenities. Cray did as he was told, and the man departed. As the door closed, he swore he heard the door lock. He rose and stared, wondering if the man truly had the nerve to lock a member of the royal family in a glorified closet. After checking the handle, he realized he had.

He was a prisoner.

He waited. What else could he do? He reached into his pocket and pulled out a flask and took a swig, then a second. By the time he heard the door unlock, the flask was empty.

"Master Cray," Sasha Scarlett's voice echoed from the hall. "So good of you to come in such times. I hope you weren't harassed on your travels?" She entered the chamber alone, her dimpled face warm and inviting. "Would you like some refreshments after your long journey? Or a chance to use the privy? I regret that I had to keep you so long unattended."

"Any other nobleman would be insulted," Cray replied, trying to remain calm. "But I am a patient man and here on important business with you. Refreshments can wait. They are a trivial matter. I am refreshed by your company."

"Have you come with recompense from the king for the four caravans I have lost on his roads?" she asked, a sly tone in her voice. "And for the families of over one hundred of my merchants and soldiers I've lost? I see you and your men, but no trains of gold?"

"My dearest Sasha—"

"My dearest Zendel," she mocked, drawing out his name as she spoke and tilting her head back to emphasize every word.

"I am not here with recompense," Cray admitted. "I am here to offer you much, much more."

Sasha sighed and looked at him, her green eyes narrowing. "May I remind you I negotiate deals for a living and no attempt at false pretense will sway me. What is it you want? And I beg you to speak plainly."

"I was sent by the king."

"Which king?"

"The only king." Cray turned his pleasant nature sour at the thought.

"You mean *Godwin*?" Her face was painted with false confusion.

"King Godwin." Cray reminded her. "And the king asks you to reopen the gates of Saracen to trade with Thronehelm. Thronehelm and Saracen have always been strong allies."

"Again, I've lost four merchant trains in two months in your kingdom without—"

"Recompense?" he answered for her.

"Yes." She leaned back into her chair and steepled her fingers. "If you do not have my gold, what is it Thronehelm offers me? I have three trains of stolen twergish gold from Von Lormarck just a few rooms from here. Payment in full to ensure my doors remain closed, and an offer of a knighthood... and a bride." Her eyes lifted and searched Cray for some reaction. "What can your king give me?"

Cray, taken aback by her brutal honesty, stopped to think before answering, "A bride?"

"Yes," Scarlett answered without hesitation. "His daughter Ember Fleury is to be my bride. Does your king send you with a better offer?"

"I must protest," Cray replied, raising one hand and shifting in his stiff chair, trying to shake off the malaise his empty flask had brought on. "You will recall Ember is betrothed to Viscount Joferian Maeglen."

"That was before the secession," Scarlett reminded him. "Your king will have to do better than this, Cray."

Cray leaned back in his chair, pondering the moment. "What is it you want? I can see the greed in your face, Sasha. A touch around your mouth and eyes, perhaps."

"I've told you," Scarlett leaned in, the smile now gone from her face, and Cray knew to dispense with any further pleasantries. "I want three trains of gold to match Von Lormarck's... and the title of Baroness of Hunter's Manor."

Cray laughed out loud, but soon noticed she was serious.

"Hunter's Manor is *my* barony," he managed with a pained smile on his face. "Are you saying you want me to be your husband?"

Scarlett sat back in her chair, seeming to ponder the thought. "No. You mistake me. I *want* a bride. I only like to take men from time to time and you're *not* of interest to me, I'm afraid."

"So, you want to marry for convenience and borrow my title?"

"No. You still mistake me. I want Hunter's Manor."

Cray tossed his head and laughed. "You want me to step down? Abdicate?"

"No," Scarlett said with a devilish twist in her voice. "Hunter's Manor will need a new lord, since their current one has failed to produce a legitimate heir. And one that will fail to return from a dangerous negotiation with an untrustworthy guildmistress in enemy territory."

Cray looked at her, at a loss for words.

"Don't worry," she said, "I will make your imprisonment as comfortable as I can while I seek a handsome ransom for you. Let's see how much Thronehelm is willing to pay for Master Zendel Cray's return. Or perhaps Von Lormarck will pay more? He may want to interrogate you himself." Scarlett rose and turned to leave, but Cray stood and reached for his sword.

She smiled and waggled a finger at him and pointed to a secret door that had creaked open behind him. "My guards have a crossbow trained on you."

Cray lifted his hand from his sword and slumped back into his chair. "I guess I surrender," he managed, as he felt the guard's hand on his shoulder.

LUCAS RANFORD LEANED PATIENTLY against the side of his wagon, his mind drifting somewhere between sleep and boredom. He had made dozens of these trips for his Guild, the Irieabor House, this trading season alone. Usually, the trips were only a few days to and from Saracen. This would be one of the last treks before the end of trading season. The Season of Colored Leaves waned fast, replaced by the Season of Long Nights. The onset of harsher weather in the mountains meant fewer trips, which translated to fewer coins. He had to make the trip count.

The small merchant caravan was set to begin its awkward trek out of the city of Vallance at dawn. The modest trading town was the merchant city of Saracen's toehold in the north, standing as a challenger to the Norsemen and twergish clans of the Dragon's Breath Mountains. Vallance had been around for half a century, serving as a way station to many human and trollborn merchants selling pelts, minerals, and, of course, the rare slate iron found only in this part of the mountain chain.

Lucas's guildbrother, Reyes, not known for his patience when bartering prices, paced in a wide circle in front of the cart, making tracks in the light snow that started to fall. His disheveled brown hair flopped in his face as he marched with hard, deliberate paces, letting his impatience be known.

"Who are we waiting for?" young Reyes demanded in a petulant voice. "What is taking so damned long?"

Lucas snapped out of his daze and turned to his young associate. Reyes had been a valuable and diligent guildbrother for Lucas, running the warehouses in Irieabor the past summer. But it wasn't until now that he realized Reyes was making his first trip out of Vallance and home to Saracen.

"Patience, my good guildbrother," Lucas replied with a calming tone. "I don't think the other brethren share your eagerness to depart without our escorts."

"What escorts?" Reyes quipped. "A few mercenaries the guildmaster hired to flank us for a few miles and then return to their warm beds? Come, let's leave this place."

Reyes stopped his pacing and climbed into the driver's seat. Turning to his friend, Lucas locked eyes with the youth, his tone much more serious this time. "The hills outside of Vallance are littered with small trollborn clans, not to mention Norsemen from Hrolt. Sometimes the trollborn ambush unguarded merchant caravans that are traveling the roads alone. Then they descend upon their hapless victims, robbing them of both life and goods, and eat their flesh for food."

The exaggerated story might've been a bit too much, but his tone carried a serious enough edge to capture Reyes's attention. Almost on cue, the two men heard the approach of distant horses.

"Ah," Reyes crowed with sarcasm. "That must be them now." He sat atop the wagon eager to get moving. But Ranford stepped away from the carriage, his eyes squinting in the snowy darkness. He raised his finger to shush Reyes and listened to the oncoming horses. The hoof falls were too many, too fast.

Lucas turned in a panic to Reyes and yelled, "Run!"

Reyes turned his head to the horizon. From the blowing flurry of snow charged a row of Norsemen invaders on horseback. A brief flash of a hand axe whirled at him from one of the riders, whooshing by his head and sticking in the door of the cart behind him. He turned to call Reyes once more, but it was too late. A second axe, then a third found their mark, and the poor guildsman fell from the cart to the snow, dead.

Lucas turned to run, heading for the lights of the town, but before he got to the edge of the caravan, the stampeding horses of the Viking invaders ran him down. The sacking of Vallance had begun.

JOFERIAN SAT ATOP A nearby hill, overlooking the town of Vallance. Argantyr, son of Atorm, rode next to him alongside Strunk, son of Helmgard Forkbeard. The attack was timed to perfection, coinciding with the first true snow fall of the season.

Below, he could hear the cries, both of Norsemen attacking and Vallancians dying. The first assault had been led by Yngwie Cnute and Bjorkmar, son of Insulgil, who led the first wave into battle. The Norsemen didn't attack like Warminsterians. There were no long lines of armored pikemen, no cavalry, and no phalanx of reinforcements if their escalated assault failed. Instead, they depended on instilling fear into their enemies, sparing few and burning all. But this time, Joferian reinforced the need to secure the town's granary and as much livestock as they could. He knew the Vallancian gold would come in time, but today he was here for the food.

The tiniest rivulet of hope and pride tricked down Joferian's throat, and he held his head a fraction higher. Not that they were assured victory, but he felt in control.

He noted Argantyr watching him rather than the raid. Though only in his early twenties, Joferian was older than Argantyr, the Norse commander and son to Atorm Stormmoeller. Argantyr watched his every move and every command over their long march to Vallance. Joferian couldn't decide if the younger Norseman did so out of admiration or something more akin to watching out for him.

It had been three weeks, but the trip should have only taken two. They hit a quick white-out a few days earlier that slowed the two thousand Vikings at their command. They could have taken an easier route to Vallance, but they would have risked being spotted by scouts or merchant trains on the road. The extra week helped them raid the town relatively unnoticed.

Joferian, who chose to take the more tumultuous route, and Argantyr had agreed in the value of the delay. Perhaps the enigmatic Einar Skullgrimsson's rune casting was correct? Perhaps Joferian was destined to command this campaign, even though he was no Norseman. What Einar saw in the lightning runes was law from their Ancients: Koss, and Ulthgar the Forger.

The first wave of Norsemen hit the outskirts of Vallance as dawn peeked above the horizon. The clashing of swords rang below and smoldering fires reached his nostrils.

Seeing the young Norseman prince still watching him, Joferian leaned closer to him, and asked, "Would you like to order the second wave to attack, Prince Argantyr?"

Argantyr looked at Strunk to his left and Joferian to his right and sounded the battle horn. The three urged their horses to the front of the second Viking wave.

"Hail and ride! To our deaths! Into the Hall of the Ancients, we ride!" Argantyr screamed in his native Wartooth. His warriors, nearly two thousand strong, raised their war cries in a song of death and rode to their destinies.

BY MIDMORNING, THE COMBINED forces of Hrolt and Hammerstead had taken the city of Vallance. The surprise attack caught the Vallancians flat-footed, and their guards never responded to even slow the assault. Joferian and Argantyr walked the streets uninhibited as the city surrendered, even if it didn't know it. Norse pillagers scrambled through the town, gathering all manner of treasure from homes and merchant houses.

Strunk, son of Helmgard Forkbeard, returned from his reconnoiter, rode to Joferian and Argantyr. "All of Vallance's granaries and food stores have been secured," he reported.

Joferian breathed a sigh of relief at the news. The golden grain was worth more to him and Warminster now than all the golden coins in Vallance and Saracen.

"Well done, Strunk," Argantyr said. "The Hall of the Ancients beams proudly at our people today."

Strunk bowed his head to his leader. "My prince, what's more is that we have captured the town's *hersars*."

Joferian didn't know the Wartooth term but understood the depth of meaning. *Hersars* were the town's leaders of sorts. Joferian noticed dripping disdain in Strunk's voice as he said it. At first, he thought it was targeted at the prisoners themselves. But as he looked to Argantyr and saw the look of disgust on his face, he realized both Norsemen saw shame in their leaders' surrender. Their people saw it as cowardice, preferring to fight to an honorable death.

Joferian thought it was an act of wise self-preservation, but bit his tongue, as to not cross his allies.

"Bring them forward," Argantyr commanded Strunk. Strunk pointed to his ruffian guards, and they pressed four bloodied figures to their knees at the tips of their spears.

Argantyr looked at the defeated Vallancians at his feet and jumped down from his horse. His bloody sword swung in front of their faces. He couldn't help but hurl a subtle but poignant insult at the lot.

"Cowards," he murmured through an air of disgust.

Joferian dismounted to join him, albeit a few steps behind. Strunk stepped back to let the prince and viscount interrogate their prisoners.

"Save yourselves," Joferian said in the common tongue.

"My friends from Rijkstag wish to have the four of you fight each other to the death. The lone survivor will be granted mercy. But I have convinced them to let you all go if you tell us what we wish to know."

"I swear by all the Ancients in the Great Hall, we will." One of the *hersars* looked up to Joferian. He shook only a little with fear, but his eyes brightened upon addressing the viscount. "I shall speak for us all. I am the reeve of the town."

"Reeve?" Argantyr asked Joferian.

"Mayor," the viscount answered back. "Then speak," he ordered the man. "What word of Saracen?"

The man looked at Joferian's coat of arms and grimaced. "My lord," he began, "I fear that I have nothing but poor news for you."

"Go on," Joferian said. He swallowed hard, steeling himself for the news.

"I fear your attack tonight may be in vain. I understand that Saracen has allied with the forces of Foghaven Vale against the baronies of Warminster. They have sent their Sentinels to war. To join with King Von Lormarck."

"King?" Joferian scoffed. "If this is true, how many Sentinels remain in Saracen?"

"Saracen has nearly emptied their barracks for the campaign. I would wager less than one thousand."

"If this man speaks the truth, perhaps Saracen could be ours for the taking," Argantyr whispered in Joferian's ear.

"I know Sasha Scarlett," Joferian replied, shaking his head in doubt. "Why would she and the other guilds allow Saracen to stand undefended?"

"You lie," he said to the reeve. "A deceit to trick us to ride to our deaths."

"Nay, my lord," the reeve bartered. "Riders came just two

days past with news of the alliance. In return, there will be a knighting. Guildmistress Scarlett is to be made Lady of Saracen, by accolade of King Von Lormarck's sword. And she is to be married."

Joferian couldn't stop his brows dipping deeply at this strange news. "Married? To whom? One of Von Lormarck's sons?"

"No," the reeve replied. "She is to be married to his bastardess, the Lady Ember Fleury."

Joferian's mouth went dry. Before he could stop himself, he balled his bloody fist and punched the reeve square in the jaw with his armored gauntlet, knocking him senseless. The man crumpled to the snow in a heap, while the other three *hersars* looked on in mounting panic.

The viscount grunted, shaking his hand and turning away. It had been an impulsive reaction, one he wished he could have controlled. The man, now sprawled at his feet, lay unconscious, useless to him.

"He has no reason to lie," one of the remaining *hersars* pleaded. "What he says is true. I saw the scroll from Saracen myself."

"You appear upset with this news?" Argantyr asked, ignoring the *hersar*'s comments.

Joferian turned from the men and sighed, taking a moment to calm himself.

"Lady Ember Fleury is my betrothed," Joferian admitted. "We must ride for Saracen in haste."

Argantyr and Strunk exchanged glances, the first and only poor news they had received all night.

"Joferian, I am sorry," Argantyr began, but Joferian ignored the words of pity and turned back to the captives.

"You," Joferian pointed at the *hersars*. "I promised to spare you and I shall. But first, I need to know the defenses of the city… to the man. You will lead us to Saracen where we will release you once you have fulfilled your oaths to the Ancients."

The leaders agreed, nodding in silence.

What choice do they have? Joferian thought.

Argantyr approached Joferian and said, "This news has unbalanced you. We will ride for Saracen, but we must choose to attack it *wisely*."

CHAPTER TWENTY-TWO

"The art of diplomacy is mastered when one can disagree without being disagreeable."
—Tribune Greyson Calder, of the Regency of Castleshire

, LABRECQUE AND HIS entourage of Jaxtyn, Hallowell and Raynor returned to the docks of Castleshire on their way to the Lighthouse Inn to find Tribune Calder. The inn was usually bustling this time of day, and today was no different.

As they entered, they spotted Calder among his guests, his brimming moustache chortling alongside a table of happy patrons. His eyes caught them entering and he excused himself to join his new guests.

"A table for four, Master Faircloth?" Calder asked. "You should have sent word ahead. Let me see what I can—"

"We are not here to eat," LaBrecque interrupted. "May we pull you away for some private conversation?"

Calder grimaced at the thought but didn't disappoint, leading them all to the spiral stairs of the old lighthouse where they ascended to the top. As they emerged from the hall, the great basin, normally ablaze at night to warn ships in the harbor, lay unlit this time of day, and the four joined Calder in gazing over the Thalassian Sea below.

"So, Admiral," Calder jumped to begin, not looking at LaBrecque out to sea, "why do you return to our shores so quickly? I can only wonder if the *Wake* is ready to sail."

"It is," LaBrecque replied. "We sail home today, I hope. But that is not why I am here."

"The war?" Calder surmised.

"Aye," LaBrecque answered. "And we need your help."

"What can an old innkeeper do to help in a war so far

away?" Calder asked.

"We have just left Lady Chessborough," Jaxtyn interjected. "She seems to think you are the man to see."

"For?"

"Thronehelm needs food," LaBrecque added. "Food enough to feed an army of ten thousand and a city of thirty thousand through a long winter."

Calder snickered. "And she sent you to see me?"

LaBrecque nodded. "She said you could arrange the supplies and that she and Thronehelm would split the payment."

"Did she now?" Calder squinted in disbelief.

"She agreed to pay for the services, but the food cannot sail on her ships or under her standard," Jaxtyn explained. "You, on the other hand, have… *other ways* to accomplish this."

Calder turned from them both and leaned hard on the railing with his considerable frame. "I have no love for Foghaven Vale, and I saw what the young Keeper did. I believe that Prince Montgomery is on the right side of this. But Von Lormarck is not one to forgive or forget. If my hands are to be on this, it will be found out by his people. If I am caught, or even suspected, I will be subject to all sorts of inquisition, including the most unpleasant means of questioning."

"King Godwin will pay—and win," LaBrecque added, sidling up to the tribune and looking out into the same sea. "At war's end, when Warminster is restored, you will be rewarded by Thronehelm. And Lady Chessborough's vaults are overflowing. She has so much gold, her spires are stained in it."

"What happens if I'm 'rewarded' by Von Lormarck before war's end?" Calder glanced over at LaBrecque. "Or what if he is the victor?"

LaBrecque broke into nervous laughter at the thought. "War forces us all to take a side. Which will you choose, Tribune?"

"Give me a minute." Calder walked away from Jaxtyn and LaBrecque, taking in a quiet moment of contemplation.

"He's not going to do it," Jaxtyn whispered. "He's a man of means and age. He prefers peace to palmettes."

"Ah, he's an old adventurer," LaBrecque countered. "It's too much to pass up on."

The two waited for Calder to return from his thoughts of and glanced back at Hallowell and Raynor, who had been making side bets on the outcome of the conversation. LaBrecque sneered at them, but Raynor just shrugged his and smiled back.

Calder spat over the side of the lighthouse and turned back. It was apparent that regardless of the outcome he reached, he wasn't happy with his own decision. "All right. I'm in. But the price I have will be steep. One that Lady Chessborough may not want to pay."

"The coffers of Thronehelm will be open to you as well, I assure you," LaBrecque offered, struggling to hide his relief. "They too are wealthy."

Calder chuckled. "I don't want laurels or palmettes."

Jaxtyn and LaBrecque looked at one another, confused.

"Then what is it that you want?" Jaxtyn asked.

"Come, lads." Calder smiled, his one arm digging into his meaty hip. "Let's go downstairs and have a drink on me so we can discuss the arrangements of our relationship."

PRINCE MONTGOMERY STOOD WITH his father, the kingdom's generals, and the leaders from Rijkstag in the war room in Castle Thronehelm. In the midst of a flurry of moving bodies and energized conversation, hurried plans were exchanged. Discussion of tactics, supplies, defensible positions… rippled through the clatter of movement.

The command to assemble the Warminsterian army on the Fields of Koss had been given at dawn. According to tradition, to appropriately honor the Ancient of War, the army had to gather at dawn and not a moment earlier. And Koss's good tidings were surely needed. Both Thronehelm and Hammerstead shared the Ancient of War, so the Norsemen sent their troops to the same field to ready for the long march to war.

Queen Amice and Baroness Cecily sat against the rails of the room, watching and listening to the leaders of both nations cobble together the battle plans.

"Any update from LaBrecque?" the king asked Montgomery.

"None yet," Monty replied, his eyes glassing over and tracking moving bodies at the same time. "The only news we have is from spies within Foghaven Vale. They claim Von Lormarck still remains at Dragon Ridge and appears to be refortifying his defenses. It appears he's digging in."

"What of our bannermen?" Godwin asked Blacwin.

"Four of the five remaining baronies have reported sending troops, or their troops have already arrived. They gather on the Fields of Koss with our own."

"Who is missing?" Godwin asked.

"Hunter's Manor, sire," Blacwin replied. "But that is to be expected. We have not heard from Master Cray yet in his efforts to persuade Guildmistress Scarlett in Saracen to our cause."

"I have sent riders to Hunter's Manor," Monty added. "In Cray's absence, we will summon their forces. The Manor borders Gloucester to the south and they have eyes in the woods watching for Baron Thessaly and his forces."

"We must assume Cray has failed then," the king bemoaned. "When will we expect his bannermen?"

"Two days hence," Monty replied.

"Atorm, son of Wolfrick," Godwin said, inclining his head to the great man. "We are ready to move out by the time the great pendulum clock is at its zenith. What of your troops?"

"We are always ready for battle," Atorm replied. His tone came deep and sincere.

Monty believed him. Was the great *konungr* ever not prepared for bloodshed? He looked to his betrothed. Freya sat nearest her father's left arm with Faxon the Red to his right. She smiled back and stood to approach him.

Monty pushed off the wall and moved to meet her. He let her lead the way in a slow walk around the war room.

"What will you do while I am gone?" he asked as the conversations continued around them.

"Do?" She frowned up at him, confused. "I will fight with you."

Monty chuckled, then he caught himself staring into the eyes of an enraged woman. She'd stopped her slow march, her left brow twitching and the skin around her eyes tightening as she did her best to not slap him across the face. He remembered her strength from their one night together, but it wasn't enough to blot out his initial question.

She shouldn't go into battle. Not as his wife.

"But I—" he started again, hoping she'd see his reasoning.

"Enough," she quipped. She leaned in to kiss him and stop his mouth, sparing them both some embarrassment if her father overheard. "I am a shield maiden of Rijkstag, and I will fight alongside my future husband."

Monty said nothing, at first at a loss for words. He steadied his hands on her waist, not sure what to say.

Perhaps she was right. There wasn't some generations-long tradition that said she *couldn't* fight. Unlike the opposing tradition for her people.

She must have sensed his conflict. She gently slid her arms around his neck. "I fight for our alliance and for our unborn child," her stern voice whispered.

Monty's eyes widened and he choked, sputtering. The words "unborn child" echoed in his ears a bit longer. He looked down at Freya. Her face was as stoic as her father's, but a kind of pride in the notion of going to war with a child in her womb turned the corner of her lips up.

"How do you know?" Monty asked, the panic rising within him. His face reddened and a cold sweat seeped onto his brow. "Is this true?"

Her eyes shifted from him, leading his own gaze to Einar Skullgrimsson who returned his look with a smile filled with rotting teeth and a twinkle in his eye.

'This cannot be," Monty breathed before he caught himself.

"Is this not what you wanted, husband?" Freya asked. "A progeny of our own?"

Monty's mind caught up with his mouth this time and he considered his next words very carefully.

"I am pleased you are with child," he said, lying to his betrothed with the steely conviction of a Keeper from the cathedral. "But I fear for your safety and the child's in battle. I would prefer you stayed here in case I do not return."

"But you will return," Einar's voice hissed. Monty jumped as the old runecaster's bald and tattooed head appeared next to his shoulder. "Your son will be a true child of war. There is no greater honor for you, Freya, and your son."

His heart leapt into his throat. "Son?"

"Aye, Prince," Einar assured him. "A son."

Monty looked back at Freya's blue eyes. She pressed her lips together hard, struggling to stifle a smile. First a marriage, then open war with his uncle, and now a child. Two months ago, his brother and cousin lived and dreamt while training in Halifax for these moments. And now, those moments were upon him. All at once. It was all coming too fast.

"CAPTAIN," A CASTLE GUARD muttered to Anson Valion, who stood outside the war room doors with a small contingent of Black Cuffs. "Come quickly."

Anson stepped away from his lieutenants and watched as an older servant of the butlery trailed the guard, trying desperately to catch up. The man was filthy and smelled even from a distance.

"What is it, soldier?" Anson replied.

The soldier turned to the servant who came to a halt and bent to catch his breath.

"We have found… *something,*" the soldier whispered to Anson.

Anson looked at the guard and saw not only fear, but tears in his eyes. He shifted his gaze back to the servant, covered in muck and feces.

Anson stepped into a side corridor to get the three of them from the entranceway. If the king or any of his court emerged, he didn't want them walking into this disgusting sight.

"What is it?" he asked quietly.

"Captain," the servant began, "I've found something while cleaning the king's privy."

Anson could tell that whatever it was, it shook both men to the core.

"What is it?" he pried.

"We do our regular cleanings of the castle privies, and as I lifted the king's wooden seat to clean, I noticed blood had stained the walls inside."

"How much blood?" Anson asked. His heart started to

race. He glanced back at the soldier who did his best not to gag at the servant's recounting.

"Much," the servant replied, nearly crying. "One streak painted the side of the walls before it hit the cesspit below."

"What did you discover?" Anson asked impatiently.

"We had to walk the outside of the castle to the collection point at the base of the wall, where we can empty the cesspit into a nearby stream. But something had clogged it."

"Come see, Captain" the soldier begged, tears wetting his shaking face. "Please."

"What did you find?" Anson pressed, grabbing the man around the bicep, nearly shaking it out of him.

"The mutilated body of the queen!" the man yelled. Suppressing his voice into a hurried whisper he added, "And the body of a maid."

Anson stopped. "This can't be. The queen has been in chambers behind locked doors since the morning with the—"

"But the queen, sir…" the servant continued. The butler's voice escalated in pitch, and the words came more quickly. "Her skin was brittle to the touch and flaked away as I tried to recover her, like a snake that had shed."

Anson removed his hand from the panicked butler and looked to the soldier, who could only nod in affirmation. Anson stood straight for a moment and thought.

"Who else knows of this?" Anson asked.

"We came to you straightaway," the soldier said. "It is only the two of us."

"Recover the bodies and have them brought to me immediately," Anson ordered of the servant. "Cover them and take care of what remains of the queen."

"And me, sir?" the guard asked, wiping his face clear.

"Quietly order all of the gates closed," Anson replied. "And when I give the order, sound the castle's horn."

"What will you do, sir?" the soldier asked.

"My duty," he replied.

MONTGOMERY SAT WITH FREYA, holding hands and chatting quietly as the war council came to an end. The plans were hatched, and he was to leave with Godwin for the Fields of Koss to join their combined armies shortly thereafter.

The initial wave of uncertainty about the news of his son washed by him and receded, leaving only Freya standing on the beaches of his mind. Her smiling eyes and rosy cheeks hadn't left her since she had spoken the words. She took great joy in the news and his reaction. But if what she and Einar professed were true, he needed to keep her and their unborn son safe. Einar was a man of magic, but he and Freya had only coupled a week ago. How could his Ancients have assured the runecaster already?

He glanced over to see his mother sitting near his aunt and then found his father finishing a conversation with General Blacwin. He wasn't sure how they would take the news, as they had just met Freya yesterday. He debated on what to say, or not, when Freya gently reached for him and pulled his face back to hers.

"You needn't say anything," she said, stumbling through her broken Warminsterian words. "We will be long on our march to battle, and beyond, before it becomes apparent."

"But we aren't married," Montgomery whispered. "And the baby shall be born out of wedlock."

"We are married," Freya scolded him, gripping his chin harder. "Under the eyes of Koss and Ulthgar the Forger. Your traditions are strange to me. Why would this make a difference to the king and queen?"

"We were not supposed to…" Monty replied, fumbling for the right words. "Until our wedding night."

Freya chuckled at the memory and kissed him. She released him then and leaned back. Her level of poise stunned the prince. He was jumbled at the thought of marriage, let alone fatherhood, and here sat his young bride, easily keeping her wits about her.

"How old are you?" Monty asked, never having gotten a straight answer before.

"Old enough," she replied with raised brows.

Unsatisfied, he opened his mouth to ask again when the groaning of the castle's horns sounded. Everybody in the war room stopped and every voice cut out.

"An attack?" Monty asked, standing up and turning to his father.

Godwin's face broke in confused fear as well. The distant and unintelligible sounds of the castle guards echoed throughout the keep as they scrambled to quarters, followed by the screeching of lowering portcullises.

The doors of the war room burst open as a dozen Black Cuffs, led by Anson Valion, flooded into the room.

"What is the meaning of this?" the king demanded.

"Your Majesty." Anson's voice was pitched and rough. "I need you to leave with the Black Cuffs immediately."

The captain of the guard had already rushed by Montgomery and was on his way to Amice and Cecily to pull them away.

Montgomery glanced around at the stunned generals and Norsemen, some of which had instinctively reached for their weapons.

His mother and aunt remained seated but shared sideways glances at each other as the captain approached.

Anson drew his sword and marched to the queen, eyes

glaring death.

"How dare you," the king grumbled, drawing his own blade.

Monty stood up, confused. He looked to Ulf Skuli who lurked far enough away not to have heard his whisperings with Freya, but close enough to come to his aid in a step or two. With that glance, Skuli stepped to his master's side and waited for instruction.

"Anson!" the king exclaimed as weapons hissed from leather sheaths all around the room.

"The queen is not who she appears to be," Anson cried, still watching the sitting Amice and not turning to the onrushing king.

Amice tried to stand, but Anson pushed her back to the bench.

"Don't move," he warned, raising his blade to her chest.

Monty leapt into action with his thrall just behind him to join his father at Anson's side. Before they reached the captain, the king's sword crashed down upon Anson's blade, knocking it from his hand.

"I'll have your head for this," Godwin roared, his blood boiling just under the surface. He grabbed the captain by his surcoat and turned to look into the man's face. His own countenance contorted in rage and confusion, but Monty stopped the king from killing the captain where he stood.

"The queen's body was found in the privy," Anson exclaimed. "This is an imposter!"

All eyes in the room turned from the spectacle of armored men jostling back to Amice, who had used the distraction to stand. With a cry, she pushed her sister to the floor and sprinted for the door.

"Stop her!" Anson yelled, and two of the Black Cuffs moved to tackle the queen.

Amice hissed in an otherworldly sound as she darted for the exit, but the guards cut off her path. Monty's eyes widened with the noise. That could not be his mother. But were the words that Anson muttered true? His mother was dead?

The room was paralyzed with the sound of her voice, and few moved to help. Amice crouched in front of the Black Cuffs and the startling sound of flesh tearing followed. From her back sprouted the bloody wings of her true form, revealing a cryptid of some kind, cornered in the great hall.

One of the guards raised his sword to swing, but she caught his arm and broke it with a single twist, casting him to the floor in pain. The other guard gasped, but his swipe of the sword was true, striking the creature on its arm, sending a spattering of purplish blood to the floor.

The cryptid hissed again in protest and returned the favor, lashing out at the man with its other talon. A scraping sound of bone on metal followed.

The guard spun and fell from the last few stairs, his breastplate split but he was unharmed otherwise.

Another tear of flesh and splash of goo fell from the creature's backside as a spiked tail grew from under the remains of Amice's gown. Two more Black Cuffs attacked, but the tail swung violently, knocking both to the ground.

"Seize it!" Monty yelled, drawing his own sword. But the creature had gained the advantage and darted down the hall.

Monty pushed his way to the door with his father near his side and in pursuit, but Ulf Skuli's powerful legs beat both men to the door.

"Stop it at all costs!" the king cried out to the attendants down the hall.

The unarmed butlery was no match for the cryptid that rambled through them, bowling them over as it passed. Monty and Godwin trailed behind in their heavy armor as Ulf Skuli sprinted ahead of them down the corridor. He gained a few steps on the beast as it slowed, stumbling through the servants that fell away.

They charged desperately by the screaming attendants and passed Skuli's lumbering shoulders. The creature turned and headed for a stairwell Monty knew led to a parapet.

"No!" Monty cried. He pushed himself ahead of his father, but he couldn't reach the stairs in time.

The cryptid bounded up the stairs with an animalistic grace, followed by Skuli only yards behind.

Monty's armored footfalls echoed in the spiral stairs as he charged up the tower, leaving his father in his wake. His adrenaline forced his legs to work faster than ever before, but still, he trailed the beast. He bounced off the tight quarters of the circular bends and heard the tower's door break at the top of the stairs. The crossbowmen on the roof yelled to one another, but Monty's mind didn't register their words. He only sought revenge.

In a foolhardy charge, he ran through the open alcove and noticed one of the crossbowmen already down and out of the fight while the other fended off the attacking creature.

Ulf Skuli made up the ground and threw a bearhug around the cryptid. His muscles flexed, but Monty could see that even Skuli's powerful frame couldn't contain the beast.

The prince charged in, but as Skuli spun, the cryptid's clawed legs kicked at Monty, knocking him flat onto his back. Like a turtle, he struggled to sit in his armor and swung his sword in wild arcs at the cryptid, missing. The remaining crossbowman dropped his weapon and tried to unsheathe his sword, but the creature's tail whipped around and smacked him in the helmet, rendering him unconscious or worse.

Skuli groaned, gritting his teeth, and squeezed the creature tight, lifting the beast only inches from the ground.

Monty managed to get back to his knees when the creature broke free of Skuli's crushing grip and his wings flapped, giving him the narrowest of space to fly.

"Stop it!" Godwin called from behind, appearing in the doorway of the tower with the shadows of others behind him.

Monty slashed at the cryptid, cutting through the membrane of a wing but not enough to ground it.

The creature leapt to the ramparts and into the air, its wings flapping as it tried to separate from the group. Monty watched in disbelief as his mother's killer was about to escape his grasp.

Then the powerful Ulf Skuli launched himself into the air and over the side of tower, his arms wrapping at the creature's legs.

The cryptid hissed again, nearly forcing Monty to cover his ears from the bloodcurdling wail, but it was too late. The strength of Skuli's arms and the weight of the giant man sent them into a death spiral, plummeting to the stone bulwark below.

Montgomery and Godwin reached the wall of the tower simultaneously and looked down. Skuli's broken body lay atop the squirming cryptid, who appeared trapped under his weight. The creature moaned in pain, pinned under the Norseman's corpse.

MINUTES LATER, MONTGOMERY ARRIVED at the grisly scene, staring down at the cryptid struggling to free himself. Behind him rushed the king, Atorm, Freya, and the others.

The cryptid's torn wings flapped in a futile attempt to loosen the corpse on top of it. Broken bones stabbed out from underneath its pale flesh. The breath from its lungs gargled, wet with blood. The beast too was broken.

Its fight to untangle itself from Skuli slowed. It only fought with its arms. Its legs, immobile and twisted from the fall, remained still, unusable.

"This cannot be real," Godwin pleaded to Anson Valion, who offered no reply. "It is dark magic, is it not?"

Montgomery grabbed his father as he staggered in no particular direction. He held him tight. The king's rage and love mixed together, not processing what had transpired.

"Where is my *wife*?" the king yelled at the cryptid, hoping for more of an answer than what Anson had offered.

Monty took an account of the beast's features for the first time. His mother's dress was shredded from its violent transformation but still clung to its torso. In her stead, a purple-skinned cryptid remained, with bat-like wings and talons for arms. It had hawkish claws for feet and legs that looked like a hairless dog's. Its face was humanoid in nature, with a smooth, bulbous head that reminded him of an upside-down egg. Its small mouth and jaw moved rapidly as it struggled to breathe. It possessed large eyes, honeycombed like an insect. It looked like no one creature, but an amalgamation, cobbled poorly together in an abomination of an assassin.

At last, Godwin grunted, throwing Monty off. He dived at the creature and lifted the bloody Norseman from it. Monty stood in horror as Godwin jumped onto the paralyzed cryptid's chest.

"Where is she?" he cried, shaking the beast.

As he did, the creature's countenance reflexively began to morph. One face after another twisted and cracked onto the beast's visage, revealing characteristics of Amice, a courtesan, a handmaiden, and then Meeks Crowley.

Godwin released the creature and jerked away in terror, not understanding what he had done. Anson helped pull Godwin from its chest while Montgomery looked into its eyes. The cryptid's head wobbled back and forth as the king stood, but it did not respond.

"To the dungeons with it," Monty said to Anson. "It still lives and may be able to change again. I don't think shackles will work. Keep it in a room with no windows or bars. It needs to be locked away until we can revive it long enough for questioning."

Anson nodded in agreement.

Monty looked up to see his father weeping and his new family, the family of Atorm Stormmoeller, looking impassively at him. Cecily Maeglen gave in to her emotions. She lunged at Monty, embracing him, and began to cry. Monty allowed her a moment, looking over her shoulder.

His eyes met Freya's, who stood at her father's arm. His body turned numb, and he wanted to cry, but instead he stood soberly above the body of his mother's assassin, emotionless. Freya watched his eyes, and he knew she saw the emptiness.

Einar bent next to the fallen thrall and whispered in Wartooth. Monty didn't understand the language but knew by its tone and cadence that it was a prayer. The runecaster dipped his crooked finger into the pool of Ulf's blood and drew on his face. The runes were mere designs to Montgomery, but when Einar had finished, he looked to Atorm.

"Ulf Skuli has been granted entrance to the Hall of the Ancients," he declared. "He is redeemed, and his honor restored. He will be welcomed there. We must share a horn of Heifenmager in his honor when the moon rises next."

Monty released his aunt and pushed by the fallen hero to kneel by his father, who shook in tears and anger. He wrapped his arms around his shoulders and tried to calm the man who was king. But Godwin crumpled, broken. A man bereft of purpose. And worse yet, composure. They were to leave today to fight a war. But now, they had a queen to bury.

FOR THE SAKE OF his father and to ignore the ever-growing thrum of numbness in him, Monty gathered up the torturer and his father as quickly as he could. The cryptid had been taken below the dungeons to a room where it could not see so much as a pinprick of light. Monty didn't speak as he led his father to the waiting man and the heavy door that led below. He yanked it open with a loud scraping that echoed down to the stone garrison.

They descended to find the creature lying crookedly on a slab of darkened, decades-old wood, stained with the blood of previous prisoners. Its flat nose twitched as it smelled their approach.

"Blood and bile," its weak voice hummed. "And fear. Fear has its own smell when it seeps from humans, like the rancid stench of aged milk."

Monty glared at the thing through the narrow bars.

"It comes from the king," It tried to smile but couldn't quite muster the strength.

"What are you?" Godwin snarled, as he looked into its eyes. Monty let him speak, as he didn't move to try to leap through the bars.

The skin-stealer raised its shaking hand and traced a line from under its eye to the tip of its chin and cackled through the blood in its lungs. Monty realized it mocked the tear tracks on Godwin's face and the pain in his quivering voice.

"Answer him!" Monty barked.

"I am Anthrobaxicari." It spit loose teeth to the floor as it answered.

"Why have you done this?" Godwin continued. "Why have you taken my love from me?"

"Father, please stop," Monty asked, keeping his tone steady and authoritative.

"I must know," Godwin demanded of his son. "Tell me."

"She tasted delicious," the cold reply came.

The king struggled to get at the skin-stealer, but the prince and torturer held him at bay. When the men stopped wrestling, the prince pushed his father to the rear of the chamber, out of sight of the mocking monster.

"I never understood why the truth hurt humans as much as it did," the thing mused. "You eat animals, oftentimes wasting much. I consume *all* of my food—their memories, their habits, and worst of all, their diseases. Healthy food tastes better, and Amice was very healthy."

Monty's gut twisted and bile rose in his throat. He locked every feeling behind a mask of stone. "Who sent you?" he asked. "Tell us, and this will end quickly for you."

The cryptid did its best to laugh but ended up choking on its own blood. "No matter what tortures come to me, I won't last long."

"When did Von Lormarck send you?" Monty asked, getting desperate. "How long have you been Meeks Crowley?"

With what little time it had left, the skin-stealer decided to play along.

"What harm does it matter now?" the monster asked, sinking lower onto the rank slab. "Months. Long enough to start a war."

"What does Von Lormarck know?" the prince demanded.

"Of Thronehelm?" it asked. "Much. Of what is to come? Little."

"I don't understand," the prince said. "What is to come?"

"Look to Ravenwood," it replied. "And the Forge. Not to

his army. Your true threat comes from within."

"Are there others like you in our midst?" the prince pressed.

"No, Prince," the skin-stealer said. "You are quite safe from my kind for a time."

"What do you mean?"

"I have spawned," the creature half-laughed and coughed. "The Moor Bog have traded that sacrament for my service to them."

"The damned Moor Bog have returned?" Godwin's temper flared.

"You shall soon meet them, King, I assure you. They will sic their honored beasts on your kingdom soon. And return their queen to her rightful throne."

"Who else have you been?"

"I am a prince of many faces," it replied. "Would you like to see another?"

Monty winced at the thought, but the skin-stealer interpreted his response as a "yes." It concentrated on its powers, limited as they were, and its face bubbled and changed. The primordial goo that was its countenance churned, forming at first Amice, then again Meeks Crowley, but before the charade ended, one last face appeared. The visage of a man Monty didn't recognize. The old face of a twerg appeared and faded into the blank face of the cryptid.

Then the pangs of death overtook the creature. It had expended the last of its energy and its eyes began to fade. Monty watched in a mix of confusion and morbid relief as the blank face of the cryptid returned, and its body stilled.

Memories of his mother flooded into his eyes, and doubts to the meaning of the final, taunting clue the beast left for him.

CHAPTER TWENTY-THREE

"I do enjoy a duel in the midst of a battle."
—Lord Admiral Valerick Labrecque

NIGHT DESCENDED ON THE shore of the Gossamer River as Incanus waited for his prey. He'd ordered Skullam to the lower deck of the now much smaller *Ashen Dragon* while the Bone elf remained ashore. He stood next to the lifeboat, his hood masking his appearance. What warmth he'd captured in his cloak was soon dispelled by the winds of the Dragon's Breaths. He'd almost forgotten how cold it truly was near his ancestral home during the Season of the Long Nights.

In the distance he saw a lone figure approaching, and his eyes scanned to see if others followed. He wished that Skullam was nearby to spy for him, but he couldn't risk his appearance, concealed by the dark trace or otherwise. As the figure drew nearer, he was satisfied they were alone.

"Excuse me?" a woman's voice whispered from the shadows of the docks.

Incanus turned to her but couldn't make out her face from under her hood. Her cloak bore the Vermilion crest and the colors of her people. He smiled.

"I'm looking for friends of mine, Arjun and Anoki," she said. "I was told they would be here."

"Yes." Incanus beckoned to her, struggling to contain his excitement. Addilyn was here with no protection. No champion. No Silencer. His journey of revenge could come to an end, and he could rest. "Come—" he motioned—"and I will take you to them."

They boarded the lifeboat, and Incanus ordered the *Ashen Dragon* to reel them away from shore, far enough that there would be no calls for help and no ears to hear her last screams.

After a time, Incanus commanded it to cease, leaving the small boat floating adrift in the Gossamer River.

Out on the river and away from any light but the moon, Incanus stood and turned to the crouching figure, her curious head turning under the cowl of her cloak. He removed his hood as he turned to face the Vermilion princess. "Addilyn, I've waited too long for this opportunity. It is time for my tale of vengeance to end."

To his surprise, the Vermilion stood and removed her hood as well. Incanus's smile fell at the sight—the sight of Addilyn's Raven elf companion, Jessamy.

"Expecting someone else?" she asked with a smug grin. "At last, we shall see who's better."

Incanus's anger rose inside of him, and his hands shook in fury. He snarled at the imposter, his eyes flaring at the deceit.

Jessamy cast her cloak into the Gossamer and drew her sword. "Come now, my steel awaits."

Incanus fought to put all speculation of this betrayal aside. He'd faced Jessamy in battle twice and stalemated both times, leaving him to flee with injuries. She was a master swordswoman, and the rocking of the ship would make his task even harder. He channeled his rage into focus.

"So, you've come to die for her?"

"I've come to end this. And to end you." The Raven elf balanced herself against the gentle swells underneath them and beckoned him on with her sword.

With a flick of his wrist, Incanus unsheathed his sword and leapt into the air, startling his opponent. He landed inches from her, his move forcing her into high guard, their swords meeting with a resounding *ping*.

The champion grunted and nearly slipped, bracing her rear

calf against a wooden seat and she pushed off, sending Incanus backward. He spun and swung, a surprise slash he expected to hit home, but instead his sword met with a second block and quick parry from his enemy.

"You are fast," he remarked as he turned sideways, limiting the swordswoman's targets. "But not fast enough."

She half-smiled at the insult and thrust her blade forward.

He returned the block and parry.

The two stepped back to riposte, the ship slipping side to side underneath them. Silence fell around them, save for the lapping of the water against the boards of the boat.

With a furious whirl, they engaged again, this time turning into one another, steel flashing and clanging several times before the action broke again. As they parted, the elf ducked beneath his guard and sliced through his cloak in a near miss.

"Almost," the woman taunted.

Incanus spat and sneered before engaging, this time feigning left and instead spinning right while jumping atop a seat for leverage. He attacked with renewed energy, but the smaller Raven elf managed to slip by him with a block, the two switching positions on the lifeboat. He turned, their eyes meeting.

"Enough dancing," he grumbled.

She didn't reply, but her countenance changed, and Incanus knew the real melee was about to begin.

The two met in the center of the lifeboat, swords dancing and clanging in near harmony, their blades rotating so quickly the clangs of their swords grew faster and faster until they became a single tone—one prolonged ring.

Incanus's blade swiped back and forth, up and down, each offensive tactic his practiced hands knew turned back at him with the perfect counter, over and over again.

Jessamy was impossibly quick. Her moves were smooth and effortless, and her eyes stayed on his, not falling aside to give him any advantage. She knew her blade better than any he'd faced, leaving him little time to calculate between maneuvers, and it was all he could do to react to her counterattacks. His aggressive moves soon met equally defined defenses.

He was losing.

Desperate to gain any advantage, he ducked low, raising his sword up behind her blade and aiming for her hands, hoping to cut off fingers in the effort. It was a trick a duelist would use against an overexuberant opponent, disarming their prey and finishing them at their leisure. He'd done so many times before, sometimes for show, other times to torture.

But Jessamy foiled the move by dropping a hand from her pommel and bending back out of the way, leaving herself parallel to the ground. Before he could lunge and impale her, her left foot rose, kicking his sword aside and sending him spinning, narrowly tumbling overboard.

He grabbed the rail of the boat with one hand and blindly swung behind him, expecting her blade to dive at his exposed flank. His sword met hers, this time with a squeal from the swordswoman.

"Predictable," he offered, recovering and moving to a second standstill in the center of the lifeboat.

The two stared at one another, seeking the slightest advantage when the Raven elf growled and lunged under his defenses. He dropped his sword to his left, catching her blade at the last second and sending it aside. Seeing the opportunity, he darted in, bringing his blade back up and nicking the swordswoman on the forearm.

Her breath hastened and she ducked under the blade, turning away at the last moment, avoiding his death stroke that swung by with a swoosh of air.

Incanus gritted his teeth and tried to counter, but the vessel rocked with the violent maneuver and he fought to maintain his balance, losing the initiative.

The Raven elf did the same, her feet more stable now, but the blood from her forearm suggested he'd gained an advantage. She still gripped her longsword with both hands, but his blade was sharp.

Her eyes rose again to meet his and the two engaged in another volley of steel on steel, blades flashing ever quicker. The two were so close, Incanus swore they shared the same air.

Block after block, parry after parry, the two parted, neither worse for wear.

The Bone elf's breathing was measured. He wasn't used to long duels, but his body was conditioned like a fine instrument. Still, he wondered if even he could outlast his opponent.

She seemed unfazed by the exertion. Her arm bled, but her movements and maneuvers appeared unaffected by it.

He had to find a weakness, an advantage.

Before he could react, the Raven elf charged one more time and it was all he could do to get his blade in front of hers. They fought inches from each other, the din of their blades deafening to his ears, and he could feel the heat of her breath on his face. He leaned in, their blades sliding to each other's pommels, and he pushed off, hoping his strength would catch her off guard.

The Raven elf staggered back but as they parted, she rammed the hilt of her sword into his nose, blinding him with the punch.

Before he could react, she swept his leg with her sword, knocking him to his knees and plunged her blade into his shoulder. Incanus felt the sting of the steel and brought his sword up with one hand, but she knocked it from his grasp.

The Raven elf scoffed at the desperate, almost instinctive parry, her blade now at Incanus's throat. "That's it?"

From his knees, Jessamy's sword hovered over him. His mind raced. How could he have lost to her?

Yet he would not be bested tonight.

Her eyes flickered, awaiting victory, and her briefest hesitation in delivering the final blow bought Incanus time to use his last advantage. Incanus reached out to the *Ashen Dragon*.

Now, he thought.

The *Dragon* hummed in obeisance at the same moment it made its move.

The lifeboat rocked hard to starboard and swung, knocking Jessamy off-balance until she fell against the side of the vessel. Incanus flashed forward and brought his booted foot down on Jessamy's wrist, applying as much pressure as possible.

His opponent cried out in pain and dropped her weapon. In one swift movement, Incanus snatched it from the floor of the boat and ran it through her chest.

The Raven elf's eyes bulged. Blood spurted from her lips like a warm sea spray onto his face. She choked and gargled, going limp on the deck.

Incanus leaned in, causing her to buckle and twitch in pain.

He smiled. "How does it feel to know your princess will soon die, and there is nothing you can do to stop it? You have failed, elf."

Most of Incanus's words fell on deaf ears, for the light had already left his opponent's eyes. Her body sagged against the side of the lifeboat, held up only by her own sword, impaling her to the deck.

When he removed it, she dropped to the floor of the boat.

Incanus smirked. Though he'd won, he wasn't satisfied, and wouldn't be until Addilyn's body lay before him. How many times could she escape his sword?

Carefully, almost artistic in his calculations, Incanus posed the Raven elf's lifeless body. He folded her arms on her chest and slipped a black rose between her clasped fingers. Jessamy's dark hair splayed out in waves on the boat's floor.

CHAPTER TWENTY-FOUR

"A traveler is happiest, be they beggar or prince, that comes home."
—Nothos, the Ancient of Good Fortune

FROM CLAN SWIFTHAMMER AND Clan Battleforge!" the twergish herald exclaimed.

He stood nearly twenty feet above the crowded cavern on a graven balcony, hewn in the craftsmanship only known to twergish masons. Below him, a throng of hundreds of twergs from both clans intermingled, a throaty susurrus rising and echoing throughout the chamber.

Tancred had promised to make the introduction that very morning, and the old coin-counter made true on his promise. Jins and Makai stood at the front of the throng, just under the balcony upon two small, octagonal rostrums that lifted them from the crowd. In front of them, the empty throne of Yrsa Dagny, the *krol* of the clans, rested atop a third rostrum.

Jins turned around, her nerves jumbled, not used to being the center of such attention. She'd hoped for a more private audience with the *krol,* but it appeared that the entirety of the subterrane was interested in rumors of a brewing surface war and to get a glimpse of First Keeper Aliferis Makai, returned home.

Then a deep groan belched its way into the hall, resonating off the cavern walls. The royal cornet, fashioned from a hollowed horn of an ancient underground beast slain long ago, hung just above the throne. When it was sounded, it summoned the inhabitants of the Forge to the throne room.

"*Krol*... Yrsa... Dagny!" the herald cried from his perch.

The room dropped to one knee and bowed their heads in

silence. Jins looked to Makai to see him do the same, so she followed suit. It was her first time in the throne room, and she was unaccustomed to its protocols and practices.

Her eyes drifted up from her bow when she heard metal footfalls entering the hall. From behind the throne walked a twergish woman of considerable size. Jins thought perhaps she was half-twergish herself, as the woman nearly matched her height.

The *krol* was young for such a position, but unlike surface dwellers, the role of the *krol* was earned by deed, not inheritance or birthright. She had replaced the previous *krol*, Messineus Tigano, who had fallen in battle a year past in their war against the Jackals. She wore the crown by achievement, and it was said she had never lost a battle, either in single combat or as an officer of Clan Swifthammer's army.

Dagny intimidated Jins. Perhaps it was the spectacle being made of her, or the *krol*, but the situation felt too big for a lowly trollborn merchant, raised high in a crowd of her peers. As Dagny sat upon the throne, Jins noticed her youthful eyes, unmarked by age and perfectly braided red hair and wispy beard, common in twergish women. Her shape was of a warrior, not a maid, and she wore a finely crafted breastplate, with the coat of arms of Clan Swifthammer emblazoned on the front. On her head rested a simple circlet of platinum, signifying her position.

The resounding noise of the twergish community rising as one signaled that their audience with the *krol* was about to begin.

"First Keeper Aliferis Makai," the *krol* said in a voice made of gravel, "allow me to welcome you home. It must be a century since you last entered the Forge."

"Perhaps more," Makai answered. "It is a pleasure to smell

the forges of the subterrane again. My childhood here brings back memories of Rawcliffe himself."

"What events bring us the honor of the First Keeper of Castleshire?" she asked.

"My associate, Solveig Jins, has been given a message from the king and queen of Thronehelm for you," Makai replied. He turned to Jins, who presented the scrolls to an attendant that then presented them to the *krol*.

"The emissary from Thronehelm is a half-twerg?" Dagny questioned, her brow knitting.

"Two emissaries, My Krol," Makai corrected her, his tone polite. "I now am the First Keeper of Thronehelm."

"Hmm, is that so?" Dagny's face turned down with the news, and she spent a moment reading the scrolls. "I see our human friends have written these in twergish for us. Your touch I assume, First Keeper?"

"Nay," he replied. "Their scribe known as Forwin. He speaks several dialects of twergish and is a learned scholar of our people."

Dagny finished reading, handed them back to her attendant, and stood before addressing the hall.

"Twergs of Clan Swifthammer and Clan Battleforge," she intoned so all could hear, "it brings me great pleasure to announce we have new allies in our war against the Jackals. It appears as if the Kingdom of Warminster has split, and five baronies now fight against two. It is Thronehelm against Foghaven Vale. The King and Queen Thorhauer seek an alliance with our clans."

The crowd cheered at the announcement, exchanging celebratory hugs.

"And we have other news," Makai added, his voice raising to meet the *krol*'s. "With the assistance of the Valkeneers of the

Bridge and the elves of Ravenwood, Thronehelm has captured our great nemesis, the general of the forces against us, Aarav Fleury, bastard son to Dragich Von Lormarck."

Again, the chamber erupted in cheers and calls for victory.

The *krol* raised her hand, and within seconds the disciplined crowd dropped from a boil to a simmer.

"I have waited several years to hear the word 'alliance,' " Dagny admitted, "but what can we expect from our new friends?"

"They are gathering their forces now and march to meet the Jackals in the field," Makai responded.

"Tell them, First Keeper," Dagny said, "that the twergs of the Forge will fight with them, but before I accept their gracious offer of alliance, I only ask for one thing."

"What is that, My Krol?" Makai asked.

"I want the prisoner, Aarav Fleury, delivered to me," she said with a snarl, "brought to his knees in chains and shame to sit before our great hall for his crimes in this unjust war of greed."

"My Krol," Makai replied, "I am not certain the king and queen would agree to such terms. Their youngest son was just slain by the Jackal's plot, and they too have rights for revenge. An eye for an eye."

"Then we have no alliance," Dagny said. "Return my answer to Thronehelm. I will await their response before committing our forces elsewhere."

"But my liege—"

"Respectfully, First Keeper," the *krol* said, "I am not your liege, nor your *krol*. You belong to the cathedral first, do you not? Thronehelm second, and then perhaps Castleshire? Where does the Forge fit in your hierarchy of loyalty?"

"That is unfair," Makai protested. "As a First Keeper, I belong to the whole of Warminster and sit above and outside of invisible lines drawn on a cartographer's map."

"Unfair, perhaps. But nonetheless true. Do you agree to carry my message back to them? I want the son of the Jackal placed before me."

Makai looked to Jins, and she bit her bottom lip.

"My Krol." Jins stepped to the fore. "I will take your message back to Thronehelm. But I, too, want something in return."

"Who is this that speaks to me?" the *krol* asked.

"I… I am Solveig Jins. Of Clan Swifthammer."

"You look like a human to me," the *krol* answered, and the crowd began buzzing with giggles and finger-pointing.

"I am trollborn to be sure," Jins said, struggling to keep a respectful tone, "but as much a twerg of the Forge as any in this room."

"And how can I trust your human half?" Dagny replied, unconvinced.

"I am not half-twerg, nor am I half human," Jins said, with a tinge of insult in her voice. "I am fully Solveig Jins. And anyone in this room that knows me can speak to my character."

A hush embraced the room as Jins realized she may have spoken too harshly to the *krol*. Yrsa Dagny glowered at her but didn't address the breach of protocol.

"Ah, some fire in the belly from my guest," Dagny said. "Is it that same fire that brought you here in front of me in the first place?"

"Unfortunately, it is," Jins admitted under her breath.

"Unfortunately?" the *krol* replied, surprised by Jins's response.

"Yes, My Krol," Jins called out loud this time. "I am not one for politics, but I do seem to find my way into extraordinary situations from time to time. A month ago, I was in Saracen, trading jewelry for coin. In the last fortnight, I was a guest in the Thronehelm court, I befriended a First Keeper of the Cathedral of the Watchful Eye, I am veteran of a battle between Longmarchers, Black Cuffs, and Jackals that led to the surrender of Aarav Fleury. And now I stand before you, great Krol. So, as you can see, I would much prefer my life of trading gems than messages. But I cannot. You need me to return to Thronehelm, for the sake of the Forge."

The *krol*, and the room, fell silent. Jins looked to Makai, but he only contorted his face and could offer no help. Then Yrsa Dagny laughed, removing the tension in the hall.

Jins sighed in relief.

"It does appear you are touched by the Ancients themselves, Jins," Dagny chuckled. "But I do respect your vim. What is it that you ask of me in return for this service?"

"Before I left for Thronehelm, Gurglestock's miners found a pocket cave that contained magical writings on the wall."

"Yes," the *krol* replied. "And yesterday, we lost three miners to a trap set for those trying to uncover the cave. I have a mind to collapse it shut so that no others are hurt."

"First Keeper Makai believes he can interpret the runes on the wall," Jins pressed. "I showed him the inscriptions. He thinks it to be an old language, perhaps of magic, and of the Ancients."

"It is too dangerous," Dagny said.

"But what wonders may await us behind the runes?" Jins said, a hopeful air to her voice.

"Your human curiosity blinds you," Dagny replied.

"But he needs the wisdom of an old friend," Jins continued, ignoring the *krol*'s warning. "A twerg Magus named Yenroar Silentall. He feels he can help with the interpretation."

"The Magus does not want to be disturbed," the *krol* said. "He has left the clan, seeking the solitude of the mountains and wishes to fade from this world there, alone. For all we know, he may already be in the Hall of the Ancients."

"The Sight of Erud has failed the Keepers," Makai interjected. "Unless he has gone to the Hall of the Ancients in the last month, I would have known."

"Please," Jins tried, "I only ask that they speak. If the runes are tidings of ill omen, then close it. But if it is something more, the First Keeper and Yen will discern it. And you will be the *krol* that legends will speak of when it is unearthed."

Dagny sat back in her throne and pondered the offer.

"Very well, I accept your offer, Jins. Return to Thronehelm with our request and this shield that will symbolize our alliance. If they accept, return with their shield, and with Aarav Fleury. But before you depart, you may leave to find Yenroar Silentall. There's an old goat path that leads up the mountain. If you seek him, and he wants to be found, you'll need to start there. I will have my geographer provide you a map. From there, you will need to find him yourselves."

LATER THAT MORNING, JINS and Makai departed the Forge and exited the subterrane, heading along the lines of the map given to them by the *krol*. The map was new but vague and pointed them in a northerly direction with few discernable landmarks. The geographer was gracious enough to explain that the Magus didn't want to be found but left hints in the event the Forge ever needed him.

This was one of those times.

The first day's journey was arduous and slowed by Makai's age, but Jins kept him safe, choosing to take switchback trails for an easier climb. This slowed their progression, but after several days of searching, the First Keeper detected the faintest hale of magic, and knew they were on Yen's trail. If the Magus used magic to hide himself, it would also be revealed to Makai in a similar manner.

They followed the map to a dead end. The goat path had become impassable with time, and even Phanna refused to traverse the dangerous crags. They found themselves on a cliff that jutted from the Dragon's Breath Mountains, overlooking Ravenwood and far in the distance, the Bridge below. It was a crow's flight from here, but by foot, it was days, if not weeks.

"I need to rest." Makai unsaddled himself and flopped his old bones down on a flat rock that overlooked the forest in the distance. "So peaceful from up here. It's a wonder that a war rages below our view, and we are blind to it from atop the mountain."

"Have faith." Jins put her hand on the twerg's shoulder. She noticed the blood stain on his white robe had faded, but the Keeper still flinched at her slightest touch.

"We have come to the end," Jins said. "What are we do to?"

"There is little we can," the Keeper replied. "If a man of his power doesn't want to be found, he won't be."

"Let me push on a little farther on foot," she said. "You rest here."

Makai only nodded in agreement, apparently happy with the respite.

Jins grabbed a waterskin from Phanna's saddlebag and took the scattered trail, slipping on occasion on the broken ground. But she was a twerg of the Forge, used to climbing treacherous terrain on the surface and under it.

She rounded a bend and found a small cave. From the edge, she could look down the side of the mountain and could even see Makai in the distance. It was a perfect vantage point to look over the valley, but also a potential home for trollborn creatures, or worse.

She decided to explore the mouth of the cave, just to get some orientation. Nearing the entrance, she could see the cave opened and shut quickly, only going yards deep. It appeared to lack any nesting or droppings, so she relaxed a bit and stepped through the mouth.

A sudden flash of light exploded in her face, and her feet left the ground as she landed on the flat of her back, inches from the cliff face. Her breath escaped her, and her eyes were dazed from the brilliance of the flash.

"Jins!" she heard Makai cry from below. "Are you all right?"

She hadn't the breath to answer and rolled over on her knees to find some air. Her lungs burned, and she fought to inhale. She could hear Makai running as best he could up the cliff side, and she raised her hands to slow him.

"Careful," she managed in a strained voice.

The Keeper wrestled with the loose stones but finally made it to her. He lifted her back to her feet where she bent over, resting her arms on her knees.

"What happened?" he asked. "Did you fall?"

She only pointed to the cave opening and shook her head, begging him not to enter.

"I sense the hale," Makai said, as his nerves calmed. "Was it magic?"

Jins nodded, coughed, then managed to stand straight again. "Don't enter as I did. It nearly knocked me off the side of the mountain."

They both looked over the cliff and shared an anxious laugh. Some cinder stained her face and smoke still rose from her hides, but for all the show, she was not harmed.

Then they both heard the scraping of booted footfalls inside the cave where no one was, until in front of them, somehow, appeared a twerg. It was as if he'd walked straight through the walls of the mountain.

Jins backed herself as close to the edge as she could and

reached for her pickaxe.

"You look the same, old friend." Makai stepped toward the stranger, as she stared at the oldest twerg she had ever seen.

"You, however, do not," the old twerg retorted.

The two shared a hearty laugh and hugged.

"You must be Yenroar Silentall," Jins said, batting the soot from the cave from her stained hides.

"Allow me to apologize for my magical wards." The Magus pointed to the cave's entrance. "I have many who try to pass inside my cave. These hills are filled with wicked creatures, and an old twerg like me requires the protection of my spells to survive."

Despite his age, Yen acted like a twerg of half the number. He stood a foot shorter than Jins, at least, and was as bald as a newborn human. The wrinkles about his face flopped lazily on top of one another, marking his countenance like the rings of a tree. His eyes were deep set beneath a sagging brow, hidden among a forest of eyebrows that hadn't been trimmed in Jins's lifetime. He wore only the slightest of garments, looking more of a townie that someone living on the face of a mountain, ready for winter's breath.

"Why have the Fates seen it proper to bring us back together, Aliferis?" Yen asked. He reached into the pocket of his waistcoat and produced a flask, one that would have never fit in the pocket from which it came. He uncorked it and took a sip, handing it to Makai for his turn.

Makai took a swig and winced, handing it to Jins next.

"What is that?" Makai asked. "A cider? A mead? I couldn't make a proper taste through the burn."

"It's a sacred liquid. It's what keeps me so young and virile," the Magus joked. "Have a try," he said to Jins.

Jins sniffed the flask and smelled honey and mixed fruits.

She took a tentative sip and felt the same sting in her mouth as Makai. She nearly gagged and handed it back to Yen.

"Don't worry," Yen said, "the potency only lasts a few hours. It will fade."

As she recovered from its effects, Makai handed Yen the charcoal tracings of the runes that Jins had made in her ledger. "This is why we seek your counsel. We cannot decipher it, even by magical means."

Yen studied the scribblings, and a concerned look appeared on his wrinkled face.

"I was hoping to die before anyone would ever ask me to translate such words again," he said.

Makai and Jins looked at each other, a nervous tension rising between them.

"Again?" Makai asked with an inquisitive tone, but Yen ignored the question.

"Where did you find these runes?" the Magus asked.

"The miners of the Forge stumbled on them as they were digging out a new vein," Jins replied.

"Please tell me they did not try to break in," Yen said.

"They did. There was a trap waiting for them that triggered a collapse. Three are missing, and the *krol* ordered the dig to stop."

Yen breathed a noticeable sigh of relief.

"So, they have dug to it, but not through it?" he asked.

"They excavated a chamber of sorts, which revealed it," Jins continued. "A pocket cave formed by unnatural means."

Yen's face turned to one of relief, but his shoulders slumped, and his head turned to the ground.

"Tell them they must seal it back up," Yen said, looking to Makai. "There is nothing behind these ruins that should be uncovered. The seal must remain unbroken."

"What do the words mean?" Jins asked, borrowing Yen's concerned face.

The ancient twerg lifted his face to meet hers.

"Nothing that should ever be read aloud," he replied.

CHAPTER TWENTY-FIVE

"Trees teach us patience, while the grass of the emerald dales teaches us persistence."
—Lachlan Barrett, Druid of the Emerald Shield

DAEMUS LED THE WAY as the group descended the vast staircase, his footing seeming a little surer. Daemus, following him, felt the opposite. Like Wilkes, he wasn't sure if he wanted to move farther in, and his body seemed almost to be moving on its own. It was hard to be certain how long they had really been in the labyrinth, but their progress had felt quick, and that sense he had been holding onto of living within a bubble of safety and indefinite postponement of his future was starting to slip through his fingers.

"Wonder how far down it goes," Katja mused, staring into the black abyss as she followed behind Daemus.

"Drop something down it and we'll see," suggested Faux, a grin obvious in her voice.

"And tip off any cryptids that we're coming?" Wilkes's mood did not appear to have improved.

Silence fell as they descended. With every step, the cavernous hole grew darker, the light from above failing to illuminate its depths. At last, in the pitch dark, Arjun made a quiet grunt and stumbled a little. "That's it. We're at the bottom."

Daemus paused. As soon as Arjun spoke, a wavering were-light rose out of the floor, revealing the circular bottom of the well and a massive archway. A single stone door covered half of it, the other vanished or destroyed, or perhaps crushed into the dust that covered the floor.

On the remaining door, Daemus could see what looked like some sort of story depicted through figures in relief, but damage or age made them hard to discern, let alone interpret.

"What could have carved this all the way down here?" Faux asked, muffled voice held a tinge of fear.

"No idea." Arjun shook his head.

"Cryptids o' some kind?" Blue Conney offered.

"There's no weather, no rain or wind or anything." Faux shook her head. "And I can't think cryptids would be able to get into the well, let alone discover it."

"I don't recognize this style of imagery," Tuttle commented, to a skeptical glance from Caspar.

"I don't recognize it either." Anoki's eyes were on a relief of a figure next to a tree, its head and torso gone. "That could be Laurent, though—Laurentia. From the poem. Don't you think?"

"Do you know where we are, Wilkes?" Daemus turned to the man, who looked almost to be hiding behind his shaggy beard and long hair.

With a brief glance, Wilkes met his white eyes. "I… I believe I do. I'd heard tales of it, but never seen."

Everyone waited with an air of expectancy.

Wilkes hesitated, then continued, "If this is what I believe it to be, we've reached the Tomb Intricata."

"A tomb?" Marquiss turned to Wilkes "In here?"

"Aye." Wilkes's dour face told the story. "It's the final resting place of many lost souls that have made it this far. Said to be the most difficult part of the journey. Wasn't sure it was real, much less that Willow's Weep led straight to it. I might have—" He cut himself off. "The only way to the heart, but once one enters, there's no way back."

"So that's why it's called a tomb?" a somber Katja inquired, looking with soft eyes at the door. "Are there people buried down here?"

Wilkes tilted his head with an air of ambivalence. "Buried may be the wrong word. None, to my knowledge, have ever made it out." In haste, he amended his statement at the looks of alarm that were forming in response. "Or so it is said."

"No sweet lies for us now." Arjun's eyes narrowed, his tone impatient.

Wilkes drooped a little more. "Once we pass this threshold, there will be no retreat. No return to safe environs to rest or heal. The labyrinth continues underground, and I've read it surfaces at points, but Trillias created this final test for the worthiest, and perhaps the foolhardiest. And the cryptids are… worse."

That single word was enough to send chills rippling down Daemus's spine.

"Worse?" He thought of the Antlered Man, conjuring memories of fear and death.

"I don't know, for certain," Wilkes retorted. "Don't know anything for certain. All just hearsay."

"Just tell us, so we've got something to go on." Tuttle's sturdy voice resonated with the group and Wilkes looked at the door again, then at the assembled party, then at the stone floor.

"Can see in the dark," he replied at last. "Stronger than the ones up above, by much. Razor pincers and claws for digging, acid breath, clever ears like bats."

"Vrykar?" Anoki interjected, and Wilkes turned his pallid eyes on her.

"You know?" Wilkes's voice was thick with worry.

"They're mentioned in the poem." Anoki nodded. "Conjured from Trillias's own nightmares, released with Laurent's tears when the well flooded. They spew acid breath. None of the other details made it in."

Faux rolled her eyes. "Poets, sources of the wisdom of the ages."

Daemus huffed and his gaze drifted to Katja, who stared back. "Acid breath?"

"It's art, not a travel manual." Anoki's delicate voice held a specter of doubt. "I am sure the poet thought the information would be preserved another way. And it was, as it turns out."

An uneasy silence fell again as they all looked to the door.

"Onward?" asked Caspar. No one responded, but with a slow turn, they all shuffled toward the empty half of the doorway. Anoki cast one last longing glance at the once-elaborately decorated door.

"Wish I could go home," whispered Wilkes, for Daemus's ears only, as he passed.

Daemus clasped his shoulder in consolation and silent agreement. There would be no way back, now, to that safe moment on the outcropping. No more scratches along the edge. No respite, no rest, no safety.

A thought occurred to him, one he hated: ...and there never had been.

Daemus rubbed the fatigue from his face. The stress and journey through the *Tomb Intricata* continued to drag on. Without Wilkes's knowledge of the above ground labyrinth to guide the way, they were forced to decide every turn by committee. And many turns led to dead ends.

The walls within reminded him of his dreams of Graytorris—and the feeling of dread that would always overcome him. Meandering through the banks of imaginary fog from his nightmares and the fear of not knowing what lay through the endless grey pricked again at his senses.

Somewhere, deep within, he felt a tinge of guilt. Guilt rising from a passing thought—or perhaps hope—that Erud may help him here. They only needed a hint of direction. Was that too much to ask of an Ancient that had tormented him since birth?

"I can't believe we're still discussing this," snapped Faux in a whisper around what seemed to be their fiftieth corner. "We need to choose a direction and just go. It's not as though we can get any more lost than we already are."

"You are being rash." Anoki's jaw tensed. "What we need is to think about where we're going so that we can remember which way we've gone. Choosing directions by the luck of Nothos isn't going to get us anywhere."

"I've always had his favor, good and bad," hissed Faux. "We've taken eight rights in a row, and I think we should take a left now."

"You're not hearing me, Faux."

"Keep it down," Caspar reminded them, glancing back down the passageway. Despite the chilly subterranean air, he was sweating, his skin clammy in the were-light. The young Keeper had tried to map their every step with a dwindling charcoal pencil and a few pages of vellum.

"Yes, please keep it down." Katja wasn't sweating, but to Daemus, she looked cold. For the first time, Daemus sensed an anxiety about her, a departure from her usual, almost divine poise. Her worried visage struck him, and a whirlpool of emotions began to swirl inside his mind. Had he sentenced his friends to a slow, tortuous death, lost in the *Tomb Intricata* with no hope to find the heart? All in the pursuit of his accursed Ancient's prized *Tome of Enlightenment?* In truth, his friends and Katja meant more.

"Daemus?" Katja's gentle touch shook him from his introspection. "Are you holding up?"

He hadn't noticed he'd stopped walking and was staring into her eyes. "I… I'm fine."

The smile returned to her face, even if it appeared a bit forced. For a moment, they shared a quiet thought.

Arjun returned from a short foray down the left path in front of them. He looked haggard but focused. "What's important is that we keep moving. The longer we stay in one place, the more likely it is that we'll be found by those creatures."

They had had a couple of close calls with the vrykar, hearing them scrabbling through the tunnels some unguessable distance away, and had only escaped notice by remaining very still. Wilkes wasn't sure they'd evaded them at all, but there was nothing for them to do but to keep going. Even if they'd questioned his warning that there would be no way out, the door into the tomb was far away enough now that turning back would be just as risky as continuing onward.

"If we keep moving without thinking, we are bound to stumble into one of their nests," Anoki insisted.

"We're going left," Daemus stated, his eyes still focused on Katja, and he began walking.

Anoki exhaled through her nose but did not argue, and everyone else followed. Daemus figured the group had assumed that his separation from Erud was not quite as definite as Trillias had said, but in truth he had picked the direction at random and hoped that they would go along. Deep inside, he knew he needed to stop their bickering, or else the infighting over their predicament may boil over. He knew in his heart they had to move.

He had to move. *He* had to lead.

He was the one that brought them all here, and for all that was good in him, he'd assure that they survived. That Katja survived. The strain in her face brought him only pain. Regardless of what happened to him, he'd give his dying breath to get her out of here.

The path turned left and turned again, straightening into a long corridor. The four directions of the compass had long been lost to them, and the corridor they chose funneled them into an octagonal chamber, each corner of the room providing another hallway to explore.

Quiet groans from those behind him spilled into the room.

"Mother of the Gods," Blue grumbled as he made his way in. "What's this? Eight hallways to be choosin' from?"

"This is good," Anoki explained, her voice hopeful. "This room can be useful as a landmark of sorts. Something we can use as a starting point on our map. Well done, Daemus."

Arjun patted the Keeper on the shoulder and Daemus glanced at Katja, who's blue eyes smiled back. He looked the hero but deep down, he knew he'd been lucky.

"Which way?" Marquiss's soft tone possessed the slightest touch of faith for the first time since they'd entered the maze. He dared to peer down the darkened paths of two corridors to the right.

"We should rest," Katja suggested when no one else in the party responded.

DAEMUS SAT STARING INTO the dark, a blank expression on his face as the were-light still hovered near Arjun like a duckling following its mother. Ancients forbid any of them should get lost; there was no other illumination to be found anywhere in this part of the tomb.

After an indeterminate length of time, someone whispered, "Did you hear that?"

Daemus tilted his head, straining his ears and closing his eyes, hoping it would help.

"Listen," snapped another whisper.

"It's coming from behind us." One of the whisperers revealed herself to be Faux. With a soft gesture, she pointed to a group of hallways to the left.

Blue drew his daggers and nodded in agreement.

"No, it's this way," Wilkes pointed, this time from the hallways across the room. He and Marquiss approached and drew their weapons, staring into the darkness.

Arjun tilted his head in the direction away from the sounds. "Let's move, but keep quiet."

The group filtered into one of the thin passageways, single file, with Arjun in the front and Faux bringing up the rear. The were-light around Arjun helped up front where Daemus walked, but when he turned, he could only see Katja and part of Tuttle before the illumination faded.

In the distance, something scratched against a wall, and the hairs on Daemus's nape stood on end. He motioned for Arjun to stop.

The scratching sounded again, louder this time, and the whole group fell silent.

Daemus's hand ran along the wall next to him, hoping to feel a vibration or any sense of the direction the noise was coming from. His finger crested over a little groove on its surface. When he felt along it, he realized it was a foot long, and right beside it was two more of the same.

Claw marks.

"Vrykar," someone whispered, as if giving voice to his thoughts.

Daemus felt his blood begin to surge and he struggled to steady his breathing. Some animalistic instinct told him this time they wouldn't escape. He looked to Katja, whose blue eyes stared back, wide as saucers. Anxiety and fear gripped at him, and with caution, he unbuckled his mace from his belt.

A hint of Faux's silhouette turned in the shadows, and she readied her bow. Arjun slid his sword from its scabbard and Anoki did the same. For a moment, no one blinked; no one moved.

Caspar raised his hand and pointed to the left. Wilkes tilted his head, looking down a hard-angled corridor to the right and motioned in the other direction. Neither opened their mouths.

"Which way?" Tuttle strained to keep his voice low, but Daemus sensed the fear in his whisper.

Arjun turned back with a grim expression and shrugged.

Panic surged through Daemus, shaking him to his core. "Where do we go?"

Arjun raised his blade. "Nowhere. They're already here."

From the darkness behind them rose a high-pitched keening, followed by a hurricane of scraping, as taloned claws cut against not-too-distant walls.

"Run!" Wilkes called. He pointed at the sharp bend nearest him and ducked alone into the darkness.

"Wait, don't—" was all Daemus could muster before he heard the *twang* of Faux's bow behind him, followed by the trailing, gurgling scream of her target.

A flash of Blue's daggers swooshed by him at hip-height, as the springheel pushed by and headed to the rear to help their companion. "I see ya, ya bastards," his rough voice announced his presence, no longer hiding in silence.

"Wilkes!" Tuttle scrambled to follow the man into the blackness, reaching for his alchemical pouch as he fled.

Before Daemus could follow, he heard Arjun grunt in front of him and the sound of his katana arcing through the air, followed by the dull thud of steel slapping into armored scales. His target, still hidden in shadow, flailed at the captain with two hooked arms, but Arjun's defenses deflected the attacks aside.

"Over here!" Caspar cried. He backed up from the turn nearest him.

Anoki stepped in his direction, only to stop inches from the sharp taloned attack of a vrykar emerging from the portal.

The cryptid's exoskeleton was almost colorless, and unlike its terrestrial brethren, it had no wings. Instead, it stalked on all fours, clinging sideways somehow on the labyrinth's walls. Its antlike head lunged in Anoki's direction, its two foot long pincers snapping open and shut, missing the Athabasica by inches.

Katja ran after Wilkes, grabbing Caspar's arm as she went, and casting a desperate glance back at Daemus. "We can't let him get lost," she cried, and Daemus turned to follow.

The distant cry of Wilkes's name echoed over the din of the battle from ahead in the darkness, Tuttle's voice many yards ahead. Daemus ran hard into the turn, hoping to find their companion. He heard a thud not far in front, and then ran up the back of Caspar, the group tripping over the fallen Tuttle, who'd slammed himself into a wall in the darkness.

"Get up!" Katja scrambled to pull the alchemist from the floor.

Caspar fought to regain his feet, pushing off the floor, but in the collision had lost his maps, slipping away in the dark recesses with the fall. Then a cry from behind them rose, a male voice, echoing down the corridor.

"Kill it!" Faux's voice followed, the *twang* of her bow not far behind.

A garbled war cry from Blue sounded off, and then more keening from the vrykar drowned out the voices of the party.

"There's one behind you!" called Anoki's voice.

More screams from his friends rose, but Daemus didn't wait this time. "We have to go back," he urged, turning to Katja. "They need us."

The healer stiffened but nodded, turning back the way they came.

Daemus ran, following the were-light from Arjun ahead. They were perhaps only a turn or two away. His hands shook in adrenaline but he readied his mace as he sprinted.

The familiar sound of Faux's bowstring plucked over and over, each time alighting a new round of screams from the encroaching nest of vrykar.

"Where's Marquiss!" he heard Blue growl as he turned the last bend.

In front of him, Arjun stood in melee with Anoki guarding his back, the two smashed between the encroaching cryptids. Before he knew what he was doing, he swung his mace at the back of the creature fighting Anoki, the iron head of his weapon cracking against the shell of the cryptid's natural armor.

Katja screamed as she emerged in the hall behind him, seeing the vrykar only a few paces away. The creature turned from Anoki and lunged at the healer, its pincers snapping as is scuttled toward her.

Daemus's eyes lit with fury, and he jumped between Katja and the beast, pounding away with his mace and hitting home more than once. With each strike Daemus heard the beast wail, and finally slip to the floor in front of him, writhing in pain.

He gritted his teeth and swore as he swung, the cracking of the vrykar's armored skull breaking away as he did. The beast twitched for a few seconds more and then stopped moving, a brackish blood oozing from the breaks in its natural hide.

"Arjun, look out!" Anoki squeezed by Daemus to engage another vrykar who'd crawled upon the ceiling and dropped down behind the captain like a spider. Her sword glinted in the were-light enough that Daemus saw it sneak between the beast's hide armor, sending it into convulsions.

Squeals of pain echoed through the corridor from the fallen monster, and Arjun stumbled back, trying to put the carcasses of two beasts between him and the gaggle of cryptids filling the hall in front of him.

"There's too many!" Faux dropped her bow, her quiver emptied of arrows, and drew her sword.

"This way!" Marquiss appeared from a darkened hallway, one that Anoki had nearly been killed in earlier. "Retreat!"

Daemus and Katja ran for Marquiss, only to see the Dale elf dart into the shadows of the hallway in front of him.

Arjun and Faux held off the beasts behind them as best they could, waxen-faced and wide-eyed, looking more panicked than Daemus had ever seen either one of them.

Tuttle, abandoning his search for Wilkes, emerged from the shadows fumbling with his alchemical kit and producing a little device that shone in his hand.

Feeling like his limbs had turned to water, Daemus ran behind Katja, hoping they'd keep pace with Marquiss.

He kept running, listening to his feet slap against the stone and keeping his fingers brushing the wall, passing several gaps in the stone where the others could have turned but hardly able to think about where he was going.

In the distance, the scraping and wailing of the cryptids filled the halls and he felt he'd go mad if it lasted much longer.

At the fifth turn something reached out and yanked on his arm, making him stumble and yelp.

Katja's voice hissed out, "Daemus!"

He gasped and ducked into a gap in the wall next to her.

The small group were all sitting on the floor just inside the gap, and slowly Daemus sank to the floor with them. The labyrinth was too dark to see anyone, but he could hear sniffling. After another moment, a loud bang sounded, followed by screeching. The faint, bobbing were-light in the distance drew closer, and Daemus exhaled in relief when he was able to make out Arjun, Faux, and Tuttle. As the dim light filtered into the small room, Daemus took account of the party.

"Where's Wilkes?" he asked in a whisper as they shuffled into the alcove, his heart sinking.

Faux's face was tear-stained and miserable. "We lost him, Daemus. I'm sorry," she said.

Tuttle's somber face said it all. "They got him. I saw them dragging him off. I—I couldn't get to him."

Daemus rested his head on his knees and said nothing. Katja put her hand on his back and sat next to him.

"How did you get away from them?" Anoki's soft alto broke the silence. "What was that noise?"

"Old potion I'd been tinkering with," said Tuttle. "Shake it and toss, and it explodes. But I only had the one."

"They scattered with the sound," Blue managed, looking down at his bloodied armor. "Scared 'em or something."

"I saw that too." Faux agreed. "When that burst, they rushed away. Long enough for us to escape."

Arjun settled on the floor, and Daemus could hear him stretching his prosthetic leg out in front of him. "Just need to rest some."

Daemus didn't move, his forehead pressing into his kneecaps, the stretch in the back of his neck from the posture growing painful. He was thinking about Wilkes, how the man had seemed so contented in his home despite his longing for more, how he might have stayed there forever if not for them. Then he thought about Kester, and Delling, who had also died because of him. And because of Erud.

His thoughts turned to Trillias and how the god had tortured them with his divine voice, the pain that had seared through his entire being at the intolerable resonance of it.

Daemus lifted his head. "Tuttle," he said, "when you used the potion, did it hurt them?"

Tuttle frowned at him. "Doesn't matter. Like I said, I only had—"

"Just think about it," Daemus cut him off, and Tuttle's frown eased as he considered the question.

"I'm not sure," the alchemist concluded. "Those armored hides of theirs still seemed pretty intact now that I think of it. But they sure did scatter."

"Can you mix up anything else that would explode like that?"

Understanding lit Tuttle's eyes. "Not quite like that. But I know I could make something that would make a noise that loud."

"Daemus's theory may be correct." Caspar moved to the center of the room. "Those creatures live in darkness. Like bats and such. I doubt they can see well, and they appear to have sensitive ears."

"Or are afraid o' big noises," Blue replied.

"Either way," Tuttle said, adjusting the bent frames of his spectacles, "I can make more… If I have time."

"How many more?" Anoki asked. "Our weapons worked little against their scales."

Daemus dropped his head back onto his knees. "Do it. Maybe Wilkes didn't die for nothing."

CHAPTER TWENTY-SIX

"Many learn harshly that the truth of treasure is found not in the gold in your coffers but with whom you share it."
—Katja Seitenwind, Simple Servant of Ssolantress

THE TRUMPETING OF ARRIVAL horns awakened Addilyn from her restless sleep. By the time she dressed and exited her room, she found the new arrivals, a second wing of Vermilion elves and her attendants, milling in the courtyard. Among them, Addilyn recognized Yala, Mir, Iolund, Eiyn, and Rasilyn. As the others stuck with proper courtesy when greeting royalty, Addilyn and Rasilyn embraced like old friends, because they were.

Ritter and Hertzog stood on the side of the courtyard, offering a warm greeting to their Vermilion allies.

"...allow me to welcome you to the Bridge," Hertzog was saying.

Even after so much time apart, Addilyn was struck by how little her attendants had changed. She felt so much older than when she'd last seen them and briefly wondered if she looked the same to them.

"It's so good to see all of you," she said.

Yala, the eldest of the group, could always be counted on. "No more than two Longmarchers to greet us?" she said. "I should think these people have no respect for the Vermilion."

Addilyn laughed. "The Bridge may be called 'Castle Valkeneer,' but it is no palace. It is a humble fortress, and Lady Amandaris and her daughters are away recruiting allies. They would be here if they could. Please don't take offense as there is none intended. And anyway, Sir Ritter and his father, Hertzog, are here." She flashed a smile to the two men.

"Very well," Yala said, turning to Hertzog. "Would you mind terribly if we had a moment alone with the princess to discuss personal matters?"

"Of course." Hertzog bowed and pointed. "I believe the drawing room just inside and down the hall will suit your need for privacy."

Addilyn smiled. "Thank you, Lord Hertzog."

The two men departed as Addilyn shared a parting glance with Ritter. Not a minute later, Addilyn ushered the group of elves into the drawing room, and her attendants didn't waste any time in catching their lady up on the latest in Eldwal.

"Your father's burial was a beautiful service, Your Highness," Iolund imparted. "Eiyn sang a prayer to the Ancients."

"Thank you, Eiyn, for your prayer." Addilyn's voice was soft.

Rasilyn clasped her friend's hands tight. "It was truly beautiful, Princess, Though, the coronelle wasn't happy with your absence."

Addilyn had expected her aunt's disapproval, and a part of Addilyn wished she had been there to send her father off to the Hall of the Ancients, but her duty still lay outside Eldwal. She would find a way to come to terms with her father's death after she avenged him. Coronelle Fia had to understand this.

"Will you not return to the safety of Eldwal, Princess?" Iolund asked.

At this, her father's Knight Hobelar, Verrigo Releante chimed in. "Your Highness, perhaps it is time for you to return to Eldwal. The Vermilion nation needs you there, not here."

Addilyn shook her head. "There is still much to be done here in the Coventry."

"Your Highness, are you entirely sure that—"

To her surprise, Evchen Vischer stepped to her side and addressed the Knight Hobelar, his voice stern. "I believe the princess has made her decision."

Releante closed his mouth as relief flooded through Addilyn.

"As for the rest of you, may I suggest you meet with Sir Ritter to find where you may best defend the castle?" Vischer continued.

As the party broke away and her aids surrounded her, Addilyn nodded a thanks to Vischer. It was only then she realized the aid she'd most wanted to see—Jessamy—was missing.

In the confusion of the arrivals and general chaos of the morning, she hadn't noticed her friend's absence until that moment. Excusing herself to the less crowded hallway, Addilyn searched the corridor and walked as far as she could in the span of a couple minutes before she had to turn around and head back. Before she did, she stopped a castle guard and asked her to find her friend and send her to her side.

With no other option, Addilyn returned to her aids. They tended to her scars and fawned over her appearance, and Addilyn allowed them, but her mind was elsewhere. She had the distinct sense that she didn't belong among them anymore. As if her place was now with Ritter and Jessamy.

The guard she'd asked to search for Jessamy returned with a piece of parchment in her hand. "This was found on your bed, Your Highness," was all she said.

With a pit in her stomach, Addilyn took the scroll from the guard, noted Queen Amice's seal, and skimmed its contents.

...Your allies will be arriving to meet you at the Bridge shortly...

The pit grew as Addilyn rushed to find Ritter.

CHAPTER TWENTY-SEVEN

"Capitulation is the greatest error, for victory awaits those that try one more time."
—Nothos, the Ancient of Fortune

DAEMUS WATCHED IN SILENCE as Katja aided Blue Conney in the dim hues of the were-light. The springheel's wounds still bled from the vicious pincers of the vrykar.

"Stings?" she whispered to Blue, as her hands pulled another barb from his flesh. Blue flinched when she tugged the final one free, refusing to admit it. "That's the last."

Blue breathed a sigh of relief, his face pale from blood loss and fatigue. "Thanks," he grumbled.

"I can't risk casting a spell," she admitted to him, her voice regretful. "Just in case it will attract them back. This will have to do for now." She handed him a flask.

"What is it?" Before she answered, he took several shots from the draught.

"It's a potion. It contains cloves, a bit of lavender spikes, ginger, and a few other ingredients you'd rather not know about. I mix it in peppermint tea to make it more tolerable. It'll help with the pain and some of the swelling, but if you move, you may pull my stitches open."

"I won't be sittin' 'round," Blue said, stone-faced. "Them bastards'll be back."

"Quiet," Arjun urged from the alcove as he stood guard. He glanced outside the small chamber they'd all crowded into, looking up and down the corridor.

"Nothing?" Anoki asked, sitting across from him.

"If they come back, we can defend the door for a time," he whispered. "But if they return in numbers…" He shook his head.

"I'm out of arrows." Faux unstrapped her quiver and laid it with care to the ground. "Besides, I lost my bow in the retreat."

"I dropped the maps, too." Caspar peered at Anoki, hoping not to send her over the edge. "I'm sorry. When we ran, I—"

"It's okay." The Athabasica raised a steadying hand with a forced smile. "We're just glad we're all safe."

"Not all of us," Daemus reminded them, reflecting on their perished friend, Renfrow Wilkes.

"We have to keep moving," Marquiss urged, as Faux rewrapped his bloody arm with one of Katja's bandages. "This room is a death trap. If they can't see well if at all, they must be tracking by hearing. And I bet they have a keen sense of smell. We must keep going."

Arjun pursed his lips and exhaled softly, looking at Tuttle, who had been working for what Daemus guessed had been several hours, his eyes focused behind his spectacles. "How much longer, Jeric?"

At first the alchemist didn't answer, instead staring at what appeared to be an armful of small glass bottles, one of which he was capping.

"Tuttle," Arjun risked in a louder voice. "How much longer?"

Tuttle sat back, fixed the mangled glasses on his face, and sniffed. He wiped his stained hands on his waistcoat and mumbled something to himself. "I think the thunder flashes are ready. Handle them with care. And watch out for your ears."

"How do we know they won't realize the thunder flashes are harmless?" asked Arjun, his gaze sharp. "Hard to be sure how clever they are."

Tuttle half-shrugged, his smile falling away.

An uncomfortable silence fell. Looking around at their grey faces, Daemus could see that everyone was thinking about what would happen if they failed. "Tuttle's devices will work," he said at last. "We won't fail."

Caspar shot him a sudden look, seeming startled. "Daemus? Is it back?"

Daemus blinked at him for a split second before realizing what he meant. "The Sight? No, Caspar, I don't have it in here."

Caspar's lips quirked. "I just thought... You sounded so sure."

Daemus paused. "We don't have another option, my friend. And..." He hesitated again. "Erud must have known about our visit to the Laurentian Labyrinth, which means it's at least possible for us to succeed. Lest we'd not be here at all."

Caspar's eyes lit. "Praise be to Erud." He cut off before saying the rest of the ritual prayer, but the way he said it and the expression on his face made Daemus feel like he'd been tricked somehow.

He looked away from Caspar and noticed the others watching him with similar odd looks on their faces. After another moment he recognized it as awe and turned away, uncomfortable. Even Anoki and Arjun had been looking at him with that hopeful light in their eyes, and it made his skin crawl to realize that on some level they all expected him to save them.

Needing no more encouragement, the party made rapid preparations. When they were finished, Arjun led the way back to where Wilkes had been lost. The trek was short, and bad memories of the chaos flooded back into Daemus's mind's eye. He fought a shudder as they entered the bloody hall.

"Where from here?" Katja looked to Daemus, who again felt the weight of the party's gaze upon him.

He huffed to himself and closed his eyes. He had no way of knowing and without Caspar's maps, rudimentary as they were, he didn't recognize one corridor from another. Yet everyone looked upon him for guidance. His brow furrowed and he sighed.

Erud, he started to pray to himself, *I've never asked anything of you before. You thrust your curse upon me, robbing Graytorris of his eyes and granting them to an innocent boy, one ill-prepared to lead, or even understand. A boy—unable to fight the madman who seeks my death for his own redemption.*

Now, the realm of Warminster rests on the sharpened edge of the blade of chaos, one you created, and I am as lost as I was as a young child. Unable to see… see my way through all your visions. And deep in the walls of the Laurentian Labyrinth, my divinations are severed by the might of your brother.

But I've seen your pain, and the pain of my fellows. All eyes, including yours, are upon me. And it is time for me to stand and fight. To embrace your curse and transform it into a gift. A gift that perhaps it had been all along.

I stand here now, Erud, lost in a tomb of horrors and I beseech thee for this one mercy. For I care not for the preservation of my own cursed existence. I ask only that you spare my friends—those that have risked all to help me and the realm by accepting the challenge of your brother's dangerous gambit. They were willing to trade their lives for mine, and now it is my turn to offer mine in return for theirs. Spare those with the courage to join me in this fateful quest, to vanquish the evil that seeks unwarranted vengeance on an innocent child, now become a man.

I ask you, the All-Knowing, All-Seeing, to free them from this torture and in return, I offer you my life, for what little it is worth to you.

And if my humble prayers do not echo in your ears far away in the Hall of the Ancients, or you deny my last wish, then may the light of your Tome never reach the cathedral's watchful eye ever again.

"Daemus." He felt a hand at his elbow. It was Katja. "Are you—"

"We follow in Renfrow's footsteps." His voice was resolute. "We go this way." He pointed in the direction Wilkes had run. He wasn't sure why, but he swore that Wilkes would not have died in vain. If Erud would not grant him the Sight, maybe it was time for him to take matters into his own hands. Or in this case, his friend's.

"But the vrykar dragged him away," Caspar whispered, "down that very hall."

Daemus shot his friend a knowing smile. "Follow me, Keeper. Erud awaits."

Caspar's face contorted in confusion before easing, a small tear forming in the corner of one eye. He straightened his sooty cassock and his visage morphed from desperate to determined. "I'm with you."

"To the end?" Daemus asked.

"The bitter end," Caspar replied.

The two Keepers turned to the rest of the group. In one hand, his mace remained ready. In the other, he took Katja's gentle hand and said, "I am ready. Will you come with me?"

Her eyes flickered as he reached for her face, gently touching the magical tattoo beneath her cheek. He could feel her shudder and then calm with his touch. "Yes."

He smiled and looked deep into her eyes. "Now let's find the heart, together."

She returned his smile and nodded.

"I'm tired of standin' 'round anyway, kid," Blue grumbled, trying to keep his voice low, "so lead on."

"I'll take point," Arjun stepped to the front of the group.

"No, Arjun." Daemus held his mace out flat, stopping the captain in his tracks. "You've done enough for me. It's my turn to lead."

Arjun thought for a second and then backed away.

"Stay close, though," Daemus said, a wry smile appearing on his face, "as I will need Trillias's pet lamp to see."

His first steps down the corridor were silent as the grave, followed by the careful clicking of his friend's boots behind him. He passed over the bloody tracks of Wilkes on the ground, then they crossed over the scratches on the wall from the vrykar.

After a few minutes of heading in one direction, Daemus noticed the were-light haunting Arjun began to flicker. With a few steps more the illumination grew in strength.

"Do you hear that?" a whisper rose from the rear of the group. Marquiss pointed to his half-elven ears.

Daemus froze, expecting to hear more claws grinding away at a distant wall, but instead he heard a strange humming on the air. His eyes narrowed and he found himself following it.

"The heart," someone murmured behind him, and he remembered Trillias saying something about the Heart making a sound. Hope surged through him, alighting his spirit and blossoming in his heart.

"Daemus," Caspar's voice wavered, "can you feel it?"

The young Keepers stood side by side for a moment, halting the group. Daemus opened his senses and felt the slightest hint of a magical presence ahead—but a hale he recognized. One he hadn't felt since…

"It's *The Tome of Enlightenment*," Caspar's voice bubbled in excitement. "Tell me you can feel the presence of our Ancient."

"Shh," Anoki warned but Daemus didn't care. For the first time in his life, he felt an emotion he hadn't recognized. One of gratitude.

Had Erud truly answered his prayers?

CHAPTER TWENTY-EIGHT

"Beware, as the greatest danger to victory occurs the moment before one declares it."
—Malgavarre the Usurper, the Duchy of Queen's Prey

ONE OF HER MINIONS interrupted as she prepared for her wedding, "the Norsemen… They are only hours away."

She donned copper-colored leather armor with a silken shirt of soft sage, matching the colors of the Guild of the Copper Wing. On the armor, above her left breast, a brand with the detached wing of a bird in flight: the Lady of Saracen's new coat of arms.

"How many?" she asked, fighting to appear calm as her handmaidens tussled with her red hair.

"Thousands," he said.

"Send for Commandant Baden," she replied. "Have her meet me here."

"Yes, my lady."

"It is still 'Guildmistress,' " she called as he walked away. "Until the sword touches my shoulders, I am still 'Guildmistress.' "

She sat, staring into her bedroom mirror, not used to attendants waiting on her hand and foot. Typically, merchants and guildsmen accosted her this time of day. Instead, three women she didn't know tried to fix her hair. She'd cared little about her appearance most of her life and found the attendants struggling. But to be a lady, there was a certain level of decorum expected, and she knew she had to reinvent her image, from commoner to noble.

Minutes passed until the women finished. Scarlett stood and looked at herself. Her wedding day was supposed to be special. Instead, she had thousands of unwanted guests at her door. She found no joy in her new raiment nor the intricate braids in her hair.

"You called for me?" Commandant Cass Baden entered with her usual gruff demeanor, waving for the handmaidens to leave. Sasha didn't fret about her breach of etiquette. She knew the two women needed to speak alone.

"My wedding has been moved up on account of the Norsemen." Sasha stiffened a bit at the thought. "I need to marry the bastardess today instead of next week as planned. And we need to win this battle. It will be an historic day for Saracen."

"Then why summon me here when there are preparations to be made?"

Baden's lack of protocol didn't bother Sasha either. The two had known each other since their days as street urchins in Saracen. In some ways, Sasha found it refreshing.

"I need to know you will be able to hold the Norsemen at our gates." Sasha's stern eyes met Baden's in the mirror. "The bulk of our forces are south with Von Lormarck."

"The walls will hold," Baden offered with her usual confident stride. "We have one thousand Sentinels of Saracen manning the gates, the towers, and the rivers. The Norsemen will have more to deal with than they did in Vallance."

"Excellent, Cass." Sasha smiled. "You will be rewarded when I am made Lady of Saracen today. You have been my closest friend, and you will not want for anything."

Baden bowed her head and clicked her heels. She left before wishing Sasha well or saying goodbye.

Such was her way.

As she departed, Ghyrr Rugalis, Von Lormarck's rogue emissary appeared in the door.

"Is my bride ready?" Sasha asked.

"You look beautiful," Ghyrr admitted.

"Is she *ready*?" Sasha demanded, ignoring the platitude.

"She is not drugged, if that's what you mean," Ghyrr replied. "She has been dressed and there are several guards at her door. She will be ready, but you may find her combative without the daily dose of Von Lormarck's concoction."

"If you give it to her, will she be able to stand?" Sasha asked.

"Possibly, but her condition will be obvious."

"Give her half a dose," Sasha commanded. "I want no incidents."

"Certainly," Ghyrr agreed. "I have Malice at my side and will be the one presiding over your accolade, as proxy for the king himself."

"That is welcomed news," she said. "For one Saracenean to knight another… I will have a painting commissioned, featuring you and me. It will hang in the halls of my new keep once it is built."

"It would be an honor, my lady," Ghyrr teased.

"Have the other guildmasters and merchants arrived?" she asked.

"Many have," Ghyrr replied, "but I must say, there is an unsettled nervousness with the approaching army. I have heard complaints about being summoned to an impromptu service from many in the hall. I am sure you understand, this is not the best day for your wedding."

"But it is the only day," she said. "A knighthood, a wedding, and a victory in battle. History can ask for no more of one person."

"As you say," he acquiesced.

"Now," she replied, "go to my betrothed and make sure she is prepared properly for the ceremony."

EMBER SAT QUIETLY IN her room, somewhere in the bowels of the Guild of the Copper Wing. She wasn't sure how long she had been in Saracen, as her bouts of sobriety were infrequent. When drugged, she lost track of time. The potion they forced her to drink would at first make her giddy, then numb, and then she eventually woke in some portion of her room.

The room was more like a cell than a comfortable living space, featuring no windows and one door, constantly guarded by Scarlett's henchmen. She had a bed, a writing desk, and a small chifforobe for her belongings. There was an attached privy, but she had to ask the guard at the door to unlock it as they didn't trust her in the room alone and unwatched.

The door swung open, and in walked Ghyrr Rugalis.

"I see you are ready for your big day." His dispassionate smirk gave her no comfort.

Ember had been forced into a wedding dress of the guild's colors and figured her time had come. The waiting was over. There was to be no rescue, no recall from her father. His mind was set, and he had moved his pawn on the chessboard of Saracen into a position of sacrifice.

"Ghyrr, I beg of you," she started, tears forming in her eyes. "You know this to be loathsome and unfair. I am not a slave, but a lady of Foghaven Vale. I am not to be bartered like a head of cattle."

Ghyrr closed the door behind him, affording them some privacy.

"Pity doesn't make for a becoming bride," he said.

"Please help me," she pleaded, her tears flowing and panic lilting her voice. "I will pay you handsomely for my rescue."

"I see no palmettes or laurels on your person," he stated with cold honesty.

"My *truly* betrothed, Joferian Maeglen," she scrambled. "He is a wealthy man and can not only pay you, but grant you lands and titles."

Ghyrr sat at her writing desk and sighed, looking at her. She was desperate. Anything to free herself from this tortuous fate.

"You will see Joferian soon," he said.

A spark of hope lit in her eyes and a wave of tension washed from her brows.

"What?" Her voice filled with surprise. "You will help me then?"

"I have no choice," he said. "Just like you. Don't misunderstand me. Your Joferian charges at Saracen this day with an army of Norsemen at his side. He is at the head of these marauders and will attack the town within the hour."

Ember took a deep breath and smiled through her tears.

"But the guilds have something planned for him and his allies," Ghyrr added. "What I meant was, you will probably see his head on a pike by day's end."

"Do you take joy in teasing me?" Ember asked. "Am I a mouse, running trapped between the paws of a cat?"

"No." Ghyrr shook his head. "If it were up to me, or even Ilidari, we would have absconded with you the night before your father gave us the order. But alas, he tricked us all, and now it is my job to ensure his wishes are granted."

"Please, Ghyrr," she cried. "Anything."

"Do this for me," he said, as he placed a small vial on the writing desk in reach of her. "Take this without trouble. It is only a half dose. It will help you, and me, get through the ceremony.

"It is time."

JOFERIAN PEERED DOWN AT the city of Saracen atop his wooded perch in the sloping mountains. From where the bulk of the invading army sat, the front gates of the merchant city were a mere hour away. Argantyr's scouts informed them that the Sentinels had reinforced the front gates not with troops, but with a small flotilla of navy vessels disguised as merchant ships. Saracen knew they were coming but wanted to appear as if they didn't. At the right moment, the frontal assault of the Norsemen would crash into the gates of the city, making their rear units vulnerable to ballistae and arrow volleys from the navy. They would be pinned down between a river and a fifteen-foot wall, fighting a two-front battle. It would be a slaughter.

Joferian had other plans.

Argantyr and Strunk would appear to launch their assault as Saracen wanted, but only after his small company of two hundred attacked the rear gate. The rear gate was guarded by Sentinels and a few war machines, but Joferian knew that their diminished ranks, the lion's share of which were off to war with Von Lormarck, left them depleted somewhere. His roll of the dice was at the rear, where it would have taken his army two additional days to march. And moving a brigade that far would certainly tip off the Saraceneans.

A small company of fast-moving cavalry could ride far enough east, away from spies, and return west to the gates undetected. A company of two hundred could cause enough chaos with the sounds of speeding horses that their true numbers would be hidden amongst the trees. It would deceive its leaders, leaving them to doubt their plans. Perhaps they would move troops from the front gates to reinforce the rear, giving Argantyr the break he needed.

And of course, a company of two hundred untrained

cavalrymen that were unaccustomed to attacking on horseback could smash into the walls of Saracen and die within minutes, falling to arrows and war machines. The plan was not without risk.

Joferian believed in the battle plan. It was his idea, after all. If it failed, he would likely not survive the first assault. He closed his eyes and heard the words of the Faxerian, Lucien Blacwin in his ears.

"Leaders always lead from the front," Blacwin would say. "Your troops need to know you will bleed with them and that you believe so much in your stratagem you will stand shoulder to shoulder with them. Defeat is not in you. If you do this, they will never retreat."

So, Joferian placed himself at the tip of the spear.

His untrained horsemen gathered themselves in a long thin row that nearly mirrored the length of the rear wall of the city. If they held the line and charged in unison, the sounds of two hundred unseen horses would echo off the rear wall, sounding like thousands.

Joferian stuck his hand in the air and dropped it, silently giving the order to turn back west. The forest was empty, as they had hoped, and it appeared from afar the Saraceneans didn't have enough troops to guard the rear gate properly.

As the distance between their horses and their destinies halved and then halved again, his steed galloped faster. He struck out in front of the long, meandering line. He drew his sword and held it high.

"Charge!" he cried, and the deafening sounds of the sons and daughters of Rijkstag followed. Their calls for the Valkyries to carry them to the Hall of the Ancients rose from the valley. The pounding of their hooves against the hardened ground sounded at first like quiet thunder, rising slowly in the distance. A thunder that grew and grew as the trees thinned and their thunder rolled.

Joferian's heart pounded in his armored chest, and he lowered his sword, pointing at the wall that appeared in front of them. He felt the reverberations of their horse's charge echoing back off the walls as they cleared the forest. He looked up through his visor to see the Sentinels atop of the walls scrambling into attack positions, but it was as he expected. His plan had caught them by surprise. It may yet work.

The Norsemen emerged from the woods behind him in a crooked line of horses and rushed toward the wall. Half of them made it before the Sentinels even had a chance to fire their first volley of arrows. The thud of dozens of arrow points bouncing harmlessly off the slate iron shields of the Norsemen below sounded like raindrops dinging off of his helmet.

The first row of his cavalry swung a series of grappling hooks, catching onto the tops of the battlements. His lightly armored troops began to climb, as the second row of horsemen returned covering fire for the climbers.

As the sounds of horses tapered away, he could hear the barking of panicked orders from above as the Sentinels fought to hold their wall. Some cries from the first row of attackers rang in his ears as ropes were cut and arrows found their mark. He watched the dead and dying rain to the ground while a second assault began their ascent.

Then he signaled to the woods and an improvised war machine rambled over the broken ground. Composed of two covered wagons, a group of Norsemen propelled the battering ram toward the rear gates. The tip of the ram was a sharpened spear, carved from a large tree trunk and dowsed in water to prevent it from catching fire.

A row of men on each side heaved the giant truck forward

while a second group ran next to them, holding their shields high in the air, offering cover against the pelting of arrows.

The final row of cavalry rode back and forth, spinning oiled lanterns on a tether of thin chains and launching them over the battlements where they would break and catch fire. It was an old Norse trick, one that Joferian learned by watching his men practice over the last few weeks. But they were unpracticed on horseback, and so many exploded harmlessly against the walls. More than a few however found their marks, setting the wooden roofs of the towers ablaze and landing on the catwalks on the other side of the battlements.

He heard the cries of burning Sentinels and equal cries to dowse the flames in the towers. More men climbed and fewer fell. The familiar sound of clashing metal cascaded over the wall. His forces had reached the catwalks.

The battering ram slowed as it pushed against the slight grade that led to the wall, but it was nearly there. A ballista from one of the war machines atop the wall launched and missed their shot, their giant bolt splintering off the ground, its remains careening off into the woods. Joferian breathed a sigh of relief. They had one ram, and it had to reach the gates.

Arrows rained down on the troops manning the ram, as an officer begged his men to target it. They were still too far from the wall. He jumped from his horse, holding his slate iron shield above his head, and ran to the ram. One more man to push couldn't hurt.

The voices on the wall were close enough to hear from the ground.

"Fire!" yelled a voice, but Joferian heard a springy *clang*.

A misfire, he said to himself. Likely a rookie guard, rushing to reload and not finishing the job properly. Sometimes it is better to be lucky, and he quickly offered thanks to both the

Ancients, Koss and Nothos. The misfire bought them time.

He ran to the rear of the ram where two of the shield bearers had already fallen dead, victims of arrows that found their marks. He leaned in to protect the men, pushing in time to hear an arrow shatter on his shield. The hardened surface of the slate iron had saved his life.

The ram crested the small embankment and was now level ground again. A small cheer from the exhausted men pushing it echoed inside the hollow of his shield.

"Almost there!" he yelled over the sounds of battle to his men, not even sure if they understood him.

"Heave!"

The makeshift ram hurtled along the ground, the men giving it their all. More arrows descended and one snuck through his shield, piercing through the side of a Norseman's helmet. He fell sharply and the wheels of the cart rolled over him. Joferian dropped his shield and filled in his spot. The ram had to reach the gate.

"Heave!"

The cart gained speed. They were ten yards, then five from the gates. Then the point of the battering ram found its mark and slammed headlong into the double-banded wooden doors with a resounding crash. The impact was jarring, knocking Joferian to the ground. A cheer rose from his companions who had already backed the ram up for its next assault. Joferian stood and leaned into the ram, charging ahead with his men. Their first assault had crippled the gate, but it remained in place.

"Heave!"

They backed the cart up and rammed in again. More splinters flew from the doors and this time, newly formed cracks shared a vision of their goal. The streets of Saracen were but yards away. He could see the scrambling of guards on the other side, fighting back to bolster the door.

"Oil!" someone yelled from above, and Joferian looked up to see the mad scrambling of troops atop the battlements, trying to target them with a vat of boiling death.

A charge of his raging barbarians rushed to their rescue. His helpless eyes looked on. If his men lost, he would die horribly in a scalding bath of fiery oil and could do nothing to help.

"Heave!"

His men felt his urgency. One more time the ram slammed into the doors. Its hinges weakened and it began to lean inward.

One of his men in the front screamed and fell under the cart's wheels, having been run through by a poking spear, sneaking through the newly formed cracks in the wooden doors. From the side rushed one of his soldiers, replacing the fallen man while another covered the small opening, pressing against it with his shield.

Joferian watched the fearless man's arms bounce back from impaling spear attacks coming from within, but none penetrated the slate iron shield.

"Heave!"

The ram reared back like a stallion and kicked forward with the victorious sound of splitting wood and bending iron. The left side of the double doors broke free and swung in, far enough for two of his brave Norsemen to jump through. The clanging of steel followed. Then two more jumped in. And two more.

The rear gates had been breached.

"GUILDMISTRESS," A SENTINEL CALLED, rushing in from the corridor. "An attack on the rear gate has commenced."

Sasha shot up and looked to Ghyrr Rugalis, who sat next to her in an antechamber holding up a slumping Ember. They waited just outside the wedding hall, which in truth, was the floor of the guild's warehouse. It had been converted for her accolade and wedding ceremonies. Inside the chamber awaited the leaders and wealthy of Saracen.

"This cannot be," she snarled in anger and disbelief, and her cheeks flushed as red as her hair.

"Should we rush through the ceremony?" Rugalis asked.

Sasha frowned, her lips going tight. Her shoulders slumped in defeat. "The ceremonies will need to wait," she murmured.

She opened the doors to the hall and walked in. Unsure eyes stared at her, waiting for her to speak.

"Citizens of Saracen," she began. "I am truly sorry to have to inform you that our city has been attacked at our rear gates."

In an instant, the room boiled with side conversations and worried rambling.

"Please," she yelled over the noise of the crowd, "return home to your families and businesses. Our walls will hold. They always have. But this ceremony will need to wait."

The sitting crowd rose nearly as one, some running, others walking to the exits. The heads of the other four guilds came together, their personal guards around them. They walked to her through the scurrying crowd as she tried to leave.

"Guildmistress Scarlett," the snotty voice of Durwin Torrence said. "I thought you had met with Commandant Baden earlier this morning. Why were we unaware of this second group of barbarians at the far gate?"

"We have no time for discussions, Torrence," Sasha responded, her tone sharp. She shoved passed him. Of her other rivals, Scarlett hated Torrence the most. As the Guildmaster of the Manticore House, they were her chief rival, and somewhere in the back of her head, she wondered if he had anything to do with the assault. He had accepted her decision to send the

Sentinels south, but openly opposed her at the time.

"I must find the commandant and ensure that our plans to defend the city are still in place," she added.

"*Our* plans?" questioned Olaf Admunsdson. "Or *your* plans? If it were up to me, we would still have the Sentinels here to man the walls."

"We do not lack for resources or troops," she countered. "I thought the Guildmaster of the Warrior's Guild would act more like a warrior in times of battle." She raised her brows at him.

Olaf balled his hands into fists and stepped toward the guildmistress. Rugalis inserted himself between them, brandishing the shiny steel of Malice in his hand.

"Play nice," Rugalis said as the other guildmaster's guards drew their weapons. "We're all inside the walls together. Let's win the battle before you fight this war."

SASHA DUCKED BACK INTO her chambers and wrestled with her wedding attire. Ghyrr followed her in and guided the wobbling Ember Fleury to a chair.

"What are you doing?" Rugalis asked.

"I very well can't fight a battle for the city in a leather doublet," she replied. "Bring me my armor!"

Moments later, several attendants entered the room, carrying a suit of fitted coin mail much like chainmail, but the outside of the armor was riveted with shiny copper sheaves, emblazoned in the lariat of Saracen.

Sasha stripped down to her undergarments, and the servants held the mail up, one in front to hold it, and one in the back to buckle it closed.

"Don't just stand there," she snapped while the servants struggled to ready her with boots and sword. "Take my bride below to her room and come find me on the front wall. I must find Commandant Baden immediately."

Rugalis shrugged. "Very well."

Just then, the horns from the front gate towers sounded, warning of the assault.

Sasha froze. "They are at the front gate?"

"Perhaps you should consider—" Rugalis started.

"Our walls will hold," she interrupted, trying to convince herself as much as him.

Rugalis grabbed Ember around the arm and lifted her from her seat.

"And Rugalis," Sasha said. "Let us not hold our prisoner any longer. The time for ransom has passed us."

"You mean Master Zendel Cray?"

She nodded, lacing her boots.

"It's my Joferian," she said, her voice soft but hopeful, fighting against her drugged stupor. "He comes for me."

"Come now, young Ember," he said. "Let us get you to safety." He led her out into the hall and away from Sasha Scarlett.

CHAPTER TWENTY-NINE

"Words that stay in one's ears are whispered, not screamed."
—Precept Radu of the Cathedral of the Watchful Eye

, ALONE IN HIS thoughts. Even from where he waited, he heard the approaching battle. As a prisoner, he had no real idea which army was at the gates. But whoever it was, it could not be good for his captors.

"Guards!" he yelled. "What's happening?"

For a moment, his usually attentive guards were silent. Then he heard the clicking sound of the lock opening and the door to his makeshift cell opened outward.

A man stood in front of him, wearing dark leather armor with a dirty cloak that at one time may have been the color of Jackal orange. In one hand he held a sword, a sword Cray recognized. One that would be recognized around the whole of Warminster.

"Only the baron of Foghaven Vale carries that sword," he said to the stranger.

"He does," the figure said, slowly entering the room. The man turned the sword on its side, revealing the mark of the Jackal, leaving no doubt to its owner.

"Then why do you wield it?" Cray managed, trying to diffuse the situation, but the figure's features remained stoic and unchanged. "Have you come to use Malice? If you have, know I am a wealthy man, who has—"

"The resources to make me wealthy too?" the man mocked. "Grant me titles? Deed me lands?"

"Yes," Cray pleaded, and backed up, his legs finding the rail of his cot.

"I have heard this many times before," the figure said. "Yet honor prevents me from accepting."

"Honor? Where is the honor in killing an unarmed man?"

The man remained silent and edged closer.

"Why does Von Lormarck want me dead?" Cray asked. "How does that serve his cause?"

"He isn't the one that ordered it," the man replied. "It was Scarlett."

"Then why Malice?" Cray asked. "Why that sword?"

The man pointed to the ground, ignoring him. "Drop to your knees and I will make this painless and quick."

"Please. I must know. It is the last request of a dying man."

Cray dropped to his knees and turned away from the sword. He tilted his head to the side, offering his neck to the man. He felt him close in, his knees brushing his back.

Then Cray raised his elbow violently, catching the man in the groin. The figure fell backwards in pain but managed to swipe the sword across Cray's back, barely missing his neck.

Cray winced as the hot burning sensation of the sharpened sword scraped along his skin. He spun around and jumped to his feet to find the man doubled over in pain but waving Malice in front of him.

Out of sheer instinct, Cray held his hands wide and charged at the man. His only chance for freedom was the open door behind him, and the man and sword stood in his way.

His charge caught the man off guard but again he was able to raise the sword high enough to clip the barreling Cray in the face. The edge cut through his cheek, rolling up his face and cutting through his ear.

Cray screamed in pain but kept coming, plowing into the man with his sizeable frame. The two fell to the ground, and the man dropped the sword and gasped for breath. Cray slid atop the man, straddling him like a horse and began pummeling him with the sides of his hands and wrists. He aimed for his head and had one of the man's arms pinned underneath his bent knee.

The man countered by reaching up with his free hand and tugging at Cray's torn face. His fingers found his wounded cheek and slid to his bloody ear. With a yank, Cray felt the flesh of his ear rip, tearing the lobe from his head.

He cried out in a desperate scream and lowered his forehead into the man's face, biting at his nose.

It was the dazed man's turn to yelp in pain, as Cray bit through his nostril and wrenched back, tearing his nose near in half. He spit the flesh onto to the man and began to pound away again, and again, and again.

Soon, blood flowed freely from the crippled assassin, covering both in a spattering of red. The man slowed, reflexively trying to block the never-ending stream of desperate fists and elbows.

Cray lunged back and grabbed at Malice's pommel, dragging it closer to himself. As the sword hit his palm, the man swung a fist, connecting with Cray's battered face. Cray felt the punch and began to swoon. His eyes rolled into his head as the man's palm pushed under his chin, forcing his head back.

With one last effort, he swung Malice at his foe. He felt the blade strike bone and the man howled in his ears. Cray's double vision hadn't relented, but his eyes revealed the nature of the wound. The blade had sliced clean through the man's left arm, leaving the amputated appendage on the floor next to him.

His foe tried grabbing at the bloody stump, feebly struggling to stave off the inevitable.

Cray turned the sword point down and pierced through the leather armor until he felt the tip hit the stone floor.

The man's body wiggled for a few seconds more, then came to rest.

He gathered himself as best he could and pressed hard against the wound on his cheek. His face was now numb to the pain, but he had survived.

Regathering his thoughts, he rifled through the man's possessions, discovering a key. Perhaps he would need it to escape the basement where he was being held.

He forced himself to his feet and staggered out the door, using the walls to hold him up. He staggered his way through the corridor, checking around every bend for a guard. Yet he found none.

He couldn't feel his torn ear but could sense the wet blood on his face and neck.

"Ghyrr," a woman's voice called from down the hallway. He stopped in his tracks, fearful at first that a guard was on her way.

"Ghyrr, please!" the voice said again, behind a door farther down the corridor.

He slid down the wall, balancing himself with every step and stopped just shy of the door.

"Help me," the feeble voice called. "You have to let me out, he's here!"

"I am here," Clay called, his own voice wavering. He slid down the stone hall to the door the voice came from. "Stand back, and I will unlock the door."

He fumbled to find the key he'd acquired from the assassin and made it fit after several attempts. He rested for a second against the door, hoping the key would work. The key clicked and the door unlocked. He tugged at the handle, swinging the door open. He found himself staring into the teary eyes of Ember Fleury.

SASHA SCARLETT RODE FROM her guild's stables atop her horse toward the front gates. But before she crossed a city block, she saw several clouds of black smoke rising from fires in the far end of Saracen. The sounds of the distant battle hung in the air, ringing like a hundred smithies hammering in discord.

She heard no such chaos at the front gate, save for a group of horses riding toward her. A unit of the Sentinel's cavalry rode by her, heading for the battle. She waved at them to stop, but they ignored her and carried on.

She looked to the nervous citizenry who had scurried in the streets like rats trying to find their way off a sinking ship. The anxiety was palpable, and she wondered where they would run to. There was nowhere to hide. Their high walls were a defensive nightmare for their enemies, but if the Norsemen did win their way through, the walls would turn into a prison, offering no simple way out.

She spurred her horse on and arrived at the front gates where she dismounted and climbed the tower to find Commandant Baden.

Baden stood with her officers overlooking the mouth of the rivers. Sasha surveyed the field. Where were the Norsemen?

"Commandant Baden," she interrupted.

"Not now, Scarlett," Baden barked then took a moment to finish giving her orders to reinforce the far gate. "I am sorry your ceremony was interrupted, but I am busy. What do you need?"

"Why have they not attacked?" Sasha asked.

"They have, just not here."

Baden handed a spyglass to Sasha and pointed at a spot

in the distance. Sasha peered through the lens to find the Norsemen, not far from the mouth of the city, biding their time.

"They wait," Baden managed with a knowing tone. "The rear gates have been breached and I have sent reinforcements to attend to it."

"But what of the front gates?" Sasha asked.

"We cannot give the enemy easy entry to the city," Baden replied. "The rear guard was sorely undermanned. They have spotted our weakness and diverted more forces to support their far assault. So, we must counter. My fear is that if we pull more troops off this wall, it will invite an attack here."

"Can we hit them with ballistae? Catapults?" Sasha asked.

"They are out of range," Baden groaned. "And it will take too long to redeploy them to defend the far side of the city."

"What do we do?" Sasha said.

"We fight," Baden replied, turning to her friend. "This will be bloody. You should try to escape while you can."

"Escape?" The thought seemed incredulous to Sasha. "You said the walls would hold."

"They will," she replied. "But I don't think your only enemies are the Norsemen."

ZENDEL CRAY AND EMBER Fleury snuck through the Guild of the Copper Wing. The place was in order but abandoned. Not a soul could be found. They had made their way from the basement into the guild hall cautiously, with Cray wielding Malice in case trouble found them. Instead, the pleasant aromas of fresh ale and untouched food greeted them at the doors, readied for a wedding that hadn't occurred.

Ember's induced lethargy was beginning to wither away, thanks to a mix of adrenaline and emotion. Her legs still wobbled, but she could stand on her own.

"We must get you away, my lady," the broken Zendel Cray insisted. "The city is under attack."

"It is Joferian and the Norsemen," Ember replied, her nerves on end.

"How do you know?" Cray's eyes narrowed, a ray of hope appearing on his bloodied countenance.

"I was told by my captor," she replied. "He teased me with the news of my betrothed."

The two staggered their way to the warehouse doors and peered through the windows. The streets of Saracen opened in front of them, and Cray pointed to a second large building next door. "Just there. It is their stables. We must find you a horse."

The two slid out onto the street and stumbled toward the stables. The larger barn doors were open, and it appeared that anything that could be taken was already gone. No carts, no horses, and no guildsmen or guildswomen to be found. A soft neighing rose from the far end of the barn, and Ember bravely stepped into the gaping opening.

"Careful," Cray whispered to her, grabbing at his back, and using the stable walls to hold him up. He handed her the sword. "I cannot go any farther."

"I don't know how to use this." She grabbed at the hilt of her father's sword.

"Use the pointy end," he joked as he slid down the wall to sit, leaving bloody skid marks.

"Stay here and I will retrieve the horse." Ember dragged Malice on the ground behind her, unable to lift it. She was getting stronger with every step, but she had never carried a sword when sober, let alone drugged. The steel was too heavy in her hands.

She made her way to the back of the barn where she found a lone pony, big enough for herself alone. It was half dressed in a saddle, as if someone decided against taking her. Ember approached the skittish horse, slowly petting it and offering it carrots from a pale outside the gate. The horse ate, and she used the distraction to fit it with a bit and bridle. Once she had gained its trust, she walked it to the front of the stables to retrieve Cray.

As she neared the door, her eyes fell on Sasha Scarlett standing over Cray.

"Where is she?" Scarlett threatened, the tip of her sword at Cray's chest.

"She stole a horse," Cray replied. "She headed toward the sounds of battle, I believe."

"I know when a man lies," Scarlett growled. "Tell me where she is, and I will spare you. I may need a handsome ransom after all."

"Your man told me you sent him to kill me," Cray teased. "Sounded as if trading my pounds of flesh for pounds of gold were off. It would be a hefty sum at that."

"Master Cray." Sasha shook her head in disgust. "A jester to the last."

"You sent him with Von Lormarck's sword," he replied. "I made him taste the steel before he died."

"*You*?" She laughed. "You killed Ghyrr Rugalis?"

"Survived him is more accurate."

"If you killed him with Malice," Sasha replied, "where is the sword now?"

"It's here." Ember marched from the stables, bloody sword in hand. Suddenly, the weight of the steel didn't feel as heavy, as she lifted it with two hands.

"There you are." Sasha turned and drew her own sword. "My lovely bride. It appears your wedding gown has been soiled. We shall find you a new one. Now, put the sword down."

Ember stepped closer, her face resolute.

"All right then." Sasha spun the pommel of her sword in her hand. "I always did like your spirit, little girl."

The two danced in a circle, waiting for the other to make the first move. Cray crawled to his knees to help, but Sasha kicked him in the face, knocking him flat to the ground.

Ember could wait no longer. She had no skill, no tactic. She just charged, rage in her eyes and hatred in her veins.

Sasha turned back at the last minute and the two crossed swords with a clash. Ember grunted with the swing and leapt, crashing into the guildmistress, sending them both to the ground. Sasha rolled over and swung, making wild cuts with her blade but caught nothing but air.

Ember swung again, and in close quarters was lucky enough to strike home. Malice met resistance as it cut through Sasha's armor, slicing through the coin mail, and into her shoulder.

The guildmistress wailed in pain and forced herself to stand, groping at the open wound. She switched her sword into her good arm and pushed her disheveled hair out of her face. With a grunt, she waved Ember on.

Ember needed no invitation. She raised Malice high above her head and ran at Sasha. With two hands she swung down with all her might. Sasha raised her sword to meet Malice, but the force of Ember's blow slapped Sasha's blade down and away. Malice dug deep into Sasha's skull with a brutal crack. Sasha's green eyes froze, and her dimpled cheeks disappeared. Her jaw slacked, and Ember watched the light dim in her eyes as she fell to the ground.

Ember let go of Malice and stepped away from the Guildmistress. She covered her mouth as she gasped. Her eyes teared at what she had done and cried until she convulsed.

From around the bend, a few merchants came, carrying

looted wares in their hands. She turned to them but their gaze fell to the corpse of Sasha Scarlett. Frozen, she waited for them to react, but they wasted no time in scurrying off, disappearing onto the dusty roads of Saracen.

Ember rushed to check on Cray, to find him dazed but alive.

"Zendel." She helped the man to a sitting position. "Can you ride?"

The swollen face of Master Cray nodded, his usual humor lost.

"Anything to get out of here," he mumbled, spitting blood from his broken nose and lips.

Ember helped him to his feet and onto Sasha's horse. She then mounted the pony she had retrieved from the stables and rode for the far gates and the war.

She rode to Joferian.

THE BATTLE AT THE rear gate of Saracen raged on, bolstered on both sides by reinforcements. Joferian watched as hundreds of Norsemen joined their effort from afar, flooding the opened gates and pouring into Saracen. He didn't know how the fight elsewhere fared but if Argantyr dispatched help, it must have been going well.

And just in time, no less.

The Sentinel reinforcements arrived. A unit of cavalrymen scattered in front of him, chasing the plundering barbarians as they started to ransack the town. Two other units on foot marched his way, but Argantyr's men, yet to taste blood and led by Strunk, charged into combat. Joferian found a respite to breathe.

He looked around for a free horse and found one just outside the gates. As he mounted his new steed, he looked to the bodies strewn on the ground. Many of his men were mingled amongst the dead Sentinels. He couldn't help but notice their faces. The proud Sentinels of Saracen, heralded across the realm, had been gutted, replaced by children not much younger than Joferian himself. Yet he felt so much older.

He fought the urge to mourn them. He didn't travel here to kill untrained teenagers, but the choice was not his. If he were to win this battle, he may be heralded for his bravery and skill. But in truth, he would have sacked an unsuspecting town of merchants in Vallance and then destroyed the town of Saracen. A Saracen guarded by boys in Sentinel armor, sent to die by greedy merchants that cared not for them, but for gold.

Joferian forced the images from his mind's eye. Thoughts of Ember raced back to him. She was here somewhere. He had to rescue her. He recalled the thanes in Vallance saying she was to be forced into wedlock to Sasha Scarlett as they pled for their lives. Ember's strawberry blond locks and her emerald eyes entered his mind's eye. He had to stop this at all costs, including his own life.

He guided the horse through the mangled bodies and broken gates, into the clear. He spurred it on, riding blindly, with no regard for his own safety, looking for the Guild of the Copper Wing.

As he rode, he found many of the streets empty, or the people of Saracen hustling away from his charging horse, offering no resistance. In the far distance, he saw smoke rising from the harbor and smiled to himself. Argantyr's forces had engaged. That fight was on two fronts. The battle was his to win.

As his steed rambled through the streets, the black smoke of a nearby fire shrouded his vision, but he pressed forward through it. As he emerged on the other side, two horses galloped toward him. Instinctively, he lowered his head and leaned forward in the saddle, making himself small behind his slate iron shield. He raised his sword and charged.

As he closed the distance, he couldn't help but notice one rider was already bloody and slumping in his saddle, while the other rode a pony. He reared back on the horse to stop yards from them and pointed at the pair with the tip of his sword. Through the blood and soot, his eyes met with the sullied rider. A small woman in a blood-stained wedding gown peered back at him.

"Joferian?" her gentle voice called to him.

He lifted his visor to get a better look and lowered his sword.

"Ember!" he cried out.

They dismounted and ran into each other's arms.

She dropped a bloody sword and threw her arms around his neck.

He lifted her from the ground with one arm and tore his helmet off with the other.

They kissed deeply and passionately, holding each other tight.

"I came to rescue you," he said, with tears of love and joy in his eyes.

"She didn't need you for that," the bloodied man riding next to her said.

Joferian glanced away from Ember to find Master Zendel Cray slouched in his saddle, covered in wounds and blood.

"Cray!" he cried. "You've made it."

"If you say so," Cray argued. "It doesn't feel as though I have."

"Come, let's leave the main streets," Joferian implored. "We must get the two of you to safety. What of Scarlett?"

"I killed her," Ember choked. "Joferian, I didn't—"

"None of us do," he said, calming her. "You are free now."

He pulled her into another hug for reassurance and held her head in his hands and kissed her forehead.

Then the low sob of a mournful horn sounded, rising above the city from the front gates.

Ember jumped into his embrace. “What is that?”

It had worked. Everything came together. He’d done it. The stone in his chest that was his heart lightened. He didn’t grin but felt the sensation all the same.

“It is the sound of surrender,” Joferian said.

CHAPTER THIRTY

"With the raven on her pommel and the sharpness of her blade, we remember her."
—Princess Addilyn Elspeth of the Vermilion Nation

ADDILYN STARED AT THE BODY of her fallen champion on the shore of the Gossamer River. The moment she'd found Ritter, they had rushed to the water in search of incoming vessels.

Now, accompanied by Ritter, Hertzog, and Vischer and standing over her champion, Addilyn couldn't help but blame herself for not being there for Jessamy as she'd faced down the infamous Black Rose.

The assassin's calling card lay clutched in Jessamy's rigid fingers, her friend's eyes still open and vacant.

"Why was she alone?" she managed to choke out before falling to her knees on the cold ground.

"An excellent question," Vischer said through gritted teeth.

Addilyn barely heard him as her vision blurred, and her body wracked with sobs. Her calm demeanor had reached its breaking point. The Vermilion Wing's arrival and their pressure along with the coronelle's weighed on her delicate condition. The death of her father and now Jessamy, both lost to the same assassin.

Unable to bear looking too long at Jessamy's face and the pain of seeing her unmoving, Addilyn focused on her hands. She removed the rose from her clenched fingers, casting it into the firth, and brought her hands together on her chest, sliding the pommel of her raven sword between them.

After all, that's where it belonged.

Addilyn thought of those hands—hands that held her after

her father's death and defended her against countless adversaries. And today would be the last time she would hold them.

A hand brushed across her back and Addilyn saw Ritter's boots and trousers in her periphery as he came around to stand next to her. He lowered to one knee beside her, placing a comforting hand on her shoulder. She kept her gaze on Jessamy's hands, memorizing the scars there.

Without warning, Ritter was pulled from her, and Addilyn heard Vischer's voice from behind her, speaking hard and clipped.

"Sir Ritter, this is not your place. You and the Longmarchers must find the assassin who committed this wrongdoing and settle this once and for all."

"We have both lost a companion today," Ritter managed in a solemn tone.

"If this castle were better secured, and you had done your duty, perhaps Jessamy would still be with us," Vischer continued with little regard to Ritter's sentiments. "Who's to say this Bone elf isn't stalking the halls of the Bridge?"

On his feet once more, Vischer spun on Ritter, almost poking him in the chest. "You and your Longmarchers must find this assassin before he makes another move. For all we know, he already has."

Addilyn continued holding her vigil, feeling numb to everything around her. "She had to have known it was a trap," she murmured through sobs, though there was no way she would ever know for sure.

Ritter took a step back, and Addilyn, registered him turning to her. She felt removed from the chaos around her. As if the men were yelling in a different room. Detached, she managed to close her friend's eyes before her own sight blurred once more with tears.

"Castle Valkeneer is under the command of the Valkeneers, good knight." Hertzog's tone was polite but stern. "If it pleases you, I will give the orders in my own home."

Vischer didn't let up. "There's an assassin among us, my lord, and it is your duty and the rest of your Longmarchers to find them." He cast a withering look at Ritter. "Your son and his men have failed. Jessamy's death—"

"That's enough!" Hertzog moved toward Vischer, but Ritter held him back.

"Father, stop," Ritter said. "He's correct."

Addilyn's ears perked up at the words, but she couldn't draw her eyes away from Jessamy's broken body.

"No, Son. He's not."

"I failed to kill the assassin before this happened," Ritter lamented. "I failed to kill him at the Battle of Rillifane's Meander. Then, at Castle Thronehelm, and again in the streets of Abacus as he and his imp evaded me. This is my fault."

Addilyn met Ritter's eyes then. He was being too hard on himself. He'd saved her in Thronehelm and Abacus, risking his life to keep her safe. Her heart twisted. She turned to the men behind her. When she looked at Ritter, she saw he was looking directly in her eyes. She saw sorrow there—a different kind of sorrow than she felt at losing Jessamy, but sorrow nonetheless. Sorrow, and the guilt of one who survives.

Before Addilyn could say anything, Ritter spoke again. "Princess Addilyn, I promise I will make this right. I will put an end to the Black Rose. Excuse me." He gave a quick bow, ordering Storm to take to the skies. Then he trudged off, returning to the Bridge with Hertzog following him.

Addilyn watched Ritter go, wishing she'd spoken up while he was still here. She stood to follow him, but Vischer took her hand.

"Are you well, my Princess? Is there anything I can get for you?"

Addilyn took her hand from his. "There is nothing I need from you, sir, other than to perform your duty to the coronelle."

Vischer appeared to ignore her indignation or be entirely oblivious to it. "The trollborn surprised me," he replied. "I didn't think he'd admit fault. He *is* to blame, Princess Addilyn. Surely, you must know that."

Addilyn rounded on him. "How dare you? That man has saved me several times on our journey." She made sure to emphasize that Ritter was a man, the same as Vischer. "I'd be dead if it weren't for him." Her cheeks burned with rage as Vischer stared at her.

When he spoke again, it was steady and low. "Perhaps you should have returned to Eldwal instead of chasing the illusive tetrine. If it even ever existed. You'd be much safer there. The Vermilion defenses are much mightier."

"The tetrine *does* exist, and that '*trollborn*,' as you call him, is worth a hundred of you," Addilyn barked. She may have gone too far, but she didn't regret her words.

Not wanting to waste any more time on Vischer, she turned away from him and back to Jessamy. "If you're quite finished, I'd like to mourn my dead friend."

Vischer stood there a moment longer, but Addilyn didn't address him any further. Whatever he thought of her outburst, he kept it to himself as he left her side.

Addilyn clasped her hands tight in front of her and closed her eyes, repeating Eiyn's words for her father for Jessamy now.

"Innuan serenitus trevitae
Melexis, joquato veresist
Opange, Ssolantress, Medige"

Her mind flicked back to the day she'd blasphemed against

Melexis in Jessamy's presence. She'd felt so comfortable around Jessamy since the moment they'd met. She pushed the memory aside and continued with her prayer.

Threnody, the Ancient of Death,
it is to you whom I lament.
To the Hall of Ancients with my friend,
I watch your dark ascent.
Turn then, most feared visitor,
from this veil of tears.
Where she, my friend, shall rest,
and forever hold no fears.

If any were worthy of joining the Hall of the Ancients, it was Jessamy.

As Addilyn dried her tears, she vowed to put an end to the Black Rose herself, but if the assassin wanted her, he'd have to come and get her. And she wouldn't make it easy for him.

CHAPTER THIRTY-ONE

"Without heroes, we shall never learn how far we can go."
—Athabasica the Poet

AFTER SEVERAL DAYS OF downhill hiking, Jins, Makai, and Yenroar arrived back at the Forge to hushed whispers and stunned glances in Yen's direction.

Tancred stopped the three on their way to the throne room. "Yenroar Silentall, you old codger!"

The two twergs shared an embrace and a chuckle as Jins and Makai waited for the two elder twergs to catch up.

"I didn't think you'd ever leave that ol' mountain of yours," Tancred admitted.

"What can I say," Yen replied, "Solveig Jins won't take no for an answer."

"Don't I know it," Tancred laughed, winking at Jins before turning back to Yen. "You heard about the runes she found then, eh? What do you think?"

Yen hesitated. "I am not sure we should investigate any further, but if the *krol* orders me, I will oblige."

Jins was taken aback at Yen's words. That was not what she had expected Yen to say. Just how reluctant was he, and what if the *krol* said no?

A few moments later, the group of four twergs stood under the throne as twergs from both clans gathered and milled about around them. Soon the hall was just as full, if not more so, than a few days prior. The inhabitants of the Forge whispered amongst themselves, shocked to see Yenroar Silentall after so long. Most had thought him dead.

Solveig Jins caught herself searching for any sign of discomfort from Yen at the crowd's scrutiny, but he didn't display any. He stood as tall as his old bones allowed him. She wanted to ask him how it felt to be back and around so many people, but she didn't have the chance.

The *krol*'s herald sounded the royal cornet, and a hush fell over the crowd.

"*Krol*... Yrsa... Dagny!" the herald cried.

Once more, each twerg in the crowd dropped to one knee as the *krol* made her way to address her people. Her face stayed impassive as she gazed out at the crowd and the returning face. When she saw Jins, she stopped.

"Solveig Jins, I see you've found your way back to us. And with company. Still looking to translate the writings?" she asked.

Jins nodded. "Yes, My Krol. I still believe we should."

Yrsa changed the subject as her gaze roamed to Yen. "Welcome back to the Forge, Yenroar Silentall."

"My Krol." Yen bowed his head. "I did not think I would have this honor again, but Solveig Jins here can be very convincing."

The *krol*'s eyes twinkled with amusement. "Yes, it is the first thing I learned about her. Her... stubbornness."

A few people scoffed at her and chuckled, and Jins bit her tongue. She chose her next words with great care. "My Krol, First Keeper Makai and I have succeeded in finding—and bringing home—our Magus, Yenroar Silentall. He has agreed to interpret the runes we've discovered in the caves below."

At her bold words, the crowd of hundreds broke into a subdued chatter, and Jins picked out a few words thrown her way.

"Insolent."

"Disrespectful."

"...half-human should hold her tongue..."

Jins took it all in stride. She'd heard it all before, if not worse.

Yrsa held up a hand, and the crowd fell silent once more. Jins's awe of the *krol*'s command for respect dissipated into preparation for disappointment. She held her breath.

"You continue to impress me, Jins. Convincing Yen here to return to us is no doubt only the start of your skills. And your persuasiveness must aid you in your merchant life."

Jins didn't allow her hopes to rise as the *krol* continued, "But as was said before, that particular mine is extremely dangerous. I don't see a way to—"

"If I may, My Krol," Yen interrupted.

Yrsa nodded, showing a deep respect for her wise Magus.

"I know a few spells that may help us ensure our safety," Yen continued. "Small enchantments that can hold back rock. As long as our group is kept small, I do not see a problem with investigating the mine."

Yrsa Dagny was silent a few moments, and the crowd waited on bated breath below her platform as she considered Yen's proposition.

"Very well. I shall escort you to the runes."

Jins released her captured breath as Tancred patted her on the back. She bowed her head to the *krol*, and a wave of pride and unexpected pressure washed over her.

The *krol* was watching her.

To the crowd's dismay, Yrsa announced that apart from Solveig's group and the *krol*'s personal attendant, no one else would be permitted to accompany them to the runes.

As her attendant cleared the way, the *krol* descended the platform and approached Jins.

Jins kept her head bowed as her *krol* approached with a clattering of armor, but she could tell Yrsa was just as intimidating on level ground as on her dais.

The *krol*'s boots stopped at the edge of Jins eyesight. "No need for that, Jins," the *krol* rasped. "You'll need a full range of vision if you are to brave uncharted mines."

Jins dragged her eyes up to meet Yrsa's deep brown eyes, unmarked with wrinkles. Her expression was one Jins expected—a warrior's fierceness that emulated her strict personality. But behind that, Jins detected a hint of warmth and kindness. And just the faintest bit of amusement as she tilted her head at her subject.

"That's better, isn't it?" the *krol* said.

Jins nodded, fighting the urge to bow her head once more.

It felt wrong to look straight into the *krol*'s eyes, but Jins reminded herself that she'd been given permission. She let her eyes take in Yrsa's features as she was unsure when she'd have another opportunity. The *krol*'s full, braided and beaded red beard hung at an impressive length. Her shining hair was twisted into one long braid and rested on her breastplate while the mane on her brown tail was tied taught in short increments, wrapped in a polished bone.

The *krol* turned to the elder twerg. "Magus, I must thank you once again for coming."

Yen placed a hand on his heart. "It is an honor, my *krol*."

The pleasantries out of the way, the *krol* turned to Jins. "Lead the way."

Jins did her best to ignore the constant eyes on her as she turned from the throne room and headed in the direction of the pocket cave.

The *krol*'s remarks about her had been an honor, but she suspected a few in the crowd did not agree with their leader. Their whispers were indecipherable, and, she admitted, could be about Yrsa herself. It would be arrogant to think she factored into the crowd's gossip.

They reached the first corridor, and the dim light was a

welcome change to the openness of the throne room. Yen fell into step with Jins, his bald head bobbing.

After a while, Jins broke the silence. "May I ask you something?"

"Another something than you already have?" Yen replied with a cheeky smile.

"Back in your cave, you said the markings should never be read aloud. What did you mean?"

"There is power in words. The wrong word at the wrong moment could…" He shook his head. "It's best I do not elaborate."

"But how will you translate the runes for us?"

"I said nothing of translating them. I shall read what I can for you, but it may not be much. I can't promise I will be able to read them in their entirety. And a part of me does want to seal the place back up so no one can reach it again."

Jins's eyebrows raised, but she said nothing as she allowed the Magus's words to sink in. Would retrieving Yenroar and convincing the *krol* be for nothing?

They journeyed on in silence, rounding numerous bends and encountering ever-narrowing tunnels. Solveig recalled her previous visit to the cave and knew they must be nearing their destination.

"I suppose—"

Yen placed a hand on Jins's arm, stopping her. Before she could ask what was wrong, she made the discovery.

The rumbling began, imperceptible at first, but as the group listened, it grew in volume until it reached their vein. The flames of the mounted torches flickered as dust and debris shook loose from the cavern's ceiling. The five braced themselves against the walls.

"It's as if the mountain is warning us," Makai braved.

"No cave-in," Dagny murmured. "But that doesn't mean we're safe. Your spell, Magus?"

Yen stepped to the front of the group and began to speak in the conjurer's tongue. "*Verhindern hohle schliessen,*" he intoned, and a sweltering vibration rose from the cavern floor.

The waves of magic pulsated around them, their ripples bouncing from Jins's chest. She blinked and held against the wall tight as the effect of the spell grew. As fast as it had come, the powers receded, and Yen dropped his arms to his side and took a deep breath.

"The mountain will hold for a time," Yen assured, "but I suggest we make haste. My powers are unpracticed."

For the next several minutes, they placed each foot carefully in front of them. Jins half-expected the rumbling to return and the ceiling to fall on them. But it held, just as Yen had promised.

With a few final steps, the group reached the mouth of the pocket cave, and they huddled around to make a plan.

"My Krol, perhaps you should stay here where it is safer," Yrsa's attendant pleaded in his Battleforge brogue. "We do not know the dangers therein."

"He makes an excellent point, My Krol," Makai agreed. "We should keep you—"

The *krol* blew out a breath of frustration and without further debate, she pushed past the four and strode ahead, her metal armor clanking as she did.

The mysterious etchings weren't that far from the makeshift doorway, but the area felt doubly unstable to Jins. And colder than she remembered. Even more so when they approached the markings.

Yrsa stopped a few feet inside the cave and let Jins guide her and Yen to the wall in question. Jins couldn't help noticing his sure-footedness the whole way. His years alone on the mountain had no doubt aided him.

Yen bent to get a closer look at the runes, his unkempt eyebrows furrowing in concentration. The dull blue glow of the magical markings remained and flared as the Magus approached.

"Is that an invitation or a warning?" Makai asked.

"A reaction to our proximity," Yen explained. "The markings are daring to be read."

Jins snuck closer and leaned over the Magus's shoulder to get a better view.

"Well, Magus?" Dagny asked. "Can you decipher the scrawl?"

"There is much to study. The magic words are both cryptic and ancient. Perhaps from a time before the Ancients departed for the Hall of the Ancients."

"Can you read them?"

"The words are not twergish, but, as I feared from the charcoal tracing, of an ancient dialect. Perhaps Vermilion."

"Vermilion?" Makai choked at the thought "Deep in a twerg cavern? Are you sure?"

"Aye, I am." Yen squinted, leaning closer. "There are two names here. The first is Laurentia."

Jins perked up at the name. "The Ancient of Dragons?" She turned to the others waiting just outside and still in view.

Yrsa stroked her beard, pondering.

Yen nodded, his eyes never leaving the runes. "And the second…" He brushed dust from the runes. "Corpsus."

His words bounced off the walls of the cavern, creating a ghostly echo.

"ARE YOU READY?"

Dromofangare thrummed in the emerald hale of Mortus's

catoptromancy. The lich sensed Johonnum at his side, but he concentrated on the throes of his invocation, alighting the mirror.

"I am." Johonnum moved to within inches of the reflective face, bathed in green from the ensorcelled surface.

"Then enter," Mortus motioned with one hand, the other holding the spell in place.

Fearless, the high watcher stepped into the sparkling rays and disappeared.

Mortus set himself on holding the spell long enough for himself to pass. The image of a darkened cavern presented itself again on the face of Dromofangare, and this time Mortus noticed Johonnum on the other side of the spell, his sword drawn.

It was time for years of planning, years of detailed articulation to culminate. It was time for Mortus. Victory was so close; the lich Keeper could sense it.

With a final thought he floated ahead, entering the grip of the mirror's power. The rush of his spell engulfed him, lifting him from one dimension to the next. The now familiar push from Dromofangare launched him forward, faster than it ever had.

Does it too sense victory was nigh?

As the sensation of weightless flight lifted, Mortus felt the presence of the mystical travel end and he stepped into the cave.

He couldn't feel the cold of the depths of the Rawcliffe Forge's subterrane any longer. Nor could he taste the dust of the twergish mines in his mouth and nose. His dead flesh no longer registered such sensations.

But he noticed the immediate effects their environment had on Johonnum. The high watcher covered his mouth and nose with the drapes of his robes and coughed. The living, unless used to the confines and claustrophobic conditions of the subterrane, reacted poorly to it, and Johonnum was no exception.

"You shall soon breathe the fresh air again," Mortus assured, "but first we must do what we came here to do. Now, ready your magics."

Johonnum coughed again and nodded in acquiescence.

Dromofangare had delivered them deep into the depths of the twergish settlement. The cavernous chamber of roughhewn walls reflected the light from Mortus's eyes, providing the dimmest of illumination for Johonnum to see.

"Come." Mortus moved toward a mined corridor in the far corner of the cave. "I feel the energy we seek. Be prepared to face resistance. I am sure the twergs will be standing guard."

Johonnum gripped his sword, and raised his other hand, readying a spell. The pair moved into the entranceway, where twergish jacks and timbers held the portal open.

Johonnum wiped his nose on his cassock and rubbed his eyes. "Master, may I cast a spell so that I may see better?"

"Nay," the lich replied. "I don't want to alert the twergs, who see just as well in the dark as they do in the light. We will need the darkness, Johonnum, to find the grave. It is warded with an evoker's glyph. We must be careful."

The two continued through the rugged cavern passageway for several minutes more, hunched in the narrow and low-cut walls of the mine. They climbed over and around loose rock piles, the green fire from his eyes lighting a space only a few steps ahead. But it was enough for them to both manage. Soon the pair entered a storage area, the dim light from an ensconced lantern revealing the way. The mine opened into a well worked and buttressed area replete with small benches, empty mine carts, and a larder. And as Mortus expected, they weren't alone. Voices chattered in the twergish tongue ahead, not far from them.

Mortus raised his skeletal hand to stop Johonnum, his osseus neck crepitating to allow him a better view. Ahead, his otherworldly eyes noticed an accidental break in the cavern wall, a near collapse revealing a hidden chamber. Twergish ramblings, incomprehensible to him, chattered on from inside.

"Guards at the grave?" Johonnum whispered, moving closer but staying hidden in the shadows.

"There," Mortus pointed, his boney finger indicating the hole in the wall. The two approached the entrance, peering into the pocket cave.

A small group of twergs stood inside in total darkness, their backs turned and concentrating on a far wall. Mortus leaned in, sensing a magical hale. The twergs in front took turns studying the wall, and Mortus notice a bluish glow scrawled along its flat surface.

"Laurentia," said one of them, then came a twergish scrabble he didn't recognize between the two aged men. Behind them stood another, one wearing a circlet on her head, outfitted in custom armor and carrying weapons that could only be made in the Forge. The last figure, the largest of the bunch, looked different. She didn't have a beard, carried no weapons and her tail was much shorter and less pronounced than the others. She looked out of place.

"Corpsus," the most venerable of the group read aloud, then turned a concerned look to the others.

The grave!

Mortus, bereft of many emotions in his new form, couldn't help but feel a sense of happiness and relief. The twergs had done the hard work and already uncovered the Great Mother. If he could, he'd laugh at the irony of it all. They'd dug their own graves by revealing hers, not knowing what they'd done.

Seeing their adversaries, Johonnum made a move to engage them, but Mortus stopped him.

"They are mine."

Jins stood at the back of the group, watching Keeper Makai and the Magus Yenroar share worried glances, unsure of the meaning of the words they'd found. She felt their unspoken emotions and the atmosphere in the pocket cave loomed heavier.

Her lips parted but before she could ask, a strange voice rose from behind her, one that sounded as if two talked as one. "Corpsus," the voice repeated.

Jins spun and gasped, surprised by the Warminsterian tongue reaching her ears. The others turned, the *krol*'s hand reaching for her battle axe strapped to her back.

Jins covered her mouth and cried out at the visage of the creature standing on the other side of the cave entrance. She looked upon a living skeleton, its tattered robes hanging from its corpse, its skull alit in a green fire rising behind its dead eyes.

The skeletal figure tapped its dark staff on the ground and muttered words she didn't understand.

The *krol* tried to move but before any could react the staff flashed a brilliant white light, blinding her, and perhaps the others.

Jins grabbed at her face and cried out, panic seizing her. She blinked over and over, rubbing at her eyes, but her sight was gone—just gone. No shadows, no distant shapes, no blurry figures. Nothing.

She fell to her knees, a reflexive moan escaping from her. Her remaining senses heightened momentarily, desperate to understand what was happening. She heard the *krol* at her side sound off in a war cry and felt the breeze of someone running by her. Then a loud bang rang in her ears, metal against metal, followed by a body landing on her. The weight of the *krol* slammed into her, knocking her prone, and pinning her under the armored corpse on the cavern floor.

She squirmed and moaned, trying to free herself, but it was helpless. Warm blood flowed from the motionless *krol*, draining onto Jins's face, inspiring one last push to lift her.

The rushing of feet echoed all around her and she swore she heard Makai's voice mumble something before she felt the sting of a sword cutting into her skin. The force came from above and the *krol*'s armor sounded once more, a blade piercing through the metal, cutting through Yrsa Dagny and finally slicing into Jins. The blade cut deep, perhaps puncturing all the way through her and hitting the stone floor at her back. The bite stung her in the shoulder, and she felt her arm go numb, hurting even more as the blade was withdrawn.

The *krol* groaned one last time and fell limp, the entirety of her weight pressing Jins flat.

"Yen, help!" she heard Makai beg, followed by a *thwack* and the sound of bones snapping.

The First Keeper mumbled in agony and a second whack quieted the noise.

Jins froze. The pain in her shoulder seared through her, but the dead *krol* atop her prevented any escape. Even trying to lift the *krol* caused more pain. She exhaled, her mind still whirling, lost in the chaos of the moment.

Something shuffled closer, and a coldness settled in around her. She fought to remain still, hoping they'd think her dead. But somewhere in her distant mind, she began to accept the inevitability of the end. Blind and bleeding, there was no escape.

"Corpsus," the spectral voice sounded, almost pleased to utter the name. "Laurentia."

"Great Keeper," a second human voice speaking Warminsterian came from somewhere near her in the darkness, "shall I prepare for the ceremony?"

Great Keeper? Her mind raced in confusion. *Is that what she'd heard?*

"Yes," the strange voice replied. "Join me here in reciting the sacramental prayers to Threnody."

Jins knew better than to move. They must've believed her to be dead. Even if she could, fear and her wound may have prevented it. Then the creature's voices were joined by the voice of the other man in unison, and the voice of Yenroar Silentall.

Yen!

The rote verses spilled from the trio.

Threnody, Ancient of Death, I beseech thee.
Let the blood of your sons empower me.
In the name of your first born, Koss, the Ancient of War,
I offer you a vial of blood harvested in battle, from an enemy slain.
In the name of your second son, Zuzual, the Ancient of Pestilence,
I offer you a vial of blood, gathered from the ruptured bowels of a frothing cow, fraught with disease.
In the name of your third son, Vraest, the Ancient of Famine,
I offer you a vial of blood, taken from a starving man as he drew his last breath.
And in the name of your fourth and final son, Requius, the Harvester of Sorrow,
I offer you a vial of blood, taken in the name of thine self.

Mother of the Four Deaths, She of the Dark Wing and Sudden Doom,
Please accept my offerings.
And in return I ask that you open this grave and bring forth the Great Mother.
Return her from her slumber in the Hall of the Ancients,
In your name, I ask only this in return.

Jins lay still. She could hear the shuffling of feet next to her but in her blindness couldn't see what the prayer had done. Then the cave grumbled, a noise she was all too familiar with but one she'd never been close enough to experiencing—a cave-in.

One pebble, then a second struck her face, and the rumbling grew, and the room began to shake. Dagny's body slipped a bit, and Jins felt her weight fall to one side. She could hear the voices of the three men in full throated prayer and knew this was her time to make a move. She squirmed until the armored *krol* dropped from atop her, the sound lost in their raised appeals and buried underneath the creaking of the cavern's walls.

She crawled on her belly, remembering the direction of the entrance, pulling with desperation and hope until she found the mouth of the cave's entrance. With the incantations of the figures behind her, she heaved herself out of the pocket cave and into the broken corridor.

She pulled herself over broken rocks, feeling the cuts and scrapes slicing at her body as she made her way. The corridor shook and she heard the cracking of the timbers holding the hall around her. A jack behind her snapped, it's metal popping in her ears. Time was short, she had to run.

Leaning against the side of the cave she struggled, her eyes blind and her body wounded and bloody. One painful step after the next, she hurried, hoping to gain distance from the skeletal creature and its dark intentions.

Her twergish senses piqued. A shuddering crack shook the hall and she slipped to her knees. The quaking continued to her side, then the other, and her instincts told her that it was too late. She heard the loosening of boulders overhead giving way and the painful impact of the falling rocks slamming into her, knocking her prone. A darkness seized her, and she spun away, her last thoughts of Tancred Abeline telling her not to let her human curiosity get the best of her.

CHAPTER THIRTY-TWO

"The most important terrain to protect on the battlefield lies within one's mind."
—Warminster, the Mage

BIT MONTGOMERY'S FACE, FORMING a crenelated rim of ice on his visor. He rode next to his father ahead of the combined armies of Warminster and Rijkstag. Their horses cut through the wet, fallen snow from that morning. It was just enough to whiten the ground and slow the war machines; a reminder that the Season of the Bountiful Harvest had passed, and the Season of Long Nights descended.

Atorm, Freya, and Einar rode at his side alongside an army of ten thousand flying banners from Thronehelm, Queen's Chapel, Hunter's Manor, Halifax, and Thunder Cove. The standards of the Norsemen, their vivid colors aching to be tainted red in blood, intermingled with the others. The two armies, ravished for their taste of violence, finally found each other on the field of battle.

They arrived at the Falkenwraths, a series of dangerous peaks on the south face of the Dragon's Breath Mountains, their unpredictable, rugged and scree slopes a danger to all that passed. It was as the runecaster, Einar, had foretold. The twin peaks rose from the landscape and were the last stretch of the mountain chain between Foghaven Vale and Thronehelm. Technically, the Peaks were in the far stretches of Queen's Chapel, or so the historians would say after today.

It was near dawn, and Montgomery watched the breath of twenty thousand soldiers on different peaks escape into the winter wind. In the distance, the combined banners of Foghaven Vale, Gloucester, Saracen, and Deadwaters Fork fluttered in the distance, alongside the scattered banners of the tribes of two thousand trollborn warriors from the Killean Desolates and the Dragon's Breath Mountains. The two armies stared at one another in near silence, anticipating what was to come.

Then the norsemen began to rhythmically beat on their war drums. Swords and spears pounded on shields and almost in unison they started to sing their battle hymn.

Ulthgar the Forger, fallen heroes embrace me.
Koss, our Ancient, a battle awaits thee.
We pledge thee our swords and swig our last ale.
We offer thee blood, so that we may prevail.
Valkyries fly, come carry us home.
To the Halls of the Ancients, where we shall forever roam.
The Horn of Hammerstead, calls us to the fore.
Where our tale shall be sung, forevermore.
The fury of war, the shattering of shields.
Glory awaits us, in the fighting fields.

Between them, a valley shaped like a bowl between the two peaks sprawled in the distance. The rocky valley would soon be home to thousands of dead soldiers and a new name, the site of the Battle of the Falkenwraths.

The first to ride out, under a banner of parlay, was King Dragich Von Lormarck.

Godwin urged his horse on, and he, alongside of Montgomery, Baroness Maeglen, and General Blacwin strode with him. Atorm, Freya, Einar, Faxon the Red, and Magnus Bearslayer followed a few horse lengths behind.

As they drew nearer, Monty recognized many of Von Lormarck's retinue: Donnar and Emmerich, Thessica Camber, Baron Kellan Thessaly. His two sons, Darrick and

Jareth, flanked him. He guessed at the presence of Field Marshal Cherica Lambert by the silver trident on her shield and Commandant Dirdrenum Tullamore at the head of five thousand Saracen mercenaries. Dirdrenum he'd expected, but Lambert was a wildcard neither he nor his father was aware of. The Tritons of the Fork were skilled cavalry and would present a problem, even for the Thronehelm horsemen.

Lastly, a half-giant trollborn general, not known to him, that must have been in command of Von Lormarck's henchmen, strode into view. By a short count, he estimated they were outnumbered two to one.

The two sides gathered within yards of one another at the base of the bowl. For a tense few moments, they sized each other up. They created a circle of flags and banners, each representing a different province, city, or barony but one: the purple and golden flag of Warminster, the hopeful standard brought by Prince Montgomery, representing them all.

Von Lormarck broke the anxious silence. "I have been waiting my entire life for this moment. I've envisioned this meeting since I was a child. A changing of the guard has finally come to Warminster."

Godwin said nothing, only stared at his opponent coldly, vengeance in his eyes.

"I am glad to see that you chose to fight instead of hiding behind your high walls," Von Lormarck continued. "Fighting is much more honorable than starvation, don't you think?"

Godwin pointed to his army on the peak behind him. "I have no need for a castle. The shields of my people are my walls."

Von Lormarck circled about, taking a few steps closer to Godwin. He paused and looked to the opposing army.

"I have but one request in this parlay," Von Lormarck went

on, "one that will save thousands of lives on this battlefield today. We fight—king to king—and the winner ascends to the restored throne."

"You are no king," Godwin muttered in disgust. "You are a usurper. But I accept your challenge, for the sake of the families of the warriors here today. I will not allow you to steal this kingdom like the robber baron you are."

Montgomery's eyes shifted to his father. Von Lormarck was ten years his younger, and recently battle-tested in his war against the twergs. He questioned his father's judgement.

"Then we have terms," Von Lormarck replied, with an air of surprise in his voice. He turned to Thessaly and nodded.

Baron Thessaly led the rest of the Von Lormarck contingent back to their army. They removed their banners and began the short retreat to their lines with the news.

"Father, are you sure?" Montgomery whispered to Godwin.

Godwin grabbed the back of Montgomery's neck and held his forehead to his.

"I must," he replied. "One day, as king, you will understand."

Montgomery turned, taking one last look in his father's eyes and commanded their group to return to their peak. He prayed that day was not upon him.

THE TWO MEN MARKED their personal battlefield with their respective flags and Godwin drew his sword and gripped his shield. Von Lormarck unsheathed his dual swords. Both men slowly danced around, taking the measure of one another.

"Before we begin," Von Lormarck said, "I need you to know that I was responsible for all of this. The assassins at the masquerade, the bandits, the sea battle that claimed your son, and the cryptid that ate your wife… painfully… from inside her skin."

Godwin fought to sustain his rage. He didn't want his boiling anger to unbalance him, but he had already concluded Von Lormarck was responsible for every plot. His admission was just confirmation.

Godwin was the first to move. His sword dived in from low guard, catching Von Lormarck by surprise, but the battle-tested baron blocked the lunge and struck high with his other blade. Godwin easily blocked it away with his shield.

Von Lormarck's strength bent the top of the shield on the first swing, but Godwin knew he could absorb the hits.

With a grunt, Godwin's pent-up anger, sorrow, and thoughts of revenge were unleashed, and the nobles fought in a flurry of violence, resounding in deafening blows and blocks as metal met metal.

Then, it ended in a frustrating stalemate.

Silence descended upon the valley again as both men took a short respite to riposte. The tension from above pressed down on Godwin and he fought to keep his attention on his foe.

The next round of attacks were led by Von Lormarck, the aggressive warrior coming in, both blades high. Godwin raised his shield high enough to block part of the double maneuver while spinning to one side, using his sword to cross blades, parrying the second.

As Von Lormarck reset, Godwin punched out with his hilt, landing a glancing blow to the usurper's helm, knocking his visor askew. Von Lormarck stepped back and tossed his broken helmet into the snow and spit blood from a missing tooth.

"I will take you one tooth at a time if I must," Godwin threatened. For the first time in the battle, his mind allowed the sounds of the two armies to invade his senses. At first, it sounded like equal sides of a gladiatorum, and he tried to put the cries for and against him out of his mind.

Von Lormarck curled his nose in a grimace and grunted, launching a new round of attacks. His swords came down one after another in rhythmic succession, pounding away at Godwin's shield and sword. The great king stepped back, returning shield block to sword block, until the baron tired and broke off his attack again.

Godwin barely breathed heavily but could see the rapid puffs of steam rising from the baron's mouth and nose.

That's it, he thought. *Tire yourself out and let us level the playing field.*

The baron's armor was well made, but still encumbering, and all those powerful, wild swings were predictable.

"I could have had you killed in bed." Von Lormarck wiped the blood from his mouth, "but I needed to defeat you on the field of battle, cousin. So that all could see. So Warminster would know who their real king is. You are but the embers of a man you once were."

This time, it was Godwin's turn to lead. He shot in, feinting low as he had done on his first attack. But as the baron lowered his left blade to block, Godwin shot in under his defense and raised the flat of his battered shield into Von Lormarck's face, sending him spinning.

Godwin pressed on through the distant hissing and oohing of the crowd. Somewhere, the Viking drums began to beat again, raising his spirits. Perhaps their Ancients could lift him in this battle.

Von Lormarck tried to recover by waving his free sword up and away, putting distance between the two, but Godwin would have none of it. The sound of steel slapping into the baron's face was the break he had been waiting for.

Blood ran from the baron's hairline into his eyes. Godwin hoped the shield concussed him but the baron, to his credit, defended with perfect form. Godwin's swing from the high guard forced the baron to drop to both knees, and he caught the king's sword in the cross of both of his.

Sparks flew from the connection of the blades and Godwin used the opportunity to charge in with his shield again. But the baron dropped a sword and spun on his knees in the snow, grabbing the edge of his shield and pulling him clumsily around. Godwin felt the strap of his shield break and the slap of a blade connect with the back of his breastplate.

A near miss, he thought. If the baron had lunged instead of swinging down, it may have pierced the metal. Instead, it was a warning that would leave a nasty welt.

Their second engagement ended in another stalemate, sending the crowd whooping into more cheers. To Godwin, it felt as if their personal battle was being lived vicariously by thirty thousand soldiers at once.

Von Lormarck circled, labored in his breathing now, while Godwin cast his broken shield aside. Both men were down to one sword.

"Your line ends here," Von Lormarck spit. "In your death, and your son's. He will never leave this battlefield alive."

Godwin reared up and weighed in, taking the fight to Von Lormarck. The king rushed him, the sound of steel clanging in a storm of swings.

But both men broke away in another draw, again to the cheers and jeers of the two opposing sides.

Then Von Lormarck grunted and charged. Godwin did not expect the move, and the baron managed to wrap his arms around the king, tackling him into the snow. They both tumbled, one over the other, and slid down the hill while they still battled.

Godwin's helmet jarred askew, and he used his free hand to dislodge it entirely so he could see. His other hand was busy digging the pommel of his sword into the crown of Von Lormarck's head.

The baron screamed in pain but blindly lifted his own blade at nearly the same time, clipping the king on his forehead. Both men slid to a stop and rolled away from one another, turning the snow red in their blood.

Godwin rocked back and forth in his clumsy armor, forcing himself to sit up. He glanced at Von Lormarck, who had done the same, but both were slick with blood and melting snow, neither able to regain their footing.

Both nobles swung at each other from their knees, exchanging awkward and unconventional blows that bashed into, and sometimes through, their armored defenses. One slash caught Godwin on the side of his neck, a second cutting a hole in his armor under his left arm. He felt the stark differences between the cold of the snow mixed with the warmth of his and Von Lormarck's blood.

Von Lormarck was cut and bleeding from one arm, and a second slash cut his left leg. He flashed his arm out, hoping to dislodge his armguard, which had been punctured by one of Godwin's blows.

The two stopped for a second, neither able to rise, and looked at each other.

Godwin was just happy that Von Lormarck didn't have the energy to keep talking. The man was worn down and bloody. To his surprise, the roar of the crowd had diminished, perhaps they too sensed the battle was nearing its end.

Then, Von Lormarck ended the mutual rest by shoulder rolling on the ground toward Godwin. The king raised his sword in defense. The two men came together, their swords flying in different directions, again finding themselves in a wrestling match.

Godwin heaved and rolled on his back, tossing the baron over his head, and watched him land hard on the snowy ground behind him.

The baron woofed on impact and he reached for his injured back while Godwin rolled and recovered his sword.

The king stood and exhaled a plume of frosty breath and spit a wad of bloody phlegm onto the snow. His armor was cracked and dented in more than one place, making it hard to move. But so was the baron's, and the Jackal's orange cape lay torn from him, half buried in a snow angel made from their flailing suits of armor.

To Godwin, they were both bleeding wretches, their once gleaming armor now tainted in the irreparable stains of their personal war.

PRINCE MONTGOMERY STARED INTO the valley between the peaks. He felt like a spectator, watching two great gladiators in a battle to the death. The distant clanging of swords and armor eventually slowed, and the growling of the two men sounded more animalistic than human.

The two, now covered in blood, mud, and snow, were indistinguishable from one another from afar. The Thronehelm shield and the orange cloak that would have told the tale of each man lay scattered on the ground. Their faces at this distance looked the same, matted hair too covered in muck to know the difference.

The combatants fought longer than Monty expected, and with each swing of a sword, the resonance of steel sounded like the ring of small chimes, ceaselessly echoing in the valley below. Each chime meant another swing, another chance for his father's victory, or death.

Freya's soothing hand lighted on his. He looked down into

his bride's blue eyes, hopeful that the melee would come to an end with his father victorious. But as he watched, the struggle between two hated rivals continued below.

He gazed across the field at the equally disciplined forces, a hodgepodge of flags quilted together, half of which he did not recognize. He wondered how his uncle was able to weave such a tapestry of divergent interests together, the threads between them as bare as they were. How could an alliance like that hold for long, let alone hold a kingdom together?

He prayed introspectively to the Ancient of War to see his father through, and to the Ancient of Death for the man who would fall.

Then, with a cry from below, the two great Knights charged at each other one last time. Their armor crashed together in a crumpling of metal. They fell to the ground as one, and rolled over and over, sliding in the slick snow like a metal sled, tumbling deeper into the valley.

Monty nudged his horse a little farther out to see, but the two disappeared over an embankment and fell into a small pocket of rocks, hiding them from view. The groans of the other army rose, and it was obvious they too could no longer see the combat.

The chiming stopped, causing tense moments of silence along both ridges of the Falkenwraths. From the scene, a lone Knight, snow covered and bloody, clawed his way slowly over the embankment. At first, he crawled on his belly, seemingly too injured, or too tired from the melee to do much more. Then the determined man took a few breaths and found strength enough to rise on all fours. He spit a pink mist into the snow, his arms trembling to hold his weight. He rested.

Neither army moved, and Monty held his breath, waiting for some sign, some signal from his father. After a few seconds, the man crawled to the two remaining flags, both flapping strongly in the winds of the sharp dale.

He stood, resting his hands on his knees, wisps of wintry wind leaving his mouth, over and over, until he could stand straight. He held no sword, no shield. His armor was torn and tattered. And then he stumbled toward the standards.

Monty's heart froze when he saw the man grab the flag of Foghaven Vale and hoist it high.

A deafening cheer rose from the opposite peak, swords clamoring from shields and the deep hoots from the thousands of warriors filled the mountain air.

The chant of "King! King! King!" rang through the valley.

Freya's hand squeezed his, but Monty could think of nothing else, save for the fall of Warminster. In two short months, he'd watched his brother killed at the hands of an assassin, his mother eaten by a cryptid infiltrator, and his father die at the hands of his hated uncle, a man that had usurped not just his father's crown, but all the realm.

And his father's promise to the thousands of warriors on both ridges to let the Ancients decide the next king stung like the wound from the sharpest of swords. They had fought in single combat under the eyes of the Ancients. What was he, a mere mortal, to do?

The heavy hand of Atorm Stormmoeller came to rest on his shoulder. He turned to look the *konungr* from Rijkstag in the eyes, but then the wiry hand of Einar Skullgrimsson grabbed him around the arm.

Both Norsemen looked at him and their emotions penetrated his soul. He heard Einar's distant words from his first night in Hammerstead, claiming there would be blood in the mountains and that the two armies would clash there. He didn't have to say it again.

"What now, King Montgomery?" Atorm asked, his voice steady and unaffected by the outcome of the battle. The weight of his words shook Montgomery to the core.

King Montgomery?

Monty hesitated, but he could no longer suppress the cold eyes of vengeance and rage from appearing on his brow. He looked to his side where the Horn of Hammerstead hung from his belt.

His father had made a promise. But the fate of the kingdom now rested upon his shoulders.

He turned back to Atorm, Einar, and Freya, all of whom had tracked his eyes to their most hallowed artifact with a silent passion.

"Koss, the bringer of the valiant dead awaits your decision, King." Atorm's steady voice was matched only by the steel in his eyes.

He raised the horn and put it to his lips.

"The Horn of Hammerstead, My King!" Einar said, a crazed look of battle frenzy conjuring in his eyes. "Let us ride into the Hall of the Ancients together in glory this day! Let us not stop until the blood on your sword is the blood of a king!"

All thought left his mind. All feeling fled from his chest. His own kind of numb war-frenzy took over. No heroic speeches left his mouth, no rallying cries. Only the sound of the Horn of Hammerstead echoed from the walls of the Falkenwraths, sending his army to war.

CHAPTER THIRTY-THREE

"From a battle i've come. To a battle i ride."
—Koss, the Ancient of War

LOOKED TO THE FAR peak. A cacophony of groaning from a Rijkstag horn bellowed through the valley. Then came the inevitable war cries from the Norsemen themselves and the thunderous galloping of the Warminsterian cavalry.

He stood alone, too exhausted to try to escape. He grinned, the already drying blood cracking on his face. He waited for the battle to come to him. It would be the shortest reign for a king in the history of the realm. But if he should fall, he would do it with a sword in his hand.

From behind him, the calls of the army of Foghaven Vale rose.

"To the king!" he heard one of his sons call from a distance.

His bloody grin broadened. Perhaps they would reach him before Montgomery could.

He looked to the matted snow, having only a minute before his fate would be sealed, and found the shattered helmet of King Godwin half buried on the frozen ground. He reached for it as the echoes of war crept closer.

With broken fingers, he wrenched the tightly fitted golden circlet from the helm. The circlet was a symbolic representation of the crown in battle. It was a far cry from the true crown jewels that awaited him in Thronehelm, but it would do. He placed it on his bare head.

The circlet did not fit. It cut into his skin as he fitted it upon his forehead. A trickle of blood seeped from a barbed edge and ran down the side of his cheek.

Godwin's last jab at him.

The scar it would surely leave would serve as a daily reminder of his old foe every time he would look into his mirror.

The ground trembled under his feet as the armies drew nearer. He looked both ways, listening for his sons' voices to rise above the roar, or to feel the comfort of knowing that his army would reach and defend him first.

Neither came.

As the armies met, a great thunder reverberated from the valley. The whinnying of colliding horses and metal chiming against metal deafened him. The roar of the fury of men and the cries of the dying surrounded him.

Somehow, Donnar and Emmerich rode to his side. The steep hills on both sides created the illusion that the Warminsterians were closer, but his Jackals surrounded him, rallying to protect their new king.

"Father, take my hand," Donnar said, reaching for Dragich. He signaled for him to jump atop his mount so they could ride him to safety. But Dragich merely stole his son's sword from its scabbard and clanged it against the bloody steel of Woe.

That was his answer.

"I shall not leave the victory of my battlefield," he replied.

One of his men dismounted, giving him a steed, and the new king mounted it and turned to his reserve troops. He lifted his two victorious blades into the air and crossed them, signaling to his bannermen to launch an aerial assault on the approaching army's rear guard.

KING MONTGOMERY SLAMMED INTO the organized chaos of battle, his sword swinging at anything that moved. A sea of bodies crashed like a booming wave on the rocky shoals around him. He had been in battles, but nothing he learned at Halifax could prepare him for this.

He led the charge despite the voice of the Faxerian behind him, begging him to remain atop the peak. His thirst for bloody revenge couldn't wait. He'd be damned to years of self-inflicted torment if he didn't sate his desire for vengeance on this battlefield today. Somewhere in the back of his mind, the runecaster's words overrode those of his most trusted general.

He needed to fight.

His horse and the horses of his Black Cuff cavalry trampled the Jackal's pikemen as they fought to protect Von Lormarck's position from the Warminsterian horsemen. The breaking of bones and the cries of death tugged at his ears, but he didn't care.

The pikemen tried to form a barrier, but the cavalry charge came too swift, rattling through their ranks and rendering their polearms ineffective. The charge was a slaughter. Swords banged against his shield and his horse's plated barding, but he pressed on.

Next to him, somewhere in the stampede, Anson Valion and the Faxerian, Lucien Blacwin, rode. He had lost track of them when he'd spurred on the charge. He knew they kept pace with the cavalry, but his eyes only saw the flag the Jackal had planted in the snow ahead.

He swung into the meaty crowd of pikemen as he rambled by, again and again and again. Each time his sword lifted, it brought the stains of fresh blood or torn flesh with it. It wasn't enough. He needed more. Wanted more. He began to worry there might not be enough blood in the enemy's army to quench his thirst.

The Jackal's flag fluttered a mere hundred yards from him. Surrounding it now was a flank of horses, forming a wall between Montgomery and his prey.

A tug on his shield came from the left as a desperate foot soldier tried to unseat him. A foolish move, one the poor soldier learned swiftly at the edge of Monty's blade.

"My king!" a familiar voice called from nearby.

It was Anson Valion, but Monty didn't turn to look. He sliced and stabbed into the hapless crowd, reveling in his steel popping through armor and the feeling of short-lived resistance as flesh gave way to his blade.

A rumbling of war machines invaded his ears and Montgomery looked quickly to the horizon. A new weapon, one Von Lormarck surely had delivered by the High Aldin in Abacus, made its presence known. Monty had heard of these devices but had never seen them in practice. Until now.

The javelin carts appeared from the crest of the hill, rolling like mobile wooden launchpads. On the top of the cart, Monty stared down nearly two hundred cylindrical holes. Before he could react, a set of triggers released from the rear of the carts in unison, similar to a trigger on the back of a catapult. The whip of the force blew snow from the ground in wisps of circular mist. From the cylindrical holes leapt hundreds of small javelins. The missiles arced above his position and most of the cavalry, soaring into the approaching ranks of the Thronehelm infantry.

In some places, other javelin carts were tilted to fire in a horizontal strip, delivering their deadly payload directly into the attacking lines of the Norsemen, who had charged in from the southern flank of Monty's cavalry charge. The mechanical hissing of the war machines at work were only emphasized by the speed in which they were reloaded. Monty stopped attacking and started thinking.

"Valion, take some horses and sweep behind those carts,"

Monty ordered. "Stop those batteries or else we won't have an army much longer."

Valion called out to a few of his most trusted lieutenants, and two dozen horses cut away from the frontal assault to put an end to their deadly practice.

Monty spun about on his steed and looked to the ground where the front line of the Jackal's assault had been destroyed. He had gotten lucky in his charge and knew it, but the result of his tactical win opened a temporary window to strike.

He called out for Blacwin but couldn't find his general in the morass. He retreated alone to regroup with the onrushing ground troops. His infantry had been stunted in their advance by the javelin carts, but they still pressed on. They were now charging uphill, on snow and ice, with the encumbrance of extra pounds of metal armor weighing them down.

"Soldier!" Monty yelled from his horse. "We need to attack into the breach we made in their lines with the cavalry. Where is your commanding officer?"

"Dead, sir," the soldier replied. "We've caught the ire of those damned war machines, and it leveled the first two cohorts. It's us and a few other units we strung together. Our shields are useless against them."

Monty surveyed the battlefield, trying to devise a plan. To his right, the cavalry swept through the Jackal's remaining pikemen. To the left, the Norsemen engaged with the Sentinels of Saracen and quickly tore through the first wave of the mercenary lines. Those lines appeared to be bolstered by the trollborn troops of Von Lormarck's army. He knew he couldn't pull troops from there to help.

They were on their own.

VON LORMARCK BEGAN TO breathe easier. He had won the death match between himself and Godwin and tempted the Fates when his sons outraced the Warminsterian cavalry, saving him. But the battle hung on a knife's edge, and he knew it.

The Saracenean mercenaries were better behind their walls. The Norsemen's escalated assault ate through them like a dragon's tooth through bone. The Saraceneans outnumbered the Norsemen at least two to one, but Dirdrenum Tullamore wasn't used to commanding in an open field. A lesson he learned the hard way at the wrong end of Urnst Jamner, Atorm's warhammer.

The Sentinels scattered, some abandoning the field altogether, others regrouping, only to succumb moments later to the forces of Rijkstag. Von Lormarck decided to occupy the Norsemen as long as he could by commanding Zendzack Jahdiel, his trollborn general, to action. Jahdiel knew no mercy and suffered none from deserters. If they wanted lands in Foghaven Vale, he would command his men to the last. But they needed some additional support to soften the barbarian lines.

He ordered a dozen hippogryphs, saddled with his own regulars, to take to the air with a new weapon from Abacus. Before departing for the cathedral, Jhodever absconded with the creatures, and he knew it would surprise their enemies. They could not prepare for what they were about to see.

The gryphs swooped down like a flock of well-trained eagles toward their target, strafing the barbarians with clawed talons and angry cries, trying to scatter their ranks. But as the gryphs broke away, their riders dropped clay jars into the crowds that exploded with some alchemical material, made only at the High Aldin. The jars shattered, erupting among the army of the north, and sending deadly metal caltrops in all directions. The pronged metal shrapnel cut through the hide armor of the Norsemen, dropping dozens of warriors with each detonating jar.

Then they swung around again for another assault.

This time, the Norsemen were ready for them. As the roaring of their giant wings soared toward them, the Norsemen fired arrows and crossbow bolts at the gryphs and their riders. Spears and hand axes whirled at them as them passed by. More jars fell and burst, but four of the gryphs were downed, and a fifth's rider was unseated, sending them each into the ground with a resounding thud.

A cheer rose from the barbarian clans and Von Lormarck watched one giant of a barbarian wrestling at the neck of the injured gryph. With a twist of his bulging muscles, he appeared to snap the creature's neck. The beast went limp. Another cheer rose from the pit of the valley, and Von Lormarck knew he would have to depend on Zendzack Jahdiel to hold that end of the line.

FREYA LEANED INTO HER slate iron shield, her legs straining not to buckle against the weight of the trollborn mercenary on the other side. The half-man drove into her defenses, bloated and war-crazed, swinging his war hammer with reckless abandon.

She grunted and blocked with her axe, turning her attacker to the side. With a swift cut, her weapon arced at the overextended arms of her enemy, slicing through muscle and bone.

The creature recoiled, releasing a blood-curdling cry, and spun away into the advancing forces of Von Lormarck's hirelings. Its yellowish blood stained her axe head and below her visor she smiled. Koss was with her and her unborn son this day.

She turned to find her next opponent amongst the chaotic rage of the battle. Before her splayed the vanguard of the mercenary forces. With each passing second, it seemed to spin anew like a kaleidoscope of death, with Norsemen, Saracenean sentinels, and trollborn warriors moshing together in the basin of the violent cauldron of the Falkenwraths.

From out of the spiraling sea of humanity, a sentinel ran at her, or perhaps away from Einar, who cackled in Wartooth, admonishing the man's cowardice from nearby. His hurried breath and wild eyes told her he'd lost control, and he rambled at her brandishing his cutlass in an unconventional stance.

Freya didn't wait for the man to gather himself and instead rushed in low. Using her shield to block the sentinel's blade, she attacked from underneath the canopy of her slate iron, catching her opponent's thigh with her axe.

The sentinel's cries were lost in the din of the battle, but he collapsed underneath her defenses, where she sent him to the Hall of the Ancients with one final blow.

An inhuman roar sounded over the battle, and she spun to find its source.

Wading through the waves of armored masses stepped the trollborn chieftain, towering over its own forces and pointing its hideous weapon at her father, Atorm. The chieftain held in one hand a club that no human could wield with two arms, its crown fashioned with the severed hand of some cryptid from the Killean Desolates. The claw, grey and mottled with mummified decay, still possessed the six fingers of the fallen beast, its razor-sharp talons splashed in the fresh blood and torn flesh of its enemies.

Atorm acknowledged the approaching menace and waved

his hammer, Urnst Jamner, at him, inviting the single combat.

Time seemed to pause, and Freya crept closer to the two combatants as the battle slowed and then stalled around them. Each side watched their champions circle one another. Her father, blood-soaked and singularly focused, moved first, earning a cheer from the Norsemen around him.

Urnst Jamner arced high, meeting the trollborn's weapon with the sound of metal against wood. The slate iron of Atorm's hammer won the exchange, weakening but not splintering the weapon's shaft. Freya saw the slightest smile curl on her father's face.

The chieftain glanced at his prized club and unleashed a second enraged roar while raising its monstrous leg to kick at Atorm.

The *konungr* ducked under the counterattack, lunging in with the flat of his hammer and landing a blow that would have felled any other opponent. But the chieftain barely moved from the power of the hammerhead, its dull thud dying in the mass of the creature's hide armor.

The two broke apart and began circling one another again, this time the onlookers breaking their anxious silence, whooping, and cheering for their champions.

Freya looked to Einar, wondering if she should help her father, but the runecaster's eyes were affixed on the single melee, seemingly lost in the devilish rapture of the moment.

Before she could move, the two engaged again. The trollborn's reach gave it an inherent advantage, and even with a cracked club, its vicious cudgel batted Urnst Jamner aside, powering through the *konungr*'s advance.

Atorm flashed to one side, evading a crushing blow, but the claw's sharp talons scraped through his armor and tore at his chest. He moaned in pain, to the gasps of his supporters and to the elation of the trollborn.

Her father staggered backward from the blow, but regathered himself, not looking at the wound, raising Urnst Jamner in the defense of his familiar high guard.

The chieftain taunted the *konungr*, leaning his cudgel on his shoulder, and with a deep, mocking laugh waved him in with his free hand.

Atorm needed no invitation and leapt into the air, Urnst Jamner cocked above his head.

The trollborn reacted by raising his club to block, but the slate iron of Urnst Jamner landed clean, shattering the shaft of the club in two.

As Atorm landed to the cheers of the Norsemen, the chieftain swore in an indistinguishable blather, holding the two pieces of his prized weapon in each hand. His eyes narrowed and a low, guttural growl rose from him. His arm drew back and he launched the clawed head of the broken cudgel at Atorm.

The *konungr* spun aside, but the broken piece hurled over him at Freya. With the quickness of a cat, she raised her shield in time. The wicked claw lodged in the crown of her shield and its sharpened talons pierced through and slashed across her forearm.

She winced in pain and dropped the shield, looking to the wound. It bled, but she thanked the Fates that the cuts were not deep. She'd be scarred, but the slate iron from Uthgar's forge had saved her from being killed.

With a roar and a cheer, her eyes flashed back to the battle. In the second her attention was turned, the two men clashed again and somehow the chieftain's bare claws had wrapped around her father, lifting him from the ground, squeezing the breath from him.

Atorm winced and with one free hand raised Urnst Jamner into the air, slamming it again and again into the head and then the shoulder of the trollborn.

The beast of a man didn't falter, even against the sound of bones in its face cracking. It just squeezed tighter.

Atorm wheezed, his feet dangling off the ground in the vice grip of the trollborn.

Freya watched as her father's strength began to wane, and she wondered how his ribs hadn't given way or how he could breathe against the strength of his opponent. She had to do something. Her eyes scrambled to the crowd again, looking for direction, but her Norsemen only stood, watching and waiting.

Atorm's eyes rolled into the back of his head and with one final surge of strength he swung Urnst Jamner a last time, connecting with the monster's face.

Above the roar of pain, Freya heard the creature's jaw crack. It screeched and tossed the failing barbarian into the air, sending the *konungr* soaring into the crowd of gawking warriors. He landed hard and skidded in the bloody snow to a halt at Freya's feet.

She dared a glance at her father, not sure if he was dead or alive but the trollborn chieftain staggered, grabbing at its face, spitting blood and teeth onto the battlefield. His jaw hung crooked, but the man's eyes, still filled with avarice, searched for Atorm. When he found him, he took one step toward her.

What felt like hours ago now, Freya recalled Montgomery watching his father die from afar. The pain on his face and the emptiness she felt for him returned to her heart. If her father was dead, she had to avenge him. If he lived, she had to protect him.

Hatred and anger rushed into her limbs. Her eyes flared, and she drew in a cold, rattling breath. Drawing back, she threw her axe at the approaching trollborn.

The giant of a man swatted at it through blurred vision, but the head turned over and landed with a thud, sinking deep into one of its thighs. He staggered and fell to one knee, bringing himself down to Freya's height. He ripped the axe from his leg and roared, tossing the weapon into the crowd.

Fear tugged at her, but she didn't succumb to it. With a tumble, she shoulder-rolled from her downed father and toward her ruined shield. Weaponless, she had one move left and used her speed to stay ahead of her lumbering and injured foe. Reaching the shield, she tore the broken claw from the slate iron. The trollborn was so close she felt his hot breath on her neck.

With a cry of a Valkyrie, she swung the claw, its deadly talons finding their mark. The sound of flesh tearing came first to her ears before the giant's murmuring grunts followed. The talons cut deep, and the improvised weapon lodged into the face of the trollborn general.

She let go of the broken clubhead and stepped back, watching the great man wobble to one side, clutching at the embedded hand. His arms slid to his sides, and he lurched forward then fell back into the darkness of death.

She dared to breathe, her eyes peeled on the fallen trollborn, afraid that he'd rise again to kill her. But only stillness followed.

Einar's voice broke the relative silence, and in the words of her native Wartooth he cried, "Freya Trollsbane!"

"MY KING," KAIL ILIDARI interrupted, "there is a hole in our defenses."

Von Lormarck hadn't even realized Ilidari had joined him until then.

"Look," Ilidari pointed into the ranks. "The Thorhauer

cavalry has left us vulnerable to their approaching infantry. They are pinned down for now, but the young prince is commanding them."

Von Lormarck peered over the battlefield at the chaos that ensued.

"They are too far for me to see." Von Lormarck balked. "How is it you can?"

"You forget I am of trollborn blood, my liege," Ilidari said. "My eyes are not human."

Von Lormarck reveled in the moment. If the young prince was leading the assault, he could truly end the line of the Thorhauers on this very hill. The prospects were too tempting to pass.

He turned his horse and rode to the pinnacle of the hill. In reserve, only a few hundred yards away, sat Field Marshal Cherica Lambert and her thousand Tritons from Deadwaters Fork. They were perhaps the realm's deadliest cavalry, and unquestionably its best riders. For a second he questioned the wisdom in sending southern horsemen unaccustomed to riding in snow and mountains down a slope to attack, but he wanted to see them in battle and knew they would rout the remaining Thorhauer infantry.

"Clear the carts!" he ordered of his artillerymen, commanding them to stand down their barrage of deadly javelins. By moving them to a rear position, he would make a clear track for Lambert's cavalry to charge over the peak and down into the valley, stampeding Montgomery and the rest of his forces.

He tasted victory in his bloodied mouth. He looked down over the slope at the waiting cavalry from the Fork and crossed his swords high above his head. He watched Lambert signal her horsemen to action, their beautiful silver and blue guidon flags lifted in the wind as they began to charge.

He smiled and watched his javelin carts rotate away and back, leaving a gaping hole for Lambert to ride through. The stomping of their horse's hooves rose like thunderous applause raining down onto Von Lormarck's pending victory. The Tritons lowered their tridents and lances as they charged through. But instead, turned and attacked the Jackal's forces atop the peak.

MONTGOMERY DISMOUNTED AND SLAPPED his horse on its behind, sending it away. He lifted his shield and looked at the eyes of his frightened troops. He braced himself for a moment and stood in front of them. His armor was in tatters, bloodied and dented, but they could still tell it was their new king.

He gazed over their huddled masses, taking cover behind every hillock and nook they could find, hiding from the raining death of javelins. They lay among and atop their dead, their numbers halved since their first assault.

Monty grabbed the horn a second time. He knew it would rile the Norsemen in the valley and remind them he was still alive. He hoped the same for Freya. But he needed to get these men over the hill, splitting the Jackal's army.

Atop the peak he saw the undulating guidon flags of the army of the Fork appear. Horses gathered and formed lines on the crest of the hill. In his heart, he knew this would be his last stand. There was no possible way to fight back that force with his remaining men. They would have to defend a downward slope in the weather against a line of cavalry.

He knew Von Lormarck had won.

He blew into the Horn of Hammerstead anyway and stood, waving his sword for his infantry to attack. The roar from the Norsemen below echoed up the valley and steeled his men, who joined in the battle cry.

They turned and charged the hill. The ascent was difficult. Many slipped on the ice or mud, or in the opened entrails of the fallen. They used their spears and swords to steady themselves as they climbed to their deaths.

Then another horn bellowed through the valley. Monty turned to look afar and saw the arriving line of the twergish army. They had come! Solveig Jins and First Keeper Makai must have met with success! His heart swelled with pride. Perhaps the day was not lost, even though he would not be around to share in the victory.

The twergish first wave covered the open ground on the backs of mountain rams, white as the snow, with golden horns lowered, and the twergish cavalry armed with two-tined spears in an assault. The rams crashed into the rear lines of the trollborn forces and were greeted by a vicious chorus of groans from their enemies. The two had been warring for years and this time, their wars were not to fight in the cracks of the mountains, but on the open field of battle.

"Sir!" one of the infantrymen yelled to the prince. "The Tritons, they are with us!"

Montgomery dared to raise his head and looked to the crest of the hill before them. Instead of impending death, he saw the Tritons fan to the left and to the right, turning against Von Lormarck and overrunning positions near the baron himself.

Another cheer, perhaps premature, rose from his men as they charged the baron's position. The Tritons had stopped the advance of the Jackal's own infantry from plugging the breach and forced them away. The hundred yards Montgomery had faced before seemed like a journey of a thousand miles. It now shrunk before him.

The day, in fact, could be won.

"NO!" THE JACKAL SCREAMED.

Field Marshal Lambert turned from him and rode into his unsuspecting infantry. His face blanched in desperation, and he turned to Ilidari.

"Take the rest of the cavalry and stop her!" he cried to his trollborn stalwart. He trusted Ilidari with his life and knew the man to be a veteran of many battles beside his father.

"Sire, I..." Ilidari tried.

"Go!" he commanded, then he turned to Baron Thessaly and his two sons. "You, take your forces and stop the prince!"

Thessaly waved at his remaining men, and they charged headlong down the hill, meeting the Thorhauer forces fifty yards from where they stood.

"Sons," Von Lormarck said. "Stay with me."

"Father, the Warminsterian cavalry." Donnar pointed.

Von Lormarck turned to see less than a dozen riders coming at them, cutting their way through black and orange foot soldiers that guarded their small hill.

He recognized two of the armored figures as they rode. One, in dull black armor, fluted in red pinstripe, was the unmistakable figure of the Faxerian, Lucien Blacwin. The other, in purple and gold-plated armor, with black gauntlets and armguards was Anson Valion. He said nothing and raised his two swords knowing they would reach them in seconds.

The Faxerian crested the hill first with Valion climbing next. Von Lormarck waited patiently with Donnar and Emmerich flanking him from each side.

"It is over," Blacwin cried, sliding from his saddle to face them on even ground. "Surrender and end this bloodshed."

"You forget, old man," Von Lormarck replied. "I am the

one who earned this crown today."

Anson Valion walked to Blacwin's side.

"I told you I would find you in this battle." Valion looked at Von Lormarck's two sons. "Come, let us speak and leave your father to treat with General Blacwin."

He circled away from the Faxerian, giving him ground and waving with his blood-drenched sword for the two princes to approach. They, like their father, didn't need the invitation. They lashed out at Valion, one attacking from the hillside, the other darting low, forcing him to fight in the middle.

Anson countered by fending off Emmerich with his shield, as he had gone low, and traded parries with Donnar, who stayed high.

For a moment, the other two combatants waited for their turn. But Von Lormarck could wait no more. He clanged his two swords together twice, sending a quick nod to Koss, and attacked. The Faxerian, spry for his age, spun away. Von Lormarck's blades caught nothing but air.

"Remember, Baron," Blacwin teased, "I was the one who taught you."

Von Lormarck, even in his weakened state, could not resist the bait. He dived in again, this time one thrust after another, stabbing low then high and setting Blacwin back on his heels. But the swarthy veteran blocked every move with proficient arcs of his sword and batted away the second with his shield.

"Come at me," the baron complained, but the Faxerian just stood his ground, waiting for the impatient Von Lormarck to attack.

Von Lormarck edged in, this time feinting with thrusts but instead cutting high with both blades. Blacwin blocked the first cut with his shield, and the other with his sword.

Von Lormarck spit into the snow and circled again.

Through his peripheral vision, he could see Valion employing the same measures, teasing his sons. He was the superior warrior by far, and it was as if he was playing with his prey before the kill. Catching sight of the old veteran, he realized Blacwin was doing the same to him.

He gathered his strength and bull rushed the old myrmidon, catching him off guard. It was a move he had used on Godwin and wasn't sure if it would work here, but Blacwin was caught flat-footed. He raised his shield in time to block Von Lormarck's lowered shoulder. The two held their ground, pushing against one another in a duel of strength, their feet not giving in the snow. Neither fell and then they disengaged.

Von Lormarck knew he had little time, his wounds still bleeding and his body at the edge of exhaustion. The clanging and dancing to his rear slowed, and instinctively he knew Valion would end the games and attack them soon. He had to kill Blacwin now.

He turned quickly and ran toward Valion. The move caught both his enemies off guard and bought him what he was looking for—an advantage.

For the briefest of seconds, Valion was outnumbered three to one, and had to leave a hole for Von Lormarck's sons to attack him. The Black Cuff captain spun instinctively, his sword and shield flailing out to stop Von Lormarck's assault.

The baron's two swords clanged viciously off Valion's shield, but it forced him to abandon his fighting stance against Donnar and Emmerich.

Donnar looped in over his father's attack and struck the captain on the crown of his helmet with a resounding thud.

Valion fell to one knee and groaned but stuck his sword out in time to block Emmerich's attack at his exposed midsection.

The Faxerian darted to his aid, giving Von Lormarck

the break he'd been looking for. He spun to the old general, surprising him, and landed back-to-back swings that glanced off his breastplate, knocking him to the ground.

Blacwin fell hard on his back and Von Lormarck pounced. He dropped one sword and used his free hand to grope at the Faxerian's shield, pulling it aside.

The general recovered quickly and grabbed at Von Lormarck's sword hand, holding it from delivering a final blow. The two men groaned and Von Lormarck spit blood through the general's visor, hoping to distract him. But Blacwin twisted violently, breaking Von Lormarck's hold, turning them both over in the snow.

Now it was the general that sat atop Von Lormarck, wrestling with him for possession of the blade.

Von Lormarck looked back to see Valion on his feet, his eyes not on the general but on his sons. Valion stumbled, dazed, but Donnar had been hit and was already bleeding from a shoulder. Emmerich dueled with the captain but did so poorly. Valion no longer played games. Von Lormarck had to free himself from the general to save them, but the weight of the hulking Blacwin had pinned him into the snow.

He reached back for all he had and punched at Blacwin's helm, over and over. The Faxerian tilted just for a second, far enough for Von Lormarck to flip him aside. The baron rolled over and scrambled for his sword, but it was too late.

He watched in dread as Valion moved in on Emmerich. He had seen the move a thousand times. One Emmerich had learned at Halifax to perfection, but Valion was faster, better. The Captain of the Black Cuffs executed it with deadly precision. He stepped to Emmerich's weak arm, his left, and as the prince raised his sword to block, the captain spun, kicking his near leg out in a savage pirouette, ducking underneath the blade, and raising his up, driving the steel through his chin and into his skull.

Emmerich gurgled for a second, struggling for life. Blood spewed on the ground beneath him as Valion recovered the blade. He grabbed at his face and jaw but fell to the ground in a bloody heap.

"No!" Von Lormarck cried, trying to gain his feet, but then he felt the vice grip of the general grab onto the vambrace on his left arm, tugging him back. With wild eyes blinded in rage, he swung his other sword at the general's grip, cutting off his arm at the elbow with Woe.

The general peeled back, grabbing at his gushing arm, fighting to stave off the bleeding, but Von Lormarck didn't care. He had to get to Valion. As he got to his feet, Donnar rushed to his fallen brother's aid, but Anson made quick work of the second twin.

Donnar, in a furor, swung his sword wildly, like an untrained squire.

Valion spun away, letting the blade fly harmlessly by. He then rushed in, leveling Donnar with a shoulder to his ribs, his entire midsection exposed from the wild swing. The prince fell back in a hard slap as if falling from his horse, his breath escaping him.

Von Lormarck charged in to try to save him but arrived seconds too late. He was forced to watch the captain, standing above his first son, slide his blade under Donnar's cuirass, the steel collar that protected his neck. His son twitched, reflexively pulling away from the blade, but as Valion withdrew it, a claret fountain of blood spurted across his chest. He, too, grabbed at his throat, but it was just the death throes of a dying man, and Von Lormarck couldn't save him.

With tears in his eyes, he rushed in on Valion, the two men tumbling down the snow-covered hill in each other's arms.

Von Lormarck felt no pain. His muscles no longer ached; his wounds no longer burned. Somewhere in the tumble, he had dropped Woe, and he and Anson struggled against one another, their only weapons were their gauntleted hands. He punched, slapped and elbowed the captain in a flurry of attacks, but the captain covered up, his armored skin deflecting much of the blows.

Then Von Lormarck felt the flat of a sword smack the side of his head. His body straightened reflexively, and for a second, his eyes became cloudy. He fought the rushing of unconsciousness reaching for him from the darkness in his mind, but he was shaken from his dazed trance when snow hit him in the face from the passing of a nearby horse. He felt an inhuman arm jerk him from the ground and ride off.

His face turned to see his dead sons, their bodies still bleeding out in the trampled snow. Then his eyes went dark as his internal battle with unconsciousness was lost.

"CHARGE!" KING MONTGOMERY CRIED as he pointed his sword at the screaming Jackals that attacked his infantry. His troops girded their loins, shouting war cries, as what was left of the Jackal's vanguard descended upon them.

Montgomery gritted his teeth, but the first Jackal slammed into his shield, and with his downhill momentum, carried both men over one another. Monty tried to rise, but was knocked from his feet a second time, and then a third.

The last blow came from a sword, and not a charging soldier. The blade slapped him on the back, his armor protecting him from the blow, but the force stunned him. He lurched forward, catching himself on the back of a fallen soldier.

Regaining his posture, he instinctively turned and blocked the attacker's sword at the last moment as it hurtled at him.

When their blades stalemated, he looked up to find the blade belonged to his uncle, Baron Kellan Thessaly.

Monty reached back and swung, their steel meeting and sending a fierce vibration up his arm.

His uncle grunted and advanced, running sideways on the hill. He lunged at Montgomery, but the new king blocked and parried, sending his uncle sliding in the snow. The man tumbled uncontrollably toward him, and Monty let him fall flat on his face.

The hands of several of Montgomery's infantrymen reached for the fallen baron, but Montgomery felt no pity and showed no mercy. Thessaly spun to try to stand but Monty was quicker and pinned the man under his boot. He took his sword and drove it deep into Thessaly's chest, piercing his armor. The baron screamed, but Monty no longer cared. He left him lying there, dying in the snow, and continued up the hill.

His men cheered at the downed noble. Emboldened by the small victory, they pressed on behind him. One of the men carried his father's banner with him, blood-stained and tattered. The unit halved the distance to the hill, then halved it again. Fifty yards became twenty-five, and twenty-five became ten.

As Monty crested the top of the hill, he saw the bodies of Emmerich and Donnar lying dead in the snow. He searched for Von Lormarck but only saw Captain Valion sitting next to the Faxerian, clutching a dark, bloody stump where his arm should have been. The old general, sprawled on the frozen ground, his eyes staring into the dawn of the new day, dead as the soldiers that laid at his feet.

Valion held his mentor as if he was his father, not letting go, even though the great general had already departed for the Hall of the Ancients.

The infantryman carrying the banner knocked the standard of Foghaven Vale down and planted the flag of Thronehelm deep into the ground. A roar from his men, who all climbed to the top of the Falkenwraths' peaks with their new king, celebrated their victory.

Monty, exhausted from the fray, collapsed to his knees, and sounded the Horn of Hammerstead once more, letting his Norse allies know of their victory.

He viewed the battlefield from above. The Norsemen and twergs had routed the trollborn henchmen, who had begun to flee the battlefield. The last of the Jackal's army had already run from the scene, abandoning their war machines, and their wounded.

And the army of Warminster had won the day.

"Shall we run them down, My King?" came an unfamiliar voice from behind Monty.

He turned and looked at the woman, sitting on her horse with a trident in her hand.

"Where is Von Lormarck?" Monty asked.

"He was taken away injured," the woman replied. "One of his men rode off with him. Shall we pursue?"

"Are you Cherica Lambert?" Monty asked feebly, his fatigue setting in as his adrenaline dissipated.

"I am, My King," she replied.

"You saved my army today," Monty said. "I owe you my life, my kingdom."

"You saved all of us, my lord," she replied. "As did your father."

"My father?" Monty said, the painful memory coming back to him. Just minutes ago, his father was alive, and had defended the kingdom honorably, only to be betrayed by his cousin. Lambert had reminded him of that.

"Lambert," Monty said.

"Yes, my lord?" she replied.

"Run them down."

CHAPTER THIRTY-FOUR

"When one seeks revenge, dig two graves, not one."
—Gyory of the Pilque

"YOUR TIME HAS COME, Incanus," the Shadow elf intoned.

"How do you—"

"We are as stealthy and as secretive as you. Be not surprised by our presence, as we are always watching from the darkness."

Incanus stepped back and looked for more corporeal places in the shadows. He knew the true elf was in there—somewhere.

"I have been spying on the Valkeneers for the Moor Bog, who are on their way here. War is coming, Bone elf, and you are needed. We are glad to see you come home to us... just in time."

Incanus gritted his teeth. "The Vermilion took *everything* from me."

"We know," the Shadow elf agreed, undulating back and forth in the candlelight of the hall. Its motion was perfect in timing, as if instinct or practice had mirrored its motion with the flickers.

Incanus went on, paying no attention to the elf. "The princess's father took my beloved for *nothing*, and my mother and father died because of him. His line must be extinguished, and Princess Addilyn is the last of it. And now, my opportunity nears. Leave before I—"

"What?" the shadow's otherworldly voice whispered in his ear. "You will serve as you were bred to."

"I serve no one," Incanus's patience wore thin.

"I heard tell the Vermilion is leaving for the woods," the Shadow elf continued, "to bury the Raven elf you slew on the river. But it is of no matter. The battle is nigh, Incanus.

I command you to help the Moor Bog… and forsake this petty idea of revenge against the Vermilion. It does not serve your masters. You are needed. Kill Hertzog Valkeneer as we command."

"Revenge is all I am here for," Incanus sneered. "It is all that matters to me."

The Shadow elf billowed with frustration. "Leave with me now and I will forgive this insolence. I will not ask again."

"I do not like repeating myself either." In the darkness of the alcove, hidden doubly by the form of the Shadow elf, Incanus unsheathed his sword.

"You dare raise a blade against your better?" the Shadow elf hissed, black smoke swirling.

"I will do more than raise it," Incanus replied.

Before the Shadow elf could move, Incanus struck out, swiping his sword across the elf's misty figure. It was an odd experience as the sword did not connect in the same way it would have with flesh. It was like striking the breeze, pushing against a strong wind, but his opponent felt it.

The Shadow elf's voice bubbled in protest, sounding an ethereal alarm that pierced the hall and stunned Incanus. It flashed forward, trying to escape into the night, but Incanus grabbed a lantern from the sconce on the wall and with its light herded the elf back into the confines of the alcove. It shrieked as Skullam fluttered his wings, the two now appearing in full form, just as Incanus stabbed it once more. Then again. And again.

The shadow diminished, shrinking against the nearing lanternlight, trapping it in a corner. Incanus's sword flourished again and again, and the dying elf diminished from a wobbling cloud into a puff of black smoke. Incanus took pleasure in watching the last protests against his revenge shrivel and fade with each blow of his blade. He didn't cease his attack until the Shadow elf's essence exhaled its last and disappeared without a trace.

Like a shadow in the sunlight.

THE REVELATION IMPARTED BY the Shadow elf of Addilyn's departure had to be true. It just *had* to be. Finally, the Vermilion princess, Dacre's heir, was within his grasp.

And there she was.

Exiting through the rear portcullis of Castle Valkeneer without her Longmarcher companion, Addilyn emerged with a contingent of Vermilion guards, adorned in a smattering of red, white, and black scale mail armor, with red plumes cascading down from the tops of their helmets. They bore a stretcher with a body, draped and covered in the Raven elf burial traditions.

Incanus almost smiled. They would stand out in all their hubris against the winter woods, somber in its greys and browns.

He watched from the dark recesses of the Bridge as Addilyn at last left from the keep. Her retinue thinned as they passed through Firstgate, with only three Vermilion guards attending her.

Clever, they must have thought, leaving under the cover of darkness. But he worked in the shadows. The darkness was his friend, a tool to use against those he sought. They wouldn't have taken such a risk if they'd known he'd beaten them to Valkeneer.

Fools.

Addilyn paused at the tree line and looked around to ensure they were alone. Once satisfied, the small party ducked into Ravenwood and disappeared from his sight.

Incanus squinted, straining to see her disappear into the forest. Yet he waited, checking to see if anyone followed. After several minutes of normal guard movements, he felt it was safe to follow. He wasn't afraid of tracking his prey at night, and four sets of footprints would make an inviting trail for his trained eyes. He moved to follow but stopped at a sudden jerk.

"Master, maybe we shouldn't," Skullam whispered as he tugged on his master's cloak. In his zeal to kill, Incanus had forgotten they'd been hidden by the imp's command of the dark trace.

He swatted Skullam away. No one would stand in his way, not even his own imp.

"I can't keep us both hidden if we run," Skullam warned, but the assassin ignored him and forced him from his shoulder, ending the spell.

"Then let them see me coming," he growled.

Skullam's ugly features contorted in disagreement, but he raised no protest. "As you wish, Master."

The Bone elf followed Addilyn into Ravenwood, pushing through overgrowth with trembling hands. Adrenaline coursed through his veins and his heart raced in the anticipation of the hunt. Within minutes he caught their trail. They'd been moving at pace even bearing the stretcher but couldn't have gone far. Alone, he'd move quicker and make up the lost ground.

"My Captain," the *Ashen Dragon*'s mental interruptions reverberated in his head, "please don't leave me."

"*Not now,*" he thought back. "*Let me finish this and I am yours… forever.*"

"I don't believe you," the *Dragon*'s tremulous thoughts shot back, almost before he finished his. "*Please, no.*"

"*Stop!*" his mind commanded, but the magical vessel, hidden well at the mouth of the Gossamer River, continued to fret. Her omnipresence started in his head like a distant memory summoned from the back of his mind, but then grew in force with every step he took, farther and farther away from her decks.

"*Leave me now.*" Captain Dru'Waith concentrated hard, and for the moment the connection receded. Shaking off the effects, the assassin realized he'd stopped in the open before Skullam shook him free of his stupor.

"Master?" Skullam whispered, his demeanor cautious. "Are you ready? You've stopped. We must continue."

Incanus shook his head and rubbed his face. "I—I'm fine. Back to the trees."

The Bone elf's eyes narrowed, a renewed determination taking hold. He cut back and forth, zigging and zagging in case any of her attendants decided to double back and protect their flank. But his keen eyes for the trail told him they hadn't.

Skullam fluttered into the air and followed behind him as he was told, staying to the trees to hide and peer ahead. The pair had hunted together for years and possessed a near sixth sense between them. Even though Incanus couldn't see him above in the skies or hidden amongst the branches of the naked trees at times, he seemed to know always where Skullam was, and the imp's mimicry of woodland animals would signal trouble as he'd done so many times before.

Time passed. How much, he didn't know. Didn't care. Incanus ran in near silence, his honed skills an advantage in the familiar confines of Ravenwood. This was home. His home, albeit a distant one.

Then he spotted a subtle change in his prey's tracks. A novice tracker may not have noticed, but his practiced eyes did.

They were slowing.

Incanus could barely contain his excitement. He looked to

the hot trail, but his eyes were far away, considering how he'd kill her. Should he kill the guards first, one by one, taunting his victim like an alley cat? Or should he injure her first, then mop up the rest, setting upon her when they were alone? He almost laughed at his luck. Addilyn alone and vulnerable. Ripe for the taking. He would delight in the sight of her blood on his sword.

"Captain!" the *Dragon* cried in his mind. *"Please come back! You travel too far. I cannot protect you!"*

Incanus gritted his teeth and fought the urge to cry out. Her voice was like an echo, bouncing around in his skull. Her tone had changed, once dour and sullen, now a near panic. He struggled to mute her, concentrating on the trail, his prey—anything but his connection to her.

But nothing worked.

"Captain… my love… my dearest, no!"

The last volley of mystical voices stopped him in his tracks. The forest grew thick, his eyes clouded and teared. His head ached.

"Stop, I beg you," he managed. Even his thoughts tremored in pain. His limbs grew weak, and he saw Skullam drop to his side. The imp was speaking but he couldn't make out the words over the *Dragon*'s booming tones.

Skullam grabbed Incanus's arm, and it took the assassin a few seconds to even recognize the gesture. And then… silence.

He blinked. When the smoke in his mind cleared, he found his hands covering his ears and he'd bit through his own lip. The tinge of the coppery taste of blood hit his tongue.

"Master?" Skullam approached, his face full of dread. "What is it? They are getting away."

"Give… give me a moment." Incanus gathered himself and took a deep breath.

Skullam glowered at him and for the first time the Bone elf could remember, the imp's face bore a mix of pity and concern.

Incanus waited. A moment passed, then another. Then another. The *Dragon*'s voice didn't return.

"Perhaps we should wait for her come back this way to Valkeneer?" the imp said. "Ambush her instead of pursuing—"

"The time is now." Incanus's thirst for vengeance swelled again, overriding any sense of caution. "This is it; don't you see? A perfect kill. She shall fall at last, atop the blood of my family. The blood of my love, long spilled in these very woods."

Skullam drew back, his face even more confused.

Incanus didn't care. He stood, then took a few labored breaths and staggered forward, balancing himself on the trunks of the bare trees.

The imp followed, at first on foot then after a few minutes he took again to the air.

The creature's departure brought with it a needed respite. No magic invaded his senses, no simpering Skullam to offer unwanted counsel. A calm soon returned and Incanus found his footing. He began to jog. The trail had grown cold with his failures, but he wouldn't be denied. Tonight was the night the princess died. Tonight was his time.

Soon, Skullam returned. Incanus felt the familiar presence of the dark trace at his waist and the imp appeared from his concealment spell.

"My liege…" Skullam's voice quivered, laced with the strangest of emotions: a cocktail of joy, anxiety and anticipation. "She's just there. They've stopped. Come."

Incanus wasted no time. His focus returned and his stomach fluttered. He unslung his deadly bow as he hustled, running with the silence of a skilled hunter.

Ahead, an ethereal green glow rose on the horizon. It was

a sight he'd never seen, even in the darkness of the Dragon's Breath Mountains. Had they caught on to his pursuit? Was the princess conjuring defenses?

He went to ground, using the forest's hulking timber as cover. His strained to listen and dared to peek ahead.

"Just there," Skullam's hushed voice met his ears and he saw the imp's taloned finger point over his shoulder to the left.

"Are they aware of us?"

"Nay," Skullam assured. "They rest. But this area has a powerful presence. I sense the remnants of a powerful necromancy, conjured long ago."

Incanus crept closer. He worked his way over a small hillock and looked upon a grove of trees, tinted in a dull green glow of necromantic magics. He recognized the hale, one that followed at his side since Graytorris summoned Skullam to his aid, but this was much more powerful, even jarring for Skullam, whose face sickened at the sight of the petrified branches.

"Unnatural," Skullam lamented. "This is the work of desperate evil."

"Why would they choose this hollow to rest?" Incanus dared to ask his imp. Neither had an answer. The pair inched closer, near enough to see the Vermilion appear through the dull luminosity of the forest.

He took a moment and considered the battlefield. There were four of them resting in the hollow among the twisted and petrified branches of this strange copse of trees. The princess was equally trained in sword and sorcery while the others he knew nothing of, but they appeared every part the bodyguards of a Vermilion royal. His arrows would pierce their armor, no doubt, but three trained warriors against his one sword would be a challenge, even for him. And if the princess went unchallenged, her spells could be a dangerous element to any combat.

"I will kill the guard on the left by bow," Incanus said to Skullam, the words barely audible. "A panic will ensue, and when they grab for their weapons, you will drop from the trees, out of the darkness and occupy the princess while I kill the other two by sword."

Skullam's eyes flared, greedy to serve his master's ultimate wish. He sneered, his serpentine tongue snapping between his jagged teeth, a strand of saliva dripping from his mouth. He didn't need to speak, and with a blink, the imp disappeared back into his concealment spell.

Incanus turned back to the hollow and nocked an arrow. The group hadn't moved, so he skulked to the right, sliding between two trees, giving himself a superior sight line and downhill path to run.

He played and replayed his tactics in his mind. Shot first. One down. He calculated the steps to the remaining Vermilion, choosing a path to flank one and limit their chances to pair up against him. If he made quick work of the first, the second would swing out to round on him, but his bloodied blade would be ready. Almost too simple if Skullam did his part. Then the princess would be his, alone and scared, fighting against the inevitability of her tortuous end.

"Captain! No! Return to me!"

The voice of the *Dragon* invaded his senses, an explosion of ethereal sound wracking through his brain. Images of the trees in front of him blurred and he lost sight of his targets below. It was all he could do to not cry out, to not fall to his knees. He closed his eyes and fought to hold his shot.

"Captain!"

That damnable boat. He'd burn it upon his return.

"You wish to burn me?"

"No!" Incanus stumbled over his thoughts, recovering. "*I*

need time. My prey is in my hands!"

"You love her more than you love me!"

"No, Dragon," Incanus implored, *"I seek her destruction."*

"You've abandoned me for her!"

"Leave me now," he tried in desperation, *"or I shall never return!"*

The voice in his head shouted, babbling in an incomprehensible blather, but her intent was unmistakable. The visions of Fala, or the *Dragon*'s replica of her, floated into his mind.

"Please don't leave me again, Incanus. Do you wish me to die again in your absence? Come home. Save me."

Incanus could smell the lavender in Fala's hair, see the silver flecks in her eyes, and feel the heat of life from her body as she neared. It was all too real. He began to swoon, losing focus on his task at hand. He slumped to the ground, his bow dropping to his side.

"Stop, stop, for the love of the Ancients, stop!" His mind capitulated and he began to shake. *"Mercy, my love."*

The *Dragon* silenced her assault on his senses, but the effects still gripped at him. He fought to recover, turning to see if he'd given his position away. The image of Fala receded, disappearing into the woods.

As he gathered himself, he searched for his quarry. The elves still dawdled in the hollow. Somehow, he was safe. His eyes began to return to him, and his breath calmed. He looked again to his foes, hoping for any sign from Skullam, but the imp knew to wait for his attack first. He took a measured breath and stood, bracing himself for his assault. He nocked his arrow again and raised his bow to shoot.

Out of the corner of his eye, Addilyn moved. She now stood in the center of the men, with her back to him. Her arms moved in circles as sparks of magic emanated from her palms.

Incanus hesitated, but she turned before he could shoot. He couldn't place her expression. It wasn't the sheer terror and surprise he had expected.

Branches snapped behind him, and he turned to see several Longmarchers with their bows drawn and ready.

When he spun back to face Addilyn, he saw even more opponents behind her. He was surrounded. He placed her expression then.

Triumph.

He rushed to move his mark from the Vermilion guard to the princess. If he were to die, he'd take her with him. Then the pain from a silent arrow tore through his side, cutting through his leather armor, and lodged deep in his torso.

His breath escaped him, and he stared at the wound, loosening the string of his bow, his arrow sailing harmlessly away. The sniper's arrow, green with the magic of the hollow, struck him from the left and as he raised his startled gaze to the forest. From the darkened branches of the trees above he saw the ghostlike glow of Silencer appear, followed by Ritter jumping down and landing next to him.

The pain was not the first thing that registered. Rather, he recognized the arrow's design—a black arrow carved into the shaft that now protruded from his side.

His own arrow.

His failing arms tried for his sword, but Ritter stood on his hand and kicked his bow away.

In the distance he heard Skullam scream, his wings flapping as he descended upon the princess. With a flash, her awaiting spell launched, striking the imp in flight, freezing him in mid-air. He squirmed against the power of the spell.

Incanus had no choice but to watch the death of his only friend. The first arrow from a hidden Longmarcher struck

Skullam as he twisted against the magic's effects, then a second arrow followed. Then a third. The arrows peppered Skullam, even slashing through his wings, as he gazed at his master in horror, helpless.

Ritter turned from the hapless assassin and took aim with Silencer. When the final arrow hit home, a flash of green ignited, and the imp burst into flames with a horrible, guttural choke. When the smoke cleared, Skullam was gone, and there was nothing but silence in the hollow.

Incanus recognized the end was upon him. Pain spiderwebbed out from the wound, spreading to the rest of his body, and blood drained freely from the wicked wound. All adrenaline left him as his energy faded. Darkness nudged at the edges of his vision, as his gaze struggled to focus on the approach of Addilyn while the Vermilion and the Longmarchers encroached from all sides. Had he the energy, he was sure fury would have risen inside him.

As he watched, helpless, the Vermilion princess stepped to his side, approaching with steady, purposeful strides. In her hands he recognized the weapons that would send him to his death. In her right hand rested her father's ceremonial sword, the one that had slain Fala so long ago. In her left, the raven sword of her champion, Jessamy.

She stood over him and Incanus awaited the final blows.

"This is for my father, and for Jessamy Aberdeen," Addilyn said, her swords diving into his chest. Incanus closed his eyes and thought of Fala.

"Goodbye my love," The *Dragon*'s voice reverberated in his mind one last time before the darkness stole him.

CHAPTER THIRTY-FIVE

"Rely not on the appearance of your enemy, but your readiness to receive them."
—Annals of Halifax Military Academy

THE LAST FAINT FLECKS of twilight were showing through the forest around the Bridge as Ritter trudged through the undergrowth and back to Castle Valkeneer. The Bone elf's bow and sword, while not cumbersome, weighed on him as he carried them. He'd carried the assassin's arrow from the day of the battle of Rillifane's Meander and knew one day he'd have the chance to use it. He'd hoped they'd lost the tracks of the man he entrapped when they left Abacus by air, but somehow, perhaps by other magics, he tracked them.

He had no choice.

He couldn't hear the Longmarchers following behind him, but he knew they were there, carrying the body of the assassin atop a makeshift stretcher. He didn't want to look at the body. He'd prefer to know he did what he had to do to protect his love, and the realm.

Addilyn walked next to him, flanked by her three Vermilion bodyguards. She too looked harried and absent, her hair tousled and her swords bloody. Every few minutes they shared a knowing glance but didn't dare to say more.

Ritter led his entourage through the tower of Firstgate and across the bridge. Morning eyes were upon them as they trudged through the courtyard and headed for the keep. No trumpets blared; no horns heralded their return.

They reached the drawing room and gathered before Ritter was his father and a scramble of servants and Longmarchers, as well as Evchen Vischer and the rest of the Vermilion Wing.

Ritter couldn't stop himself from looking for his mother and wondered when she and his sisters would return. The fog of the coming war wore on his brow.

Before he reached his father, Vischer intercepted them with a balled fist. "You dare use my princess as bait, trollborn?" he spat through clenched teeth.

"It was my idea." Addilyn corrected him. "He merely followed my orders. Stand down, Evchen."

Vischer's fist relented, and his face contorted in confusion. "Princess, why—"

"He wanted to kill me," the princess admitted. "He's tracked me from Thronehelm to Castleshire, from the capital to Abacus, and now to here. He was never going to stop unless… unless we offered him what he wanted."

"You offered yourself up as bait?" Vischer's brow knitted and his eyes sank. "You must know how foolish this was."

"But necessary," Addilyn added. "And our plan worked to perfection. Both he and his cryptid were slain by Sir Ritter and his Longmarchers."

Vischer looked to his troops that had accompanied Addilyn that night, including the Knight Hobelar, Verrigo Releante, and none offered any contradictions.

"The princess is being modest," added Ritter. "It was her plan to trap him in Ghostwood, and her skill of sorcery that held his creature fast, making it easier for the Longmarchers to kill."

"You?" Vischer's pale features reddened, but Ritter couldn't tell if it was from anger or sheer embarrassment. His eyes narrowed as he stared at Addilyn. "You engaged in combat?"

"I've been trained by my father in many arts, combat being one of them." Her face tightened and she stood tall. "And I fear there will be much more fighting before I return to Eldwal."

Vischer's flat expression froze, caught somewhere between

outrage and confusion. His shoulders slumped and his head cocked as he began to absorb the weight of what his princess just explained. After a moment of silence, he said much more quietly, “I only had the interest of my beloved in mind.”

Addilyn’s eyes seemed to glow with the crimson fire of her soul. “We are not in love. We are not courting, we are not betrothed, and we never will be.”

Ritter’s eyes widened in shock, while he felt his stomach do somersaults, wondering what she might admit to next in her rage.

“How did he die?” asked Hertzog, interrupting the rocky exchange.

“I shot him with his own arrow,” Ritter replied. “The one I found unused at the battle of Rillifane’s Meander. Then the princess finished him.”

Behind them, the stretcher bearers brought the body of the Black Rose into the room to gasps from the crowd.

“Bone elf,” someone said.

“Foul beasts,” said another.

While the Vermilion remained stoic, the Valkeneers and their townsfolk voiced their concern.

“Where there’s one, there will be more,” Hertzog meted out, his tone deflated of its normal vim. “They are proxies for the Shadow elves.”

Vischer re-entered the conversation, still recovering from Addilyn’s tale and turned to face the lord. “If that’s true, then the Moor Bog will be unstoppable. The Bridge with our meager defenses won’t hold.”

“The Bridge has never fallen, and it shan’t under my watch.” Hertzog Valkeneer stepped to the fore and put his hand on Ritter’s shoulder. “Tell me everything.”

“Of course, Father. Any word from Mother?” Ritter asked.

Hertzog took a deep breath. "None."

The crowd murmured, frothy in a nervous anxiety, until the susurrus was extinguished by their lord's deep voice calling them to attention.

"While this is a victory for the Bridge against an enemy who has grievously wronged us and our allies the Vermillion, now is not a time for celebration. Ritter, you shall take the place of Captain Driscoll as Captain of the Longmarchers permanently. You've earned it, Son. Double the guard around the castle tonight. I want everyone as sharp as ever. War comes to the Bridge once more, and it is our duty to defend our borders for the realm of Warminster. The Bridge will rise strong as ever. There is much to do."

Vischer interrupted from the lord's side, stepping forward until he was toe to toe with Ritter. "Captain, you will have the full support of both Wings of the Vermilion."

"Thank you," Ritter said, surprised at the speed in which Vischer shifted positions. The plague of politicians, and no one was immune.

Addilyn turned on her heel to face Hertzog, followed by a slight bow. "I apologize for my outburst, as it has been a rather long day. I will now retire to my chambers and ask that Sir Ritter escort me."

Hertzog nodded his ascent and Addilyn marched from the room. Ritter made quick eye contact with his father, his face revealing nothing, and then followed Addilyn and her entourage.

The farther they walked through the keep, the slower Ritter had to walk to keep up with Addilyn. She seemed to almost deflate, as if the rush of energy from defeating the Bone elf and admonishing Vischer had evaporated from her, and only the sadness of losing Jessamy remained. He did not dare touch her in the open corridors, though he felt she needed the comforting reassurance of his hand in hers.

Addilyn's shoulders slumped as soon as the door to her room shut, and Ritter closed the distance between them. She pressed her forehead into his chest, and he wrapped his arms around her shoulders, letting her lean into him for support. Her hair smelled like honey and sweat and the forest. She inhaled a big breath, and he loosened his hold on her, but she didn't step back or look up at him, as he expected. She just stood there, like all she had strength left for was keeping herself upright.

"Sit," Ritter murmured, keeping one arm around Addilyn's shoulders and steering her in the direction of her bed. He sat her down and helped her out of her boots but hesitated to undress her any further. She swung her legs up into the bed, shoving her feet under the covers and laying back on the pillow, paying no attention to her muddy gear. Ritter pulled the covers up to her shoulders and fiddled with them, tucking them around her middle and pushing a stray hair out of her face.

"Get some rest, okay?" Ritter's voice was soft.

When Addilyn didn't respond, he touched her shoulder and got up to leave.

He was halfway to the door when she called his name, and he came back to her. She had sat up, the covers still up around her torso but arms out of the blankets. She beckoned to him. He sat back down on the side of the bed, and she wrapped her arms around him. She brushed his cheek with her lips, then found his lips and kissed him. It was a kiss like a promise.

She hugged him one more, her cheek pressed against his.

"I love you," she whispered.

Ritter's heart jumped and fell at the same time, as he

squeezed her tight against himself. He kissed her mouth again, looking into her eyes. "I love you, too."

She smiled, exhaustion evident in her countenance, and she laid her head back on the pillow, closing her eyes.

Ritter exited her chambers, seeking a few moments of silence and solitude. He felt his love for her deep in his soul, but it was not a hopeful feeling. It was an aching, longing love.

He thought of Vischer and his public display just moments before. It wasn't just Vischer he was truly thinking about, but an entire realm full of men like Vischer, a place that Addilyn would return to after the war was over. He belonged here at the Bridge, where people didn't call him a trollborn, and she belonged in Eldwal, where she would be the princess of the most honored elves.

Their love, however strong, would never work.

THE NIGHT SKY WAS purple and soft, almost time for the sun to set on the day of the winter solstice. The Bridge stood fast on high alert. Captain Ritter of the Longmarchers had dispatched his best troops to scout the fields for any signs of the Moor Bog's approach and the return of the Black Vicar. His father still held the vicar's son, Amaranth, in their dungeons alongside Aarav Fleury. The dark cultist killed Driscoll, his friend and mentor, as a warning, and everyone in Valkeneer knew as this day ended the Black Vicar would not relent on his threat. With dusk upon Castle Valkeneer, Ritter knew the leader of the Moor Bog would show en masse, and in force. But when?

A heavy snow began to fall, the first true storm of the Season of the Long Nights, and Ritter hadn't slept more than a wink in two days. He walked to the keep's trophy room, hoping to find some solace in their family's history there, where he could wrap himself in the comforting memories of kin.

As he opened the door, the warmth of a new fire in the hearth caught him by surprise and he saw his father standing alone, looking upon the flames. He twitched as Ritter entered but didn't turn, instead choosing to take a deep swig from his beer stein.

"Are they here?" Hertzog asked.

"Not yet." Ritter approached, placing his lantern on the tabletop next to the small library that housed the short but valorous history of their low noble family. "Any word from Mother, or the Raven elves?"

His father took another swig and a deep breath before shaking his head.

"Don't worry," Ritter tried to reassure him, "Mother knows the woods better than anyone this side of Ravenshire. I am sure she's fine."

Hertzog finally turned to his son, his eyes full of worry. "I am sure you are right."

A few moments passed between them in silence, both their family's welfare and the arrival of the Black Vicar weighing on both.

"Will they fight?" Hertzog asked, returning his gaze to the orange flickers in the fireplace.

"The Longmarchers?" Ritter was shocked by his father's question. "Of course, and to the death if we must."

"No, son," Hertzog explained, "the Raven elves."

"Grandfather—" Ritter caught his misnomer and corrected himself, "I mean the Coronel will come to our aid. He won't leave us to die. Not with Mother in his ear."

"His people…" Hertzog continued as if he hadn't heard Ritter's reply. "Her people, I mean to say. They owe us nothing. They think differently than we in Valkeneer. I must admit, son, the reason I sent your mother and sisters there was to protect them, get them out of here, in case her father turns his back on the Bridge."

"What of reinforcements from Thronehelm? Halifax?" Ritter's face fell and he took a few steps closer to Hertzog.

His father, still watching the flames, motioned to an open scroll that sat on the table next to the lantern. Ritter hadn't noticed it until now and when he picked it up, he saw a cracked seal of purple wax, the signet of the Thorhauers.

Before he could read it, his father said, "They aren't coming. A messenger from Queen's Chapel delivered news of a great battle in the Falkenwraths. The Norsemen and Thorhauers met the Jackal in the field two days ago."

"And?"

"The queen was assassinated, and King Godwin is dead, killed by Von Lormarck on the field of battle."

Ritter let the scroll slip from his hands and his eyes widened with the news. His heart sunk deep in his chest. He dared not say a word as his father poured him a glass of beer and shared it with him.

"Prince Montgomery won the battle, however, and Von Lormarck's forces retreated to Dragon Ridge, where the prince lays siege. They've taken the city of Krahe and the Thessalys are all dead. Gloucester routed."

"But what about the Bridge?" Ritter wondered aloud. "Surely Montgomery must know Von Lormarck's tied with the Moor Bog and by pursuing Von Lormarck that far west they've left their flank and Thronehelm to the south as open as the Thalassian Sea."

"I don't think so." Hertzog took a deep swig and wiped his beard on this sleeve. "We sent word of Aarav's capture and the connection to the cultists, but I believe the king had departed to meet the Jackal in the field by then. They don't know. Or won't know until it's too late."

Ritter stared hard at his father and placed the stein on the table. He wouldn't be drinking this evening.

"So, you see, my son, no one is coming to reinforce the Bridge." Hertzog's voice was strong, but Ritter detected deception in his words. "And when the Moor Bog attack with their cryptids and whatever horrors from the Dragon's Breaths they've gathered, it will only be we Valkeneers to stop their advance south. Only the Bridge… one last time." He finished his mug and flung it into the flames.

"Have faith, Father." Ritter approached, putting an arm around Hertzog. "We have trained and practiced for moments like this. The Longmarchers are strong and deadly, and we have not one but two Wings of the Vermilion with us here. Mother will rally the Raven elves, of that I am certain. We are not alone."

Ritter wasn't sure if he believed the words tumbling out of his mouth, but he knew the people of Valkeneer and their strength. This town survived despite the treacheries of the Dragon's Breath Mountains, a beacon to humans, twergs, huldrefolk, and elves alike. In his heart, he knew they'd rise and fight.

"Vermilion," Hertzog echoed, looking his son in the eyes. "I see you've spent some time with the princess since you've returned." He smiled like a knowing father.

"Is it that obvious?"

"To those that know you." Hertzog cracked a forced smile and hugged his son. "I know what you're going through."

"I love her." Ritter found it hard to believe he said it to someone other than Addilyn or himself, but this evening wasn't made for patience. It was for moments of truth.

Hertzog nodded in agreement. "Your mother was the one to open my eyes to it. And of course, your sisters."

Ritter exhaled with the thought and leaned against the table. "It's not in the stars," he said.

His father sat next to him. "Your mother and I made it work." Hertzog's demeanor changed from worried lord to wise father. "When I married your mother, it was forbidden by the royals of Thronehelm and the elves of Ravenwood, but once both sides realized we were inseparable, they both conceded."

"She's Vermilion," Ritter lamented. "It's—"

"Different?" Hertzog interrupted. "Sometimes the heart calls stronger than your head. You love who you love, Ritter. Amandaris and I made the right decision, and as a result we've pulled two nations closer together, even if against their cultures and wills, and I have had a family that I can be proud of."

"But you've suffered so much for your trollborn—"

"Suffered? For my *family* you mean?" Hertzog said, his face dropping to look into Ritter's eyes. "Duty be damned when true love calls."

Ritter studied his father's gaze and found no deceit in his countenance.

"If this is my last lesson, then I hope you've heard loud and clear. It's your decision to make, and hers of course."

"Father, please don't—"

The lord ignored Ritter's attempt at reassurance. "Now, regardless of what happens tonight, you must get the princess to safety. No matter what may transpire here. No matter what you see."

"Please don't ask me to abandon the Bridge."

"This is your lord ordering you, Captain." Hertzog's tone changed, becoming more authoritarian for effect. "She must survive, even if the Bridge falls."

Ritter contemplated the gravity of his father's words. With a sigh, he unslung Silencer and offered it to Hertzog. "Take it," he implored. "Silencer belongs with the lord of the Bridge."

Hertzog refused the gift. "That bow belongs to you, Ritter. From the day it passed from my failing hands, it's been part of you. Carry it like a torch, nay a beacon. If it's in the hands of a Valkeneer, the people of Warminster will always know the Bridge stands with them, for them, even if it's walls fall. It embodies who we are—nay, who you are. Carry it well. And may your arrows fly true."

The groan of horns from the castle's parapets sounded, interrupting their brief respite. Ritter knew in that moment the Moor Bog had arrived.

Five days had passed since LaBrecque set sail on the *Wake*, leaving the friendly shores of Castleshire on his way back to Thronehelm. He'd passed by the Horn of Seabrooke early in the evening the night before and made their way east along the coast to the capital.

Doom's Wake sailed like never before. Her new rudder stretched her legs, and he had to drop sail a few times to ensure he did not lose the *Sundowner*, who was drafting behind him. He felt his sea legs returning, the familiar boards of the *Wake* at his feet. And, most importantly, he was returning home with good news.

"Ahoy!" a crewwoman yelled from the crow's nest above.

LaBrecque pulled his spyglass out and looked in the direction the woman pointed. His mind wandered at the thought of having to pull alongside a merchant vessel and exchange news. As a man-o'-war, he didn't have to, but never really minded. You never knew what information you might glean from a ship passing in the night.

But today, he wanted no part of it. He wanted to get back to Thronehelm and greet his king and queen with good news. Castleshire's help was there for the taking, even if it was being delivered in the most surreptitious of fashions. And he had to confirm the king and queen would accept Calder's help under some pretty unique conditions.

As he unfurled his spyglass, his thoughts changed in an instant. Along the horizon floated the remnants of a naval battle. His heart raced in fear at first, thinking he had missed a conflict and somehow the fleet from Seabrooke was lost without him. But as he scanned the sea, he recognized the flotsam and jetsam of Norse vessels, ones that brought the prince and viscount home. They were scattered from east to west as far as the eyes could see. Bodies littered the sea, untaken by the predators or sunk with water filled lungs. The battle was fresh.

Off in the distance beyond the wreckage, an armada of tall ships flying the flags of the Sea Kingdom blockaded the entrance to Thronehelm's port. Their numbers were thrice that of Seabrooke's fleet and their ships, were all man-o'-wars.

"Turn about," he called to Tamsyn.

"Aye, aye," came her reply.

LaBrecque knew he had to get home to Seabrooke and launch the royal navy. They would be outnumbered and outclassed. But he was the Seawolf. Thronehelm depended upon him. And he had some ideas of his own.

CHAPTER THIRTY-SIX

"A path without challenge is the wrong way."
—Erudian Proverb

"WHERE ARE THEY?" DAEMUS murmured, mace in one hand and a vial of Tuttle's thunder flash concoction in the other. His eyes strained, peering into the darkened hallway, impatient for the return of the vrykar.

"Shh," Anoki warned as he stepped to the side of the Keeper. The corridor ahead widened, allowing for two to stand abreast, and the humming from the Heart of Laurentia grew louder, yet still distant.

The pathways began to grow somehow darker. The were-light flickered and dimmed. There was a tension in the air, and everyone seemed to be nervous, but no one suggested they turn back.

Daemus knew they wouldn't if he forged ahead. They were following him, and he knew it, and in a perverted way, he was glad.

Beyond the point of hoping they were close to the end of the labyrinth, he kept walking. Daemus believed they were because he had to, because anything else would have been intolerable.

Arjun slipped next to Caspar with his red-edged katana drawn and at the ready while Caspar curled two thunder flashes, one in each hand. The thrumming teased a rhythmic pattern, and to Daemus, it reminded him of a strange heartbeat.

Tha-thump thump. Tha-thump thump. Tha-thump thump.

"Behind," Faux said over the beating of the Heart, not risking a whisper.

Speaking in a normal tone could mean only one thing:

the vrykar had found them. That notion brought both terror and relief to Daemus. The mix of emotion, now a bit more common to him, could only be found in the spirit of a soldier at the coming of a battle. The kind of odd symmetry found between the utter chaos of combat and the knowledge that the wait for it was over. He gritted his teeth, resolute to end this game—this divine challenge—set for them by Trillias. He'd gotten them this far. The Heart was within his grasp, as was salvation. He wouldn't fail his friends, or the realm.

High-pitched squeals of the approaching vrykar rose from somewhere in the shadows behind them, followed by the all-too familiar scrambling and scraping of their wicked talons against the halls and walls of the labyrinth.

"Here they come!" Faux called. "Hold your ears!"

Before Daemus could cover up, Faux hurled the first of Tuttle's thunder flashes into the darkness. The vial exploded, echoing throughout the maze. The impact jostled him, shock waves ricocheting off the walls, sending him to his knees. He twitched and groaned before an otherworldly shrieking arose, seeming to hang in his ears as the creatures reacted to Tuttle's improvised devices. He grabbed at his ears, unable to stop from crying out in pain from the inhuman wails. In seconds, the shrieking trailed away, the cryptids retreating behind them in the darkness.

"It's working!" he heard Tuttle cry over the noise, the sound of his voice now dulled and hollowed with the physical effects of the blast.

Daemus's head throbbed and the cryptid's piercing cries reminded him of Trillias's voice, when the Ancient punished his insolence on the beach. The pain was as unbearable then as it was now.

With a thrust of a hand, Anoki urged Daemus forward

down the hall. She was saying something, her mouth moving, but the pounding in his ears prevented him from understanding the words. Regaining his feet, he started a slight jog, not yet sure of his balance when a small hallway to Anoki's right appeared in the wisps of Arjun's encroaching were-light.

In a blur, the Athabasica ducked and spun, her katana flashing up at an onrushing cryptid appearing from a nearby corridor. Her blade slipped through the flailing creature's defenses, slicing between its pincers, and impaling itself in the beast's mouth.

She turned away and withdrew her katana, the vrykar falling dead inches from Daemus's feet. Anger, surprise, and fear flared in her eyes, but before she could recover, they both noticed a shifting of movement in the shadows down the same corridor. More vrykar began to hiss, crawling over one another to get to them. Like mindless beasts they scuffled nearer, pincers clicking and sharpened hooks grating at the stone as they approached.

Daemus had little choice.

Without hesitation he lobbed his lone thunder flash into the clicking throng of armored cryptids. The flask exploded only a few feet away. The force of the explosion knocked him from his feet and for a second, he seemed detached from his body, his ears deafened in the blast.

Time stood still. He forgot where he was. An arm grabbed at him, pulling him back to his feet. His legs wobbled and his stunned eyes found Arjun's free hand holding him up. The captain pushed him forward, away from the crowded ambush. Arjun pointed his sword down the main hall, his voice lost to Daemus's deafened state. With a forceful tug, the cradling arm of Katja pulled him down the corridor. He staggered forward in his concussed stupor, concentrating as best he could on

Katja's blue hair, her glowing face tattoo, her touch.

Seconds blurred by. He glanced back, trying to stitch it all together. Arjun ran down the retreating Vrykar to his right. Katja pushed him forward.

Caspar raced by and tossed another thunder flash past Anoki in the darkened hall in front of them. Seconds later, the denotation knocked both Daemus and Katja over, on top of one another. Emotion and fear left him. Daemus was numb, his thoughts still piecemeal and blurry.

He thought he heard Blue Conney screaming, but his voice sounded like he was calling out through a pillow. Then the arcing of Arjun's sword slashed by him, and the keening of the creatures returned. He fumbled his mace and instead of picking it up, he reached to help Katja, whose ears were bleeding. Her face, stoic and cold, stared empty eyes at him.

"Katja," he slurred, reaching for her, not sure how to help. He shook her shoulder, trying to pull her back from wherever she was, and for the briefest of seconds she blinked. "C'mon."

He managed to pull the healer to her feet and his mind started to regather. Then a splash of blood slapped him in the face. His eyes fluttered and turned, where he saw Anoki's blade cutting down another vrykar—one that was a foot away from him and the healer.

"Go," Anoki's mouth was forming, the words silent to him.

He reached down and hoisted Katja to her feet. The healer leaned into him, struggling to stand on her own, so he threw her arm over his shoulder and carried her away.

Arjun's were-light slipped away behind them as he made his way with Katja through the darkness. His blurry eyes failed him, but he pressed on, Katja in his arms. Blindly he managed, bumping into walls as he went, stumbling from time to time in the darkness. The farther he moved ahead, the more lost he knew they'd be. The thought of his companions making it out skipped through his mind, but his sole focus was getting Katja away from the cryptids.

As the light dissipated, he found himself alone in the shadows with the healer. Her head bobbed with each step, fading in and out of consciousness, but he wouldn't give up. He leaned to the side against the wall to take a breath. The distant battle still sounded but he'd cleared enough ground to rest. The slightest of hearing returned.

Tha-thump thump. Tha-thump thump. Tha-thump thump.

His mind cleared a bit, and the noticeable beat of the Heart grew louder. He could feel the thrumming as he leaned into the wall. They were getting closer.

The fog in his mind began to clear and he had a thought. If they couldn't see, perhaps he could *feel* their way through the maze, using the humming of the Heart in the wall.

"Can you continue?" Daemus asked Katja, but when he looked down into her face, the blue tinge of her tattoo illuminated just enough for him to see her eyes nearly closed. She was alive, but delirious.

Tha-thump thump. Tha-thump thump. Tha-thump thump.

He grunted and lifted Katja, the pair staggering into the shadows alone. He closed his eyes and leaned on the walls to feel for the beating to lead them.

Tha-thump thump. Tha-thump thump. Tha-thump thump.

At last, he saw four pinpricks of light, and when he approached it he saw that light was streaming out of four holes in the wall that were just far apart enough to be the size of a hand. Moving without thought, he slotted his fingers into the openings and tried the wall. It slid to the side easily, and light bathed them all as they entered through the opening.

"This is it," Daemus said to Katja. "This has to be it."

The gravity of the moment gripped Daemus, and Katja felt weightless under his arm. She moaned as the doors to the chamber opened, stirring her from semi-consciousness. A blessed light flooded onto them, one that brought with it a distinct and unforgettable sensation Daemus recognized. It was the holy light of Erud, golden rays that had filled the skies over Solemnity for a millennia before the hands of Graytorris dimmed it.

He closed his eyes, bathing in the brightness, letting the warmth of the light wash over them. Katja started to mumble, and he laid her just inside the door, gently kissing her forehead as he did. She blinked, staring up at him from her stupor, confused. Her trembling ceased, a calmness seeming to overtake her.

Daemus smiled down at her and then glanced over his shoulder. He squinted and shielded his eyes against the powerful illumination. In the wake of his god's presence, his ears no longer rang, and his fatigue dissipated, replaced with a peculiar rush of adrenaline. His hands shook as he peered onto *The Tome of Enlightenment*, the source of the light, lying on the floor in the center of the room. The *Tome*'s ancient cover remained closed, but its golden light seeped from its pages like an unstoppable breath.

"Daemus," Katja's weak voice reached his ears, "is that… the Heart of Laurentia?"

Daemus registered her words, but his eyes only pored over the artifact of his god just a few feet away from him. His Ancient's essence called, its radiant beams sweeping by. Yet he managed to break away for the briefest of seconds, lifting his gaze to find a glowing amethyst the size of a ground floor cornerstone of the Cathedral of the Watchful Eye. The violet orblike heart pulsated, levitating a full yard off the maze's floor, though its light was dim in comparison to the *Tome*'s.

For the moment, he ignored the inestimable beauty of the beating gemstone, and set his attention on the recovery of his sect's great book, the one he lost in the struggle against the fallen Keeper. A vague sense that others had entered the chamber tugged at his senses, and he thought he heard Caspar crying quietly behind him. Daemus half-wished he could cry too, feeling as though he might burst, but his eyes were bone dry, as if they didn't want to occlude his vision of the *Tome.* He shuddered as he approached the relic, taking one careful step at a time.

Is it real? Is this another of Trillias's tricks meant to deceive us? Is... this...

When his fingers fell onto the cover, he felt the power of Erud surge through his every limb, every fiber of his being. This had to be real.

His eyes widened and he lost his breath. With one heaving motion, he threw open the diamond-shaped grimoire, unleashing a rush of brilliance that filled the room around him. He stood still, a timelessness capturing his senses, as he basked in blinding light of Erud. Euphoria flooded through his veins and he almost swooned.

A Presence—Erud's *Presence*—blasted into his mind like one of Tuttle's thunder flashes, and in a sudden burst of emotion, blessed tears streamed from his white eyes. Memories of his uncle Kester, streamed back to him, blinding him to the *Tome*'s passages for a moment. He saw glimpses of sentimental birthdays, where only his dear uncle cared for him. Flashes of their travels together, to and from the great cathedral and then finally his uncle's vicious death at the hands of Misael of Clan Blood Axe.

Watercolor images of other lost companions, Chernovog

and Burgess flashed next, laughing together around campfires, riding hard on the plains of the Vilchor Highgrass and then dying for him at the second battle of Homm Hill. One after another, more specters came, the visage of Disciple Delling emerged, riding with him along Harbinger's Run, imparting nuggets of wisdom and then falling at the hands of the Antlered Man.

Part of him wanted to look away, but his gaze, resolute, stayed on the glowing pages. Flashes of the deaths of Precept Radu and First Keeper Brecken replayed in front of him, followed by the sacrifice of Captain Hague in the streets of Abacus. He hadn't seen Hague die, but the *Tome* revealed it anyway.

It was then he noticed the memories were not in his mind. They instead poured from the pages of the magical book resting in his hands. They felt real and time seemed absent, the past and present jumbled together in indeterminable dimensions hidden in the aged pages of the *Tome*. A second dragged on for what felt like hours. The presence of his companions beside him melted away until there was nothing left but him and the great book.

"I did not want you to come back," Daemus muttered to his patron deity, aloud, or so he thought. "I did not want you back."

The glow from the book took a distant, brilliant form, like a star shining through a canvass of other stars, brighter than the pages themselves.

Erud knew, of course.

Then came an answer, perhaps the first direct reply Daemus could ever recall. It floated into Daemus's consciousness as if on a wave, rather than the hammer and nails that had been Trillias's voice. *"I am sorry."*

Daemus heaved a breath and began to shake with sobs. He dropped the *Tome* onto the labyrinth floor, and with his eyes affixed on the blinding starlight, he didn't move to pick it up. Instead, his body wracked in uncontrollable awe, love, and understanding. Again, the young Keeper lost track of time and raised his hands to cover his face. He slipped to the floor on both knees and rocked back and forth, fighting to find a grasp on the *Presence.*

"I only see, Daemus, I do not ordain," the voice in his head came again. *"But I am sorry for all that has happened."*

"You meddle!" he screamed back, unable to stop himself. Eighteen years of pain blurted from him, and he felt his face reddening, his brow sweating. "You torment. I never wanted the Sight. I didn't ask for any of this."

"This had to be, Daemus. You now are the sole possessor of our infinite knowledge. You now see where no others can. Use our knowledge wisely. We shall speak again."

The Ancient's voice fell away, and Daemus squinted at the diminishing light, torn between an unbalanced rage and the silent lucidity of the knowledge the Ancient had bestowed. The room fell quiet, and his physical sight returned to him. *The Tome of Enlightenment,* lying still on the floor, filled the chamber with a tolerable glow.

Daemus let out a single breath and rubbed the tears from his eyes. He was left in an unfamiliar peace, if not solitude. He blinked for a moment, waiting for more, but nothing came. The image of Erud remained in his mind and he somehow became aware that the Sight, the whole order's Sight, had been restored. With the *Tome* in his hands the Keepers of the Forbidden could once again see.

"Daemus, look," whispered Caspar, a sense of excited urgency in his voice.

Daemus dared to glance away from the overwhelming magical hale rising from the pages and realized he was on his knees. He hauled himself to his feet, the *Tome* in hand.

Caspar's face beamed with pride, his wounds gone, his cassock refreshed as if it were new. For a moment, Daemus thought his best friend had died, a ghost returned from the pages of the great book, perhaps as some twisted lesson for him to learn.

But instead, his friend rushed in and hugged him. "You've done it, Daemus."

Daemus didn't know how to respond but scanned the gawking gazes of each of his companions, all of whom had been restored to health by the magic of Erud. He couldn't prevent himself from wondering and glanced to Arjun's prosthetic leg. Even though it remained, there was an aura about it, one he'd not seen before. One of gold and white, the colors of his Ancient.

Am I seeing the hale of magic now? Was this ability somehow imparted to me by Erud?

"Your… leg?" he managed.

"It's… I don't know." Arjun's face twitched and he rubbed at the device. "It's metal, but it feels… real."

"By the Ancients." Anoki's eyes welled with tears, and she hugged the captain who returned her affection with a kiss.

Katja covered her face with her hands, fighting back tears. "Ssolantress," she said, her voice quivering. "The Blue Lady blesses you, Arjun."

Daemus's newfound power gripped him. His eyes left Arjun's magical leg, and stopped next on Katja's blue mark, the mark of her goddess. It too glimmered, nearly dancing on Katja's face when she turned to him with a half-smile.

"At last, you've succeeded, Great Keeper." The familiar boom of Trillias's disembodied voice returned to the room, carrying the air of the disappointment of a small child who had been denied a treat on market day. "I commend you. The *Tome* and the Heart are yours."

From behind the Heart the Ancient appeared in all his grandeur and approached the group.

Daemus winced as the hale of magic seeped from Trillias's image, an aura of five distinct colors: red, green, black, yellow, and blue. He didn't know how to interpret the varying hues that followed the god, so he tried, and as kind as he could, said, "My lord, I am not the Great Keeper."

"That's not what the *Tome* has decreed, is it?" the Ancient's voice grumbled at the perceived insult.

Daemus's face quirked, and he felt the *Tome* flare in his hands.

With a flick of his finger, Trillias's magic reopened the *Tome* for him and Daemus fumbled with the ponderous book, using both hands to hold it fast. One after another, pages of aged text flipped on their own, guided by the god's magic, until it came to the page upon which the names of the Great Keepers had been scrawled by Erud.

"As it has been, from the time the Ancients left Warminster for their Hall in the heavens," Trillias added.

Trillias's hypnotizing glare shimmered with the words and Daemus felt a rush of anxiety skip inside him. He scoured through the glowing text, scrolling past a thousand years of names and stopped at the final entry, Great Keeper Nasyr Tagabunlang.

Appearing below it, shimmering symbols began drawing themselves and a new name appeared—Daemus Alaric.

The young Keeper's gaze froze on the page, unable to move, unable to breathe.

No. Please, no.

Caspar moved to help his friend, a concerned gaze upon

his countenance. He peered over Daemus's shoulder. "Great Keeper." His voice was both awestruck and resolute.

With a cautious step back, Caspar dropped to one knee in a traditional genuflection offered to those that held the exalted position. "I am here to serve thee."

One by one, the rest of his friends shared knowing glances and followed Caspar's lead, taking a knee and offering a respectful bow.

Daemus's eyes turned from the *Tome* and looked to the group in front of him. "Friends, rise."

Daemus reached for Caspar's arm, and his old cloistermate stood and with reticence, raised his eyes to meet his.

"It's me, Caspar. I am no Great Keeper. We found the *Tome* together. Not just I."

"Your Ancient has chosen you." Trillias stepped into the center of the group, his fiery eyes aglow. "You, amongst all the others that have tried, have proven yourself worthy. You've bested my creatures and found the center of my labyrinth where all before you have failed. And as such, you have earned your freedom from my labyrinth and a return to your realm, wherever you shall choose to go."

"Thank you, Lord," Katja said before anyone else could reply.

Daemus turned to her, finding her soft stare comforting.

Faux dared to stand next and pointed behind him. "The Heart of Laurentia," she managed through a tremulous voice, the corners of her mouth lifting in a gentle smile. "Is that ours too?"

"I've never seen it's equal." Blue Conney's eyes were as wide as saucers, and he and Marquiss both approached the pulsing amethyst. The thrumming cadence of the heart continued.

Tha-thump thump. Tha-thump thump.

"It is," Trillias assured him.

"What in the name of the Ancients is this?" Tuttle brushed his disheveled hair from his face. "Tt's no gem. It's *alive*."

Trillias squinted at the alchemist before moving on. "You have reconciled with Erud?" Trillias asked, looking to Daemus. "Perhaps you should seek knowledge from the book you possess?"

Daemus turned back to the *Tome* and flipped through pages hoping to catch a glimpse of Trillias's meaning. As ill-prepared to use the manual as anyone else in the room, he rifled through it, sending whisks of hale into the ether as he turned each page.

"I—I don't know how," he admitted.

"Perhaps concentrate," Caspar said, pointing at the *Tome*. "Think of Erud. Search for the answers in the signs of our Ancient."

Daemus blinked. He recalled what little time he'd spent with Great Keeper Nasyr and closed his eyes, trying to remember how she'd used the relic. He drew a deep breath and calmed himself. "Erud, the All-seeing." His prayer was unpracticed, but he pressed on. "I beseech thee. Show me the tale of the Heart."

His body trembled. The familiar angst of his Sight returned, at first slow, then the surge of energy spread like tendrils through him. His limbs went weak, and he felt himself slip into a meditative state, one familiar to him. It was a waking oneiromancy—not asleep as his Sight had always required—but not fully awake either.

The voice of Erud didn't return, but instead an image of the beating, violet Heart floated and spun from the glowing sheets.

Tha-thump thump. Tha-thump thump.

The whirling gem disappeared, replaced by a primordial sludge that began to take shape. From the gelatinous mass transformed a dark and terrible creature and it was all he could do to not gasp.

A skeletal dragon, its flesh melted away, reared on its hind legs and spread its broken wings, with its raised maw to the sky. With a crouch and powerful leap, the fleshless creature took imaginary flight from the *Tome*, creeping skyward with a batlike motion, soaring toward a small castle tucked into faraway mountains.

"Laurentia." The name came into his mind, and he recognized the voice of Erud returning. "Corpsus."

"Laurentia was a mighty Ancient." Trillias interrupted Daemus's reverie. "The Ancient of Dragons."

"What?" Arjun asked, his voice laced in confusion.

"Aye," the god answered, sneering back at the captain. "Before Laurentia could leave our terrestrial world for the Hall of the Ancients, she was slain by her own worshippers for abandoning them, her heart torn from her bosom by the black blades of resentment, fear, and despair."

Tha-thump thump. Tha-thump thump.

"How can mortals kill a god?" Anoki asked, finding the courage to approach Trillias.

"Slain? Nay." Daemus answered for him. "Her heart still beats, but her body lies buried by the magics of those that betrayed her. I have been shown this by… Erud." He couldn't believe the words as he spoke them.

"So, what are we to do with this?" Blue Conney asked of the group, including Trillias.

"It's a priceless prize you've won," Trillias replied. "Her heart has the power to restore her, if you learn how to do so. Or you can destroy the gem and kill her, forever ending the divine life of an Ancient. But I warn you, dangers come with both paths. The choice is no longer mine."

Daemus sensed much more than just a simple meaning in the Ancient's words. "Who is Corpsus?"

"Corpsus is what has become of Laurentia." Trillias's somber tone carried even more weight than before.

"Why would we want to restore her?" Marquiss's unapologetic tone stunned the room. "I say we stab the heart and end this."

Trillias's eyes narrowed. "Are you sure you want to be the one that slays a god?"

Marquiss stepped back, his arms raising slowly and his hands empty.

"If we restore her," Katja interjected, "will she return to the Hall of the Ancients?"

"I know not," the god replied.

"But she flies to a castle." Daemus glanced back at the *Tome* to find the image gone. "She must be stopped."

"Who would release such a beast?" Anoki asked.

Daemus could only think of one person.

Graytorris.

EPILOGUE

"O dreadful chimera, swift vengeance awaits thee. For I am your instrument of retribution."

EVERY PART OF JINS'S body ached as she crawled out from under the debris, and from under the *krol*'s body, which saved her from the worst impact of the cave-in. Her face was torn, her bones broken in places, and her lungs felt as if they were filled with soot. Heaving breaths left her gasping for more, her mouth dry and full of cavern dust.

Somehow, there was light. This far down—this deep in the mines, it made no sense. Her left arm was numb, but she crawled her way, propelled ever so slowly by her bloodied legs and her twergish tail, pushing her forward. She used her right hand to move rocks and pebbles as she could.

Her hearing came back to her. At first, there was a constant ringing, distant but steady. Then the sound grew closer and louder before it ceased, making it possible to discern a little more than a hollowness to every sound.

She followed the light. That's all the hope she had. Pulling her weight over broken rocks brought excruciating pain with each motion. She tried to cry for help, but her weak lungs and dry mouth left her rasping.

One tug closer, she told herself after each pull, some of which were better than others. Ahead, the smoke began to clear, and she registered the faintest of breezes reaching her face. The cold winds of the Dragon's Breath Mountains never felt better. They brought with them hope, a chance to live. It renewed her spirits and her pain diminished, even if only a little.

Fighting her way down the remnants of the once-proud artisan hallway, she saw the tunnel give way to the outdoors. A broken smile formed without effort, and she coughed in pain, trying to clear her mouth and throat. Just a few more pulls and she'd be clear. In truth she didn't have any idea how far she'd come and where the collapse had brought her.

Thoughts of the carnage the cave-in must've done to the Forge invaded her mind. She tried putting them out of her head, thinking survival first, recovery later. Then the screeching sound, one she'd never heard before and one she'd never forget, echoed down the hall, shaking more rubble free, forcing her to duck for cover. The piercing wail sounded like the scraping of a whetstone on a giant's sword mixed with the release of pent-up rage, bottled for centuries.

She trembled, her heart raced, and her eyes filled with fear. She couldn't stay in the ruined mine, but nor did she want to see what may have escaped it.

Ahead, the light brightened as she crawled closer, and the smoke began to clear. With a few final tugs, she reached the outside.

She lay prone on a jutting rock formation created by the eruption. She squinted in the afternoon sun and propped herself between two boulders to gain a better view.

Standing in front of her, not a thousand paces from the entrance of the subterrane, rose the animated skeleton of a dragon. The creature was fear made manifest.

Unable to turn away, she peered down at the undead horror, who's eyes glowed with the same green magic of the man who'd released him. The clicking of its bones echoed through the valley and off the walls of the great mountain when the dragon spread its wings. Its bones, ancient and grey, were suspended together by strands of the same green magic found in its eyes.

It cried out again, sending waves of its hideous noise throughout Ravenwood below. Trees swayed back and forth, cracking and bending underfoot.

Jins ducked for a second behind the boulders, hoping the monstrosity hadn't seen her escape. She quaked in fear, unable to flee. Was the creature breathing?

"Corpsus!" a voice called out from the valley beneath her. "I, Mortus, have freed you from your slumber!"

Jins recognized the voice. The same ethereal voice of the skeletal man that entrapped them at the ruins moments ago. It was unmistakable. She grunted in pain and rolled, gaining a better view of the scene.

The man stood at the feet of Corpsus, undaunted by the vile creature. He raised his obsidian staff above his head with both hands and began chanting in words she didn't understand. A black smoke leaked from the staff, surrounding the man and his companion, who held a sword by his side.

"This can't be real," she said aloud, hoping her words would wake her from this nightmare. "Please, Renshaw of the Rock People, let this not be true."

Corpsus spun, its osseous tail snapping trees as it turned to face the one called Mortus and the man with the sword. Its neck sank and its green eyes flares as it closed in on the men. Jins thought for sure its skeletal maw would swing open and grind them in its teeth, but instead, the abomination waited as the two men approached.

"O, dreadful chimera," Mortus called, "swift vengeance awaits thee. For I am your instrument of retribution."

To Jins's abject dismay, the death dragon spoke, its voice belching through the valley, spreading like a plague as it reached her ears. The swordsman standing next to Mortus might have called out in pain, but the dragon's spectral voice drowned it out. He twitched in the pale magic for only a second before she watched him disintegrate, sword and all, in the wake of the dragon's voice.

"Hubris," the beast said to the remaining figure, "for I am an Ancient."

Corpsus reared back and let out another unholy, screeching hiss. It puffed up its chest and exhaled a cloud of black smoke this time, spreading onto the valley like a creeping doom, destroying everything. Trees wilted, leaves withered, and death became the valley.

Jins covered her face, trying to block out the horror surrounding her. But it was no use.

"You live?" Corpsus's eyes flared as it stared at Mortus, who had somehow survived its apocalyptic breath.

"We are one," the skeleton called, cracking his staff on the ground, "we are death incarnate."

The undead dragon's spine popped as its skull turned, seeming to consider the words, lowering even farther to stare at the skeletal man. For a moment, it pondered the curious figure, then it unraveled its horrible claw long enough for the skeleton to climb onto what remained of its appendage. The dragon moved, saying nothing further, and lifted the undead man to its back.

It was then she heard distant shouts and screams, emanating from somewhere below, coming from the Forge. Both Mortus and the dragon turned, and the beast leaned in, focusing its breath into the cracks and crevices formed in the mine's destruction.

Jins's jaw dropped, helpless, and watched the destruction of all she knew. With a powerful magic, Corpsus lifted and began to levitate above the valley of death, then a blast like nothing she'd ever heard before as it began to fly off.

Then, all was silent, the silence of dust and bones.

ABOUT J. V. HILLIARD

BORN OF STEEL, FIRE and black wind, J.V. Hilliard was raised as a highlander in the foothills of a once-great mountain chain on the confluence of the three mighty rivers that forged his realm's wealth and power for generations.

His father, a peasant twerg, toiled away in industries of honest labor and instilled in him a work ethic that would shape his destiny. His mother, a local healer, cared for his elders and his warrior uncle, who helped to raise him during his formative years. His genius brother, whose wizardly prowess allowed him to master the art of the abacus and his own quill, trained with him for battles on fields of green and sheets of ice.

Hilliard's earliest education took place in his warrior uncle's tower, where he learned his first words. His uncle helped him learn the basics of life—and most importantly, creative writing.

Hilliard's training and education readied him to lift a quill that would scribe the tale of the realm of Warminster, filled with brave knights, harrowing adventure and legendary struggles and help his people.

He lives in the city of silver cups, hypocycloids and golden triangles with his wife, a ranger of the diamond. They built their castle not far into the countryside, guarded by his own two horsehounds, Thor and MacLeod, and resides there to this day.

Made in the USA
Monee, IL
10 August 2023

40728195R00256